Pussy
Productions

Mark D K Berry

Pussy Productions by Mark DK Berry
Copyright © 2019 Mark DK Berry

First edition: Feb 2019
Second edition: Dec 2023

Ebook: ISBN: 978-0-6486197-0-3
Paperback: ISBN: 978-0-6486197-1-0

Animus Est Solvo

Part I

Part II

Part III

Part IV

PART ONE

An Attempted Take-over

A golden Rolls Royce pulled into an industrial estate in Deptford and came to a halt outside Pussy Productions headquarters. The rear door flew open, and shortly thereafter something attempted to squeeze and gazumpf its way out. Hoots, the most loyal of South African chauffeurs, appeared around the rear of the car a moment later to assist.

"Allow me to help you, sir," he said, grabbing at an arm, then putting a shoe up onto the polished wing to pull at the beast within.

"Get your damn hands off me, you inbreed!" came the gruff reply from the lump of sweaty, reddening flesh that was now trapped in the door frame.

Eventually extricating itself from the vehicle through a series of grunts and twists, he brought himself to his full five-feet-one-half-inches and bore down upon the waistline of the six-and-a-half foot South African, while grunting like a baby rhino.

"Bloody wogs, always meddling in our affairs," he murmured between huffs.

"I'm white South African, sir," replied Hoots.

"Still a bloody wog, and a turncoat to boot," came the reply.

Sir Stott waddled his way towards the glass entrance of his empire. Shaking off his chauffeur's help as he struggled to put one foot in front of the other.

"I can do it, boy. I'm not a bloody invalid!" shouted Sir Stott.

"He's a bloody invalid," said Rigby, to himself more than the other man in the room.

They were watching with some amusement through the tinted glass, as Stott huffed and puffed like a demented badger and slowly made his advance upon the building where they now waited.

"He calls an emergency meeting and then takes most of the day to get to it," continued Rigby.

"We all know your views, Rigby, but for now it would be more astute of you to keep *schtum*, especially in view of our current crisis. Anyway, the more crippled he becomes, the better."

It was the commanding voice of Mr. R. Hazelhot. Ex-paratrooper and commander of the guards until caught trying to sodomise a recruit. Since then, the only work he'd been able to consider was in the lower industries as a managerial viper. Something he excelled at. Hazelhot was currently sitting a distance from the window in a darker part of the room, as he didn't like the light. A cloud of cigar smoke occasionally billowed out and was sucked into the air-conditioning system above.

Rigby made nervous glances back and forth from the scene outside the window to the darkened corner where Hazelhot lurked.

"I hope you know what you are doing," said Rigby.

"Trust, Rigby, trust. And wipe that sweat from your brow. You make me wonder if it isn't you who might be the weak link in this impending engagement."

"It wasn't me that caused it," muttered Rigby, thinking Hazelhot wouldn't hear.

"And it isn't you who has to deal with it. So park your shivering butt on some leather and speak only when you are spoken to," replied Hazelhot. "Yellow belly," he added, as he eyed Rigby in the way a puff-adder might view a mouse.

A moment later the office door swung open, and the rotund Stott stumbled noisily in, followed by his chauffeur.

"How delightful to see you, Sir Stott," said Hazelhot, rising from his seat and heading towards Stott with his arm outstretched.

"You bloody snake!" bellowed Stott, wasting no time to express his thoughts. "Think you can slither round behind me and try a takeover, do you?" he bellowed, as one eye closed and the other got larger, his hand then making a rapid snaky gesture that distracted everyone for a moment. "Hmm?" he finally added into the pregnant silence that followed.

Stott's face was reddening as he continued to ignore the outstretched hand of his business partner, instead holding him in what he felt certain was a steely stare. His body, at that moment, reminding him he was in no state to be standing for long periods, and so he made his way across the room towards his chair; a commanding leather Chesterfield that was kept empty should he ever need to visit.

He misjudged his trajectory, and shot across the room in a stumble that failed to place him in the central location, designed by the maker to nurture the human buttock. It was

5

a miss, and he went crashing down behind the chair, sending a large yucca plant across the length of the window until it was lying prostrate on the office floor beside him.

"Hoots, you damn buffoon, get me up at once!" he shouted, but Hoots was already towering over the flailing turtle, struggling to find a safe part to pull him up by.

It was an interesting moment, and it reminded Hazelhot of the time he had tried to push a large jelly fish back into the ocean around the shores of Tahiti as a child. The damn thing was just too slippery. He was enjoying the recollection of kicking the thing to death as an alternative, when Hoots finally got Stott into a safe landing upon the Chesterfield. Once done, Hoots positioned himself like a faithful dog a little behind the chair and stared straight ahead like a member of the Queen's guard.

Hazelhot eyed them both, weighing them up, before breathing a sigh and wandering back across the room to stand in front of his own slightly less commanding desk and chair. Rigby nervously took the signal as his cue, and positioned himself upon a third, thoroughly uncommanding office chair. Everyone then eyed everyone else suspiciously, except Hoots, who continued to stare straight ahead.

Stott tried to speak, but he was still struggling to catch his breath. Hazelhot waited with an angelic look of patience on his face. On Stott's third failed attempt, he took the lead, though he did so with a pre-emptive cough equal in its angelic politeness to the look on his face, and just as false.

"*Huh-huh-rum*," he began, as gently as he could so as not to rile the odorous beast further. "Sir Stott..." he then began, pausing a moment to allow the humility of his demeanour to sink into the cantankerous old bastard. "I believe you are referring to the attempt by Quaker and Quaker to buy a large portion of Pussy Production shares that were floating on the stock market yesterday. Now, before you fall into the obvious error of judgement you were about to make, allow me to delineate for you just what plan Quaker and Quaker had in mind."

The irritation that Hazelhot's fey display of integrity was having on Stott's senses brought on a new display of wrath, and he let Hazelhot know it.

"You bloody what? Good god man!" bellowed Stott. "I don't wish to hear your slithering excuses."

Both Stott's hands made snake shapes as his face puckered up and spittle sprayed from his mouth, but he had overdone it and the air wheezed back into his lungs as he struggled from the exertion.

Rigby looked at Hazelhot and shrugged his shoulders. The display of Stott imitating snakes confused him. And while Rigby was lost, Hazelhot wasn't. But Stott soon continued.

"You and I both know what your bloody game was," he said. "You saw a chance to steal the company out from under me. Admit it, snake!"

Hazelhot was indeed driven by an innate reptilian psychology, but was also incapable of admitting to anything. Denial, deception, and a total fabrication of events was his pathological forte.

"No, no, no, no, no," replied Hazelhot, adding a false laugh. "Oh, how funny you should see it that way."

As he spoke, he moved a paperweight a few inches across his desk. It helped draw the focus away from his defensive lying, or so his subconscious thought.

"No, no. Quaker and Quaker were saving the day. There was another takeover bid. A company called Stop It Don't Rocket. They were after those same shares and had they got them, we all might have fallen."

"Stock it, don't rob it?" shouted Stott. "What sort of damn silly name is that? Who in hell's name are they?"

He was frowning, one eye now deucedly low against the other. He smelt a rat and knew damn well it was coming from Hazelhot's corner. In which direction he now stared unblinkingly, looking for the telltale signs of deceit.

Cracks in the armour, hmmm. Damn irritating fellow that Hazelhot. Should never have let him in at all. Wot. Hmm. Slippery snake of a chap. Slippery.

His thoughts meandered about his ageing mind. Images of snakes with Hazelhot's head on them drifted by.

Fangs too. Big ones. Like Borneo, fifty-four. What? Snakes, big hairy snakes, ready to plunder the ripe flesh of young...

"Sir," Hoots was tapping his shoulder. "Sir, the takeover, sir," he whispered quietly, so as not to embarrass Stott, who had drifted off.

"Take over? What damn take over? Oh yes, the takeover... HAZELHOT!" bellowed Stott.

"Right here, Stott," replied Hazelhot in a tired monotone, as he wondered about the medication Stott was taking and if he could lace it.

"Damn it man, don't stand so close, you oaf," Stott barked at Hoots, to cover up the fact that he had dozed off. "Hazelhot, I suspect there is more to this scandalous situation than meets the eye, and I don't for a minute trust either of you degenerates."

A squeak came from Rigby, surprised to be having the attention pointing his way.

Hazelhot's eyes rolled upwards in his head in disbelief at the cowardice of the man. Stott looked at Rigby and then gave him the infamous steely Stott stare. Beads of sweat could be seen forming on Rigby's forehead, and he shivered noticeably.

"Hazelhot," said Stott, and because of the unexpected success of his stare, he kept his eyes locked on Rigby as he spoke.

"Stott?" came the lackadaisical reply.

"I suspect if I grilled this mouse under a low flame, then a lot more information than you or I want to hear would come to light. Hmm?"

Stott had assumed incorrectly, it would not take a low flame to have Rigby spill the beans. Just a stern look, or a small "boo", was more than enough.

"As it is," Stott continued, now turning away from Rigby with a sense of victorious satisfaction to look back at Hazelhot. "I know damn well you are after the company, and am more than prepared to fend you off. So, give it up Hazelhot. No good will come of it."

And with that, he signalled Hoots to help him up. He was done.

They spent the next five minutes in much the same way as they had spent the first five minutes, just in a reverse order. This time the yucca plant sailed in the opposite direction, as Hoots fell backwards while trying to keep his employer balanced in the vertical plane. When Stott finally made it out into the sunlit day, it was with a sense of achievement. Though he'd left behind him an atmosphere so thick, it could be cut with a knife.

"You really are a pathetic maggot," said Hazelhot, as the gold Rolls Royce gently sparked its engines before gliding smoothly towards the exit of the industrial estate. Rigby cowered as Hazelhot moved towards him like a reptile going in for the kill.

"And yet," he said, pausing mid-stride to casually stroll the last few steps. "Inadvertently, you have brought about a situation that could now be of benefit. The old bastard was getting his rocks off, giving you that pathetic Stott stare. He would have been in here for hours if you hadn't squirmed like an eel. As it was, he left in a curiously good mood. I realise now he just wants someone to bully, and you, my timid little mouse, fit the bill perfectly."

Hazelhot put a hand on Rigby's shoulder in a brotherly way and squeezed it lightly while smiling at him. He was developing a plan. He *um'd* then *ah'd*. Thinking. Nodding. Pleased with his thoughts. Rigby didn't dare move. But as his master seemed to relax, he risked straightening up and breathing again. Hazelhot looked almost joyous, and that came as a tremendous relief.

"Yes," said Hazelhot. "Yes, this really could work out rather well."

He looked back at Rigby, cocked his head to one side, to observe him for a moment. "Rigby, if you ever behave like that again, I *will* kill you."

Rigby then dropped to the floor like a sail dropped from a ship. Hazelhot brushed his hands together, as he liked to do after all his acts of violence.

"Hmm," he mused, looking at his hands with admiration as he squeezed the thumb and index fingers together, marvelling at the simplicity of such powerful skills. He loved the opportunity to perform a pressure-point grip. It was always so devastating in its effectiveness.

Stepping over the unconscious pile on the floor that masqueraded for a human being, he pressed the buzzer on the intercom and leaned over the desk.

"Miss Jones, Mr Rigby appears to have fainted again.

Kindly bring the smelling salts."

He let go of the button and looked down at the crumpled wreck.

"You may be a bumbling maggot, Rigby, but a maggot that may yet help me catch that old trout, hook, line, and sinker."

An Unwelcome Acquisition

How Sir Stott came to be head of a corporation specialising in pornography was a curious tale and a running joke throughout the mess halls of England. It all began one afternoon, *post-argumentus* with his wife, a well-bred lady of high social standing, who - and she frequently made this perfectly clear - he had been damn lucky to get. One afternoon, as they often did, they had argued. This led Sir Stott to seek solace in a little hideaway drinking parlour favoured by the upper echelons. There he found himself in the un-consoling company of the Earl of Cavendish, a known gambler and cad. Pretty soon Sir Stott was blind drunk and losing at a game of cards.

"Spott," said the Earl, eyeing his latest victim with the look of a salivating wildcat.

"God damn your rapscallion hide, the name is Stopp, I... I mean Stott!"

Stott was losing his rag and his hand.

"Spott, Stott, whatever your name is, play your hand and stop dithering, man," said the Earl, feeling satisfied his opponent was now on the back foot.

Stott had never been so insulted in his life. Well, not since about 4 pm that afternoon when his wife had ejected him from the love nest with venom that was positively acerbic in its delivery. He shuddered at the memory and wondered just how he might win favour with his beloved pet tarantula once again. Initial anger had now given way to a mild homesickness, or was it indigestion, he wasn't sure. Either way, he knew he had to get back into her good books. Even if only to attain the comfort of being able to walk safely around the house without fear of crockery, missiles, or sharp lashings of the tongue. He laid his hand, and once again found himself in the losing seat.

"What Ho! That's three hundred quid and my deal!" said the Earl. "Stott, you really are a super chap you know, damn sporting of you to give in so easily. Anyone would think you were doing it to make a bloke feel at one with the world and himself. Really jolly decent of you, old sport."

Stott couldn't reciprocate the emotion that was spewing forth from the far end of the table. In fact, he was pretty peeved with his day. He glared at the Earl. It was a calculated look, designed to send shivers down the spine of one's enemy.

"I say. Are you okay, old chap? You look a little queasy, one eye appears to be limping a little, how strange," said the Earl, knowing full well what was going on.

Stott adjusted himself. He would not take this from anyone, especially a whipper-snapper who clearly didn't know his place. It was time to up the ante. "Three hundred pounds is chickens feed," said Stott. "Care to play for men's stakes?"

"Quite what do you have in mind, old fruit?" asked the Earl, stiffening slightly, rather more in excitement than fear. And a plan formed in the philistine mind of the Earl of Cavendish. Stott spoke first.

"I have a small cottage in the lake district, worth eighty thousand pounds. Anything you care to put up against her?" Stott dared the Earl.

This was, in theory, a smart move from Sir Stott. The thing was costing him an arm and a leg, and if it wasn't listed in the Doomsday book, he would have raised it to the ground long ago and put up a hotel. As it was, he was bound by law to look after the damn thing, and it had simply become a curse he could well live without. He had also lost five times on the trot at this damn silly poker game. He knew as well as anyone that statistically the chances of him winning the next round were well in his favour. Or they should have been, but for the fact he was one drink to the wind and hadn't noticed that it was the Earl's cards they were playing with, and they were marked.

The Earl took the bait like a hungry trout, except he knew damn well it was bait, and he knew the cottage too. He'd heard of Stott's headache one afternoon on the golfing range while he was caddying for his father, the late Earl of Cavendish senior. But the Earl younger had a thorn in his side of his own; a rather sad, though semi-lucrative company that he couldn't put into liquidation. The reasons were complicated but involved a small but extremely violent group of thugs who were using it to launder their dirty money. Hence, the Earl was required to keep said company alive. In return, he got to keep his legs. A fair swap, maybe, but one that didn't sit well with the Earl. In one of his meetings with the thugs, who called themselves Bulldog Security and even sported black bomber jackets that said so, he enquired how he might retire from their service, if such a thing had been his want. The answer was provided to him by Basher Bob, the guvner of said firm.

"In a body bag, mate. Or by handing ownership over to

another toff that is more rich, lordly, and stupid than you."

And so it was that the Earl had at last spotted his champion. All he had to do was convince Sir Stott that the business was reputable. That business was Pussy Productions, and it did exactly that, on video and any other media form it could find to distribute its smut.

"Stott, I feel humbled to be before such a hustling card-sharp as yourself, and I can only offer as matching ante my little known, but splendidly versatile company, Pussy Productions," the Earl waited with bated breath for the response.

He'd expected Sir Stott to laugh the house down, but the long silence that ensued kept the Earl on the edge of his chair and locked him into the most difficult poker face of his career. It was with shocked relief, mixed with incredulity at his good fortune when, from the far end of the table, he heard Sir Stott's reply.

"God damn it boy, you are on. Deal those cards!"

With a brash confidence, Sir Stott watched the cards arrive at his quarter. He couldn't lose, or so he thought. On the one hand, he would rid himself of the rat-ridden hell hole that cost him a small fortune each year in the Lake District, and on the other, he would return home to inform his wife that he was now the proud owner of a cattery. She would certainly be overwhelmed by the gesture, especially since she knew how much he hated cats. Back in her good favour, with the peaceful tranquillity of home life restored, life would be simple again. He smiled to himself, picturing her tending to their feral feline needs. She would also be out of his hair and kept busy. A most excellent result, he thought, as he promptly received a Royal Flush and bagged the game.

This turning point in Sir Stott's career - not to mention his life - led first to divorce, and then swiftly on to the collapse of most areas of his life that hitherto seemed unchangeable. He had correctly assessed his wife's excitement at such a gift and things really seemed to go exactly as he'd hoped they would. Right until Lady Stott arrived at her new company.

Wearing her favourite mink coat, she sashayed in as if she owned the place, which she did, or at least, her husband did. The young woman on reception - who she noted looked far too cheap to remain in service now she was in charge - asked what business she had there. Lady Stott raised herself in fine ladylike splendour and looked down the bridge of her nose at the woman, as was the custom when questioned by such lesser mortals. Pausing elegantly just for a moment, she then informed her.

"I, madam, am Lady Stott," she said grandly. "My husband, Sir Stott, has recently purchased this company and I should like to see the cats and their condition. Now, run along, there's a dear, and see they are prepared for inspection immediately."

Miss Jones, realising her mistake, and terrified that her new boss hadn't taken a liking to her, did as she was told. Once they were ready, she re-appeared and invited the Lady to carry out her task.

Lady Stott took one step inside the office and the shock of what lay before her was imprinted on her mind for the rest of her days, suppressed only minimally by the powerful drugs she would become addicted to in attempts to quash it. After the briefest of moments, when one has been locked inescapably into a view that will never diminish in intensity, one often reacts assertively, and Lady Stott did just that. Instinctively, she took off at a pace in the opposite direction from that which she had just been staring, absolutely aghast and in terror. Unfortunately, she neglected to open the large glass door as she passed through it. Where she was going was anybody's guess, just away somewhere, anywhere, but there.

In the room, spread out before her, had been naked women, their legs akimbo and their vaginas bared for display. Some shaved, some hairy, some large, some small, but all prepped and glistening, ready for inspection. Just as she had asked. Smiling up at her was an insane mockery. An Hieronymus Bosch of dystopian proportions that she had never known existed. Not even in the deepest, darkest reaches of her upper-class mind did what she witnessed that day make any kind of sense. Not then, not later, not ever. Only powerful medication would keep it from manifesting into her consciousness, day or night.

But the trouble didn't end there for Sir Stott. On hearing that his new company wasn't quite what it was supposed to be, he immediately went round to find those responsible. He had plans to bring about some Etonian justice, but instead he found Bulldog Security, who had also recently arrived to find out what was going on. Sir Stott was one sentence into his lecture when a fist the size of a melon laid him flat on his back in the same spot that his wife had stood while requesting to see some pussy. When he came round, he thought he was dead. A throbbing told him his nose was somewhere it didn't belong, and the sight of four large and ugly dark angels confronted him. A voice somewhere behind him outlined his situation and what would be required of him in the future. He took it all in quietly, and was promptly ejected from the premises by air.

After that, he went home to find his wife's solicitors had beaten him to it. The locks were changed and legal process was already under way. So, he went instead to the hospital to have his nose fixed and x-rays taken of the other parts of his body that had received additional attention from the Bulldogs. It was during his time in the hospital that he found an apparent solution to his problems.

"It 'as been an 'umbling experience," Stott said hazily to the gentleman in the bed next to him.

He'd come round from surgery to discover a splint taped to his nose. It made talking a little difficult. Normally, he would have found himself in a private room with all mod cons. On this occasion, he was incognito because he had to avoid the press, so he had booked in as Mr Spiff. He couldn't say Smith because of the clotted blood and the bend in his nose. Neither would he usually have spoken to any members of the public, merely barked orders at various navies to get whatever he needed. As it was, the drugs they had injected him with - and the gas that he kept breathing in - were acting something like a truth serum. Stott was happy to talk about anything that came to mind, and there was quite a lot on his mind that day.

It was a Mr R Hazelhot, ex-paratrooper and buggerer of anything young and male, that quizzed him in an extremely zealous manor from the neighbouring bed. Sir Stott was oblivious to Hazelhot's machinations. In fact, he was oblivious to anything except the pleasing gas that he sucked on like a hungry guppy.

"Tell me more, Mr Spiff," said Hazelhot.

"Well, my name's not Spiff, it's Snott, Sir Snott actually."

"Really? Go on."

Hazelhot's interest was so piqued by all he was hearing, he found it hard not to rub his hands in glee.

And so it was, Stott told Hazelhot everything about himself and his unhappy situation, and plenty more besides. Hazelhot had recently gone through a similar and equally violent situation, but in his case it had been a little more deserved. He had recently received a beating, followed by swift ejection from Her Majesty's forces. During the time he had been with them, rather than perfect the inner soldier, they had effectively turned him into a highly trained and extremely dangerous pervert. Instead of becoming the protector of Queen & Country, the country was now more at risk with Hazelhot at large. But Stott was blissfully unaware of the creature's less salubrious proclivities, as he offloaded his life story upon him.

"...and that is 'ow I came to be like this. I really don't know what to do about it," said Sir Stott as he finished his tale.

Before he'd finished speaking, Hazelhot knew exactly what he was going to do. Craning his neck as far as he could in order to get a good look at Sir Stott through the plaster-cast that currently covered his head, he outlined his plan, or at least a portion of it. The portion which he hoped would appeal to Sir Stott in his hour of need. Sir Stott listened eagerly. Despite his higher state of consciousness, he knew a good plan when he heard one, and besides, he had very little alternative. Help from this strange, plaster-cast saviour was certainly a welcome change to his recent run of bad luck. He had no other friends left to turn to. No family, and now no wife. Hazelhot was indeed his saviour in that moment. Though in future months Sir Stott would have course to consider the phrase; *out of the frying pan and into the fire* in something of a new light.

Acts of altruistic salvation were also not passing through Hazelhot's mind as he stood overlooking the wretched Rigby laying prostrate in the main office of Pussy Productions as Miss Jones attempted a revival.

"Should I give him mouth to mouth?" she asked, after administering the smelling salts to Rigby, which had first made him writhe, then sent him into a catatonic state.

"Mumma," dribbled Rigby.

"Don't be ridiculous, Miss Jones. He is perfectly fine and just needs a moment to recover."

Miss Jones looked disappointed. Hazelhot wondered how any woman could want to have anything to do with such an inept creature as Rigby.

"Go back to reception, Miss Jones, thank you. I can take it from here."

Rigby went through the full spectrum of emotions as he regained consciousness. It began with the soft delicate voice of an angel calling to him through the meadows. He followed the sound and presently saw the face of his long departed mother. She was smiling down at him as she floated a little way above the coloured flowers. Soon she seemed to change into Miss Jones, and Rigby knew then he was safe. He was home in Narnia. But what was that? Dadda? Rigby turned around in the meadow. He could hear Dadda somewhere, too. Then a darkness fell, and the thunderous voice of the Devil brought the scene crashing down around him as pain entered his head and settled there to throb.

"Get up Rigby, you ridiculous buffoon," said Hazelhot, kicking him lightly after the doting Miss Jones had reluctantly left the room.

"Okay daddy," replied Rigby, still in a dreamworld.

"What?" asked Hazelhot.

"Nothing, just a dream, sorry," said Rigby, waking back into the painful reality that was life trapped in a business with Hazelhot. He rubbed his head. It thumped ferociously. "I wish you wouldn't do that to me," he added, somewhat bravely, considering what he had just experienced.

"Shut up Rigby," replied Hazelhot.

It had been Hazelhot's intention to take over Pussy Productions from the start. And this recent attempt was no different. Since expanding the company into Europe and America, they had grown it into one of the world's leading specialist suppliers of porn.

Quaker and Quaker were a small but well-funded company that did nothing other than float around the stock exchange like a deep-sea shark, looking to snap up anything that might be edible enough to feed it. One of its silent partners was a Mr R Hazelhot. The other silent partners were so silent they had no say in the affairs of Quaker and Quaker. In fact, they were all dead, so it afforded them no perks where the company was concerned. They were dead even before the company was born into existence, which was probably better for them since Stott and Rigby could attest to the fact that to be living and mixed up in a company with Hazelhot was tantamount to facing imminent death, anyway. Hence why Stott had employed the loyal henchman Hoots, his South African chauffeur and bodyguard. What Hoots lacked in personality, he made up for in loyalty and capability. What Sir Stott lacked in card-playing skills and drinking, he made up for in survival and business acumen. He knew damn well that Hazelhot was out to get him, and he knew he would likely kill Stott if he had to. In fact, that was what he had been trying to do, one way or the other, since the day Stott signed the contract with him, thus handing over one third of the company to the reptilian creature. Of course, at the time, it had looked like Hazelhot was bailing Stott out of trouble for a share of the franchise, but a third share just wasn't enough for a psychopath. Hazelhot now wanted it all.

Hazelhot desired absolute control simply because that was how he functioned. He had instantly seen the value of the business Stott had unwittingly become a part of. All that really stood in his way was Bulldog Security, and after he got rid of them, he planned to get rid of Stott. Then, he felt sure world domination of the porn industry would be his for the taking. Hazelhot had worked all this out soon after meeting Stott and hearing his tale. And what better way to feed one's own nefarious desires in life than to be knee-deep in smut on a daily basis? Unfortunately for Hazelhot, it hadn't turned out exactly as planned. Yet. Stott had had other ideas, and had proved less than easy to dispose of, especially now he had Hoots in tow.

As for Bulldog Security, well, they had learnt a few lessons about thuggery, not to mention buggery, that no sane man would have wished his worst enemies to endure, let alone a team of ne'er-do-well villains masquerading as a Security firm from Peckham, South London. And that is where this story begins.

PART TWO

Bulldog Security

"Bulldog Security. Basher Bob. I'm the Guv'nor," said a man into a large wall mirror.

He'd been practising that introduction since he was a nipper. Christened Boppy Beans, Basher had pretty soon discovered two things in life: first, that stupid names get you picked on at school, and second, that beating the crap out of people puts a stop to it. With a good dose of the second, Basher completely got rid of the first. He hadn't heard the name Boppy since he was twelve years old. Whenever he *had* heard the name Boppy, it had mostly been associated with the phrase *queer cunt*. So the name Boppy associated itself in his mind with that phrase, and thus he had sought to eradicate it from his world. Basher Bob was not a queer.

He tried it again, this time with the head tilted back, and a little more gold tooth showing. Yea, that was it, nice.

"Bulldog Security. Basher Bob. I'm the Guv'nor."

He was standing in his bedroom in a pair of under-sized y-fronts with the British flag emblazoned on them, looking at himself in the mirror admiringly. After each butt-clenching, hard-man stance, followed by the introduction, he did a little foot shuffle and a quick bob and weave. It felt good. He was a fucking Tyrannosaurus-Rex, and he knew it. A quick growl at his reflection. Move in close. *Boom, boom!* Double-punch and shimmy to duck away, then head for the door. Basher Bob had just performed his daily morning mantra of introducing himself to himself via the mirror, and he was now ready to face the world. The world was his kingdom, and he was the fucking king.

Basher loved Basher. It was in his walk; a swaggering, over-emphasised walk. It was in his talk; a deep, throaty, rhetorically loud talk. It was in the way he ate. It was even in the way he sat down to take a shit. Like the world fucking knew he was there the whole time, and it awaited the return of Basher. The world couldn't wait to wipe his arse for him. Basher Bob. King of Peckham. There was no one he loved more, except maybe his dear old mum.

Everything was where it belonged; his jacket, his cereal bowl, the house, the roller, the belt, the money, the guns, the drugs, the birds, the boys, and, of course, his lovely mum. Everything was in its place because everything had its place, and Basher Bob was at the top of it all. Move one of those things, and you would have to answer to Basher. Something you didn't want to do. His name was known, alright. He was the face; he was a nutter, a don, a geezer, a hard man, a gangster, the boss.

Basher Bob ate the cereal, kissed his mum, donned the jacket, checked the gun, grabbed the money, kissed the mirror, left the house, got in the motor, and went to see the boys.

Basher's boys - as they were known in local circles of underworld crime - were a motley crew of ex-cons and hard-men without necks. Just huge shoulders, biceps, muscles, and egos. They had enemies, sure, but since crewing together and going legit with Bulldog Security, they also had protection in numbers. No one messed with a geezer wearing the black jacket with the insignia of a bulldog chewing a wasp as it guarded a bowl with some Latin words on it. Some said it looked like Basher's mum. That was one of those jokes you told once you'd checked over both shoulders; just like a good nigger joke. People laughed at them, but you didn't want to get caught telling one.

But Basher was not a racist. There were as many blacks in Bashers crew as there were whites. He had grown up in the days of mixed race London schools. His father, on the other hand, had been a brown-shirt, hard-line fascist. He had tried to bang the blessings of white supremacy into Basher daily. Unfortunately for Basher, with his school being mixed, he had no choice but to deal with the *nig-nogs*, as his dad had called them. Basher soon found out it wasn't a term they much appreciated. Not only that, but the fuckers could fight.

By the time Basher's dad came out of the nick, where he had been for most of Basher's formative years, Basher already had black mates in the schoolyard and he respected them. As far as he was concerned, it was a wise decision and something of a matter of survival. He wanted them on his side, and he had fought with them to get their respect, and in doing so, they had gained his. Any racist stamp that was going to be put on him was coming too late, and so it didn't sit right on Basher's now self-forming opinions. So his dad had despaired of him and beat him relentlessly for being a *nigger-lover*. And though Basher stood up as much as he could to his dad, it wasn't long before it didn't matter. Basher's dad went down in a bungled raid on a Post Office in North London, shot by armed police as he was trying to make his getaway out the back. He never got back up.

"All right, you Muppets!"

Basher was stood in the doorway, puffing himself up like a cane toad. He hoped he looked like the silhouetted figure he had seen in a movie the previous night.

Nice move, thought the boys in unison. And they all made mental notes to try it the next time they had the chance. This was what made Basher the leader. He was always one step ahead.

"A'wight Boss." came the chorus not long after his brilliant execution of the new move. The room was full of grunting, testosterone-overdosed, silver-backs, of mixed breeding. All were wearing regulation black bomber jackets, and all looked larger than life. The only body part that remained the same size, despite over-enthusiastic gym work and steroid abuse, was the head, but none of them seemed to notice this anomaly.

Basher broke his pose, grinned his gold tooth smile, and then moved into the room to lay his briefcase on the desk. It contained nothing of importance, but it looked good, made him seem intelligent and official, and that gave him the fucking horn. And with that, the regular morning meeting of Bulldog Security got underway.

It was during this morning's meeting that Basher discovered Pussy Productions had recently had a change of ownership. Basher grinned to hear it. He knew that the Earl of Nonce would eventually find some woolly woofter to palm his business off onto, and that meant an extra step up for Basher. He hoped it wouldn't be the last he saw of the Earl. In fact, he knew damn well it wouldn't be. The protection racket was not one you ever got out of alive, despite what you got told by the Fuzz. He could let him off for a while, though. Give the Earl time to rebuild his confidence and his coffers before he pounced on him again. He'd always loved to give the toffs a kicking. They scared so easily, the fucking rich. Smarmy, silver-spooned bastards that they were.

"So, who is the new owner?" asked Basher.

"His name's Sir Archibold Stott," said the man who had been updating the group on the latest news about the business.

Sounds great, thought Basher. "Sounds like a cunt," he said, and the boys chortled.

Basher picked a few of the boys out, including himself, to visit Pussy Productions to meet its new heir. First, he dealt with a few other bits of business; drug deals, door work schedules, bar scuffles gone wrong, news of other gangs and who had court visits that week. It was the usual Monday morning problems. And then he left with a team of four, headed for the offices and studio warehouse of Pussy Productions that was housed on an industrial estate in Deptford.

On arrival, he found pieces of glass door strewn across the path and for a moment Basher wondered if he had brought enough firepower. Maybe this Sir Stott had a crew waiting inside. But any concerns - that he didn't actually have because he thought he was invincible - were squashed anyway once he heard what had happened.

The boys were still laughing and cracking jokes when Sir Stott himself appeared in the doorway, showing all the signs of a short, fat badger gone berserk. A startlingly accurate analogy. His wife had just been assaulted and insulted, and he had just discovered he was the unwitting owner of a porn company. He was livid, and he was rabid, as he stepped over broken glass and into the front reception. There, he intended to deliver his verbal decimation to the lower classes and teach them a thing or two.

"I am Sir Stott, and who the bloody hell are you hoodlums?" he bellowed in a patronising, better-than-thou, Etonian kind of way. It was Basher himself who stepped over and did the honours.

When Stott came too, they had carried him into the back room so as not to attract further attention from the other industrial estates inhabitants. Normally Stott might have noticed the pictures of naked females in bizarre poses on the walls, but on this occasion he was preoccupied with the large gentlemen who held him pinned to the desk like a frog ready to be dissected. The images instead slipped into his subconscious where they gestated, awaiting the day that they might reappear again.

"Archibold Stott, you don't know me... yet," came a voice from behind his head, "but you are going to wish you had never met me for the rest of your living days."

Basher loved to give his speeches. He felt the power, and he felt the exhilaration. He felt like the Angel of Death or maybe a Herculean God, and that really pumped his nads. Especially when people squirmed beneath those threats.

"You are the fucking fly that just walked into the spider's web," he continued. "Stupid, stupid move, but such is life. As there are flies, so there must be spiders. Every man makes mistakes. Mistakes that never can be rectified. That is his fate. It is your fate to have crossed our path," said Basher, then he paused, and just to be sure everyone had understood it, he added, "you are the fly. I am the spider."

Stott had understood this the first time and didn't see why it needed clarifying, but kept quiet none the less.

"Now this leaves you two options," continued Basher. "The first option is that you take our offer. The second is the stupid option. The stupid option involves deciding not to take our offer."

Again, that seemed obvious to Stott, and superfluous, but again, he felt it best to say nothing. Though he was feeling an insistent urgency to correct such terrible use of English, he quashed it. When no further response came from Stott, Basher assumed the message had gone in and outlined what was going to be expected of him.

"We hear you just bought this here company for yourself from one Earl of Cavendish. A cunt. I don't know what a toff like you is doing wanting to associate his-self with a nobbing company, but that isn't my business."

This was too much. Stott had to butt in and correct his grammar at this point. It really was going too far to use the Queen's English in the way he had been. He instantly regretted it as a gloved hand pushed his already hurting nose further across his face. Stott screeched in agony and fell obediently silent. He wouldn't make that mistake again.

"Good," said Basher. "Now you get it. I don't like people who don't learn their lessons quickly, Archy."

Stott doubted that the person who owned the voice he was listening to had ever been to a lesson in his life, but decided it probably wasn't relevant at that moment to mention it, either.

"Now, my boys here noticed some very unhealthy-looking folk milling around outside with baseball bats a little earlier. These folks were not looking for a game of baseball. So you tell me, Archy, what do you suppose that is worth? My boys keeping people like that away from you and your dirty little business?"

He moved his head closer to Stott, who managed a throaty whimper as he choked on the blood that was oozing down the back of his throat. It tasted metallic and disgusting.

"I agree," said Basher. "Good boy! I knew you would see sense. I think we are going to get along just fine, Archy. Don't you boys?"

There were grunts of agreement all round.

"Now I suggest you leave the running of this little business to me and my boys. All we need from you are a few signatures and to be at the occasional meeting for financial reasons and, you know, to make it look good. We aren't robbers, we are businessmen. You understand that, don't you, Archy, me old mucker?" he patted the chest of Sir Stott, maybe a little harder than he needed to, but it added to the effect. He knew what he was doing.

"Now, I suggest you get yourself down to the hospital and get that nose looked at. I think your wife was here earlier, too. You might find her there waiting for you, given her exit through that there glass door. She didn't seem the sort, but she wanted to give the girls here the once over. Don't you find that strange, Archy? Your missus wanting to look up a bird's gusset? You lucky boy!"

There was a ripple of guffaws from the no-necks.

Stott had never heard such base commentary in all of his life. Was he was losing his mind? How in God's name had such thugs ever come to be in the same room as him, let alone involved in a business he didn't even want? All this from a game of cards! It seemed impossible, and yet here it was. Happening. How could he, an old Etonian, a true-blooded pedigree, a British subject and a knighted one at that, ever have lost command of the situation enough to end up being man-handled onto a desk by lower-class thugs while suffering the indignity of a broken nose? What the hell had become of England? The old world was crumbling. He knew it now. He had seen the signs, and now the great British Empire, such as she was, was fast falling into the hands of mindless... god they had such enormous bodies... and yet what small heads.

Stott was being raised up off the table and back to his feet. He didn't feel at all well. The police would have something to say about this, and he intended to make them his next stop. But Basher was reading his next thoughts well, mostly because this wasn't Basher's first barbecue involving the roasting of a toff.

"Now Archy, if you think going to the police seems like a good idea, then let us remind you of a couple of things. Firstly, your nose, and secondly, your family and their noses. Just a little thought for you to take away with you. If you consider it, Archy, a lot of guys wouldn't give you the generous offer we have today, but today I was feeling nice and generous. This way you get to make a little spending money for yourself and keep your family happy, keep the wolf from the door, so to speak. This way, everybody wins! I think you see my point."

Basher then stepped in closer to tower over Stott like a dark storm cloud, as he brushed his tweed jacket down a little for him.

Stott couldn't see his point at all, but he now knew better than to mention it, and instead remained silent while hiding the look of defiance that burned in his eyes. He was not finished yet, or rather, his life was utterly finished, but changes were taking place in Stott's being. He was physically broken, but he had seen enough of life that he was made of a tougher stuff. It was going to take a lot more than threats and beatings to crush him. For all his apparent over-fed weaknesses, Stott was a leathery-skinned old bastard.

Basher seemed satisfied they had done enough, and so Stott was shown to the door and given a few extra wallops on the way out before being unceremoniously launched through the air to land on his face on the ground outside. As the door closed behind him, minus the glass, a roar of laughter came from within as they relived the event, adding to his shame and to his inward-developing rage.

And so it was, that a strange dishevelled man, who some would say looked remarkably like an over-fed and rabid stoat, could be seen covered in blood and limping his way down the path towards an expensive car. He opened the car door, got awkwardly in, and then quietly drove off.

The Archibold Stott that left Pussy Productions that day was a different man than the one that arrived there. He had discovered for the first time in his life that the power of the Etonian tie was a frail, naïve, and possibly cowardly thing. He now knew Blighty had changed. God bless her. Times had changed. She had lost her men of true standing; her educated officers, gentlemen, and warriors of integrity, conscience, and compassion. Also lost was the basic tenet of decency, uprightness, and respect. Those simpler times of Earl Grey tea and cricket on Sunday afternoons, along with the hours spent discussing politics at the club, were obviously at an end. Instead, a malaise had been permitted to creep into her heart, and she was dying. The rats had taken over the ship.

Sir Archibold Stott had just had his first brush with the creatures that inhabited the murky depths of the underworld. Those same creatures were symbolic of the change that was happening to the country that he so loved. It was a change that he determined there and then somehow to fight. It was an unfamiliar and ugly world that Stott found himself in, and it had happened so quickly it was hard to digest, but he wasn't done yet. No, sir! He was a British subject, knighted by her Majesty the Queen. Goddamn it, this was far from over!

Signed And Sealed

A week after leaving the hospital, on a typically English mid-summer day. Warm, but a little wet. The rain had drizzled persistently through the morning, and a light smog filled the grubby streets of London town. Sir Archibold Stott made his way along Piccadilly and then headed on towards St. James park. His long Moss-Bros coat afforded him some protection from the elements. A giant umbrella that his bank manager had given him made him look like a badger attached to a large, multi-coloured parachute. Unperturbed by laughing cabbies, he continued on and presently ducked into a small pub hidden slightly from the main drag. Once inside, he made his way to the bar and looked about. His intended meet was easy to spot.

Hazelhot was dressed in a flasher mack and an ill-fitting trilby. Normally, the trilby sat well atop his head, except on this occasion, his head was still covered in bandages. He looked like the invisible man, albeit a little more creepy. Something that a small group of young city gents had also noted, and were busy heckling him from further down the bar. Hazelhot ignored them. He was used to taking jibes.

"Let's find a cubicle," said Hazelhot after Stott approached.

Stott was happy to be out of earshot for the things they needed to discuss, and followed Hazelhot to the back of the pub, where they sat down on opposite sides of a table.

"Right," began Hazelhot once they had both settled.

He drew some papers from inside of his jacket and placed them on the table in front of him.

"Here is the deal. I'll get these thugs off your back, and you give me one third of your porn company, Pussy Productions."

"Shhhhh!" said Stott in a harsh whisper. "I'm known in these parts, for god's sake, man!" he admonished sternly. "Can we refer to it as the cattery, or something?"

"Alright, alright, keep your hair on. I want a third of this… *cattery*," said Hazelhot, accenting the word while making quotation marks in the air and rolling his eyes at the banality of it.

"Yes, well, fine. I didn't want the bloody thing in the first place," said Sir Stott. "But it seems it is also going to be my only source of income for a while. They have thrown me out of every old boy's club in London. I have lost my wife, my home, my social standing, and absolutely everything I loved. It's outrageous how much damage this incident has done to my good name."

Stott was feeling sorry for himself and Hazelhot was the first person that he had the chance to offload onto. He had yet to understand the complete lack of emotional empathy in the creature that sat opposite him, who now stared at him coldly.

"I am not interested in your fucki…"

Hazelhot remembered that the man who sat before him had not yet signed anything. He checked himself.

37

He looked at Stott's nose. It was jetting off at a different angle to the perpendicular, and was held in place by white tape and a splint that looked like it wouldn't easily to be removed. Hazelhot breathed in to calm himself, then continued.

"So, the kingdom of Stott has fallen. It's hard. Life is hard. I am sorry for you. Boo-hoo. But we must act fast if we are going to regain the advantage," he urged.

"It's more than my bloody kingdom," replied Stott. "My entire family tree is being uprooted and burned in shame."

The depth of the whole affair was still in the process of hitting home. Stott had been realising just how far-reaching this matter was going to become now it was public knowledge. Each day, he found new and profound depths of inner turmoil and despair to sink into. So much so that he had returned to his GP and demanded stronger medicine in order to deal with the emotional impact he was experiencing.

"Well, I am sure there is a light at the end of this tunnel," Hazelhot said, quoting a get-well card he had once seen. He was not one for diplomacy or sympathy. Hazelhot had little use for either. The only acts of human connection he practised with any fervour or natural talent, other than distinctly degrading sexual ones, were violence and coercion.

"It's not a bloody light," muttered Stott, still wallowing around in self pity and loathing. "It's the train."

Stott was unconvinced that Hazelhot could help him. Basher was bigger, tougher, better protected, and he wasn't wearing hospital wrappings. It was time to point this out.

"How the hell do you expect me to believe you can deal with an army of thugs when you are covered head to toe in bandages yourself? Your last battle obviously didn't end in a victory."

Stott had a point.

"My last battle was with a truck," lied Hazelhot.

Though it was partially true, the truck didn't make it to his battered body, only because the Sergeant Major happened upon the fracas just in time to save his life.

Hazelhot continued, "Look, you sign over one third of Puss… the *cattery*, and I will sort this problem out for you, I assure you. If I can't, you can have it all back, and I will refund you for time wasted," he lied again.

Just then, a woman leaned over the table to give it a wipe and empty the ashtray.

"I'd sign it over, love," she said like a typically nosy London barmaid. "From the looks of you two, those cats are a bloody menace. What you feedin' 'em?" she asked.

"Bonio," said Stott, saying the first animal product that came into his head, and not paying much attention to the irritating woman other than saying enough to get her to leave.

"They are bloody feral wild animals. Look at what they did to us," said Hazelhot, playing with her for his own amusement since she had insisted on interrupting them.

"Gawd, love a duck," she said, and moved on to another table.

"'Ere, Harold," she said to her husband, the landlord, when she got back to the bar. "Them two oddballs down the end got cats or lions or something, and they's feedin 'em dog food. D'you think our Pipkins is eating the right meats? You know with all this genetic wot not going on, you don't know what it's doing to these poor animals. I mean, look at them two. Can't be right, can it?"

Mrs Miggins, Mr Miggins, and three people at the bar who had overheard the landlady's conversation, leaned out to have a look at the two suspicious-looking characters sat at the far end of the pub.

"Okay, I guess I can accept that," said Stott, reaching the conclusion that, like it or not, the stranger before him was his last chance at salvaging his rapidly disintegrating life. "What was it you said you did again?" he asked, as he mulled over the documents Hazelhot wanted him to sign.

"I worked for the Government," said Hazelhot. "The Paras," he added.

"Ah, the real killers," mumbled Stott in admiration of Her Majesty's more specialised paratroop fighting corps. Maybe there was hope after all.

Mrs Miggins, who had returned briefly to collect some non-existent ash from one of the nearby tables, returned to the bar.

"They works for the Government," she said excitedly, "and they got killer parrots. I just heard 'em say it, clear as day!" she added.

The gathered group looked at one another, and then back down the pub. As the two gentlemen continued their business dealings, paperwork could be seen moving back and forth between them.

Stott signed the document and pushed it back to Hazelhot, who smiled. It was a smile befitting the devil claiming his first soul after a long abstinence from sin. He tapped the pen on the table after he seconded the signature and then slotted both pen and the papers into his inner pocket. They felt warm and wholesome, and he knew with a doubt that he had just set himself upon the road to fortune, and hopefully with plenty of perversion along the way.

Stott didn't feel so confident. In fact, he needed another

drink to steady his already shattered nerves. He looked round for the barmaid and had the uncanny feeling that, at that precise moment, the entire pub had turned away from looking at him, and burst into a babble of conversation.

Odd, he thought, *I must be hallucinating with those damn tablets*, and he made a mental note to visit the doctor at his first available opportunity to double check the dosage. He then changed his mind and decided he wouldn't get another drink, and it was time to leave.

"I don't care what you bloody do," he said. "Just get those damn gorillas sorted out, and get my name clear of this evil, bloody mess. But above all, keep me informed. You've got the address of my hotel. I am in room 667. So, are we done?" He asked, preparing to stand up. "If so, I've got other business to attend to."

Hazelhot nodded and smiled to confirm that Stott had indeed been done, and with that, Sir Stott left.

As he passed the bar, he couldn't help but notice both the barman and woman were staring at him strangely.

Shoddy damn service and not what it used to be in here at all, he thought.

His last vestiges of upper-class snobbery, mixed with a loss of rationality and declining social graces, not to mention strong medication that he was currently taking, all urged him to stop and comment on the lack of quality table service and general state of the country too. Once he got started, the awareness that he had the attention of the entire pub inspired his narcotically inebriated sense of superior breeding, and he let them have both barrels.

"Absolute bloody abomination," he said as he began his speech. "What is happening to the once civilised *Homo Sapiens*? What are we creating here? I will tell you what. A nation of bloody killers, low life cretins, and dastardly monsters to be unleashed upon the innocent, hither and thither! End of days, I tell you! End of days! Mark my words."

Stott then laughed somewhat maniacally, but then, seeing he still had a captive audience, gave them his infamous steely Stott stare. After that, he huffed once, and since he had run out of things to say, promptly left the pub.

Even the usually cynical Mr Miggins was now convinced by what he had previously thought was just his wife's passion for gossip and tall stories. He picked up the phone and dialled a number.

"Fred. Alright, yea, fine mate. Look, you know you said that if ever I heard something I ought to call you? Well, I might have got a result for you... yea, if you're quick, one of them is still here. The other has just left. You may pass him on the way in. He looks like a fat badger in a long overcoat and bright umbrella, can't miss him. He's got tape across his nose. I'll tell you more when you get here."

Fred put down the phone and grabbed his jacket. He looked at his watch. If he was quick, he could make the pub in under five minutes.

"Hold my calls," he shouted to his secretary. "And tell Bob to get the first press out ASAP. The write up is on my desk."

He looked through the door as his secretary held up a picture. "Yea darlin'... lovely... maybe better in pink though, shows her tits a bit more... we'll get page three with that, no problem."

And with that, he left, headed towards where a story hopefully awaited him.

Meanwhile, throughout the pub, the seed of misconception had found its way into the egg of imagination, and from its incubation was about to be birthed a mutant bastard of journalistic incompetence. A story would be born that would far surpass that of the disappearing world-war-two bomber allegedly found on Mars.

Hazelhot sipped gently at his lager and lime that had finally arrived. He was happy with proceedings. As he did so, Fred arrived in the bar and nodded to Mr Miggins, who beckoned him closer and whispered the tale of genetic modifications and human sacrifice to breed governmental killer parrots and crazed gorillas into the journalist's ear. If Fred could have masturbated at that moment, he would have done.

Unbe-fuckin-lievable, he thought, as Mr Miggins shared the tale.

Knowing himself to have made a few liberal mistakes in the past, he thought he better check with a few unrelated witnesses before he dived right in like the rabid vulture that he was. Fred thanked Mr Miggins for his help and - checking that Hazelhot wasn't on the move - he went over to a random part of the room and asked a couple of people if they knew anything about the story.

It was unfortunate for Fred that he hadn't considered the speed at which gossip travels round a traditional London pub. His error was to assume that someone on one side of the room would not communicate with another, unknown person on the other side of the room. As it was, the story had twisted and fabricated itself around the pub at least three times already. It had escalated into quite a grand tale by the time it reached back to Mad Moby, the brick-layer from Essex, a place renowned for its tall stories. And that is where Fred now listened, incredulous, as his dreams came true in large Essex flavoured portions.

Christ, I've got a raging hard-on, he noted, and he angled himself a bit more discreetly to avoid poking it in his orator's leg.

It was at this point that Hazelhot noticed the journalist. He was about to leave when he saw the strange way in which the gentleman was standing. It was as if he wanted to pee desperately, but couldn't tear himself away from the conversation. He looked at the man he was talking to, trying to gauge what was causing it. The man Fred spoke to was a bulky gentleman wearing a loud pink t-shirt and lots of unnecessary gold chains, both round his neck and on his arm. Arms he flailed back and forth descriptively, as he described something to the man struggling to contain something in his trouser pocket. Hazelhot wondered what on earth two such bizarre looking creatures could have in common to talk about, when the one dressed, not unlike himself but minus the bandages, turned, and made his way towards him.

"Excuse me, sir," said Fred, wrestling his erection into the elastic of his y-fronts to keep it in place.

Hazelhot didn't like the way he had made his approach. Anyone who walked like that was not to be trusted. There was definitely something in the man's pocket. Could be a weapon. He eyed the man, weighing him up, as they had trained him to do. His mind instantly jumping to *action-stations*, his army training coming instinctively into play. Hazelhot clocked exits, movements, people who might be armed, his radar scanning for any other signs of danger. Everything checked. He was fully alert, and he was ready.

God, that really felt good. thought Hazelhot, after feeling the rush of adrenalin brought on by the execution of his dormant training. It was enough to instigate an erection of his own, and he shifted in his seat to adjust to a more comfortable position.

"How can I help you?" he then asked calmly, prepared now for anything.

"Don't I know you?" asked Fred, somewhat amateurishly fumbling for a way in that wouldn't arouse suspicion while achieving the opposite effect.

"I think that highly unlikely," replied Hazelhot, watching the man.

The word *pervert* was the only description that seemed to fit from his dressage and weird movements, and since that fit his own description pretty well, he realised the creep was probably into the same bag he was, and was after a connection.

"I am sure I know you from somewhere," repeated Fred.

He was trying to push for a clue from Hazelhot to give him something to work with. Anything that might start him in on the path to talk about the governmental underground genetic work that this man was privy to. Hazelhot was acting cagey, and the way he had shifted about when he came up, something was going on. His journalistic senses knew it.

"Sorry, but I have never seen you before in my life," replied Hazelhot.

Fred could tell he was going to be a tough nut to crack, and that was a good sign. It wasn't supposed to be easy. He had to break cover, just a hint. It was a gamble, but he had no choice.

"I know where I have seen you," said Fred, sitting down without an invitation.

Hazelhot wasn't falling for it and made to leave, but as he did so, Fred grabbed for his arm. Hazelhot had been ready, and his fingers were closed around Fred's jugular before he had finished blinking.

"You make another fucking move and you won't be leaving this bar, got it?" said Hazelhot, cold as ice.

If Fred had been uncertain before, he was no longer. He nodded vigorously, as his cock got even harder in anticipation of what might be the story of the month.

Hazelhot relaxed his grip and looked to make sure no one had seen the event. Everyone had seen, but no one was about to show it. Hazelhot looked back to Fred.

"What the fuck do you want?" he asked more aggressively.

"I know what you are up to," said Fred, half afraid, totally excited, and with a small amount of pre-ejaculate emitting into his pants.

"Oh really, and what would that be exactly?" asked Hazelhot, wondering which one of a multitude of evils he was referring to.

"You know, with the dogs and cutting 'em up and all that."

Hazelhot breathed a little easier. For a minute, he thought he was going to have to discuss his homosexual rape exploits.

"Oh that," he said, relaxing a bit. "What about it?"

"Well, I think we should talk. I could help you," said Fred.

"And why on earth would I need your help?" replied Hazelhot, unconvinced.

"Coz it's wrong, init, what they've been doing."

"So they have been working on you too, have they?" asked Hazelhot, still not sure how he was involved.

"Not directly, but I've seen their work. It's pure evil," replied Fred.

Hazelhot now wondered if the Bulldog network was a lot larger than he had at first assumed. They must be working inner city London too, not just Peckham, if this guy knew about them. He considered it. That was big. He wondered how he hadn't heard more about them before. Maybe this fellow could be useful to him, after all.

"Alright," said Hazelhot after a moment, and Fred smiled. "But to be sure I can trust you, I assume you must know about other work they have done in London, then?" Hazelhot asked.

"London? It's bloody world-wide ain't it?" said Fred, acting like he knew everything there was to know about genetics in the current political climate.

Hazelhot stared at him.

Shit! he thought. *Just my bloody luck.*

What appeared to be merely a local gang protection racket was seemingly a global syndicate.

Fuck-nuts. This is going to call for much tougher measures, he thought.

"So who's behind it, then?" he asked Fred, in a tone that suggested he needed to prove himself further.

"How the hell should I know? I thought you could tell me," said Fred.

"And that's why you approached me?" asked Hazelhot.

"I need more information," said Fred, deciding that opening up was probably his best bet at this point.

"Why? Who told you I had anything to do with it?" asked Hazelhot.

Fred paused. He didn't want to blame Mr Miggins, but he thought quickly.

"Fella who just left. Long jacket, broken face. You had a meeting with him, right?" he said, using the info Mr Miggins had given him without ever having actually seen Stott.

"What, Stott?" said Hazelhot, falling for it.

"Yea, Stott." said Fred, repeating the name in his head to remember it.

"Bloody idiot," muttered Hazelhot. "Did he cut you in on the deal too?" asked Hazelhot.

Fred, seeing an opportunity, pushed on it hopefully.

"Actually, it was him suggested we work together on this, pool our resources, so to speak," said Fred.

"The bloody fool has panicked," muttered Hazelhot, thinking about how emotionally weak Stott had been. It always made people over react. "So how are you able to help me then, exactly? And is anyone else in on it I should know about?" asked Hazelhot.

"Not sure. Don't think so. But if you give me the lowdown on the whole thing, my people can cover you, and if anything untoward happens or you think they are going to target you, then *boom!* We spread them all over the bloody place the next day!" as Fred said it, he animated the power of the press with his hands. A story this big would easily make front page news in the National papers.

Hazelhot looked shocked. He hadn't seen that coming from the creepy-looking gentleman at all. Sure, he'd known some weasels in his time, and he was one, but this guy took the biscuit. He didn't look like a bomber, let alone a connected one. Hazelhot decided he had completely misjudged the man. The world was full of surprises these days. He observed Fred with a new sense of awe. His mind was already at work in light of this new information.

"Alright then," said Hazelhot. "I could certainly do with that sort of fire-power behind me. But just how big is... *boom?*" he asked, making the same movement with his hands, but not wishing to use words more expressive than the man had done. He was trying to ascertain if the man was ex-IRA or ex-mercenary.

"Ha ha!" laughed Fred, feeling like a big journo all of a sudden., He'd completely reeled in this massive fish and lent back in a much more relaxed manner as he elaborated exponentially.

"When I say boom, I mean global man, the entire fucking world if necessary, especially if it's a big enough deal. But if you want to make it really count, then you take it fucking inter-galactic, if you catch my drift."

Fred was bragging. He hadn't broken the bomber on Mars story at all, but the man he was trying to impress didn't need to know that.

Hazelhot recoiled.

This fucker has nuclear technology, Jesus Christ Almighty! he thought.

If his people were allowing guys like this to wander round offering nuclear weaponry on tap, there couldn't be long left for the planet. And offering inter-galactic action, too. What did this all mean?

Hazelhot thought hard for a minute. He obviously needed to think a lot bigger than he had been. He needed to think bigger than he had ever thought. The whole thing was escalating way faster than he had ever imagined. If the Bulldog crew were as big as this weasel was suggesting they were, then the only way to deal with it was to hit them hard and fast and get it done. Though the smart move would be to get out now, tear the contract up, and leave Stott to it. But nuclear? intergalactic? Global syndicate gangs. Holy shit! A war at that level made Hazelhot wetter than a cougar on Graduation day who had just slipped Viagra in the punch.

"Well, if we do it," said Hazelhot. "We've got to take them all at once, every single last one of them. We can't leave a single one of those dogs alive. If any of them get loose, we are going to be fucked. And I'm going to need help for that. These guys don't mess about, as you well know. Has your lot seen much of this level of action before?"

Hazelhot looked at Fred. This was heavy hitting. He was going to need some re-assurance that this chap's mob was going to be there to back him up.

"Of course we have. I mean, not me personally at this scale, or as sick as this, but we've covered it all as a conglomerate, believe me."

Fred looked at Hazelhot, a little surprised that he was asking. "Don't worry, mate, they won't dare touch you once they realise we are behind you. They will shit bricks, they always do."

"And just who *are you*, if you don't mind my asking?" asked Hazelhot.

He now needed to know if it was the IRA he was getting mixed up in, a mercenary group, or some Mafia. Whoever it was, they were big time, if this was for real. But Fred knew better than to give the name away, in case Hazelhot made a bid with another paper. Trust had to be earned, and this was only their first meeting.

"Ha ha, amigo, if I told you that, I would have to kill you," said Fred, joking. "Let's just say we are in the top three, and not just nationally, I mean, globally," he added and folded his arms, leaning back. Then he raised his eyebrows twice to suggest Hazelhot should be impressed.

"Really?" replied Hazelhot, still uncertain about trusting this stranger. "You'll be telling me we could take Mars next."

Fred, dropping to a whisper for effect and leaning forward conspiratorially.

"Already have, mate," he whispered. "That Mars one. We

got to that first. It was us. My idea, in fact, just took a little push and the right weight behind it, and they went for it. Total success. I admit it surprised me, but fuck, who knew it would be so easy? And the people loved us for it, crazy, huh!"

Fred knew it would be best to appear to be less interested in Hazelhot's story from that point on. He'd got his result. Fred knew when a fish had taken the hook, all he had to do now was reel him in, but do it slowly. He pulled out a pad and wrote a number on a page, ripped it off, then handed it to Hazelhot.

"When you're ready to move, call this number. The name's Fred. Night or day, I'll be there. We'll give you whatever you need. And we have the money and all the clout you need to make this happen. Let's make history, but most of all, let's get the bastards!"

And with that he tapped Hazelhot lightly on his plaster-cast shoulder, got up and walked straight out of the pub, giving a subtle two-handed thumbs up to Mr Miggins as he left, along with a hand movement to suggest he'd be getting a fair bit of cash for it too.

Hazelhot sat staring into space. He couldn't quite believe it. People were living on Mars, and mob conglomerates had nuclear weapons and didn't care who they sold them to, just so long as the target was mutual. This meant something. The world was changing. He hadn't seen it happen. It had caught him off guard. And if Fred's mob could use nukes without a second thought, then the planet must be really on the edge. That must mean they were just looking for the opportunity to leave the planet themselves. Mars… wow… This went deeper than he had ever considered. Technology had raced ahead of him, and he suddenly felt out of touch. When had things changed? When did interplanetary missions become part of contract hits? It was a brave new world, and it seemed like he had just found himself accidentally invited into a VIP position.

As he sat there staring into space while thinking about space, it didn't take long before his look of non-plussed confusion turned into a subtle grimace, and then to a huge grin. Once again, Hazelhot had a plan formulating. He pulled the prescription medicine bottle from his pocket, knocked a couple back, and contemplated the various ways in which he was going to deliver hell to Bulldog Security. It was now going to happen in ways they could not even imagine existed.

Lucy Lovelips

While Sir Stott laid low at a London Hotel, Hazelhot busied himself with some detective work on Bulldog Security, which for a man dressed in flasher mack and head bandages proved somewhat challenging. Fred, meanwhile, went in search of the name Stott and tried to find associations between it and any suspicious governmental departments. Though he found some recent business purchases that were questionable, and the reference to a knighthood, he had no luck connecting Stott to anything sinister, which led him to the conclusion that they must be covering their tracks.

Meanwhile, deep in the heart of Pussy Productions, the glamour girls were concerned about their job security after discovering about the recent change of ownership. Lucy Lovelips, one of the star ladies at the company, elected herself as a spokesperson for the others. She was the only one who had previous experience with company business and was unafraid of violent men. No one minded her taking the lead in the slightest.

There were over twenty principal ladies on the books at Pussy Productions and several other extras. They could be called upon for various duties, and at various times of the day or night. Mostly, it was film work, or photography for the porn magazines and movies that the company produced. Several of the ladies did the more hardcore footage which had its outlet on the black-market and, of course, in Europe. Lucy covered the entire spectrum of the trade. She was tall, busty, blond, and elegant. Lucy did in, out, up, down, front, back, lap or crack, lesbi, bi, multi, gang, pussy, tits, or anal, she could even do donkey, horse, dog, eel, ferret, pig, or marsupial, if the money was right. Lucy was a professional and knew what she was doing. For this level of professionalism, she didn't come cheap, but she was no bimbo and certainly was no slut. Lucy worked on her own terms and made a lot of money by allowing her body to be abused in front of the camera. It looked like abuse, but what people failed to realise was that Lucy was in charge. Always. She even took a cut of direction and production when there was time for her to be involved on both sides of the camera. Lucy Lovelips was a name known and highly respected in the industry. She'd won plenty of awards for her work. A two-foot high gold penis sat on her mantelpiece at home as proof. And these were the points she brought up to Basher as he sat in the head offices of Pussy Productions while the new front doors were being fitted.

Basher really hated dealing with the feisty tarts, but he knew that if he didn't for the next few days, the place would turn to chaos. Too many hens running round screeching, preening, gossiping, and whining. It gave him a fucking headache. Porn wasn't the glamorous world it appeared to be from the outside. It was more like trying to herd cats. Bloody hard work, and you spent most of your time wondering why you bothered.

"We've had a change of ownership. What did you expect?

Don't worry about it," he said, trying to keep his cool. He wanted to be down at the gym, not in there answering a dumb broad's questions.

"The girls have a right to know where they stand," said Lucy, unwilling to be brushed off so easily.

"Lie down, would be more like it," said Basher, wishing the boys were there to laugh at his jokes.

Lucy glared back at him. She wasn't about to be dismissed, and she certainly wasn't about to humour him in his immature machismo and misogyny.

"Look," said Basher, as he leaned forward in his chair, lent across the desk, and eyed Lucy's long legs that stood defiantly before him. "Give me a couple of days to see how this new owner is going to pan out, and then come back and see me. Meanwhile, just get the girls to do the work as usual. You're still getting paid, for fuck's sake. The bitches should be grateful."

Basher let his eyes wander up from the calves that he had been staring at while he spoke, to the top of her legs, up over her curves, until he met her eyes. The look she returned made his testicles wither. Basher looked away. He was surprised Lucy wasn't ripping her clothes off to get at him and couldn't understand what her problem was. All women fancied Basher Bob. They just pretended not to.

Lucy knew otherwise.

Fucking lesbian, he muttered under his breath as he sat back.

"And why exactly should *we* be grateful for keeping *your* business running?" Lucy came back at him, knowing full well the effect she had just had on him. "The girls are distressed. That snotty tart in the mink had them on inspection yesterday and they feel violated. They need some time-off to recuperate and you better pay them for it too."

Basher saw where it was going. The geese were clucking for free holiday time and extra cash.

"Get out of it," he said, waving his hand as if to shoo her off. "The slags scared the hell out of the old bitch. Why do you think she belted through a glass door? She was trying to get away from them."

"I don't appreciate your tone, mister! The girls are not slags, the girls are human beings with feelings and needs, and they deserve more respect from the likes of you. How would you like it if you had to go through a prick inspection like that? We are not your bloody animals."

Basher liked that idea immensely. He thought he was a stallion amongst men.

"Nothing I wouldn't feel proud of," he replied.

"My girls are professionals and you best treat them like it. Else we will up and walk to where the money is better, and we don't get messed around."

Basher didn't like threats. Had Lucy been a man, he would have got up and smacked her. As it was, he had to show her leniency, but he was annoyed. He didn't like to acknowledge that he needed them more than they needed him.

"Don't push it, Lucy. Don't you threaten me. You girls kick off with your amateur dramatics at the slightest chance, and you know I put up with it. This is business. Shit happens, roll with it and we will get along fine, but fuck with me and you are gonna look pretty stupid sucking cock with no fucking teeth. *Capiche*?"

Lucy paused before responding. She knew they had no choice. She also knew to put on a show of defiance all the same. Men hated it when women challenged them.

"Big man having to threaten the women to get his way, huh?" she said in a mocking tone, but relenting all the same.

She knew when not to push too far, and she had made her point.

"Good, you get it," replied Basher.

Basher sat back and eyed her once again. A sheen dropped over his eyes as his testosterone levels rose a notch, mistakenly thinking a woman had just submitted to his superior strength.

"Now, how about you come round here and show me you mean it?" he said, turning his chair to the side and patting his leg.

"I don't fuck closet homosexuals, so how about you swivel on this!" replied Lucy, extending a finger vertically and thrusting her arm in his direction. She didn't wait for the reply.

Basher hated being snubbed, but more than that, he hated being accused of being a queer.

"Slut," he said as she left the room.

"Prick," said Lucy, as she walked back through to the studio where the other girls were waiting.

"Well, I tried," she said, shrugging her shoulders.

They knew it wouldn't work, but it had been worth a go. Silently they all wished Basher dead, as they went back to putting on make-up, padding blusher over breasts, and apply glint to the nipples and lips, and lips and rings, and things. None of them knew that only a few miles away, their wishes had found a home.

Finding A Way In

A shady looking character hovered in the shadows near to the rear of Pussy Productions warehouse. When a group of people came out, he snuck in through the fire door before it shut. Once inside, Hazelhot manoeuvred round curtains at the back of the warehouse. There he looked around for some tools to help him. Finding a brush, mop, and bucket, he then edged his way towards the main studio area, sweeping nonchalantly as he went, in case anyone was looking. His disguise wasn't perfect, though he had got the plaster-cast off from one of his arms, his neck was still in a brace, and bandages were wrapped around his head. This meant his eyes and mouth were visible, but not much else, and though one leg worked well enough, the other one had a drag to it. To the casual observer, the impression might be that the hunchback of Notre Dame's had a troubled understudy. Coincidentally helping to set the scene, some orchestral music from a phantasmagorial opera was being piped through loud speakers spread around the building. With the accompanying soundtrack, Hazelhot portrayed an eerie sight.

An Italian porno was currently in progress. The script was a one page epic and involved grunts, groans, and a few *"Que bella!"* all expressed to a rousing piece of opera. The rest was just shagging. Scripting the thing was unnecessary, but the director was famed for his work, and he liked to think it made him an actual movie maker. As it was, the two dwarfs couldn't read a script, and nor could the Labrador. Randy Andy could, but wouldn't, and Janice and Janine, the nymphomaniac twins, had little time to read. They were blond and Swedish, not that it made an ounce of difference, just that they looked good, and it wasn't common to have genuine twins, so added a certain something to the shoots they were involved in. The back drop was elegant, or so the director thought. From the right angle, just over the thrusting buttocks of Randy Andy and through the fake window, could be seen the Leaning Tower of Pisa. The cameraman thought it made for a cultured shot and panned back a little. As he did so, four movie moguls watched a colour monitor, where they could see the two mounds of Andy's cheeks rising and falling, up and down in time with the music, as he went into the behind of Janice. Or it might have been Janine. In the background, the symbol of Italy stood proudly erect, albeit leaning. In the monitor it appeared, then disappeared, as if from the very cheeks of Andy's butt. The movie moguls were stood in staunch and manly poses as they observed this creation of cinematic history, destined, more than likely, for the cutting room floor. But in that moment, they thought they had reached the dizzy heights of pornographic excellence.

"Absolutely wonderful framing," said one mogul, and the rest agreed in unison, and turned back to watching Janine. Or was it Janice? No, it was definitely Janine.

"Oh yah," went Janine.

"Ugh, ugh, ugh," went Andy.

"*Que bella!*" said a voice that was probably a dwarf.

He was out of shot but currently chewing on the mound of one twin.

"Oh yeah," said the movie moguls. All except one, who slowly lifted his hand to point at the colour monitor and ask,

"What the fuck is that?"

A white masked creature had just stepped into the frame in front of the Leaning Tower of Pisa backdrop, just the other side of the fake window. It paused for a moment, looked left, looked right, then moved once more out of the shot.

"CUT!" screamed the director, and the opera music stopped.

Hazelhot, realising his error, put his head down and swept vigorously.

He thought it a little unfair that they should throw a cripple out onto the street so roughly, but in the end, it served his purpose. By the time two of Bashers boys had sent him on his way - more downward and into the gutter than forwards and up the road - Hazelhot had gleaned all he required from their pockets. A security pass, a wallet, a door card, a set of keys, a patch with the Bulldog logo, and a condom, unused. The last item had been a mistake. He had got carried away and was grabbing anything in the scuffle. It hadn't been difficult. Hazelhot was well practised in the art of rummaging around in men's pants uninvited.

"They're lucky I left them with their balls," he said to himself, and after getting up and dusting himself off, he left.

When Hazelhot arrived at the hotel on the Euston Road the next day, with a plan to meet up with Sir Stott at the hotel he was now living in, he looked pretty shabby, and certainly not the type of person to frequent a reputable establishment such as the five-star London Hotel he now stood before.

"Sorry, sir, no drunks," said the top-hatted valet, who doubled up as a security guard at the front entrance.

"I'm not drunk," replied Hazelhot, who had not thought to tidy himself up a bit.

"Of course not, sir," replied the valet, who remained one step above him, blocking his entrance, as he looked down upon him.

"I am here to see..."

Hazelhot paused, remembering that Stott was there incognito.

Damn it, he thought, realising he hadn't got the name that Stott had booked in under.

"Look, I am here to see the gentleman in room 667," he said, and tried to look as *prince-disguised-as-pauper* as he could.

Unsurprisingly, the ruse didn't work.

"If you don't step back down to the pavement, sir, I shall be forced to summon the police," said the valet, getting bored with the man.

For the valet, it was a daily ritual of discrimination, and though he enjoyed it, he didn't like to dally over engagements for long.

"Bloody hell, man, I am dressed like this because I have to be. I am an actor," lied Hazelhot, coming up with the best fib he could.

"What you are is a pest, sir. Now *shoo*," said the valet, tired of the persistence from this lying low-life.

"I don't *want* to be going inside your rotten bloody hotel. I *have* to be!"

Hazelhot was raising his voice, but the valet remained

61

unruffled.

"You are not having to be going inside this hotel at all. This is a five-star hotel reserved for gentry and lady of the..." but he got no further.

Hazelhot had heard enough, and grabbing the man by the balls - since they seemed to be the nearest items to him - he stepped forward with his right foot, while thrusting backward with his left arm. The propulsion effect sent Hazelhot gliding effortlessly up the stairs and into the hotel lobby, while the valet, top hat and tails was sent, crushed testicles and all, catapulting down the stairs and into the lap of a lady who was at that moment alighting from the rear of her Daimler. She duly screamed.

Hazelhot barely noticed the noise as he shot past reception with all the stealth of a blundering white robot in a flasher mac. Speedy movement in the leg department was attained by keeping both legs locked and going for it. This he did with such gusto that he might easily have been mistaken for a whirlwind, more because of the effect he was having on the people he passed, than the fact that his movement created a blur. He wasn't invisible, he was extremely visible, and he created a mess in his wake. People and furnishings were knocked left and right like skittles as he passed through. When he reached the lift, he turfed the bell-boy out of it, and nodded politely to a lady who was now cowering against the back wall. Swiftly pulling the door shut, they began their ascent. Her mouth was still hanging open in horror at what appeared to be the invisible man gone mad when she heard it speak.

"Which floor, madam?" it asked with a gentle, if curiously sudden, politeness.

"Three, please," she managed.

"Certainly, madam," said the thing, and circling a finger thrice in a clockwise direction, it pushed the button number three. The button was already lit, but this seemed not to matter to the creature.

"Lovely weather for this time of year, so clement, don't you think?" it said, turning to her briefly, before returning to its forward-facing stance.

"Quite," replied the lady, still aghast, and a little uncertain of the response that would be required of her.

As the lift stopped at the third floor, the doors opened and the thing helped her gently alight. She didn't look back, for fear it might have followed her. As it was, Hazelhot had more pressing engagements on the sixth.

"You did bloody what?" said Sir Stott, but Hazelhot had no time to repeat his brief explanation, as a banging on the door echoed around the room.

"Bloody hell fire!" said Stott, and after scowling at Hazelhot, waddled down the hallway to deal with it.

"Excuse me for disturbing you, sir, but we believe an unsavoury gentleman may be loose on this floor," said Inspector Stump.

The debris of people, plants, plates, and plaster that littered the reception area had given the manager cause for concern. Having had the displeasure of dealing with rock stars and renegades in the past, he had opted to let the police handle the issue on the sixth. This allowed him to busy himself with the slapping of cleaners and bells boys to rid himself of the embarrassment he was feeling because of the litany of complaints that were now befalling him on this most unfortunate shift of duty. It would no doubt reflect on his monthly appraisal sheet, and subsequently, his salary.

All of which made him mighty peeved. While he went off to take it out on staff members, Inspector Stump took charge of the hunt, since he was in the hotel for other reasons when the call came in. The inspector then went to deal with the problem, now loose on the sixth.

"Well, as you can see, I am fine and there is no one else here, Inspector," replied Stott, "but I appreciate your concern and will be studious and alert to unwanted intruders. Thank you and good day."

Stott shut the door and waddled back to the main room. Hazelhot had disappeared. He looked in the bathroom, nothing.

"Strange," he said, and was about to sit down when the cupboard door opened and Hazelhot fell out backwards.

"By Christ man, is that necessary!" bellowed Stott as he struggled to keep his soul in its cage.

The commotion brought the Inspector back along the landing at a rapid rate and they heard the same knock perforate the momentary silence in room 667.

"Dear god. I'm not a jack-in-the-box!" shouted Stott at the door as he made his way towards it once again.

"What now?" he roared as he opened it.

"I thought I heard a commotion, sir," said the Inspector, trying to look past Stott and into the room. Stott was having none of it.

"Look, I am trying to get some well-earned rest, and between you and my infernal neighbours in 666, I am not getting a bloody wink. Kindly forward any problems to the management, old chap. I shall deal with them on my arise from slumber for dinner this evening. Thank you."

And with that, Stott shut the door again.

"I still can't believe I own a bloody knocking shop," said Stott, after hearing Hazelhot's highlights from the previous day.

"With the right people behind it, that knocking shop could earn us a decent sum," said Hazelhot.

"Filthy money, made from filthy habits, by filthy degenerates," replied Stott, dismayed at the sorry affair he was now mixed up in.

"No money is clean, nor any soul, nor creature innocent," said Hazelhot in an odd moment of philosophical meandering.

"Hmm," replied Stott, eyeing Hazelhot suspiciously, and not having a clue what he was talking about.

With these many developing perplexities he was being forced to deal with, Stott was seeing how absolutely nothing was sacred, nothing at all. He breathed in, sighed, then continued. He didn't *want* to ask, but he knew he had to.

"So, what is your plan? And I still don't get this bit about Mars. What the hell have the planets got to do with all this?" asked Stott, wondering whether the sherry might be disagreeing with his new medication. He pulled the medicine from his pocket and looked at the bottle. It seemed like potent stuff.

"I could have sworn you said something about rockets and planetary buses," said Stott, confirming he was not having auditory hallucinations.

"I did," said Hazelhot, who often wandered some way into his imagination to camp out there for a while.

Hazelhot was dosed up on his own medication for various injuries, and a little more than he should have been. Seeing Stott check his medicine bottle reminded him of his, and he took out the bottle and shook a pill or two into a hand. A couple of extra ones fell into his palm, but rather than put them back, he threw them to the back of his throat and swilled it all down with the remnants of Stotts sherry glass. He then shook it at Stott, requesting a refill.

Stott watched this display with curiosity but chose not to comment on it. Attempting to stay focused, he tried to bring the conversation back on track.

"I would much rather you kept your notions of interstellar travel to yourself, at least until we have a firm grip on what is happening down here on Earth," said Stott.

"Alright, but I just thought you might like to know the reasons behind the planning stages," replied Hazelhot.

"Bugger the reasons. Get me results!" shouted Stott.

Keywords brought about strange movements in Hazelhot, and 'bugger' was one of them. Whether it had been because his father had liked to shout it repetitively as he did exactly that to the young Hazelhot, or whether it was Hazelhot's personal bent of nature, was impossible to know. It often made him react with a twitch and a scratch, followed by a thrust of the left arm. Hazelhot had grown used to it, and didn't even know he did it. Stott hadn't, and this was new to him.

"What was that?"

"What?"

"That odd movement with your arm."

"What movement?"

Stott imitated it and looked back at Hazelhot.

"*That,*" said Stott.

"I didn't do that."

"Yes, you did."

"Nonsense."

"Good God, man, I just saw you do it!" shouted Stott,

frowning and eyeing Hazelhot, wondering which of them was the more insane.

Stott gave up trying to make sense of anything and reached for his pills again. After that he topped up Hazelhot's sherry glass, took another glass for himself, filled it, and knocked half of it back. If he was going to lose his marbles, he may as well be drunk and pain free.

"Whatever," replied Hazelhot, realising that he must have twitched, and changed the subject before Stott could question him further on it.

"I grabbed some things that might help us get close to Bulldog Security," he continued.

"Oh really, like what?" asked Stott, eager for any bit of good news to help raise his spirits from the depths they had sunk to.

Hazelhot produced the items and laid them on the table. The first thing Stott noticed was the condom.

"Are you planning to fornicate your way in?" he asked, though nothing would surprise him with Hazelhot, despite only knowing him for a short time.

"I didn't mean to get that. This item is interesting, though."

He handed something to Stott. It was the Bulldog logo patch. Stott moved the lamp nearer and looked at it, then peered at it, and finally looked back to Hazelhot with an incredulous look on his face.

"Care to translate... *Pedicabo Ego Uranus?*" asked Hazelhot.

Though he knew exactly what it meant, he wanted to see Stott's face as he explained the meaning of it.

"No one in their right mind would want to translate it," said Stott, who already had. "It clearly says, and I use it in the loosest sense, *I Bugger Uranus.*"

Hazelhot twitched and punched Stott's sherry across the room. Stott was on his feet in no time, fists to the fore.

"Good God, man! If you know what's good for you, you'll stop your damn clowning around. I boxed at Eton, you know."

"Calm down, grandpa," said Hazelhot, more intrigued by the translation than bothered by any threats made by a man who looked like the runt of a badger litter. "I've got a nervous twitch, is all."

Hazelhot absent-mindedly took the medication from his pocket again, popped the top, and knocked another two pills back. Stott huffed and sat back down, pouring himself another sherry in a fresh glass, and moving it well out of the reach of Hazelhot.

"Why on earth do they have that on their logo?" asked Stott, calming down, and considering the meaning of it.

The truth behind the logo was not that much of a mystery. Basher had, at one time, in his employ a Latin Master who had resorted to becoming a printer after Latin ceased to be a subject taught in schools. On one of Basher's rounds to collect protection money from said printer's business, unfortunately, the man had chosen to spend his protection money on a nag. The nag had keeled over half way round the track, leaving the *Latin-teacher-cum-printer* without the money required to keep Basher at bay. Basher had broken his fingers, but not before he had hired him to design his company logo for free, to cover the loss.

At that time, Basher had been only a small time thug planning to go legit, and he figured that some matching jackets would help his boys look like a firm. On the next and final time they met, Basher demanded the money, which once again had found its way into the bookies, and on to the wrong nag. Especially tough, since the printer now had severe difficulty in working without full use of his fingers. This time Basher hadn't been so lenient and had taken a set of printing plates to the man's head. He died on the third print, leaving only the cut of the jackets, and the design of the logo in his passing. Knowing his day had not been far away at the hands of Basher, the printer had got his own back in the only way he could. The inscription was supposed to read, *"Together, the Planet"*. Something that fell in line with Basher's wishes to be gangster number-one and a global firm. Basher knew Uranus was a planet, and he knew Latin was weird, so he assumed it was an accurate translation. It wasn't. The fact his entire army now wandered round by day and night with the words *I Bugger Uranus* upon their breast, was lost on him. The printer no longer got much of a laugh out of it, either. Though he had, maybe, had the small pleasure of dying knowing that the bigger that Basher's firm got, the more likely they would one day fall to ridicule when someone was brave, or fool enough, to translate their logo for Basher. So far, no one had.

These finer historical details were unknown to either Hazelhot or Stott. They both took it to the distant dimensions of their own respective medication-addled brains, and there made sense of it in their own ways. Hazelhot assumed it related to the story about the planetary escape Fred had alluded to and the extra-terrestrial habitation of Mars, along with the subsequent plan to nuke the Earth. The longer-term aim being to get to Uranus. He had tried to guess at the link to why buggering came into it, but couldn't join the dots with any certainty, so didn't bother, and instead took another swig of his own glass of sherry. Stott, meantime, had come to a firm conclusion about it all. It seemed obvious to him, and sickening, too.

"Damned homosexual pornographers," muttered Stott. "Can't keep it to themselves, always got to wave it about. Perverted bloody poofters."

Stott stood up, discarding the patch onto the table. He'd had enough of the day already. It seemed that Hazelhot was continually delivering dirty bones to his door, like some hopeless, hapless, stray dog, eager to find a master. He was beginning to dread their meetings. Stott waddled over to the window and looked out over the spires and regal architecture of some of the older buildings of London, hoping to find some sanity there.

This fair seat of Britain, Her Majesty's own city. Each day her furtive bosom being plundered and ruined by the rectal-rogering rapscallions of rapacious intent. What in god's name is becoming of this country? he thought to himself, as he grew wistful.

The old roof tops stood high and proud, and he gazed upon them for inspiration. He wasn't beaten yet. Oh no. Not Sir Stott. He'd been shocked and dazed. Brought down a bit, sure, but he wasn't over and out. He had some fight left in him. He was made of sterner stuff. British, through and through. You didn't just stomp on a knighted subject of the realm and get away with it. He would get through this infuriating time with old-school British bloody-minded determination. Discipline, that's what was called for. Discipline!

Stott's previous homophobic comments, which Hazelhot assumed had been directed at him, did not bother him one bit. Hazelhot knew he wasn't gay because he knew he was a pervert, and so he had no problem with the label or anyone who used it. Hazelhot liked domination and control. The gays liked to submit. At least, that was how he saw it. After wandering briefly over the memories of the various young male bottoms he had plundered to date, he soon came back to thinking about how best to tackle the problem of Bulldog

Security. What he needed was a Final Solution.

"I am going to need some money," he said.

"So get some," replied Stott.

"I need to join Bulldog Security. Get on the inside," said Hazelhot, ignoring Stott's tone.

"You need to get this bloody mess sorted out and stop making matters worse," replied Stott.

"If I can get on the inside, I can find out what their plans are. Then once I know what their movements are going to be, I can set a trap and neutralise them all in one go."

"Actually, that is something I wanted to discuss with you," said Stott. "Just how *do* you plan to 'neutralise' Bulldog Security?"

Stott left the reverie of his window daydreaming and returned to his chair. The medicine mixed with sherry now gave him a bit of a wobble, but he got safely sat down without too much trouble.

"Well, from what I have found out so far," said Hazelhot, "they have their fingers in quite a few pies. I did some checking and found plenty of dirt on the leader, Basher Bob. He's the one you met that day at Pussy Productions. He's my primary target, but it is no good striking him until we know just how big the group is. I have it on good advice that it goes beyond just our shores, and that is where it gets difficult. I need to find out who is behind this, where they are, their global numbers, and all the head honchos. First, we follow the trail to the source of this whole rat's nest, then, and only then, do we call in the troops."

Hazelhot liked to voice his theories out-loud. They always sounded great, even if they rarely bore fruit the same way coming out as he had imagined them going in. Which brought him neatly back full-circle to thinking about his buttock plundering, and he smiled as the drugs and sherry took a stronger hold on his state of mind.

Stott didn't share his confidence, and was rightly dubious. He realised Hazelhot was now intent on expanding his, and everyone's, problems beyond the shores of Britain, possibly even the planet. Given some of his more insane ramblings earlier in the conversation, it worried him. The man seemed hell-bent on creating ever more unmanageable carnage. Stott felt it was time to point this out.

"I think you need to deal with things in smaller chunks, or else we will get nowhere. Forget everything beyond the limits of the M25 for a minute, and let's decide how best we are going to extricate Puss... that bloody company, and ourselves, from the clutches of Bulldog Security. Then, you may return to your task of planetary invasion and global warfare, or whatever the hell it is you keep insisting on babbling about."

Stott clearly didn't grasp the severity of the situation they were in. Hazelhot was wondering how much Fred had told him. It sounded like Fred hadn't told him much, so Stott clearly knew nothing about the risks, or the firepower, that Fred had at his disposal. Hazelhot decided not to burden Stott further with it. It was obvious he would rather not know. If Stott felt happier living in denial, so be it. He would not involve him further with the escape to Mars, and the planned Armageddon, nor expand on firepower now available to them, all thanks to Fred's crew, whoever they were. Hazelhot decided he would act on his own, and would give Stott reports as and when he asked for them. It was time to get on with it, and so his next move would be to inform Fred that he was ready to rock and roll. As of this moment, *Phase One* was a go. But Stott had been right about one thing. It would take him months to track down all the leaders abroad. So instead of Mohammed going to the mountain, Hazelhot would do something that would get everyone's attention. Hazelhot had a new plan birth itself into his mind. He would create a furore that would be heard throughout the free world. He would light Bulldog Security up like a beacon. But first, he needed to gather intel.

Feeling inspired, he put some effort in to focusing, and then looked again through the stuff he had stolen from Basher's crew when they threw him out. Cash cards, a couple of family photos, a gym pass... they all used the gym, so that would come in handy. He then found the door-swipe with 'Pussy Productions' written on it and played it around in his hand as he sat back and considered his recent visit.

"I think I'll visit the studios again," he said.

"Did you not just get ejected from there?" asked Stott.

"Incidental," replied Hazelhot. "I'll tell them you hired me."

"Right-ho, but it's Basher's mob we need to focus on," said Stott.

"Well, I think I'll give it one more reconnaissance, and after that join their gym and get a head count. I want to get a feel for their business, exactly how many of them there are, and what we are up against."

If Hazelhot had been aware that he was overdoing the medication, it still might not have occurred to him that a radar for perversion was what drew him to think about getting back into Pussy Productions warehouse.

"Not sure about you revisiting Puss... the studio. But I think the gym plan is an excellent idea," replied Stott. "Get what you can. Meanwhile, I'm meeting with Basher in a few days at the office there."

Stott shivered to think about it, then added, "I don't expect

I am going to enjoy that meeting one bit. I would like to go in there knowing that my suffering will not be in vain. Don't fail us, Hazelhot. I am counting on you, old chap. Whatever you need to do, now is the time to do it. But for god's sake, keep it focused."

With that, Stott ushered Hazelhot out of his suite. The medicine and sherry were kicking in, and he'd had more than enough of the fellow.

It was with a renewed sense of purpose that Hazelhot descended in the lift. Instead of getting out on the ground floor, he continued to the basement car park. There he wandered about for a while before breaking into a suitable vehicle. After fumbling about beneath the steering wheel, it sparked to life, and he drove out onto the Euston Road. Though not before reception had spotted him on a camera and rung the police to give them a description of the car, the number plate, and its current occupant.

First Man Down

Lucy Lovelips was preparing for the next shoot in her dressing room at Pussy Productions. She looked at herself in the mirror. The round bulb lights surrounding her face gave off a pleasing hue, but she knew her modelling days were numbered. Lucy was ageing. She wanted to deny it, but wasn't the kind to push obvious realities to the back of her mind, nor was she willing to turn to padding and plastic in an attempt to re-capture her youth. She had made a lot of money in her time at Pussy Productions, but it was time to consider moving on. Lucy didn't have kids. She had never felt the urge to settle into the house-wife role. Not that she didn't like the idea, but her life had been too busy. Her life, and her work, had been a whirlwind that simply never stopped.

Lucy was gazing at her reflection in the mirror, thinking about what direction she should take, when the call to assemble came over the loudspeaker system. She sighed and snapped out of her reverie. Giving a brisk tweak to both of her bullet sized nipples, she then made her way out into the corridor and on toward the set.

"Okay people, let's go!" shouted the director, Larry,

through a megaphone. Though he was only a few feet away from those he was addressing, this didn't seem to stop him. Lucy jumped a mile as he blasted it at her. Larry was the sort of man who wouldn't know civility if it choked him in his pink polar-neck jumper. She controlled her reaction, counted to ten, and then continued onto the set. Making a mental note to keep her eye on his whereabouts, and keep him a suitable distance from her person. Larry's whereabouts were something that everyone got to know about all the time, and loudly.

"Chop chop Maurice, powder." Larry was now clicking his fingers, looking to his left and right frantically. His gopher Maurice appeared with a glass mirror containing an enormous pile of cocaine, which duly found its way up the director's nose with an enormous snort. Only then did he stop talking for a second, mostly to adjust to the impact as it went down his throat. Larry shook himself like a manic baboon that had just ejaculated after a long week of abstinence. His face returned to the mirror one more time as he finished the pile off with a second hoof, after which his eyes goggled in opposite directions. Lucy watched the grotesque display and wondered what the hell she was doing working there. She'd had enough of the lowlifes, the freaks, and the criminals. She wanted out.

"Okay, girls and boys, let's get dirty," growled Larry, drooling with a lascivious perversity, as a spray of white powder emitted from his nostrils in a snort. Lucy shook her head. She had been observing that blob of high blood-pressured obesity with an unspoken but incredulous disbelief for many years. She was surprised that he'd not yet died of a heart attack. It would not be a pleasant shoot when he was high like that, and of late, he had been getting worse. Still, she was a professional, and it was time to switch her emotions off and let her body go to work while she put her mind into a dormant state until it was done. Any other course of action, and she would end up killing the indulgent coke fiend of a director, along with several other incompetent perverts that insisted on hanging around the shoots.

The gopher Maurice padded a small towel over Larry the director's brow to disperse the sweat beads that were building up there like shiny pebbles under the heat of the lamps. Larry, the fabulous, barked orders and instructions in all directions. The closer the object was to his megaphone, the louder he seemed to project his camp, demanding oratory. He finally plopped back into his personalised director's chair and surveyed the set for a moment. Satisfied everything was in place, he finally shouted.

"ACTION!"

Lucy walked onto the set and twirled once to give the camera a full view of the skimpy white latex skirt she was wearing. Three cowboys looked up from a pool table over which two of them had been faking an argument. The jukebox - that was supposed to stop when kicked from behind by the runner - had instead jumped onto a Christmas carol. The second and more hefty kick silenced it but also catapulted it from its moorings. It took off across the set, coming to a halt near a cowboy, who stared at it. For want of something better to do, he tapped a couple of numbers into it, trying to make it look as if they had planned it all along.

Larry dropped his head into his hands. Then, looking up, he gave a signal for everyone to keep going. Hell, it was porn, no one was going to be worrying about some god damn jukebox.

Get on with it, he mouthed silently, and everyone did.

"Why are you boys wasting all that energy arguing?" asked Lucy.

She was pretending to chew on some gum while holding a provocative stance. The bland scripts were awful, but the pay made up for it, and acting, was acting, was acting. Though, of course, this wasn't acting, this was porn, but it was nice to pretend.

"Why don't you put some of that energy to good use and spend it on a lady looking for a good time?" she asked.

The men looked at each other, raising brows and nodding in a cheesy, machismo way. Then they sidled up to her, circling her, checking out her wares like randy dogs.

Lucy was tired of faking porn, but she knew how to put on a display. The public assumed all the women who worked in it were sex maniacs, but the truth was the complete opposite. It was all about the cash. It was as boring as factory work, maybe even worse, because at least they didn't have to pretend they were enjoying it. But that was what separated the porn star from the average glamour model. Lucy was a porn star. One of the best. She could fake it so well that she could even fool her own body, and that was why she was so good at what she did.

Lucy focused her energy into character. She felt a little wetness developing, though the industrial sized tube of lube had probably helped. A waft of pheromones and the musky scent of the men arrived at her senses, overheating as they were under the hot lamps. As much as it made her baulk, so it did something else. From there, she could launch into her wilder nature. It just seem to come naturally to her to do it, but of course, it was all faked. Always. Every time. But she could now feel a show coming on. It was time for her to show them why she earned the big bucks.

Lucy was famous for turning a drab, run-of-the-mill porn-flick into a hot brazen shag-fest that might win a coveted golden penis award. Everyone wanted one. Very few got them. All she needed was the right mood, something to trigger her senses, and after that she could fake it well enough to go off like dynamite in an untapped gold mine.

"Oh yeah," she purred. The energy inside her warming up. She liked the challenge of being out-numbered, and though these boys were young, extremely crap actors, they were fresh and uncorrupted. The industry had yet to suck them dry.

Testosterone was in the air, and it worked on her senses. She looked at the men, capturing their attention with her tractor beams, like the queen of sexual energy. She had control of them. They were hired dicks, but they were still dicks, and dicks couldn't help themselves. The thrill of the power went through her. The sense of drawing all that attention. Knowing it was in her hands, she engaged it. Successfully redirecting her frustration and concerns into a sexual performance, as she unleashed everything upon them.

Lucy moved in towards a man. Resting her talons on the skin that showed at his open shirt, she scratched down lightly, and he smiled. Pushing her butt out towards the two behind her who watched hungrily on, she gave it a twerk and their eyes lit up in excitement. Lucy knew what she was doing. Larry the director looked pleased. He was seeing more cash for cocaine floating around in front of his eyes. Clicking his fingers at Maurice, he powdered his nose again.

Lucy pushed the man back to the pool table. With an exaggerated sashaying movement, she teased the others to follow, giving a brief look over her shoulder before letting her hips do the talking. The men followed like obedient lapdogs until she reached the table and slammed the man into it. Grabbing a pool cue that lay across it - a specially made dildo designed to look like a pool cue - she swung around, spinning on her heels, to lean back into him. Then she eyed the other two who stood before her, eagerly waiting for permission to dive in. Lucy licked her lips and ran the pool cue over herself seductively. She pulled it up against her thighs, lifting the bottom of her short latex skirt to reveal a shaved bald pussy. Gradually, teasing the end of the pool cue up between her legs, she let the two men take hold of it, as she controlled the movement of it into her. Focusing her mind to prepare herself until she could let it edge further in. With gentle, controlled strokes, it went deeper. Finally, in a deliberately over-acted display, she pulled it from her and threw it across the room, where it smashed through part of the set with a loud crash. Larry waved excitedly for everyone to keep going. It was too good to stop now, just keep it all rolling. Lucy grabbed for the first cock she could see, and dropped to take the man into her mouth, holding still for a moment to let Camera One move in closer. She then bent her body and waited for Camera Two to get into position. Once they were ready, moving her ass up, she slowly pushed against the throbbing male that was standing erect behind her. The owner slowly easing it in to her glistening behind - a runner having oiled it during the brief pause for camera positioning. But this was Lucy, and the show was only just getting started.

Hazelhot stood mesmerised. He'd missed the activities of the porn shoot the day before, despite being an involuntary extra in it. So, this was his first porn movie in the making, and it sent his medicated being reeling through feelings he had not previously known existed. The scene sent him into a place beyond, launched there by the events he could not now tear his eyes away from. It was different in the flesh. It was glorious. Religious. It was *[cue the music] Gloria In Excelsis.* He watched Lucy work it. He'd never witnessed a performance so enlightening or engaging.

Hazelhot didn't much like women, as a general rule. They just never seemed to appreciate the dizzy heights found through the level of depravity that he liked to aim for. He had tried them once or twice, but they were prissy, wanted wining and dining, and then demanded emotional connection and nurturing. Before and after. They also cried and complained a lot. The only women he'd ever become involved with had hung around longer than he liked, and ended up demanding expensive purchases in order to let him have access to the only parts that interested him. He'd concluded that he did not understand the female of the species. They were altogether different. Incapable of thinking in a straight line, and emotionally unpredictable. They were not worth the time and effort. He'd found rape to be so much more fun, but with women, it was almost too easy. So, after a few goes at balaclava'd fornication with the creatures by leaping out on them in parks after dark, he had given up trying, and never bothered with them again, preferring, as he now did, the more formidable fight that a young male buck could put up.

But in watching Lucy, he became transfixed. He had seen the change come over her as she deftly, and firmly, took control of the situation. Seeing her dominate the men - whom, by the look of them, should have been the ones in command - it had moved him. He could appreciate what he was seeing. It was power. It was command. It was glorious.

And it touched him in a way he had never been touched before. Hazelhot was, for the first time in his life, smitten by a woman.

The scene came to an orgasmic crescendo, and Larry shouted.

"CUT!"

The entire cast and crew then turned to view a bandaged man near the fire exit, who was clapping for all he was worth. Hazelhot had momentarily forgotten his undercover purpose and let go of the plot. When he realised his mistake, he dived on his broom to begin furiously sweeping, adding in a whistle in the hope it might all be forgotten. Doing so enabled him to go into denial, as he did whenever he felt overwhelmed by a situation. He was the cleaner, and nothing was going to make him think otherwise. Worried that he would likely now be recognised from the previous day's events, but the shoot was a different crew, and none of them had been there the day before.

Lucy strained to see beyond the glare of the studio lights at who this admirer was. Shading her eyes, she could make out the figure of a cripple sweeping the floors. Her heart went out to the poor fellow, who was obviously one of her physically challenged fans, and she made a mental note to show her gratitude to him before she left. She knew how much her work was a source of solace for the lonely and dispossessed. The creatures that lived at the edges of society often wrote to her to tell her how much she made a difference in their lives. Often she was their only connection to a woman that didn't insist on mothering them. She was well aware she had a large fan-base in their ranks, and acknowledging this was important to her.

An hour later, having got away with his outburst, Hazelhot was making mental notes of the construction of the premises and how best to make use of it in combat scenarios. As he was doing this, Lucy appeared behind him without his noticing. The lights were lower, as most people had left, except for one of the Bulldog Security staff, who had arrived on site to protect the premises overnight, though he was oblivious to the usurper in their midst.

"Hello," said Lucy, softly.

Hazelhot jumped, surprised by the interruption. He had been leaning on his broom, chin resting on the top of it, while counting rafters. The surprise sent him on a pivoting circle around the broom handle, promptly tripping over and landing in an unceremonious heap on the floor. He struggled to get up, which wasn't altogether easy with the remnants of his plaster casts. All the while observed by a smiling Lucy.

What a sweet little man, she thought to herself.

When Hazelhot finally got to his feet, he wiggled like a star-struck puppy. It was just one of those things, and there was nothing he could have done about it. Lucy's presence brought on the effects of chemical debilitation. Nature had ordained that she had all the right qualities to render Hazelhot completely and utterly inept, and it threw him into a star-struck state that confirmed to her he was probably retarded. This was helped by the medication that was delaying his return from the bizarre behaviour he was currently exhibiting.

"Well," she began, once he had calmed down a little. "I noticed you enjoyed my performance, and I thought I would come over and say thank you. I always appreciate it when someone notices the efforts I put in."

She smiled at him, feigning coyness.

Hazelhot couldn't manage a word. He mumbled and gibbered, and saliva came from his mouth and a bit ran down his chin. After that, a sort of whinnying sound emanated from him. He soon gave up trying to speak and just nodded his head eagerly. Thrusting his hand forward, almost violently, he tried to initiate a handshake. Lucy went one better and moved around it to plant a kiss on his cheek. She then turned on her heel and threw a large fur coat grandly about herself. Feeling for the reaction she knew she would create, she walked away in her best slow-motion, hip-swinging gait. As she reached the door, she turned for a moment to give him her well practised movie-star look. Her chin was slightly low, her arm high on the door, her eyes smouldering, her essence seductive. Conveniently, a light above her set it off rather well. She paused and gazed at him for exactly the right amount of time to burn an image of herself forever into his soul. Then she smiled once, threw her head back and laughed, before turning and disappearing through the door.

Hazelhot stood motionless, matching her elegance and self-assuredness with his own inelegance as he swayed a little heavily medicated, in an apparent state of near rigor mortis. His normal condition of complete insensitivity meant he didn't really know what was happening to him. The female of the species had never had that effect on him before. He had no point of reference for it. Hazelhot had fallen for Lucy.

He was still staring at the spot where he had last seen her, when the Bulldog Security guard finally appeared to make a last check prior to locking up for the night. Seeing the catatonic state of the cleaner, Barry tutted to himself before engaging the customary Bulldog swagger, and made his way over to tell the imbecile to leave. As he reached Hazelhot, he circled around the front of the man and looked at him. Waving a hand over his face, there was no response. He didn't know quite what to make of it.

"Time... to... go," said Barry slowly, as if talking to a patient in a lunatic asylum. He decided it must be a half-breed employed by Basher to squeeze a bit of extra cash from the welfare. Waving his hand in front of the man's face again, looking for signs of life, the retard just stared straight ahead, still smiling. Barry looked at his watch, sighed, and then went to take his sleeve to usher him out.

"Come on, mate, it's time for you to go home," he said.

As his fingers curled around the arm of Hazelhot, it triggered a reaction that Barry could not have predicted. With Hazelhot's rude awakening from distant summer meadows where he had been skipping with Lucy like a frolicking Labrador, he was suddenly back in a squalid grey warehouse on the outskirts of Deptford, with his medication wearing off. Barry had just found himself in the wrong place at the wrong time as the beast woke from its slumber. A darkness descended on him, and he wondered for a moment why the lights had gone out, and then he was walking through a soft penumbra, making his way towards the exit.

Meanwhile, Hazelhot was returning from the other direction, to find he had just performed a temple punch, followed by a throat-grip and tear of the jugular on which he still had a hold. Blood was spurting in all directions from what was left of Barry's throat.

"God damn it!" muttered Hazelhot, annoyed at the thought of having to throw out yet another set of clothes. He still had a hold of Barry, and he turned the now limp body back and forth in his hands, taking a moment to admire what he had done. After observing the precision of his subconscious's deadly accuracy, he released his grip and let the body drop to the floor. Hazelhot - now back from his Venusian meadow skipping adventures with Lucy - checked for witnesses, but there were none. It was a record even for him to have crossed the entire spectrum of human emotion with such rapidity. It took him a moment to return to himself.

"Hey ho?" he finally said most casually and then looked at the bloody mess on the floor and considered how best to approach addressing it.

Hazelhot's reptilian mind came quickly to his rescue, as was so often the case. He removed his own clothes, and after that he removed the clothes from the body. Then he dragged the dead Barry to the toilets, stuck his head in a large bucket and propped him upside down inside a cubicle to let the rest of the blood drain out. On the walk back into the warehouse, he practised the Bulldog swagger, which - given his lesser bulk and bandaging - looked more like a naked cripple suffering a fatal colonic rupture. He dressed, then picked up Barry's jacket and cleaned it of blood before putting it on to make his way around the building, securing the exits while practising his new walk. Satisfied that the place was empty and secure, he stripped naked again, collected the bucket of blood, and then began daubing the walls of the studio. The fates had decided the course of events, and there was going to be no turning back now. Hazelhot took to his work with a whistle and a skip, and a definite sense of *joi de vie*.

An aged rat entered through a small hole in the wall on the far side of the warehouse building. Spotting the strange creature skipping and prancing naked at the far end of the warehouse while whistling and splatting blood over walls, it knew itself to be in the company of something far more sinister than any human it had seen before. A moment later, the rat took off back through the hole to inform the other rats that the end was nigh.

The Writing On The Wall

Inspector Stump sucked in through his teeth. It didn't look good. He had known about Basher's operations for some time, and the money they gave him to turn a blind eye had been a handy little earner. But the scene that met his eyes when he entered Pussy Productions studios told him he was going to have to cut ties with Basher's firm and erase any evidence that might link him to them.

Stump was Peckham's finest, and though Deptford was out of his jurisdiction, Basher's gang hailed from Peckham, and since top-brass knew he knew them, they had requested the Deptford squad put him on the case. Given the sight now facing him, he knew Basher's days as top-dog of the Peckham underworld were numbered. Every crooked cop and criminal was going to be washing their hands of Basher as fast as was humanly possible. Events like this were precursors to gang take-overs, and he knew it. While the Inspector stood surveying the scene, Basher was at that moment in a car heading their way, and he was fuming.

"Tell that fucking solicitor to get his ass over there right fucking now, or I will rip his head off and shit down his neck," he shouted, then threw the mobile phone on the dashboard and put his hand back on the wheel.

"Fucking rats leaving the sinking ship," he muttered, as he jumped red lights and swerved through traffic.

By the time Basher arrived at the Deptford warehouse, the Inspector had gathered enough information to know who had been there the previous day, and was instructing his officers to get them down to the station for interviews. Deptford squad was more than happy for him to take it over, it meant the press would likely focus on Peckham instead.

"Ah... Basher," said Inspector Stump when he saw him enter the studio that was now a crime scene, and he gave Basher a moment to take it all in.

Basher was shocked by what he saw. Staring at the walls, he took the Inspector by the shoulder and led him out of earshot across the warehouse.

"I need your support here, Stump," he said, thrusting money towards the Inspector. But Stump coolly declined. He wasn't about to incriminate himself further.

"Basher, much as I want to help you and have enjoyed a good relationship with you in the past, this is out of my hands now," he said.

"Don't you fuck me..." Basher said, but was hushed by the Inspector before he could finish.

"You fucked yourself, mate. I didn't write this. How the hell did anyone get this kind of information on you, anyway? Is any of it true?" he asked, pointing towards the walls.

Basher couldn't bear to look again.

"Just get it washed off for god's sake," he pleaded.

"It's evidence, Basher. I can't fucking touch it. More importantly, a man of yours is dead, for Christ's sake!"

Stump knew Basher was of no threat to him now, and too

many people had witnessed the writing on the wall that included pictures of blood-daubed stick people in compromising positions. Basher's leadership was facing an implosion, and Stump planned to distance himself from it as best he could. Running the investigation meant he might help achieve that.

An officer came in at that moment and called to Inspector Stump, who took the opportunity to escape the fuming Basher. Basher braved another look at the walls, and he didn't like what he saw. As he stood staring in horror at the work, it was at that moment Fred appeared, licking his lips and snapping photographs. Basher went for him like a snake unleashed. The Inspector dashing back over, got between them both before Basher could make the situation worse than it already was. He ushered Fred back outside. Shouting, as he did so, to his officers to seal off the building and let no one else in or out. But Fred had got enough. He'd been tipped off by an anonymous phone call. A voice he had known immediately was Hazelhot pretending to be an Irishman, had sounded more like an Australian gargling mouthwash. Fred had then made his way straight to the scene. It was going to be front page stuff, and he was itching to get back and write it up.

Hazelhot was parked a short distance from the building on the industrial estate. He was still in the car stolen from the hotel and had returned to keep a vigil and watch for Basher's boys. The plan being to make a head count and take notes. He also couldn't resist returning to the scene of the crime to see the effect of his handy work.

Inside the building, Basher was trying to think. Several of his crew had now arrived, and his solicitor too. He gathered his cohorts and, one by one, sent them on their way to start the hunt for those responsible. He gave the keys of his car to Justice Jerry, another one of his crew, with orders to gather the rest of the boys and set about hounding every known crook and criminal on the payroll, using whatever means necessary to find the culprits. After which everyone had orders to convene at Peckham HQ. Justice Jerry then left, and Basher spoke to his solicitor.

"You've got to keep me out of the nick," he said.

"It's going to be difficult. These writings clearly implicate you in some pretty dubious behaviour, and the Police are going to want to ask questions."

"I don't give a fuck. I pay you to do a job, now do it," said Basher, not used to hearing the word no.

"Er... actually, you don't pay me," said the solicitor, cottoning on to the fact that Basher might not be the fearful force he once was.

"So what the fuck are you doing here?" asked Basher, racking his brains to recall why this man was his solicitor.

"Because you said you'd harm my family if I didn't work for you," replied the Solicitor.

"Oh... right... well, that still goes, so do your fucking job and get me out of this, or I will."

Basher couldn't remember, but took his word for it. He had threatened so many people and their families in his time. How could he be expected to remember every one of them? The solicitor duly went over to speak to the Inspector in order to see what could be done.

Hazelhot was growing tired of waiting and decided it was time to leave. But before he did so, he couldn't resist the urge to drive past the front of the building and have a peek. He chose the exact moment that Basher appeared outside, and

Hazelhot ducked down to avoid being spotted. Hazelhot had gone home to change into fresh clothing before returning, but he'd worn the trophy Bulldog Security jacket stolen from Barry. Basher spotted the familiar crew jacket and stepped out into the road, slapping his hands on the bonnet, forcing the car to a screeching to a halt. Hazelhot cursed himself for being so stupid, but Basher was caught up in his own problems and wasn't thinking straight. Before Hazelhot could reverse out of the situation, Basher was squeezing himself into the passenger seat and demanding to be driven to their HQ. Hazelhot, not sure what to do, turned the car around and made his way out of the industrial estate.

"What a fucking mess!" said Basher, who still hadn't looked at his driver. He couldn't control his temper and smashed his hand into the dashboard, breaking the sill. Hazelhot didn't say a word, just drove and kept looking straight ahead. It was a few minutes before Basher realised something was amiss.

"Where the fuck are you going?" he asked, finally looking at Hazelhot.

"HQ... sir," replied Hazelhot, feigning a subservient manner.

"H fucking Q is in Peckham Rye, you numb nut, and this ain't the way to Peckham Rye."

Basher then realised he didn't know the man sat next to him.

"Do I even fucking know you?" he asked.

Basher then noticed the dried bloodstains on the Bulldog jacket and looked at the plaster and bandages wrapped around the man's head, along with the neck brace.

"What the fuck happened to you?" he asked.

"New, sir. Barry, sir. Fresh recruit, bit of an injury, sir," barked Hazelhot, adopting his chosen role on the spur of the moment, that was so bizarre and unbelievable it was hard not to believe. He then turned and gave Basher a salute before turning back to stare straight ahead, as if nothing was amiss at all.

Basher stared at him, but then suddenly relaxed.

"New Barry, hey?" he said, as he got back to thinking about himself. "Fuck it if I haven't had enough Barrys causing me problems for one day. Well, *New* Barry, turn this heap of shit around. I'll direct you."

Hazelhot gave Basher another salute and did as he was told.

By the time they reached Peckham HQ, New Barry had been given a list of jobs to do for Basher, who had made a mental note to bring a new rule to bear amongst his crew - he wanted to be referred to as *sir* from now on, and he wanted the men to salute him. This new boy clearly had the right attitude.

"Good work, New Barry," he said as he got out of the car. "Now you go wash that jacket, you're in Bulldog security now boy, respect yourself, and report back here when you're done. As of this moment, you're my designated driver. What the hell happened to you, anyway?" he asked, pointing at the various wrappings.

"A truck hit me. Hit and run. But the fresh blood is from my dog. He got hit by the same truck just this morning, sir. Serial dog-killing trucker, they think," said New Barry, wondering how the bullshit just seemed to flow out of him without trying.

"Get the number?" asked Basher, distressed by the thought of losing a creature so faithful.

Hazelhot thought for a moment. "Yes, sir, I did," he replied.

"Well, when you get back, you give me that number. That driver is going to regret the day he ran over one of my boys and his dog. What was it, a Rotty? A Staffy?" asked Basher.

"A Pomeranian, sir," said Hazelhot, not really sure why said that. But when he saw Basher was looking at him incredulously, he added, "Hell of a fighter, though, sir. Little chap had a lot of spirit. Found him in the street fighting a pack of foxes. Was bleeding everywhere, nearly dead, had to patch him up. He wouldn't leave my side after that. Couldn't get rid of him. Heart of gold, though... until the truck hit him, obviously... sir."

Basher was nodding, appreciating the tale, but still struggling to understand the choice.

"Right, well, you get us that number and let's get that driver sorted out. Can't have that," he said finally. Then Basher slapped the top of the car, turned, and walked into HQ feeling a little more confident knowing the likes of New Barry were out there soldiering for him, regardless of their choice of pets.

In his new role as New Barry, Hazelhot was now being sent to sacrosanct venues and home addresses of some of the top members and connections associated with Bulldog Security. He was either passing on requests from Basher, or collecting people and items to deposit them elsewhere. His duty that day was to serve as driver and runner. All the while, he took notes of everything and everyone he came into contact with. As far as Basher was concerned, the firm had to be seen to be business-as-usual while he dealt with the impending disaster that lay ahead of him, wholly unaware that the source of his disaster was currently running errands for him.

By the time New Barry finished his tasks, including getting his clothes dry cleaned, it was late afternoon, and he drove back to Bulldog HQ in Peckham, this time hiding the stolen car in a nearby driveway. He then limped into the building to be greeted with suspicious looks by the other lads, none of whom knew who he was. The jacket he was wearing was too large for him, and the walk he tried to muster made him look like a dysfunctional and constipated alien. It was clear to everyone present that this man was not a gym regular and had never injected steroids, since his head was in proportion to the size of his body. Despite the plaster and wrappings doing a good job of hiding his features, he stood out like a sore thumb. It was only when Basher greeted him like a long-lost friend that the tension eased in the room. Basher had assumed all the boys knew him from the confident way New Barry had thrown finger guns at a few of them, but because all the boys now assumed Basher knew him, not a word was said. New Barry did his best to puff himself up to meet the standard neck and chest size of a man who worked for Bulldog Security, and then he limped over to where Basher was currently standing.

"New Barry, my boy," said Basher, clapping him lightly on the back as he got there.

"Yes, sir," replied New Barry, affirmatively, as he straightened up and threw a full salute.

Basher smiled and looked at his crew to make sure they all saw it.

"This is my new right-hand man, right here, boys," he said, then turned to New Barry and asked, "did you do you get it all done, son?"

"All done, sir!" barked New Barry like a soldier on a drill parade.

Hazelhot was enjoying his new role immensely. It was clear he had been accepted and things were working out better than he ever could have planned.

"Great work, New Barry, great work, lad," replied Basher.

Basher then turned to his men. It was time to deliver his speech of the day.

"It is a sad day, boys, a very sad day. We lost one of our own today, fallen in the line of duty. His ending was bloody, and it was violent. These are tough times we are living in, and tough times call for tough measures. Men, it is time for us to prepare. Because as of today... we are at war."

In the time that followed, Hazelhot sat in on discussions and meetings as the full extent of Bulldog Security, and all they lorded over, came to light. At least within the limits of London boroughs. Basher was the UK's top dog, that much was obvious. Though he never seemed to stray outside his area, that ranged from East Dulwich to Nunhead Cemetary, with Peckham Rye HQ in between. The only interest he seemed to have outside of that was in the Porn Production business on the Depftord industrial estate. There had been mention of a hideout, but as yet, Hazelhot didn't know where that was. The line of work Bulldog was involved in was mostly racketeering a few local businesses and running security at clubs and warehouses. Hazelhot assumed this was just a cover for something bigger. He planned to wait until he could get more information on who Basher was connected to beyond the limits of the M25. After that, he could strike the blow and unleash his Final Solution.

As he waited, he stayed focused on his new role and character, and it didn't take long before the person who was Hazelhot ceased to exist, completely replaced by New Barry.

Which was curious, given it had only been a day since he took on the role.

Further Humiliation

Sir Stott sat down to his evening meal. The hotel was beginning to feel like a prison and he had not heard from Hazelhot in nearly twenty-four hours, which concerned him. Hazelhot could get up to all sorts of mischief in that amount of time. Stott had to meet with Basher in the coming days, and he didn't feel confident that his life was going to look any brighter because of it. He tucked his napkin into the top of his shirt and switched on the early evening news. What he saw there caused him to choke on his chicken and send the tray of food flying across the room as his body shot vertically upright, launching him into a standing position.

"JESUS GOD ALMIGHTY FUCKING CHRIST!" he shouted, as the camera panned to reveal Hazelhot driving past in a car with Basher in the passenger seat.

Stott stared at the screen, his mouth agape, bits of chicken hanging from his chin, as a female news presenter began pouring further fuel onto his disturbed state of mind.

"Basher Bob, an Executive Director at Pussy Productions - the semi-lucrative pornographic franchise recently bought by ex-Etonian turned porn king, Sir Archibold Stott - was allowed to continue his work today while investigations are underway to discover just what happened at this..." the female presenter turned to point to the building currently owned by Sir Stott, "... one of the whorehouse warehouses where sex-crazed perverts carry out their filming of cheaply made smut and bargain basement filth."

She paused long enough to shake her head, so the viewers knew that the television channel was against that kind of thing, though the truth was most of them were paid-up members.

"We managed to get a brief interview with a porn star who works here. Let's go over to that now," she said, and they cut to an earlier interview.

Stott fell back down into his chair. A chicken leg held in his hand shook uncontrollably, as if it was trying to escape his grip.

"Miss Lovelips," began a male interviewer, "may I call you Miss Lovelips?"

His body language giving away his obvious excitement at meeting her.

Lucy nodded from inside her large fur coat and strategically dabbed a hanky below one eye, giving a little sniffle before replying.

"You may," she said.

"Thank you. So, Miss Lustyhips, tell us in your own words, what happened at the studio yesterday evening?"

"Well," she began, smiling at the camera and presenting a shy, nay, virginal look. "We had just finished the last scene for my upcoming release, *Luscious Lips and Copulating Cowboys*. We'd closed down for the evening, and I was one of the last to leave. When Barry, the poor soul..."

Lucy stopped talking to dab an eye once again before continuing, "Barry had arrived for the night duty, as one of Basher's security crew always does. Then, as I understand it, some hit-men broke in and murdered him in cold blood."

Lucy dabbed at each eye some more, this time with a bit more feeling, but still careful not to smudge her make-up. She continued, "And...and... they threw his blood on the walls and wrote nasty things about Basher. Things that shouldn't be written. Sexual things, if you know what I mean. Very depraved things. Things he might have done to young..."

"Thank you, Miss Lustyclit," said the interviewer, cutting her short before she said something incriminating.

The scene on the television that Stott was currently watching returned to the female presenter standing outside the studio.

"We have just been informed that the police now have a number of people helping them with their inquiries. Inspector Stump, in charge of the case, is with us now. Inspector, just what can you tell us about this incident? I understand they found the man naked, drained of blood, with his throat ripped out. Is it a vampire killing we are dealing with here? What can you tell us?"

At this, the interviewer shoved her microphone toward the Inspector. Stott then recognised the man who had been at his door the previous day looking for Hazelhot.

"We are keeping an open mind at this stage," Inspector Stump began. "Obviously, this is an unusual case. We believe it to be a local gang we are looking for. We suspect they meant this to serve as a warning. Arrests are imminent, and we are confident the matter will be cleared up quickly."

"What about the allegation of vampires? Inspector, was the victim drained of blood?" asked the woman again, now licking her lips, eager for a break that might push her ratings up, and not shy to embellish a little if necessary.

"Speculation and imagination," replied Stump. "There are no vampires. It is a simple case of one gang making a hit on another gang. We will know more after we interview those who were at the site here yesterday. Thank you, that is all we have to say at this stage. Thank you," said the Inspector, and he pushed his way past the other reporters who clamoured for more information. The news jumped back to the main desk.

Sir Stott was feeling dazed and barely heard the next news item.

"… And in other news. Maidstone in Kent saw an event tonight that has sparked fears of mass rodent infestations. A farmer said a host of marauding rats attacked his sheep. They left behind them a trail of devastation in their wake, and are now, seemingly, headed for the coast. We go now to Maidstone, where a reporter is at the scene."

"Mr Giles, could you tell us just what you witnessed?" asked the reporter there.

"Well, I was just getting to bed when I heard a disturbance from the yard. I got up and found some of my sheep had been massacred. Looking to the east, I could make out the shapes of at least a few hundred thousand rats heading towards the coast. They were making noises, sort of raspy whistling noises, and I could see them sort of prancing…"

"Er… yes, thank you Mr Giles…. well, back to you in the studio."

There was a delay in switching back to the studio, and during the pregnant pause the reporter stood motionless, staring as he had been trained to do. While behind him could be seen a drunk Mr Giles, staggering as he lifted a bottle of homemade Scrumpy up to his lips before turning towards the camera and mouthing the word "ratsssssss," before falling over and passing out of the shot.

Stott switched off the television. Feeling the doom and despair of further dark apprehension getting a grip on his heart. How much more could he take? And what the bloody hell was Hazelhot doing dressed in a Bulldog jacket, driving Basher around? He was running out of hope to cling on to. The madness was taking its toll. Stott reached for his pills and washed a handful down with a shot of sherry. The phone rang, and he answered it.

"Sir Stott," said a voice on the other end.

"Unfortunately," replied Sir Stott.

"This is Peckham Police Station, sir. We need to talk to you about an incident that occurred at your studios in Deptford yesterday."

Sir Stott slumped down in a chair and readied himself to answer the questions posed to him by the police officer.

Hazelhot felt confident that an apocalyptic end was looming, though not for him and Stott, but for Basher and his boys. He listened as Basher drew up plans to clear his name and restore the firm to its former glory. For every plan Basher made, Hazelhot quietly added his own. It was running like a dream. All he had to do was brief Stott, and then he could set it all in motion. Hazelhot put a hand up in the air.

"Permission to use the toilet, sir," he asked Basher, and held the position while he waited for a response. The room fell silent. Only Basher's face had any kind of normal look on it, as he turned to the man who had just made the request.

"Of course, New Barry," replied Basher in a fatherly way.

Hazelhot got up, saluted, and then marched out of the

room with military precision.

All the other men in the room watched him go, envious of the adoration he was receiving from their leader. But instead of going to the toilet, Hazelhot went to a phone box just outside the HQ and called the hotel.

"Room 667," he whispered to the woman on reception who answered.

"Certainly, sir," she whispered back.

"Who is it now?" barked Stott into the receiver, after the receptionist had put Hazelhot through.

"Stott, it's me, New Barry... I mean, Hazelhot," Hazelhot whispered loudly.

"... Hazelhot!" bellowed Stott. "What the blazes do you think you are up to, man? Are you stark raving mad? You are on the bloody news! And what in god's name has happened at the studio? I have just put down the phone to the police..."

"Listen, shut up a minute. I haven't got time to explain. Just come to the meeting tomorrow and agree with everything. Don't look at me. Don't acknowledge me. I am in with Basher and he doesn't have a clue. Pay no attention to whatever I do or say. Have you got it?"

"... Okay, but I don't understand..."

"No time to explain. Gotta go."

Hazelhot put the phone down. He had noticed a police officer wandering around outside and realised that the stolen car had just been spotted. He went to greet the officer before he could radio it in.

"Evening officer," said New Barry.

"Is this your car, sir?" asked the young officer.

"No, belongs to Basher," he replied.

"Really? Not yours then, sir?"

"No sir, I am just the driver. He told me himself he picked

it up from a friend at a hotel."

"And you are?"

"Jerry, sir, Justice Jerry to my friends," said New Barry, hoping the officer didn't know any of Basher's crew.

"Right," said the officer, eyeing him suspiciously, then undoing his top pocket to retrieve his notebook and pencil, which he dabbed on his tongue before getting ready to take some notes.

"Got to go inside, busting for the loo, back in a minute," said Hazelhot, and before the officer could speak, he legged it inside, ran to the toilet, and went out through a window in the back.

At Peckham Police Station, the information passed through to Inspector Stump, who put two and two together and wondered just what the hell Basher was up to getting his boys to run amok and steal cars from Central London hotels. This meant whoever he had been looking for at the hotel was also somehow tied into this incident with Basher. It was Sir Stott's room he had heard noises coming from, and Sir Stott owned the premises where the recent murder had taken place. Something was afoot. Since the news story blew up before they could get much information, he was now under orders to hand the entire show over to Scotland Yard the next day. Before he did that, he needed to make sure that there was no chance of his own dealings with Basher coming to light.

Hazelhot next rang Basher from a more distant phone box, to say that he had seen the truck that ran over his dog, and he was in pursuit. Before Basher could offer his help, Hazelhot burbled some rubbish and slammed the phone down. Basher put his mobile phone down on the table, and looked around the room at his tired, muscularly over-developed army. They looked tough, but now the shit was hitting the fan they were behaving like a bunch of gym-bound fairies. There was not an independently useful thought coming from any of them. Normally Basher liked that. Today he did not.

"If you lot only had half the gumption that boy has, I would not be in this bloody mess," he said, pointing to the phone he had just put down. No one said anything. He sighed, then got back to dictating his demands for action over the coming days.

Hazelhot rang Fred next. It was time to bring in the big guns, and since he now had the address for the secret hideout where Basher's boys would be meeting, he could get his Final Solution underway.

"It's me," he said, when Fred answered.

"Right, back in England, are you?" joked Fred, referring to the bad accent Hazelhot had attempted the last time they spoke.

"What?" asked Hazelhot.

"Thought you went down under, or something," replied Fred.

"What are you babbling on about?" asked Hazelhot. "You said to ring you when I was ready. Well, l am ready, so let's talk."

Fred switched on the tape recorder and swivelled in his chair. He was going to hit the big time with this one. He could feel it.

"Okay, fire away. What do you need from us?" asked Fred, referring to the National Paper.

"Basher is meeting our man, Stott, tomorrow. It's a big meeting and most of the crew will be there. It's the perfect opportunity to hit them all at once. I can't wait any longer, otherwise they are going to cotton on to what I am up to. But I need you to get me and Stott out before your lot goes in."

Fred wasn't sure what any of this had to do with him. How would sending the press there do anything other than cause everyone to clam up or run a mile?

"I don't think it will work," replied Fred.

"What the bloody hell does that mean? Are you backing out? What the hell do your people want? I have put this in your lap, gathered them all together in one place, and now you say you won't do it?"

Hazelhot was getting annoyed. He needed action and was getting resistance.

"Alright, calm down. We can do it. It's no big deal. I just don't see what is to be gained from hitting this meeting tomorrow if it's only Basher's lot going to be there, or are the higher-ups going to be putting in an appearance?"

Hazelhot thought about it. If he got Fred's people to wipe out the English contingent, it would be a good start and might flush the higher-ups out of hiding.

"Of course the higher-ups will be there. Why do you think I called you?" he lied.

"Oh, okay. Like who?" asked Fred, knowing better than to agree to the first thing he heard.

"I can't name names, or I might have to kill you," said Hazelhot, using the same trick back on Fred that he'd used at their first meeting.

"Then no can do," said Fred, reading Hazelhot's desperation correctly.

"Look, you slimy Irish bastard, you agreed, and I have held up my end of the bargain."

Hazelhot was one step away from destroying the phone

box.

"Jesus mate, keep your hair on," said Fred, "I just need to know that it's worth our while putting in an appearance. It needs to be big to justify me calling everyone out. We can't afford to have some no-show, or worse, all the top dogs slip through the net. If they then go to ground, we'll never get them out in the open again. I'm a professional, and this is not my first time. You need to respect that. There has to be a bloody good reason for me to call it. This has to be big, real big. It's my reputation on the line otherwise."

"Rats!" exclaimed Hazelhot, covering the receiver as he said it and trying to think of a way to trick Fred into agreeing. He tapped the phone on the booth as he thought for a moment. But Fred had heard him, though Hazelhot didn't hear what he said next.

"Bloody hell! *Those* rats?" said Fred, realising that the story he had seen on the news about the rats in Maidstone held a lot more significance than he had at first thought. "Well, fuck me, of course!" he said as it landed for him. "Those marauding bastards are your lots creation. What the fuck did you do to them? They said they were whistling and prancing and mass-murdering sheep! What kind of killer rats prance and whistle? What have they let loose on us? Those rotten bastards!"

Hazelhot was still dangling the phone in his hand, trying to come up with something. If Fred's army were not willing to come in on this one, maybe they just needed proof of *his* willingness to go the whole way. He could do that. Then an idea occurred to him. He put the receiver back to his ear just as Fred was tailing off.

"Listen," said Hazelhot. "Here's the deal. Get your people set up tomorrow and I will blow the whole fucking show. Maybe then you'll see I mean business, and we can set about getting the rest of them. But I still need you to get me and Stott out. If the Police are there in the ensuing chaos, which I am sure they are likely to be, I need to know you can keep them off our back and get us away from there. Can you do that, at least? We need to know you are going to protect us. The bigger this goes, the more we risk our necks and we need something from you to prove that you aren't going to just fuck us when the time comes. I want in on the Mars deal, you got that? If you can take tomorrow as a proof of my willingness, then we are all together on the big one. Deal?"

"The big one, eh," said Fred, wondering what the hell could be bigger than that. But he agreed on the spot, then made a mental note to cut that bit out of the recording, so there would be no record of his agreeing to anything.

"As soon as we get a good look at who is present, then we'll get you clear," agreed Fred. "Anyway, don't you worry about the police. They're not a problem. They're terrified of us. So, we'll be there, but this better be good. Impress me, or we won't talk again, and you do not want to end up on the wrong side of us. One thing we don't like is expensive time-wasters, and believe me, we never forget."

Hazelhot gave Fred the details of the time and location and then put the phone down. A big smile appeared on his face. Finally, things were coming together. He knew he could get enough gear to put on a good show. Basher had had him running boxes round all day, and they didn't all contain papers, that was for sure. But what had surprised him was the way Fred could be so casual about manipulating the Police. He reminded himself that he was just a pawn in this game, and Fred's army was used to playing for higher stakes. These were big fish. This was a whole new league for him, bigger than he had been used to dealing with, and he needed to adjust to that. Of course, he was going to have to prove himself to them. It made sense that they would need to see that he was worthy. He shivered in the excitement; it felt good to be going to war again. If he impressed them now, it meant he was one step closer to a seat on the shuttle to Mars when the time came. He would be a part of the future of humanity, out there in the cosmos. Things really were falling into place. Hazelhot popped the cap on his medication and knocked a couple back. He was feeling pretty pleased with himself.

The Hide Out

Everyone awoke to a bright and sunny day. Stott had his rain-cloud to deal with, which stopped him from seeing anything other than doom ahead. Hazelhot hadn't slept. He had been too busy gathering items for his forthcoming bonanza after stealing another car. Basher had slept fitfully and dreamed of the good old days. Fred was the only one who had slept the sleep of angels and bounced out of bed to make himself coffee and toast. The sight of such a gaunt creature parading around in filthy looking underpants gave his neighbour's children the scare of their lives. He wasn't usually up at that time, but Fred was oblivious as he wandered around his kitchen singing Irish songs and feeling pretty pleased with himself. Even Lucy awoke feeling fresh and youthful and wondered about the sweet little man she had met during her shoot at Pussy Productions before everything had taken a turn for the worse. Something about his puppy dog ways had struck a chord in her heart. She realised that at long last she might have met a man that she liked. He seemed so... romantic. She readied herself for the day ahead, determined not to let the lines on her almost unblemished face get her down.

It was 8 am when the newspapers arrived through each person's door. The reaction was life changing. Stott looked at The Times, aghast. A picture from his school-days adorned the front pages alongside that of Basher Bob with a question.

Has The British Empire Finally Fallen To The Mob?

A tear fell down Stott's cheek as he read it. England was dying, and he was now irreparably tied in to its passing. Had suicide ever been a word in Stott's vocabulary, he might very well have considered it at that point, as he stood there shaking with remorse and rage at the effrontery of it all.

Basher, on the other hand, had received The Daily Star, and the photographs that greeted him were of an entirely different flavour. Shots of bloody etchings on the wall made the man's shoulders droop and the puff of his chest diminish. What was once a great and fearsome tyrant was now reduced to a weakened caricature of himself.

London Gangland Boss In Murder And Massive Bender Shock

Blared the headline. Below which were photographs of the blood daubed walls of the studio and a picture of Basher stood beside them, looking suitably bereft of masculinity as he took it all in. Through teary eyes, Basher Bob read his epitaph. His fall from grace, and maybe even fall from sanity, was underway. He began to read the accompanying story.

Basher Bob, known to his school chums as 'Queer C*nt Boppy Beans', looks set to face charges when the true reason for Barry Miller's murder finally becomes known…

It went on to reveal how he had fought and threatened his way to the top of Peckham Rye gangland. All the while, allegedly, hiding a penchant for homo-erotic murder, which wasn't true, of course. Fred had been careful to focus heavily on the homosexual connotations that the story represented, knowing it would sell to his homophobic readers far better than just a run-of-the-mill murder story ever would. He'd peppered it all with '*allegedly*' and '*sources told us that...*' because he didn't have any sources at all, but needed to get a suitably convincing story out. Fabrication was never a problem. It was part of the job.

Hazelhot had hoped to create something of a reaction when painting the allegations over the walls of the warehouse in Barry's blood. Though most of it was sordid imagery conjured from his own depraved life experiences. But he'd had no idea how effective it would be. He had correctly assumed that the current climate would make the press jump on it like the hungry vultures that they were. It didn't need to be true, just allege controversy, and it was often enough to sink a man. And he'd been right. Done on an inspired whim, he could not have planned it any better. The impact was explosive, and everyone in England was waking up to the story.

The morning news then revealed to the entire country just what *Pedicabo Ego Uranus* meant. This not only added to the incriminating suspicions hanging over Basher, but now impacted his entire crew by association. The press could only guess at the reason for this bizarre choice of motto being used so overtly, but everyone had a go at solving the riddle of why they had used it. It was the talk of every morning TV show with a phone-in poll asking viewers to call and give their suggestions as to what it all meant. Everyone had an opinion, and the phone lines were soon lighting up.

And so it was that the crew of Bulldog Security was thrown into total disarray. Mental, emotional, and spiritual chaos ensued. What had, the day before, been an outfit of black-jacketed hard-men; a firm on the up and up; men united under the symbol of a Bulldog chewing a wasp; and a gang who had run parts of London through fear and violence, had overnight turned into a global laughing-stock. Panic set in and they flocked to one another like dazed sheep. Confused phone calls went back and forth as they tried to work out what to do, who to turn to, how to proceed. Basher was no longer answering his phone, and without their leader, no one knew what to do next.

Basher was sat transfixed at the breakfast table in his mum's house. He was staring at the writing on the wall, that was the writing in the paper. He didn't move, mostly because he couldn't move. What was currently taking place in his brain - in the part where reality got put together - was an effect not unlike a short-circuiting. He had never felt this way before. So he carried on staring at the paper. His phone rang, and then rang off, then rang, and then rang off. Before long, car-loads of reporters could be heard screeching to a halt outside the house. Vans with television station names printed on the side setup satellite dishes in the street. A small, but growing crowd of neighbours gathered, waiting excitedly for signs of life within. Basher just went on staring at the paper. The short-circuiting completed. His mind was now completely blank, and his body didn't move. The paper in his hands shook only slightly as his eyes stared right through it and into the void beyond.

As Bulldog gang members continued to phone each other, at some point, the hideout was mentioned. More calls went back and forth, and soon everyone agreed - the hideout was the place to go. After all, it was a hideout. Gathering in the one place supposedly known only to Bulldog Security members and designed to be used in the event of a gangland crisis seemed to make sense. In shock, fear, and with the inability to think for themselves - the one thing they all had in common - a decision got made. Everyone then headed to the hideout. Something that the danger in their midst had predicted correctly, since he had also been the one to first mention it.

In Kentish Town, at a small greasy spoon cafe that opened earlier than most, Hazelhot was roaring with laughter. He sat in the middle of the room, with a double table to himself, reading each of the six major papers he had bought that morning at first press and which were now spread out before him. He bellowed with laughter each time he read a new paragraph, holding his sides as he relished it again and again. Oblivious to the looks he was getting from the other early morning waifs, strays, and vagabonds that were in there. Most sat staring into their eggs on toast while giving the curious creature shifty glances. They had also read their respective papers, and now were observing one of the insane members of the now infamous Buggering gang. The problems likely to arise from wearing the Bulldog Security flying jacket in public were not lost on Hazelhot. He was enjoying himself stupid. Of all the members of Bulldog Security, he was the only confirmed psychopathic sex pervert amongst them, and at that moment he could not care less who knew it.

Hazelhot folded the papers into a neat pile. His chortling diminished slowly as he sipped at his tea. Now and then he would start laughing again, and it would escalate for a while until he'd calm down enough to take another sip. He was playing events over in his mind. He'd enjoyed being a member of Bulldog Security, and what made it all the better was that he knew the best was yet to come. His grand finale was approaching; his Final Solution. Hazelhot looked at his watch. It was time. He quaffed down the last of his mug of tea, stood up, and looked about the room. Eyes that had been on him moments before went back down to their food. Hazelhot laughed again, bathing for a moment in the attention, and then he left.

He drove first to Stott's Hotel. It took a while finding a parking spot, but he thought it best to avoid the cameras of the underground car park this time, given the issues on his last visit. When he eventually found one, it wasn't far from the hotel. He removed his Bulldog jacket, placed it over the boxes that were in the back, and smiled to himself. He then set about removing the bandages from his head. After that, he pulled out a small saw he had purchased, and carefully removed the remains of his plaster cast. He took a flat-cap that he had brought for the occasion and tried it on, checking himself in the rear-view mirror. Happy with his look, he got out to head towards the hotel entrance.

As he neared the entrance, he saw the same valet he had dealt with before, who was still looking a little the worse for wear. Hazelhot had to stop and face the other direction for a moment to avoid being spotted laughing. Once he had settled down, pulling his flat cap down, he waited for a group to enter the hotel, and chose that moment to slip in with them. Making it past the valet unnoticed, he carried on toward the lift. Arriving at the sixth floor, he walked to number 667 and knocked the code on the door.

"What the hell are you up to now?" asked Stott, after answering. Though Hazelhot's current attire looked as ridiculous as usual, he was referring to recent news events.

"Impressed?" asked Hazelhot, tipping his hat and brushing past him to head towards the drinks that were sitting on a trolley. Stott shut the door and followed him in.

"You killed that man, didn't you? The papers said it was a rival gang, but it was you."

Stott was still coming to terms with the psychopathic potential of the various maniacs he was involved with, none of whom he wanted to be involved with any longer.

"No comment," replied Hazelhot.

"You absolute bloody nutter. Do you plan to kill me, too?" asked Stott.

Hazelhot thought for a moment.

"It hadn't occurred to me," he said honestly, which made Stott even more nervous and so he changed the subject.

"I thought I was supposed to be meeting you later. Why are you here?"

"Change of plan," replied Hazelhot. "This morning's news forced the situation a bit, but I couldn't have done a better job if I tried. Basher's mob is in disarray. They couldn't organise a cockfight in a Mexican barnyard. I dropped the hideout into conversation and we'll be meeting up there. It's almost too easy. Basher hasn't been answering the phone. He's probably lost his mind and hiding somewhere, and so the rest of them are like lost children. It's utterly pathetic. With the news in The Daily Star, which is his favourite paper, and by far the worst of all the stories, the entire gang has fallen to pieces over it. They painted him up as a violent homosexual maniac. The journalist went to town on him. Basher must be in pieces, though I could see the cracks forming yesterday. It just needed a bit of a push and today, after that outing in the press, I really hold little hope for him. But if he emerges, it will be to head to the hideout where everyone else is going. So... I came to get you. Get your things. We're going to the hideout."

"Well, that explains why I haven't had a call from him," mused Stott, now understanding better what Hazelhot had been doing infiltrating Basher's crew.

But Stott had no intention of going anywhere with the lunatic. He wanted to know what was going on all the same.

"I thought for a moment you had joined them, but what's your plan then, hmm?" asked Stott, raising a suspicious eyebrow, readying himself to hear something insane and despicable, given how it usually went when he asked Hazelhot to explain himself.

"I got in with them by accident. It was the perfect cover, really. I nearly blew it a few times, but Basher was too distracted to realise the obvious. He'll work it out eventually, but it will be too late by then. That's why we need to act now. We are safe until he talks to the others, or the cops. Once he does that, then it's over. So, we need to strike them now, and strike hard. We need to get to the hideout before he does. So, time to go, old man, I need you in on this one," said Hazelhot.

"Hang on a minute, old chap. There is no *'we'* in this. You're a bloody maniac, and if you think I am helping you..."

Stott had no intention of going anywhere, but Hazelhot cut in before he could finish.

"Listen, you decrepit old toad, you are balls deep in this already. You have no choice. If you think the biggest gang in Peckham is going to just let you off the hook, then you are more naïve than I took you for. You've nothing left, me old fruit, *nada*. I'm your only hope for staying alive right now. And to be honest, I am quite put out that you are not thanking me for my troubles. There is only one way out of this mess, Stott, and that is the tough way. You signed up for this, you even authorised it, and so you best get with the program to get us both through it. If we don't deal with this now, once they put two and two together, they will be coming for both of us. This is it. We have to end this today."

Hazelhot knew he had Stott over a barrel.

Stott didn't like it one bit, but he'd experienced enough from Basher's crew to know Hazelhot was right. They would hunt them down and kill them both without a second thought.

"But you killing a chap like that?" said Stott, "My god, man, this is serious stuff! It's not war-time Germany or ancient Sparta. That was bloody weird behaviour. It was the most psychopathic kind of murder I have seen since the Pacific theatre, Hazelhot."

Stott was nervous. It was completely out of hand and way beyond anything he was used to. Everything had a nasty habit of escalating with Hazelhot, and he wasn't certain there was any kind of ceiling to it, either. He wanted the madness to stop. Hazelhot had other plans.

"And you call yourself a soldier? Are you sure you served?" asked Hazelhot, deliberately testing Stott, who stiffened at the insinuation.

"Damn right, I did! Borneo and then Angola. Two tours. In the sixties. And what of it?" replied Stott, roused by the suggestion that he was a lesser man.

"See any action, did you?" asked Hazelhot, maintaining a sceptical air for effect.

"The damn bloody cheek of it. Of course I saw action. Shot and blown up to boot."

But Stott's experience of action was a tale in itself.

Stott had been in the army for many years, but only saw action when he annoyed his superiors so much that they had him posted to Borneo. There his first tour ended abruptly, when on a jungle reconnaissance he was clawed viciously, then bitten in the ass, by what the rest of the squad would later swear was an alien. They had to sign the official secrets act to stop any risk of a leak, just in case. The injured Stott was placed into quarantine, where he stayed for over two weeks with no outside contact at all. Medics in Hazmat suits injected various toxic cocktails into him until they finally caught the unidentified creature. It turned out to be an angered sun bear suffering from alopecia. Thinking it to be some alien creature was an understandable mistake to make, and though it wasn't an alien, it had been extremely pissed off at the time of meeting Stott. The question then became why it had been driven to attack Stott's ass. The subsequent mess-hall stories of the incident left Stott no recourse but to apply for another tour of duty in order to prove himself. Though this led to bets being taken as to what would bite him next. He chose Angola, but it went no better for him there when a grenade promptly blew him out of a truck on arrival. Luckily, he was minimally injured, and since it officially qualified as action, there was not much fighting required of him after that. He was given a medal for taking part, and then sent home to recover. Though his time in the Borneo jungle often came back to haunt him in his sleep and his daydreams. He told his wife - the only other creature that had the misfortune to see his ass - that the claw marks were caused by ricocheting bullets, and he stuck to that story in the hope the truth would eventually disappear. This was the version he shared with Hazelhot.

"There you go then. You know what we are dealing with

here. What *is* this, if not war?" asked Hazelhot, though he was still not convinced Stott had ever had been fighting material.

Stott was forced to consider his bind. Hazelhot did have a point. He hadn't signed up for it, but it was fast becoming apparent that the universe didn't much care what he'd signed up for. It was coming for *him*. He considered other ways out of it, but could see none. Basher and his cronies were on one side, and the psychopath Hazelhot was on the other. If neither of them got him, the Law or the press might. He had little doubt that Hazelhot could deliver chaos, which might then take the heat of him, somewhat. He could claim to be an innocent party later, dragged along by the psychopath Hazelhot under threat. What he wasn't sure of was how to avoid becoming collateral damage in the process. The way Hazelhot had looked when he asked if he had plans to do away with him, added a new angle to his conundrum. Once Basher was out of the way, would Stott be the next in line on Hazelhot's hit list? He rather feared he might. The man was a menace to anyone living. Stott decided he would play along for now so that he might buy time, but he needed to think of something and a way to extricate himself from the mess. He'd bought the wolf to get rid of the dogs, but clearly the wolf was rabid and planning. Stott sighed. He could see no alternative but to go along with the man he now knew to be a homicidal maniac, and possibly a serial killer.

"I can't believe I am agreeing to this," replied Stott.

"Oh this is nothing, I've only just got started," said Hazelhot with a relish. "Now get yourself dressed. We're going to the hideout."

An hour later, the two men turned onto the road of an industrial estate in West Thurrock, Essex. Hazelhot slowed the car down to a glide, pulled his Bulldog jacket from the back seat and put it on. He drove, using his knees as he did so. Stott watched him and wondered how his life had come to this. For a man of his standing, it was preposterous that he was stuck in a car on a way to some gangland hide-out with a homicidal imbecile at the wheel. Hazelhot then outlined to Stott what would be needed of him.

"Okay. So the story is that I am *New Barry*. Don't, for God's sake, call me anything else once we get in there. Just New Barry, right? Or better still, just don't speak at all. Got it?" asked Hazelhot.

"Got it," said Stott.

Though he had little idea what was going on, he felt the less he knew, the better off he was when it later came time to explain it to the police. The car turned into the entrance of what looked like a chemical plant.

"This is it," said Hazelhot. "Welcome to Bulldog Security's hide-out."

There were several cars parked up, and Hazelhot pulled in behind them after turning the car around so that they might make a quicker escape, though he hoped Fred would have something planned and he wouldn't need it. He got out and looked about. No one was around. The place was quiet, and the plant looked disused but for the cars. Hazelhot counted them, looked around to make sure they were alone, then pulled a stolen mobile from his pocket that he had gleaned from Basher's crew during his various duties and rang a number.

"New Barry here. What's the word?" he whispered.

Stott could hear a voice on the other end, but couldn't make out what they said.

"Has Basher called in yet?" asked Hazelhot. "Okay. Be there in a minute," he added, and put the phone down.

"Everyone's here but Basher. I don't think they are onto me yet, so we are good to go."

He looked at his watch, then looked about again, concerned about something.

"What?" asked Stott.

"No sign of our man yet," replied Hazelhot

"What man?" asked Stott, confused by the comment.

"Fred and his crew. We made a deal, but he shouldn't be long," replied Hazelhot, and just at that moment a van came idling into the road. It was unmarked, but those inside were clearly on the lookout for something. Hazelhot spotted them first.

"Aha. Here they are," he said, and rubbed his hands together. "Time to get this party started."

Stott had managed to get himself out of the car, and Hazelhot clapped him on the back, then walked towards the main warehouse through the industrial yard, warming up to his newly mastered Bulldog swagger as he got himself into character. Stott stared after him for a moment, then shook his head and crossed his chest with a quick prayer before following on.

The van pulled up and two gentlemen sat in the front watched on as a man who looked like a small, fat badger, and another fellow, with a strange walk dressed in an over-sized Bulldog Security jacket, disappeared into the industrial complex.

"That must be them," said one of the men.

"Looks like it. Best setup the broadcast equipment and get ready," replied the other.

Moments later, another car came in behind them, and then another. The two men gave the thumbs up out of the window as both vehicles went by.

"Fred must have called every paper. This is going to be big," said one of them.

It was a good sign to see others arriving. It had to be huge if Fred was getting everyone in on it. They climbed into the back of the van and started to prepare the equipment. More vans and cars soon pulled up outside until there were news teams everywhere. All summoned by Fred, and all with strict instructions not to enter until Fred could confirm it was safe. He wanted to honour his part of the deal to get his source out before the press went in. Everyone was happy to work to Fred's command. They knew the drill. Fred had been clear there were risks. Something about mutants, DNA, and germ-warfare, and since this was clearly a chemical plant, everyone was cautious until they got more information. The eerie stillness added to their excitement. It felt big, and everyone knew it. They quietly took their positions to wait.

As they got to the main door, Hazelhot told Stott to wait behind a large container and stay out of sight. He then disappeared around the outside of the building for a few minutes. When he returned, he looked pleased.

"It's all so perfect," said Hazelhot, barely able to contain himself.

"What's all so perfect?" asked Stott, still uncertain why he was required to be there at all.

Hazelhot ignored him, and knocked three times on the door, then another two taps given more rapidly, and then three. He mouthed the words "*secret code*" to Stott before pulling the door open and entering.

There was no one there, which made the code seem superfluous, but Stott said nothing. They walked down a corridor that led into a large room. Inside were about forty men, some standing, some sitting. The babble of voices became hushed as they turned to look at the two late arrivals.

The effect of seeing the imposing sight of Basher's crew, en masse, and all dressed in Bulldog Security jackets, made Stott freeze in his tracks. He teetered for a moment as the breath expelled from his body. The last time he had been in a room with those jackets, it hadn't gone well for him, and his body had not forgotten. Hazelhot puffed up noticeably in response to seeing the gathering, though several members were obviously far from pleased to see him. But without Basher's orders, action from anyone was impossible against another Bulldog, else one or two might have started towards him with menacing intent. They were trained to take orders, not to think for themselves. Thinking was Basher's domain. But today the snake was missing its head. Unfortunately for them, Hazelhot was more than enough reptile, and he stepped into the role of assumed leadership with an immediate forte.

"Men, on me!" barked Hazelhot, as he walked into the room to take centre stage at the front and clap his hands together as he did so.

After that, he put his hands on his hips and looked around the room before motioning the terrified looking Stott to take a seat in a nearby chair facing him. This was done with a click of his fingers, pointing to Stott first, and then the chair. It was a display of command. The terrified looking Stott obeyed it on instinct. He wasn't likely to disobey an order from a Bulldog Security jacket ever again. It was etched into his subconscious.

Hazelhot looked around the room with a look of pride on his face. He was already fully immersed in the role of leadership. All the men just stared back at him, confused and incredulous. Two men even started laughing, but Hazelhot continued, unperturbed.

"I am the one they call *New Barry*. I have met some of you, but not all of you. And today we are without our beloved leader," Hazelhot began.

He was just warming up, but none of the men seemed very convinced so far, and they looked at one another, wondering what the hell was going on. Several of the tougher guys scoffed at the impostor in their midst. A palpable tension began to mount in the room. Stott felt his buttocks clench tighter. It was only Hazelhot who seemed wholly unaffected. He looked down at the ground for a moment and breathed in. He'd been looking forward to this moment for quite some time. Then, abruptly, and extremely loudly, he launched into a wholly unexpected and powerful speech worthy of a Shakespearean actor.

"Men! For we... are... men. Today we have lost our leader, but *we* are not yet lost."

Hazelhot looked up to the heavens. Slowly lifting a hand, he clenched it into a fist, then held it in front of his face until it shook with tension and rage as it whitened. Shutting his eyes, a strangulated but powerful sound emanated from his throat. In other settings, it might have been the start of an exorcism, but soon the sound formed into words. And so it was that Hazelhot launched his greatest ever speech upon the men of Bulldog Security.

"What Basher called the Battle for Peckham Rye is over. I

expect that the Battle for London is about to begin. Upon this battle depends the survival of our very civilisation. Upon it depends our own British life, and the long continuity of our institution, and our Empire. The whole fury and might of the enemy must very soon be turned on us. Our enemy knows that he will have to break us in this island, or lose the war. If we can stand up to him, all Peckham Rye, East Dulwich, Nunhead Cemetary and some surrounding boroughs, may be free and the life of the world may move forward into broad, sunlit uplands, maybe even Peckham itself and the Isle of Dogs too. But, if we fail, then the whole world, including north of the river and… well… maybe even some parts of Wales and Ireland, including all that we have known and cared for, will sink into the abyss of a new Dark Age made more sinister, and perhaps more protracted, by the lights of perverted science. Let us therefore brace ourselves to our duties, and so bear ourselves that, if the British Empire and its more honest gangs last for a thousand years, men will still say, '*This… was their finest hour.*'"

It was a speech worthy of Winston Churchill. Stott knew it was worthy of him because he was the only one in the room to recognise the speech, now doctored and butchered by Hazelhot. As silence descended and expanded into a colossal void, Hazelhot stood with his one hand held in a furious fist above his head, his eyes to the floor in an overly dramatised pose that just needed a well-placed spot light to make it Biblical.

Stott turned to look around. He expected to see a mass of men preparing to charge the blithering idiot, but instead he saw men slowly standing and, one by one, they began to clap. It was hard to digest. Obviously, none of them had a clue who Winston Churchill was. Certainly, it had been rousing, in a cheap, theatrical kind of way, but anyone with half an education knew it to be a speech plagiarised beyond belief. Hazelhot clearly knew his audience. He stood like a pardoned Brutus on the steps of Rome, as one by one, Bulldog Security came forward and shook his hand. Stott sat watching the bizarre event unfold, incredulous at the incomprehensibility of it all. The world really had gone stark raving mad, and for whatever reason, he had a front-row seat for it.

Hazelhot knew it had been a triumph. He hadn't had it so good in a long time, and he knew the best way to remain a winner was to know when to call it quits. The high he was feeling as the men came towards him and offered themselves at his feet was a powerful drug that could not be trusted. He'd studied Rome, being a big fan of the gladiator pits, and was reminded of the story about a servant that would ride in the carriages at the height of the Roman Empire to whisper in the ear of Caesar, *"All adoration is impermanent, only Death is assured."* Words Hazelhot had also memorised, and now quietly repeated to himself, as he fought to resist the urge to fall fully into the role he had just filled in Basher's absence.

He looked dreamily over at Stott as the men that surrounded him shook his hand. *His* men now, albeit just for a moment. It would be so easy to believe, at least until Basher showed up again. He then thought about Stott. He had almost grown to like him, the mad old badger. But the task ahead had not been forgotten, and as clarity expanded into Hazelhot's mind, he knew that the overfed and confused looking stoat ultimately stood in his way too. As he touched heads and hands like a recently elected Pope, he felt the buzz of a burner phone vibrating in his pocket. Pulling away from the adoration of the men, he took it out and held it in the air.

"I have to take this, guys," he said. "Back in a mo..."

And with that Hazelhot left, but not before giving Stott a peculiar look. Very peculiar, Stott felt. Even more peculiar than normal. It reminded him of the time his father left him at the gates of his first boarding school after saying he would be back in a moment, then never returned.

After Hazelhot left the room, he pushed the door firmly shut behind him. Then he pulled down a bar and locked it. He checked it was in place and then left the warehouse through a side door and went to the back of the building, talking on the phone as he did so.

"You ready?" he asked the man on the other end.

"Ready," confirmed Fred.

"Okay, a slight change of plan. It's just one person for extraction. Me."

"Alright," said Fred, "and are *you* ready?" asked Fred, for want of something to fill the gap.

"'Like when Norman D. Cota hit Omaha Beach, soldier,'" quoted Hazelhot, in a bizarre American accent as he reached the corner of the building. He was still caught up in wartime roles and television repeats as he added, "... take a squad of men, and you and your men watch carefully. I'll show you how to take a house with Bulldogs in it."

And without waiting for a reply, he rang off.

Fred stared at the phone for a moment, put it to his ear once more, heard nothing else, and so put it down with a puzzled look on his face.

Stott was getting nervous. The Bulldog crew were still animated by the effects of the speech, but before they turned their attention to him, he decided to get out of the madhouse. Hazelhot had disappeared, and he saw no good reason to stay there a moment longer. He wanted out. He quietly got up and made his way to the door Hazelhot had just left through, but it wouldn't open. That wasn't a good sign. What was the bloody maniac up to now? He saw a corridor at the back of the room that lead to a fire exit, but when he got there, that wouldn't budge, either.

This is all a bit bloody rum, he thought.

With each second that passed, he got more nervous. Hazelhot was up to something. He'd noticed a small open window a little way back down the corridor, and there was a table near it. Stott went back and pulled the table beneath the window. It didn't look like something he was going to fit through, but he was getting desperate and could see no alternatives. He needed to get out of there. Back in the main room were dogs that would tear him to pieces once they calmed down from the speech that the madman Hazelhot had numbed them with. That odd look Hazelhot gave him before leaving now gave him further cause for concern. He was now certain that Hazelhot had them all in a rat-trap and whatever was coming next would not be good.

His attempt to get onto the table and out of the window went wrong on the first go. Not only did he not reach the window, but he hadn't checked the validity of the table legs, and only discovered that one was broken when it slipped under him as soon as he put weight on it to reach for the window. The table folded in towards the wall, and Stott went straight down behind it. The table was solid, even if the legs were not, and as it slipped forward, so it sandwiched him there, and he was stuck between the solid table top and the outer wall.

Then, without warning, there was a bright white light, and a searing pain went through his entire body. It felt similar to an experience he had once had on a ride at an amusement park. Everything in his stomach stayed put, while his body achieved what felt like the speed of light in an instant. There were colours. Spinning. More spinning. Then even more spinning. Then feathers, some more feathers, and after that something furry hit him in the face. And then there was nothing at all.

Gathered in the main room at the chemical plant stood the entire crew of Bulldog Security. All except for their leader, Basher Bob. These were tough men, who together had ruled most of the land between East Dulwich and Nunhead Cemetery. Men together. Men who now stood inspired by a new potential leader, and they discussed tactics and shared thoughts as they prepared for the coming war with an, as yet unknown, adversary, but one they all felt sure could be beaten now, if they all worked together. Their mistake was in assuming their enemy was not already amongst them, and that he had already won.

Outside the building and smiling to itself, was a creature so fearsome and pathologically driven that - if it could be captured, and it really probably should be - it would have eminent psychologists, anthropologists, and even eschatologists, perplexed for decades in studying its behaviour. This creature currently stood a fair distance from the building, breathing in a happy sigh, on what had been quite the most exciting and exhilarating few days in many, many years. And as the closing ceremony reached its penultimate moment, the creature pressed down on a T-shaped handle that jutted out from a small wooden box. On its face was the look of immense satisfaction, but it had made one small misjudgement.

The resulting explosion not only turned the building and all of its human inhabitants to vaporised dust, but also launched the creature itself into the air. It then flew, still in an A-frame standing pose, with legs spread wide and a hand on what would have been the T shape of a detonator had it still been present, sailing through the air for over 500 meters, with chemical burns on its face and smoke issuing in an arc trail behind it as it went. Finally, it ricocheted off a passing oil tanker with a loud ding, and then landed with a resounding splosh into the river Thames. Curiously maintaining a beatific smile as it went.

In the road out front of the building, the scene was no less rich in symphonic, catastrophic, chaos. The blast sent every car and van tumbling through the air, spinning until they met more distant, solid objects, robust enough to stop their trajectory. Anything that was not firmly held down was launched by the blast, no matter the size or weight. Amid this escalating scene of carnage, and following an upward curving trajectory in the opposite direction of the currently flying Hazelhot, was Stott, who was now flipping round and round, attached by centrifugal forces to a solid wooden table top. The top gained some uplift through its flight, probably because of the fast spinning action afforded it by the forces that had launched it. It cleared the ensuing drama that was occurring below - of flying metal piping and vehicles - and kept going until it eventually ploughed through the canopy of trees in a park some way beyond. As it careened powerfully through the foliage, still spinning like the rotors of a gigantic flying lawn mower, leaves, branches, nests, squirrels, crows, and sparrows could be seen launched outward from its flight path. Finally, coming to rest when it became embedded in the trunk of a large oak tree, and from there a short moment later, the table top dropped its contents. Unconscious, broken and barely alive, a burned mass fell into the soft support of a large pram. One that had, thankfully, just recently been emptied and left parked beneath the tree, while its owners carried the original passenger to the swings nearby, and whom now stood motionless and aghast, staring in the direction of the explosion, as clouds of coloured, noxious gas swirled up into the air in the aftermath.

Catatonia Espanol

On the morning before the blast, Inspector Stump was going over the Basher case. He was sitting at a desk in Peckham Police Station, sipping at a cup of tea. Some things didn't add up. He looked at the photos of the bloodstained walls and at the still shots from the scene. It just didn't look like gangland work. This looked like something else. And then there was the car stolen from the hotel the Stott fellow was holed up in. It was the same car that one of his officers found later near Basher's HQ, and that 'Justice Jerry' had allegedly claimed belonged to Basher, before making off. But the description the officer gave of Justice Jerry, who the Inspector knew all too well, didn't add up either. There were several discrepancies that made little sense, but Stump felt certain it was all connected.

He was thinking about this and leaning back in a chair when someone brought the papers in. As he read The Daily Star and the article on Basher, his brow furrowed. Much as he liked to see this kind of thing being served to a low-life gangster such as Basher, his concern was more for his own loss of earnings, and even more worryingly now, was how it might implicate him. If Basher lost his mind or tried for a plea bargain to get a lighter sentence, he could easily take Stump down with him. What was clear from the news article was that Basher's time as a gangland leader was well and truly over.

"Where's Basher right now?" bellowed Stump from his desk.

There was a pause and then a reply came from outside his office.

"At his mum's house since last night, the news crews are there waiting for him to appear. He hasn't left yet, else we would have heard. Got two of our lads out there, sir."

Before the voice had finished the sentence, Inspector Stump was up, had grabbed his jacket, and was walking towards the rear car-park with the remains of a morning croissant in his mouth.

He sped through streets to get to Basher's mum's place. He thought of flicking the siren on but in the end didn't need to as he didn't hit any bad traffic. As he pulled in to the road, he could see news reporters sat around looking bored, clearly not getting anything from the house yet. Stump relaxed. As long as Basher wasn't talking, there was no need to panic. But he knew after the shaming Basher had taken in the press that morning that he was going to be struggling to cope with what he read. Stump had Basher down as a talker. And once he talked, that might be it for the Inspector too. No dream in the sun, no hacienda in Spain, no... *señorita*... Stump felt an episode coming on. He slowed the car down and got it to the curb before he entered a curious catatonic state.

Stump had been in the force a long time and had finally made inspector after a lot of hard work. It was the only profession he had ever known. He was now in his fifties, and too near retirement age to be plodding around the grey inner-city cesspit that was Peckham and its surrounding boroughs. Dealing with the daily filth of gangsters, crooks, crims, hoodlums, scumbags, and shit-heels was not a happy world, it was soulless. He'd seen the changes of the seasons. The 1970s had been a simpler time. It was everyday firms run by everyday all-white gangsters that, back then, at least pretended to have a code of honour and pedigree. But that had changed through the decades into racially tense and warring factions, with no rules, no code, and no honour. As the African and Jamaican cultures became more entrenched, as well as the Indian, Asian, and Muslim, it bled into the once all-white suburbs, until it became a multicultural swamp. The resulting conflicts had been mostly behind the scenes, as gangs fought for turf. But for Stump, it had been his daily grind to deal with it all. Those cultural power struggles really defined the last thirty years of life for him. He was sick of it.

He'd started out a fresh faced rookie with boyish dreams of doing good for his community and country, but now he was just another tired copper; a bitter old bastard with a nasty streak when it got disturbed. He was sick to the hind-fucking-teeth of the whole miserable, stinking business and what it had done to him. The bitterness was all that was left. That bitterness was his incurable hell, and he made sure he unleashed it onto the low-life creatures that inhabited his borough every chance that he got. It was they who had made him into what he now was. They deserved it.

Stump had realised, probably about twenty years into the force, that there was no way out for him. He was as much a prisoner to the Peckham Police force as the gangs and thugs were bound to their life of crime. It was a symbiotic marriage of dysfunction. And after a few more years of mulling it over, he finally decided he'd had enough of being the good guy, taking a basic wage, and facing nothing but more of the same. And so he turned to the dark side. Stump became a dodgy copper.

He'd started by taking the back-handers offered to turn a blind eye, or to favour certain outcomes. It soon turned out that he was a better criminal than he was a cop. But not yet so good as to get himself a decent enough retirement fund stashed away, nor to get himself out of the shit-pit of grey, concrete, despair that was London, as far as he cared for it. But he was working towards it.

As each year passed, so did his small tenure of remaining hope. A hope that was eventually replaced by a vacuous sense of hopeless inevitability. And somewhere in the depths of all that dank ambivalence, in the darkest stinking corner of it, a seed planted itself and began to grow. Then one day, it sprouted.

It was on a grey and cloudy day, much like all the others, that found him walking his usual beat on the streets of Peckham. The bland, inner-city relentlessness of a tired London consumed him as usual, and he was feeling pretty grey on the inside. Suddenly his entire being came to an abrupt stop, as he became mesmerised by a picture in a travel shop window across the street. It was of a scene, somewhere in Spain. The advert had a man on a Spanish white horse that was rising on its hind legs. The man was dressed in a large round-brimmed black Cordobes hat and black clothing, as he rode atop the horse and waved. To Stump, the man looked not unlike the Lone Ranger, and he was waving to a beautiful young raven-haired *señorita*, stood on the sun-drenched patio of an adobe hacienda. She was waving back at the man on his horse with a look of unbridled joy on her face.

It hit Stump somewhere in the heart of his embattled soul. All that colour, all that hope, all that... perfection. It was everything that he was not. Everything that he would never be. Everything that he could never have. It all lay before him in that brightly coloured picture. It was the forbidden jewel. The vision burrowed like a toxic worm into his subconscious, and it found root there in the septic depths of his despair. And there it festered. Before he knew it, cars were honking and screeching to a halt around him as the somnambulated Stump wandered into the traffic amid his daydreaming vision. Somewhere in his mind, he was stumbling toward freedom. In reality, he was walking like a catatonic zombie, over the busy road and towards the picture that was burying itself forever in his subconscious, emblazoned there, and taking on an embellished definition of its own. It became Stump's unobtainable utopia; his Nirvana, his Heaven, his Garden of Eden.

"Get out of the road, you stupid bastard!" shouted a cabbie as he drove around the idiot.

Stump was oblivious to all external stimuli as he reached the shop window and pressed his face against the glass. Only then did he show any kind of human response, and it was simply to sob. Falling to his knees, he knew then just how inexorably lost he was, and he knew there was no escape. Not in this life. Not unless something drastically changed.

It was the one and only time he was nearly pulled off duty and given psyche leave, but he buried it almost as quickly as it had surfaced, or so he thought. What happened was that he now had strange moments of seismic disruption. Moments where it would rise in him to manifest, expand in his mind, and create a frozen state in his conscious being, as he left and went off into a full-blown dreamscape that existed somewhere in his depths, perfectly preserved. It was the ultimate delusional vacation. A Spanish horse and a *señorita* fantasy that would bubble up and envelop him. He could neither stop it, nor refuse it, and he would disappear into it until it was done with him.

A therapist might have said that his logical mind became triggered when it felt threatened, caused maybe by a sense of extinction, or worse, the possibility of hope. It was a safe place, a happy place, that was buried deep inside him. Somewhere for him to hide out, and to protect himself from the inevitable sense of failure and doom that his real life had become. But the idyllic dream was the end of hope for Stump. Though somewhere within its mirage, he still believed it lay out there, awaiting him in Spain. He had to believe it, because the alternative was dying in Peckham.

So, he decided it was not mental illness, and that he did not need help, and that what he needed was money, and lots of it. It was an epiphany, a vision, a divine sign-post, and not just a mirage or delusion. He knew this because of how much he longed for it. The longing was the proof. Just how much he felt he deserved it was what made it symbolic of his future reality.

And ever since the day that he first fell to his knees to cry in front of a Peckham travel agent's window, he had determined that he would have it, and at any cost. With that determination - and obvious sense of denial - he worked on getting enough filthy money to eventually make his escape. But with it there now came the endless debilitating episodes which he had learnt to cover up. His catatonia dogged him, but he believed it was his version of stigmata. It was the Lord telling him that eventually he *would* be delivered to paradise. This belief is what had kept Stump going through the years since. And today was just another one of those episodes, as Stump went off into a fully fledged vision, prancing on horseback into a catatonic utopia set in sunny *Espanol*...

Rising on his white horse, in a perfectly performed slow-motion *pesade*, he waved with his free hand to *her*. He was dressed in cream coloured jodhpurs and a gallant, fiery-red shirt, open just enough to display his chest hair. The glint of a gold medallion lurked beneath. The immaculate display was for his one true love. So long he had been away from her in the bloody, but grey, wars. Now it was over, and he was returning home to *Espanol*. He pulled back on the reins and his horse dropped obediently to all four hooves, down from two. Then it began the gentle cantor towards the walled entrance of his opulent Spanish hacienda, the horse lifting its legs high in an accented trot as it moved slightly side-on. Another show of his supreme command over nature and the world; a hero returning to his home, to his family, and to her - his one true love.

She ran towards him from the hacienda with their two young children following on at her feet. Her raven-black hair flowing long behind her, in the light summer breeze and the warm Spanish air. Her colourful dress lifted above the floor with one hand, her loose but ample breasts swinging from side to side beneath the half undone lattice top that she wore. As she ran towards him, her perfectly smooth, tanned skin showing, the clothing could barely keep it all contained. A Flamenco guitar could be heard playing powerfully somewhere nearby to an unseen hand. Tears running down her cheeks of joy as she ran to meet her husband returned. Down the grass and dirt driveway, that was lined with tall and perfectly placed Italian Cypress trees.

"*Señor Stoooomp,*" she cried, jubilant and joyous. Emotional in his triumphant return.

"*Señor Stoooomp, Señor Stooooomp…* Inspector Stump, sir?"

A man's voice replacing that of the *señorita*, as a tapping on the window replaced the sound of horse's hooves.

Stump was brought back from his condition, as he shook his head and looked up wearily.

"What do you want?" he asked, winding down the window.

It was a young police officer who had been trying to get his attention for several minutes.

"Just wanting to know when we will be relieved, sir? We've been here all night. Basher is still holed up inside. Won't come out for anyone, and won't talk now that he has seen the papers."

"Okay, alright," said Inspector Stump, still shaking the experience off, and coming to terms with being back in the land of the grey. "I'll take it from here, son. Call for some replacements and then you boys go get some rest."

He rubbed his face and got out of the car to walk towards Basher's house. Passing the press stationed outside, and then opening the gate and walking up the garden path to the front door. Stump banged on the door but got no answer. He pulled his phone out and tried the number for Basher, but got no answer there either. He looked around, thinking for a moment. Spying the letter box, he pushed it open and checked inside. He could see down the hallway to the kitchen and could see Basher, still sat staring at the papers. Stump stood back up again.

"Fucking retarded prick," he muttered to himself.

Then he pulled the knees of his trousers up, knowing he was likely to be bent down talking into a letter box for a while. Stump spread his legs wide enough to support his posture, and he bent down to hold the letter box open as he spoke into it.

"Basher. It's Inspector Stump, son," he said. "Listen mate, I know it's tough. I have been there. God knows I've been clobbered by the press enough in my time too, but we need to talk. So how about you let me in, and I can help you work through this? Come on now, son. See sense here. Let's talk, have a chat and a cuppa, and see what you want to do next. No pressure. I'm here as a friend."

He pulled back to have a look through the letter box, but was met by a dog that nearly took his nose off and he fell backwards into the dirt and a flowerbed.

"Motherfucker!" he exclaimed.

A chorus of camera shutters went off a distance behind him, catching the moment for the paper run the next day.

"Fuck you too, you god damn vultures," he said, but this time at a lower volume. He knew better than to express it loud enough for them to hear. A photo of him falling ass-over-tit was one thing, but a police officer losing his cool at the cameras was a whole other problem he knew better than to invite into his life at that moment.

Stump got back up, brushed off his trousers, and sorted himself out. Then, fetching a stick from the garden, he came back and used it to prop open the letter box. The dog appeared again and barked, but it couldn't reach Stump, and the stick presented nothing for it to get its snapping jaws on, much as it tried. Stump looked in, trying to see if Basher had moved. As he did so, the dog was pulled away and he saw it getting shut into a side room. He moved forward to take a better look. A broom handle came through the letterbox next and hit him in the face, sending him reeling backwards again. The same chorus of camera shutters going off.

"Piss off you journo bastards. Leave my boy alone!" came the voice of an old lady, scolding him through the letter box in a broad East London accent.

"It's me. Inspector Stump," replied Stump, now clutching his eye and hoping she could hear him above the various expletives she was still expressing through the letterbox.

The old woman paused for a moment, then an eye appeared in the aperture.

"Oh, it's you. I thought it was the press again. What do you want?" she asked, recognising him as someone that had been to her house before.

Stump rubbed his face and responded from a safer distance. He knew her well enough to know she might launch a second attack at any moment, so kept well back.

"I need to talk to your boy. We need to know what he wants to do next, that's all. I'm not here to arrest him. Just here to talk and help if possible," said the Inspector, his hands now held up to imply a treaty.

"Wait there a minute," said the woman, and she disappeared inside. A short while later, coming back.

"He doesn't want to talk to you," she said.

Inspector Stump hid his annoyance. He wouldn't get past this stubborn old bat easily, and he knew it. As he stood there thinking, she spoke again.

"Nice to see you again, though. I am just making a cuppa. Would you like one?" she asked.

Stump said he would, and she went off. When she returned, she unlatched the door's various bolts and handed him a cup of tea in old china, with a biscuit on the side.

"There's a nice Rich-tea biscuit for you on there too," she said.

After making sure he had hold of it, she went back inside, shut the door, and locked it all up again.

"You can leave it on the step when you are done," she said through the letterbox.

It was going to be a long day. Stump sipped at the tea. He smiled a little, brightened by the quality of a good old English cuppa, then looked up at the grey clouds. It wasn't sunny, but it would not likely rain either, so there was that. He considered how at least some of the old ways were not dead yet. A nice cup of tea in the middle of a stand-off. It was standard British etiquette and always had been, once upon a time. Even during a proper shoot-out, you might get a cup of tea off one of the nanas. That was just how it was with the firms of the old days. At least it was until the other lot started showing up and doing things all out of kilter. No class, no understanding of the British way of things. It really changed then. Nothing was sacred any longer, and he knew that now, but he missed it all the same. Basher's mum was a dying breed, but then weren't they all? Him, her, Basher. There weren't many white folk left at all in some parts, and that was a fact. Not that it mattered all that much. Everything changed eventually. It was just the way of the world. And you couldn't stop progress even if you didn't much care for it.

Stump stood in the garden having a nostalgic moment, thinking how much the Britain he knew as a kid had disappeared. Even for him, a lower-class nobody from South London, who never left Peckham except for occasional visits to Margate or Southend, it had all changed from what it was once. He missed old England. Old dears like Basher's mum, you just respected them and that was that. They could walk through the middle of a gunfight back in the day and deliver a paper, a cup of tea and some biscuits, and no one would consider it strange. Both sides would respect it because it was someone's mum, and you respected that. The Matriarchs had the power, and they had tea and biscuits too, and who didn't like a break for tea and biscuits? Killing each other was not enough of an excuse and you could always get back to it right after. But with these bloody new types of gangster coming in, harking from other countries and setting up shop and taking over things, they respected nothing. They just took. And then the endless whining about racism when they were getting a traditional copper beating. It was pathetic. Taking and whining, taking and whining. A bloody travesty, really. But Stump cared little about that anymore because crims were crims whatever the colour of the skin. All that really mattered to Stump now was taking money off them and realising his dream...

"Stooomp," came the distant echo of her voice.

Stump shook himself before it pulled him in again. He put the cuppa down and fumbled about in his pockets until he found the pills, took out two, and knocked them back, making sure the press could not get a photo as he did so, then washing it down with the last of the tea. As long as he didn't get nostalgic, it wouldn't trigger. Though it was like asking someone not to think about a blue horse.

The drugs helped, but the stronger ones had left him dribbling on his desk at the station and he had to stop using them. These new ones were a lot weaker, but they did the trick if he could catch it quickly enough. He breathed like the doctor had showed him. *Pranyana,* or some stupid thing the Indian twat had suggested, but still, it worked in a pinch.

Stump checked himself and then looked at his watch.

There was no way past Basher's mum, so he was going to have to remain until Basher decided to re-surface all by himself. He had no choice. Too much was at stake. He sat down on a garden chair beside a gnome that stared at him, a laugh on its face, while it pissed into a garden pond.

He was still sat musing about events, when two hours later a loud explosion shook the air from somewhere distant. Everyone looked to the skies, but nothing could be seen beyond the houses. Moments later, a police car came screeching into the street and pulled to a halt. Two officers got out and ran towards the house. At the same time, reporter's mobile phones started going off in unison, and moments later press jumped to action as they all ran for their vehicles and started them up. Reversing, beeping, as chaos ensued until they careened away, as if a race meet had just been called somewhere. The street was emptying by the time the officers reached Stump, who was still sat in the garden next to the pissing gnome, sipping at another tea delivered by Basher's mum, this time with a slice of cake that he was finishing up as they got to him.

"Really excellent Victoria sponge this," he said, as they stood to attention, waiting for him to let them speak.

Stump was used to the endless drama, and it rarely made him move if he didn't want to. A distant explosion was not common, but it wasn't enough to move him. Finally, he bid them to speak, but what he heard made him stand bolt upright, then turn towards the Basher's residence.

"Okay boys. Let's get him out of there."

Stump booted the front door in. He'd learnt the method from watching The Sweeney, and never missed an opportunity to apply it. Double security bolts and locks went flying through the hallway as splinters exploded and shot off in all directions. The door collapsed inward, finally knocked off its hinges by a second hefty kick. Stump stepped back to let his officers through. He then turned to finish his cup of tea, downing it in one go. After that, placing it down gently on the step to the left of the entrance, as requested by Basher's mum. He started walking back towards his car, as behind him the two officers could be seen wrestling with Basher back and forth across the kitchen, his mum setting about them with a broom as they went, and a dog clamped on the ass of one officer, as they fought for their lives. Four more officers arrived and ran past Stump, giving a brief acknowledgement as they did so, to get stuck in to giving support to their men inside. Meanwhile, somewhere in Essex at a location well known to Stump, shit had just gone medieval.

Dance With The Devil

At Peckham Police Station, Inspector Stump was listening to the news reports and hearing the stories from his officers about events in Essex. It had been cordoned off and listed as a *chemical explosion*. After that, the Hazmat suits had arrived along with Counter Terrorism Command, who took over the scene. From that point on, the police were no wiser than anyone listening in on a radio scanner regarding what was going on there.

Powers given to Counter Terrorism Command after the London bus bombing had allowed for the fast-track push through of the Terrorism Act of 2006, and with little resistance. This had provided CTC with new powers, such as holding suspects without charge for 28 days, and the freezing of their assets. It also gave greater opportunity for *Stop And Search* methods to be applied liberally. Now, a nod from the higher-ups was enough to unleash seven levels of hell on a potential suspect, regardless of cultural denomination, status, position, or crime. The *powers-that-be* could re-define a dog farting as an "act of terror" if they so wished. CTC became the toolkit used by the Government to do whatever they liked, to whoever they liked, whenever they liked. They could also do it *wherever* they liked. If someone didn't like *that*, they could whisk them out of the country, and do it to them somewhere more solitary instead, with specialised equipment and fewer laws protecting what little human rights they'd previously thought they had. It was all quite convenient, and they had the Americans to thank for it. Though Britain was considered a democratic society run on a specific set of rules based on civilised behaviour and the power of a vote, it was, in reality, one of the most militant countries in the world, and the complete opposite. But that was the beauty of the powers implemented in the wake of 9/11. Applying these new powers meant the British Government could order the CTC into action whenever they deemed it suitable. The *Free world*, as they liked to call it, was only free so long as the CTC had no interest in you.

Unfortunately for Inspector Stump, with the CTC now involved, he was shut out from all further investigation. He would have loved their powers, and once upon a time, localised to Peckham Rye, he'd had them. But that had all changed, just as the world had changed. Now the Police were mostly there to provide a service as whipping boys to the manipulative so-called "minorities" found on South London councils, or the foreign religious and cultural groups that were fast becoming the majority in many London boroughs. The Metropolitan Police took all the public and press flak, which helped take the heat, so the CTC could do whatever they liked without anyone noticing. The police were now so heavily bound by protocol and red-tape, that they hardly had time left for any actual police work. To make matters worse, they got it in the neck from the CTC too. Nothing was ever good enough for them. But it didn't stop there. When they got home from a hard day of being a London copper, they often heard it from their wives and children, and their wive's friends, and their children, too. Everyone had an opinion, because everything the police did ended up on the Internet. It was also never anybody else's fault, always somehow the police were to blame. Everyone was innocent but the police. Where once the police could demand answers and apply a bit of pressure, now answers were being demanded of them. Being a copper in London truly sucked balls. There was no power in being with the police anymore. They were as powerless as anyone to do much about anything. The Government just used them to keep the public and Press satisfied. The Police were just a punch bag; staged monkeys targeted by the social media campaigns where protesters loved to protest, and loudly. Thus, all power had now been quietly transferred to the CTC.

But there was one small perk of being an old school copper, if you could call it a perk. They often had acquaintances that had climbed up the ranks, and sometimes all the way to *High Command*. Stump had been in the game a long time, and he had connections in several places. But one in particular came to mind, as he sat wondering how to address his most recent problem. It was a connection that went back to his childhood days, and who was now a member of MI6.

Stump secured Basher in a cell, and put his best man on duty, with strict orders to stop him from speaking to anyone. He then returned to his desk and sat down, thinking how best to approach his next move. Stump tapped on the phone handset, considering the risks entailed in what he was about to do. He hadn't called in a favour in a long time. It was risky because it would come at a price, and that was never good. But this was a pivotal event. Stump was facing an insurmountable problem, and Basher was in no fit state to be trusted, and silencing him more permanently was now out of the question. Stump needed access to inside information on what was going on. There was only one person who could help him with that, but to call him was to dance with the devil. He had no choice. Stump lifted the receiver and dialled the number, and he hoped the inevitable price to be paid would be worth it.

Stump sat down on a bench beside the river Thames, opposite the Houses of Parliament, and waited. A gentleman soon appeared along the path wearing a long black Moss Bros over-coat, well dressed beneath it in a custom fitted Saville Row suit and tie. He stopped beside the bench, wiped a hand across it, then sat down on the opposite end without looking at Stump. Casually removing his gloves and laying them over his knee as he briefly studied his perfectly manicured hands. Both men then looked out over the water.

"Been a while, Roger," said the man, after a time. Then he glanced briefly at Stump before returning his eyes to the river. "I assume this is about the Essex incident."

Stump nodded almost imperceptibly. The man continued.

"I understand a Peckham mob was inside the place, or what's left of them, and I wondered if I might soon hear from you. Something got you spooked, old chap? What *have* you been up to, Roger?"

Stump wasn't happy to be there, but he needed his help. He also knew beating about the bush would only encourage Sir Michael to enjoy himself at his expense. Bastards of his calibre always seemed to win, where Stump was the type of bastard that was only ever running away from endless failures. He'd never understood that about the upper classes;

how they seemed to get away with so much, or what their secret was. He needed some of that magic now, so he got straight to the point.

"I've got the gang's boss in the cells at Peckham, but I think he's being set up. He's... well, he is a mess. I don't believe this was a local gang. Not the murder, nor this. Someone else - or something else - is behind it. I've had involvement with that Peckham firm for years. This wasn't brewing. It has come out of nowhere. But if he talks, with the state he is in after all this, it could become problematic for me. Then there's the power vacuum going to be left in Peckham after this. There's a lot of low-life foreign scum are going to want to fill it. And we both know how ugly it will get while the various gangs work it out," said Stump.

"Ah, I see," replied Sir Michael, grasping his tentative position amid the mess. "The old, *'dirty cop gets caught taking backhanders'* saga. I always felt you should have done better for yourself, Roger. You have better contacts than most, but maybe one day you will surprise us. But the irony, old chap - and I think you will enjoy this part - is that I was just about to contact *you*."

Stump glanced at Sir Michael, surprised to be hearing it, and then he quickly looked back over the water again. Sir Michael continued.

"That surprised you, huh? Well, the truth is with this recent incident, we don't know who is behind it either, and that concerns us. We need eyes on the ground for this one, Roger. Seems to have come out of left-field and that makes us nervous. Just when you think you know everyone and everything in play, this happens. So, here is the deal. You keep us fed with whatever comes to light that might help us work out who is behind these events. The problem with our end is that we are under scrutiny again by the PM and need to keep everything tickety-boo and above-board. Despite our ridiculous powers, we do still have to answer to people. You, on the other hand, can fiddle around in the dirt, and no one is going to mind much or even notice. So, my suggestion and offer is this - we'll take your boy and put him on ice in some convenient oubliette for a bit. He seems to be the only remaining survivor of this, and since it's gang related, we can call it protecting a witness for his own safety. If necessary, he can later serve as fall guy, too. So that suits us all round. But don't worry, anything he says while under our protection, we can wipe from the records long before the press gets to hear about it. That gives *you* time to do what you need to do. And in exchange for this rather large first favour, we need you to do a little something for us. Okay so far, Roger?"

Sir Michael looked briefly again at Stump, who nodded, after which he continued.

"Good. Now, there is another source who has brought forward some info on this, which has made us even more nervous. We now fear it may be a play from more powerful enemies trying to distract us, and we are looking into paperwork and back-tracking records at MI6 trying to trace its legitimacy. It seems we may have some sort of *Jason Bourne* on our hands. Can you believe that? A cheap journalist for the tabloids brought the story to us, but odder still, he said the operative involved asked him to do so. It's all very peculiar, and we need to get to the bottom of it. Does the name of 'Hazelhot' ring any bells for you?"

Sir Michael looked again at Stump for confirmation.

Stump shook his head in the negative.

"Okay, well, this journalist fellow says this chap Hazelhot came to him, and that he is an agent in a mutant adaptation program. The chap was babbling about killer rats and plans to populate Mars and god knows what gibberish. The thing is that, as wacky as it all sounds, it is exactly the stuff we were working on back in the 1980s at Porton Down. I am not at liberty to discuss all that, but, of course, suffice to say that the damn stuff got out occasionally. When you are fiddling around in genetics and viruses, there is bound to be the odd hiccup that gets rapidly hushed up right after. I mean bloody idiots, but what can you do? The problem is that tracking down paperwork of that nature is a dastardly task, and so full of red-tape and red-herrings, it is nigh on impossible..."

A jogger came by a little too close for their conversation to continue, and both men sat pretending not to be together, while looking at opposite parts of the river. Once the jogger had gone by, Sir Michael continued.

"I don't buy this journalist's story for a minute. The hallmarks are all wrong. So, I wonder if it's the Russians or Chinese trying to create some distraction for us, while they do whatever it is the Chinese and Russians do. Christ, sometimes I almost don't think anyone is doing anything other than thinking the other side is doing something. But right now, all we have is a gang boss in your cells, the remains of his crew turned to vapour on an industrial estate in Essex, and a bloody chlorine gas cloud floating around making people sick. All of which is going to be causing us a royal pain in the ass with the press. And tied into all this, behind it, is one very odd story about a maniac operative from god knows where, who seems now to be loose in London and unaccounted for after the blast.

"So, Roger, what I need from you is to find your way to this Hazelhot chap, assuming he is still alive. Dead may actually be a lot better, but he's currently off the map and missing. We don't think he went up with the explosion because of the info from this journalist chap, who claims he was the cause of it. So, we need to find him, and after that, figure out who he is connected to. You have your ear to the ground and finger in multiple pies, so to speak, so there is a good chance someone, somewhere, knows about him or can lead you to him. If and when he pops up, there is a good chance you might hear about it first. Then we can nip this whole damn fiasco in the bud, and that's us happy. Can you do this for us while we put your chap on ice and await the outcome?"

Sir Michael once again looked to Stump for confirmation. Stump nodded. Sir Michael smiled, then thought for a moment before adding,

"Might I suggest you let this power vacuum in Peckham play out? In fact, it may behoove you to stir it up a bit, see if you can't encourage some chaos. This may seem like an odd recommendation, but in our experience, it's best to keep the press busy watching your left hand while your right works the magic. The struggle of a turf war might help keep them distracted while you get on the hunt for this Hazelhot chap. With bloody social media these days, we have swarms of these damn annoying Lefty do-gooders fucking around with our operations constantly. They are like wasps. No sooner you get rid of one, than ten pop up behind with their damn phone cameras pointed at your b-team. Despite all the powers we have over them, the little shits remain relentless. Well, anyway, and getting back to the point, it would appear that we can help you, Roger. So, do we have a deal?"

Sir Michael looked one last time at Stump, knowing he had very little choice.

"We have a deal," replied Stump, surprised at how well it had worked out for him.

"I am sure you don't need reminding, that we can't let anything you do come back on us. So, try not to fuck it up,

Roger. I like you, and it would be a damn shame to lose you."

Sir Michael then clapped his hands on his knees, picked up his gloves, and stood up.

"Toodle-pip then, old chap," he said, still looking toward the river.

Then he left, and as he walked, he whistled the Colonel Bogey March to himself. Stump stayed on the bench for a while longer, enjoying the view for the first time. He was relieved. And now he had MI6 on his side, maybe things weren't going so badly after all.

The Essex Ward

Ambulances arrived one after the other at St Thomas's Hospital in Lambeth, where the broken bodies, some still smoking, were rushed in to ICU. It became apparent that an entire ward was going to be needed for the recovery process and be able to expand, as required, to cater to the numbers. Doctors and nurses worked over-time to help. Many were called back from days off to attend to what soon looked like a war hospital on the front-line.

By the time the influx finally dropped off, there were forty people who had been injured, but were able to leave after being checked, and a further thirty that could not be released. Once the thirty were in a stable condition, they were moved into the temporarily renamed *Essex Ward*, so named on account of the location where the injured had arrived from. As the ward was recommissioned for the role, trolleys arrived post-surgery, and the occupants took up residence in vacant spots until it was full.

By the following morning, things had calmed down at the front desk, and most of the patients were through surgery and onto the ward. Miraculously, there had been no further loss of life other than those who died at the scene - which had been everyone inside the building when the blast went up. Despite the ensuing carnage laying waste to vehicles on the road outside, somehow not a single life was lost there.

It had taken fire crews and ambulance staff some time to cut people from the wreckage, and their work had been made more difficult by the lingering gas cloud from the chemical plant. Some reports said chlorine, others said caustic soda. One report said a group of people had smelt donuts and could now hear colours after being caught up in it. The emergency services that attended the site had worked quickly and done a commendable job. The first CTC agents to the site had been given instructions to tell everyone who was leaving the scene that it was "a random chemical explosion at a chlorine plant," which they duly did, sometimes a little too forcefully. Given they were armed with machine guns, grenades, and wore helmets and masks that made them look more like they were ready to launch a new Steven Seagal movie, it had the opposite effect and confirmed people's more outlandish fears. Though they need not have bothered. Most of the press that might have been on the scene to report it were now on The Essex Ward.

By 10 am the next morning, the ward was full and the emergency surgery doctors were finally heading home. Bodies were in plaster casts, many from head to toe, and some with limbs held up by wires and rigging. Near the door, and the last to come through surgery, was one of the worst affected. They had found him early on, but because of the damage received, they had not dared move him from the scene immediately. Eventually they used the pram he had been found in as a stretcher, and four ambulance staff carefully navigated him to the nearest vehicle before working out how to get him safely into the back of it. Finally, hoisting him up with the pram still attached, as there was some concern his back might be broken. Strapping was used to hold him in place and the driving was done at a careful pace. They got him to St Thomas without causing further issue, bringing him out of the ambulance, the same way he went in. Some freelance reporters were stationed at the hospital entrance, and they snapped cameras at the curious sight as it was retrieved from the back of the ambulance. Stott was oblivious. Having spun so many times in rapid succession, he did not know who, or where, or even what he was. He just mumbled incoherently about poisoned monkeys in Borneo and occasionally shouted other delirious inanities.

"He's a bloody maniac. Get away, get away! Fields full of poison bloody monkeys. Baboons, sir, necks like tree trunks!"

They drugged him, patched him up, drugged him some more, and once they were convinced he wasn't about to die, they wheeled him onto The Essex ward, and parked him in one of the last spaces left near the entrance.

The ward stayed that way for the next few days, as inhabitants dipped in and out of consciousness and gibbered, or shouted incoherently, mostly thanks to the strong medications they were on. The police asked questions of anyone they could get sense out of and kept an officer stationed on the floor for protection.

As patients gradually started to regain their senses, they discussed the event they had witnessed. There was surprise expressed at how the police were being so relaxed about the whole thing. Some had expected more of a grilling, and they speculated as to why CTC had arrived on site. It certainly suggested sinister goings on, as per the story Fred had called them out to cover.

Fred was not on the ward. And this sparked concern as to his safety, or whether he had survived at all. His absence fed the rumours as to just what they had uncovered at the plant. No one present knew anything more than what he had told all of them. Everyone had been working according to Fred's brief that it related to genetic mutant killing machines. Though few had believed it possible, now the place had blown up just as they were there to report it, it made the story a lot more plausible. And given all they knew of the situation, everyone had expected CTC, or MI6, to arrive heavy handed and make their usual aggressive attempts to squeeze information out of whoever they could. So far, only regular police had shown up, and that was mostly just to check in on them and confirm events. Someone must know something. The ward conferred, and calls were made, but it seemed no one knew anything. Still, no one had seen or heard from Fred.

Meanwhile, the Essex site remained in lock-down, and fresh batches of reporters that arrived there were told *"no comment"* by CTC still stationed there to guard it.

Since there was not much else to go on, the papers said nothing other than what they were told to say by their bosses. Since no journalist could prove it was anything other than a disused chemical plant going up, the public soon lost interest in the story. Without further drama to feed it, there was nothing to feed the public's insatiable desire for increasingly worse news. This was, of course, how MI6 expected it to play out, since they had engineered it.

So the news reports that played on the television in the ward said nothing of any further developments. And the same story was repeated on each channel. There was one survivor from the gang known as Bulldog Security, and that was Basher Bob, their ex-leader and possible homo-erotic serial killer. He was now being detained "for his own protection". The screen showed stock footage of police vehicles driving through prison gates, since they had nothing more recent to offer. It was known that Basher had been held at Peckham Police Station initially, but had since been moved to an undisclosed location. A previous interview showed an Inspector Stump reporting on this event. The Inspector went onto say that Peckham probably was not the best place for him to be, given the circumstances, and that CTC had taken him and that was as much as he knew. This comment produced a unison of murmuring from the ward beds. Reading from a piece of paper into fifteen microphones, Inspector Stump offered the viewers the only information anyone had.

"After this sad and unfortunate incident, our focus now is to get back to serving and protecting the local public and businesses," said the Inspector. "Bulldog Security was the dominant gang that worked the areas round here, mostly between East Dulwich and Nunhead Cemetary, with their HQ in Peckham Rye - the epicentre of their domain. With them now gone, this has created a power-vacuum in Peckham, and we need to make sure we don't have other gangs from surrounding boroughs, thinking this is an easy opportunity to step in and take over. Nothing more to comment. Thank you."

He'd finished up to a clamour of questions, but he ignored them to duck away and disappear inside Peckham Police Station.

"That's going to put the idea in their heads, you bloody idiot!" shouted a plaster-cast figure towards the television.

Everyone murmured their agreement, unaware that was exactly the reason Inspector Stump had said it.

A police officer appeared on the ward at that moment and

stopped beside the bed that contained Sir Stott.

"Mr Archibold Stott?" he enquired.

"*Sir* Archibold Stott," came the husky reply from somewhere inside the bandage wrappings.

"Very good, sir," replied the officer. "You are the current owner of a company called Pussy Productions. Is that correct?"

The reminder worked its way through the heavy sedation that Stott was currently under, and caused a spasm in his body, which hurt, and he cried out in pain.

"God damn it, sadly yes, thanks a bunch for reminding me," he replied.

"We have received some concerning reports from our Social Media department," the officer said. "Some hard-line feminist groups have made the porn industry something of a target this month, sir. Given the circumstances, we thought it might be best if you consider hiring some personal security."

"Good lord," said Stott, not unsurprised to be hearing that things could get worse than they already were. It was becoming something of a standard. "And how do you propose I go about doing that from a hospital bed, exactly, officer?" he asked.

"That's why it was suggested someone come and see you, sir. We recently heard a rather excellent security man has come free from his previous employ. Might I recommend you talk to him about taking on the job? He comes recommend by Mandela himself. A white South African gentleman by the name of Hoots. Known in the trade as one of the best, if not *the* best. Damn lucky timing, really. He is rarely available like this. Take him on sir, trust me, this is the guy you need by your side at a time like this."

Stott thought for a moment. His concern was not of disgruntled females, but that of his psychotic last partner, Hazelhot. If there was any danger of him having survived the blast, Stott was going to need all the protection he could get. Stott knew Hazelhot had been the cause of it, though he wasn't about to share that bit of information with anyone. Though he was not eager to risk introducing any new killing machines into his employ, for a police officer to be concerned for his safety and to be recommending the chap, that counted for something. If it was going to keep him safe from Hazelhot, it seemed like a good idea. But violent feminists? Really? Surely women could not pose much of a threat.

"Exactly how bad *are* these feminists, officer?" he asked.

Stott was expecting to be told they might scratch his car, or picket the hospital, or possibly break a window or two at the studio. The police officer pulled a slip of paper from his pocket.

"Well, if the Social Media posts are anything to go by, sir, they intend to, and I quote… *rip his testicles off and feed them to him, then hang the bastard naked from a tree with a five-inch wide cudgel shoved up his ass. See how he likes it. Then choke him on week-old period blood, before feeding his carcass to a pair of female Doberman pinchers.*"

"By Christ!" shouted Stott, who was struggling to deal with his reaction, trapped as he was in the plaster. "I thought you said these were women?" he managed, as he got himself under control.

"Er… correct, sir. All of them *are* women," replied the officer, checking through his list.

"Women do that sort of thing nowadays?" asked Stott, finding it hard to imagine the fairer sex doing much more than crying, seeking attention, or being overly-emotional.

"And far worse too, I am afraid, sir. They see it as the Patriarchy to blame for everything in the world today, sir," said the officer.

"The Patria… my god man, do they not know who killed all the bears and created the civilised world that they now indulge themselves to luxuriate in?" replied Stott, getting animated again.

"Quite agree, sir. Hence my being asked to come and see you. So, shall I contact our chap and get him to give you a visit, then? I assure you that you couldn't do better, and he will snap up quickly."

"Get him in, officer. Yes, please. Don't hesitate. And thank you very much for bringing this matter to my attention," replied Stott, now convinced without a doubt that a security detail would be essential.

"Of course, sir. And if it is not too presumptuous, might I ask for a signed photo from Miss Lovelips. The wife is a huge fan of hers, you see," said the officer.

"Sorry, Miss who?" asked Stott, with no idea what he was talking about.

The officer looked a little confused, but at that moment, a gentleman appeared behind him and interjected with a subtle cough.

"Ahem. Absolutely, officer, we can get you that. If you would like to give your address to Miss Jones here, our secretary, then she will get one out to you in tomorrow's post. How does that sound?"

The man who had just arrived on the ward was dressed in a boorish grey suit, stood about five-feet and six inches tall, and had an air of accountancy bookishness. There was also a certain sense of weakness that one couldn't quite put a finger on. And standing just behind Rigby was Miss Jones. She was quietly unnoticeable and looked exactly like a secretary should. If it were not for the company she worked for, it might be easy to assume she was the most plain Jane. The police officer nodded a thanks to Rigby and then turned back to the bed.

"Thank you, Mr… Sir, Stott. I'll get the chap in to see you right away. His name is Hoots, a big bloke, you can't miss him. But don't be put off by that. He's loyal as they come, and the very best in his trade. You have a good day now, sir."

And with that, the officer stepped over to give Miss Jones his address.

"And who the bloody blazes are you?" Stott asked, looking through his bandages at Rigby.

"I'm Rigby, Sir Stott. Lawyer-cum-accountant for your company, Pussy Productions. And this is Miss Jones, secretary and receptionist. We thought we should come down and introduce ourselves. Since Bulldog Security have… er… relinquished control, we assume that leaves you fully in charge of things. I thought it best we make your acquaintance in person, and to ask if you are going to be keeping our services with the changes that surely must now be taking place."

Stott had happily forgotten that he owned a porn company until the officer had brought it up, but now it seemed the entire company was bent on chasing him down. There was clearly to be no getting away from it. But he had to consider the future. Basher and the Bulldog Security would not be coming back, Hazelhot was missing, presumed psychotic enough to have survived, and this indeed meant Stott was now left in charge. Stott also knew he had no source of potential income other than Pussy Productions. He had no wife, no friends, and he'd been ejected from the members list of every club in England worth being involved in. The press had since run his name through the dirt. There were photos of him trapped bloody in a pram, suggesting he was a pervert, and now he was flavour-of-the-month for a bunch of feminists. He was also going to be facing crippling hospital bills before his recent issues were over. Stott had no choice but to accept the role and cling on to Pussy Productions as he might flotsam floating around a recently sunk boat.

"Not a psychopath, are you?" he asked Rigby, as he considered the situation.

Rigby laughed at the suggestion.

"God, no. If only, haha. No, no. I don't think anyone has ever accused me of that before. Quite the opposite," said Rigby.

"What about her? She's not a feminist, is she?" asked Stott.

"Not as far as I am aware, sir. Never said boo to a goose, but a damn fine secretary and very good with... pencils and answering the phone," replied Rigby, not really sure how to respond.

Rigby was feeling nervous. It felt like a job interview, and he wanted to keep this job, as did Miss Jones.

Stott eyed him. There was something weak about the man. Though he didn't feel he had much choice but to keep them on, he liked to keep people hanging at such times - it gave him the opportunity to read them. Rigby was a sweater, and Stott did like to bully sweaters. It gave him a sense of superiority while putting the weak in their bally place.

"Hmm," he said, after an extended pause. "Alright, you can keep your jobs. Let's begin by discussing the balance sheets, profit and loss, expenses, and how the whole sordid thing works. As you probably know, Basher did not exactly outline the workings of the company to me in our last meeting, so start from the top. And the first thing you can do is explain to me who the hell Miss Lovelips is?"

From Russia With Love

Hazelhot woke to the sound of men's voices. His lungs burned and his skin was raw. He looked around to get his bearings. A stocky man in a thick polo-neck sweater, clearly a seafaring merchant, stepped in through an open metal door and loomed over him.

"Kak ty sebya chuvstvuyesh?" he asked.

Hazelhot couldn't speak and could barely move. The man bent down and picked up a bottle of water, then helped Hazelhot to sip from it. Still groggy and in huge amounts of pain, he spoke a reply to what he assumed must be his rescuer, but his memory was foggy. He could not seem to recall how he had got there.

"Ya v poryadke. Spasibo," replied Hazelhot.

"Ty govorish po-russki!" said the man, laughing, and he shouted out of the door to his comrades. "On govorit po-russki!"

Hazelhot then had a pained conversation with his new Russian friends, in an in-elegant, but workable, version of it. In between moments of lucidity, and passing out, he got enough info to find out roughly what had happened. Much of his memory eluded him except for his name. He was at least certain of that. Winston Churchill was easy to remember.

The Russians let him know that an air-ambulance had been called, and should soon to be *en route* once the transfer between nations was authorised. His arrival on the tanker had been officially labelled *"by air"* in the log books because of the limited number of options they had available to select from when reporting incidents. It seemed to fit the best. They'd finally agreed on it, because his first point of contact with the boat occurred just before contact with the water. It had taken an argument and some amount of vodka to decide, but they eventually got there. Now it was just a case of the relevant countries having the relevant consulate conversations, and that was already underway.

Handing a person back to England - and one who had just joined a Russian oil tanker uninvited by air - was an extremely complicated procedure. It was so wrapped up in red tape, he would be in Russia before it was done. But the consulate had understood the urgency, and they also tied it into the explosion. This coincidental timing fast-tracked the process directly upwards, and to MI6.

MI6 had received the details of this request for clearance, along with the request for an air ambulance to collect a burned and injured man. The man was believed to be English, but the Russian translator was probably drunk, because they claimed his name was *Winston Churchill.*

Sir Michael received the request after it was patched through to his office inside the Vauxhall MI6 building overlooking the Thames. He wasn't alone. Some top-brass decision makers were there too. Men rarely seen together in the same space, but because of the mysterious events surrounding the explosion, an emergency meeting had been called. Sir Michael pushed the loud-speaker button so that the entire room could hear the conversation. When the diplomat on the other end finished the request, he waited for Sir Michael to authorise the process. Sir Michael asked him to wait on the line, and he put the phone on mute.

"The plot thickens, gentlemen. What do we think?" he asked of the gathering.

A gruff but commanding gentleman then spoke.

"Winston Churchill? Is this some kind of bloody joke? What are the Russians up to? Not only do they have translators on board, but they have enough equipment to monitor a rat fart in a thunderstorm from fifty miles away and translate it into forty different dialects, if they so wished. Get the name of the tanker and let's get some satellite footage. I want to see if it was involved in the blast. Certainly no coincidence it was going past that exact spot when it received this passenger, but why admit to it? As for this alleged Mr Churchill, we can't be seen to be reacting, but let's not lose track of him either. I suggest we get him shipped to the same ward as the rest of them, and get a man-on-the-ground to keep tabs on him there. Keep a low, but well-defined police presence monitoring the ward, and let's see how this plays out. We don't want whoever is behind this thinking that we are interested in the chap, especially with that ward chock full of bloody reporters. The police being there will be considered normal, but MI6 agents being there would create too much of a stir."

Everyone agreed in nods and grunts, and Sir Michael unpressed the mute button, and authorised the request for an air-ambulance and a visa to permit the unknown gentleman onto British soil.

Moments later, an air-ambulance chopper launched from London City towards the Russian oil tanker with all the paperwork on board for a handover. Russian counterparts in

Moscow prepared paperwork on their end to allow it to land on their tanker and officiate the extraction of one unregistered English visitor by the name of *Winston Churchill*.

The Russians had been watching events closely via spy satellite, and they too were concerned about why someone was trying to make it look like the Russians were involved in the blast. Stranger still, why was this person now using World War Two monikers as a cover? Was this a message? A warning? A code? What exactly did it mean? Heads of the FSB - who were once heads of the KGB - were being roused in the night from their slumber to be informed of the risk of escalation on a global scale if there was a negative response from Britain. Lists of anti-Russian terror groups were gathered ready to be located, monitored, ruled out, or set under closer observation, and, if need be, murdered. Specialist Russian forces were put on standby, just in case. Questions were then asked of what the Chinese were up to? Could it be them attempting to make it look like the Russians? Russia needed to be ready, but they also needed to avoid creating so much movement that it panicked any of the other world powers that would be watching them, looking for just such an event.

Of course, the moment things got underway in Russia, the USA immediately received notification that various Russian persons-of-interest were *"on the move"*. This triggered similar events in the White House, as well as in China, and even North Korea got a little excitable. The US president was woken, just in case, and a short while later, the Pentagon saw generals arriving and barking orders for various bits of information to be brought to various offices. A central monitoring room was setup. Soon, large screens showed several CCTV and satellite surveillance visuals covering each country of interest.

It took one hour from the moment that Hazelhot announced he was Winston Churchill, to the moment that every world superpower was waking up, running to action stations, preparing for the worst-case scenario, and arming nuclear weapons, *just in case.*

This reaction alerted various well-funded terror cells around the world, who excitedly started monitoring all the channels to catch snippets of code or information. This would help them target their next incident in order to get the best advertising exposure for their particular cause. The singular key piece of information that went around the world, created puzzled looks, and caused memos to be sent to decipher the meaning of it was the use of the name *Winston Churchill.* It was a code that, at that moment, no one seemed able to crack. This caused a frenzied scurrying in academic hot spots around the world, as relevant code breakers and high IQ contacts were roused from slumber and engaged to interpret it.

A short while later, an intelligence report came in to the MI6 building and the phone rang. Once again, Sir Michael answered it and put it onto loud-speaker. The sound of a computer generated voice could be heard on the other end.

"Every. First. World. Nation. Currently. On. Nuclear. Stand by. Reason… Unknown. Def-con. Code. Orange. Notification. Recommended. Response… Tactical Defensive."

This was the human-ish voice of a super-computer. It was the latest in Artificial Intelligence, and something that monitored all the activity fed into it. It then calculated potential outcomes, made a logically based decision, and recommended a course of action. This would arrive by phone to a meeting somewhere in Britain, as it had done on this occasion. Those few men in the room would then discuss the AI's conclusion before disregarding it, or calling for it to be actioned.

AI had proven to be useful, but it had an irritating way of always suggesting everyone nuke everyone else into global extinction. For AI, this was a first resort rather than a last resort. Nothing that the extremely well paid programmers had done could stop the damn thing suggesting that human extinction was the best outcome. In the end, they had to disable the option, just to tone it down. So it was not given access to anything serious, and was only ever used for strategy, and to suggest ideas, so that top-brass could then mull over it at the relevant meeting. The suggestion they heard from it that day was Plan B. Plan A was always, *"Launch. Nuclear. Attack."* So the programmers had coded it to always suggest Plan B first. So far, the AI hadn't got upset about that.

Plan B met with approval from the humans. *"Tactical Defensive"* was actioned without further question and the United Kingdom went into a state of *Code Orange*. Russia, China, and North Korea duly noted this and set theirs accordingly. Shortly after, a smatter of other world powers and terrorist cells primed themselves in readiness too. The USA already knew all about it, since they had hacked into the British AI system the first week it was set up.

Extinguish All Threats

They wheeled a new arrival onto to the Essex Ward and stationed him in a bed at the far end, the last remaining free space. Covered head to toe in plaster-cast after surgery, it was impossible to tell who he was. All the other patients watched him get wheeled in, but assumed him to be another victim found somewhere near the site of the blast. It wasn't Fred, else they would have heard he had been located, but since no one else was missing from their industry, they asked no further questions. The man was sedated, and seemed unaware of his surroundings, mumbling incoherently for a time before falling asleep. When he awoke, he didn't speak, but looked around as best he could, quietly noting others on the ward.

Sir Stott was running Pussy Productions from the bed nearest the entrance. Now that he was free from the danger of any further thuggery, he had taken to his leadership role with a gusto. It was also likely to be his only source of income for the foreseeable future. Rigby arrived each day with bits of paperwork that needed signing, and Miss Jones followed on behind him like a silent, but ever present, shadow. A recently arrived Hoots was also on hand. He'd had a brief interview with Sir Stott that involved Stott asking him a bunch of questions, to which he replied, 'sir'. Hoots then said he had no qualms about the work that Pussy Productions was involved in, nor did he have any qualms about what they might ask him to do while in service. This seemed to work for Stott, and he promptly agreed to hire him and to meet the salary Hoots had requested. All this was to be arranged through the Pussy Productions wage roster, and they signed-off on the relevant paperwork. Stott could not hold a pen in his current condition, so he pushed it around while it was in Rigby's hand who, as his lawyer, assured Sir Stott that since it was witnessed - and given that his current condition was on record - it would not matter too much that it didn't look like his usual signature. Once signed onto the team, Hoots quietly stationed all six-foot-six-inches of himself in a chair beside the bed. He seemed happy to maintain that position day and night, quietly and without a fuss.

Hazelhot, meanwhile, watched events unfolding from the opposite end of the room. Yet to speak at all, and mostly going unnoticed by anyone else in the ward, he had decided not to announce his presence until he knew the situation better. Some memories had returned, and he knew full well what was going on in Stott's corner. Stott clearly thought Hazelhot to be dead, since they were signing off on Pussy Productions legal documents without him. Since Hazelhot was one third of the business, he was legally required to be involved. Unless dead. He could deal with that later. What he didn't like the look of was Stott's recent recruit, Hoots. Hazelhot knew military training when he saw it. Even if the man was acting like a docile pussy cat at that moment, he was dangerous.

The six-foot-six-inch fresh development made Hazelhot keep to the anonymous option, at least until he could fathom the impact of recent events that he also now remembered he had caused. His own current situation was not something he had accounted for in his planning. Learning from the television, and nearby conversations, that he'd turned the entire Bulldog Security team to mist and molecules was satisfying. That part had gone exactly as planned. But he'd misjudged the amount of explosives required, and the subsequent impact on the chemicals that were in the pipes of the building. He had recollections of colours and movement, along with a burning sensation all over his body, and then hitting something. He also recalled leaving Stott to his fate. A fate that the old stoat had somehow defied. That part mystified Hazelhot somewhat. Especially since he had so successfully vaporised all the other living beings he'd locked in the plant. Hazelhot had clearly misjudged the old bastard's tenacity for survival. How had he achieved it? The blast should have killed him. But what concerned Hazelhot more was that Stott would know his intentions had been less than empathetic, and possibly what they really were - which was psychopathic. The fact he had hired a giant security guard-dog, spoke volumes. Staying quiet bought him time to figure out a half believable, but utterly bullshit, cover story.

There was one other memory which he couldn't quite figure out, that of telling some Russians that his name was *Winston Churchill*. Why he had been speaking to Russians he could not figure out, but odder still, was *how* he had. Hazelhot didn't know any Russian. Anyway, he knew Winston Churchill wasn't his name, but according to his bed notes, the hospital thought it was. He would play along with that for a while. For now, amnesia was going to be his friend, and since his face was wrapped again, it hardly mattered who anyone thought he was. But seeing the name had also brought back the memory of the brilliant speech he had delivered to those stupid mutts just before he blew them all to kingdom come. It had been a supremely excellent moment, and one he would treasure for years to come. Then Hazelhot wondered what had become of Basher, the loose end in the equation, but it wasn't long before he found out.

Inspector Stump arrived on the ward with an officer following on behind him. He made his way through the rows of plaster-cast bodies to the one at the back who had yet to be interviewed. This one had not yet spoken to anyone, and no one was sure who he was. There had been no clues. The name on his bed-card read *Winston Churchill*, but that just suggested he was suffering amnesia and was too unwell to speak, so no one had bothered him, leaving him to recuperate.

Inspector Stump stood looking at the man for a moment, then he pulled up a chair and sat down close to Hazelhot, who continued to lie motionless with his eyes half-shut. When the inspector didn't leave, Hazelhot opened them slowly to peer out from behind his plaster. The two men locked in a gaze. Powerful predatory instincts stirring in both of them. They knew exactly what they were looking at. Inspector Stump continued to assess what his radar was picking up, then after a moment, he spoke.

"Mind if we ask you a few questions, sir? Just formalities trying to clear up events. We've had statements from everyone else in here, just you left," he said.

Hazelhot nodded in the affirmative. The Inspector turning to point to the board at the end of his bed.

"It says your name is *Winston Churchill*," said the Inspector.

"Is it?" asked Hazelhot.

"That *was* my question, sir," said the Inspector.

Hazelhot didn't respond immediately. But the Inspector had a nose for criminals, and his nose was going off like a sniffer dog at a squirrel orgy. Hazelhot did his best to play the concussed invalid, but was eager to fish for information himself.

"I've no recollection of what happened, sorry. Were many people hurt?" he asked the Inspector.

The Inspector told him exactly what he had been told to say by Sir Michael.

"Well, sir, as far as we know, it was a hit on a local gang. Mostly killed, unfortunately. All except for their boss, who is currently being detained for his own protection. We're still trying to tie the pieces together, so anything you remember would be of great help to us. We are going to keep the police on site. Nothing to be concerned about, again, just a formality. But if you remember something, just get them to contact me so we can keep abreast of any information. Sorry to have bothered you, sir, and we wish you a speedy recovery."

Inspector Stump didn't wait for a response, but got up and left the ward. As soon as he was outside, he rang the number Sir Michael had given him and spoke to the voice that answered.

"Southern Goose here. The fish is slippery, no catch, but it looks like the trout we are after."

Stump put the phone down. He had forgotten his officer was still behind him, who was looking at him with a peculiar expression. Stump smiled, realising his mistake.

"I'm going fishing this weekend," he said, but he wasn't

concerned if the officer believed him or not.

He had bigger things to worry about, like how to kick-start a turf war in a Peckham Rye power vacuum.

Several days passed before Hazelhot felt he had enough information to make his move. He saw little point in delaying things further. As soon as Hoots took his fifteen minutes break to get lunch, he set his plan in motion. Hazelhot started by thrashing about like a trapped eel inside his plaster-cast. The racket soon had everyone in the ward turning his way to see what was going on.

"Shouldn't someone hit the emergency button?" a voice from a distant bed asked.

"I don't think he is having a seizure. I think he is just trying to move," replied a bed closer to the event.

Hazelhot got his limbs free and flapping enough that he could wobble his bed. His thrashing soon drove it towards the wall where a wheelchair had been placed. Hazelhot then dragged himself off the bed and planked his body across the wheelchair. He jigged some more, and turning around, he tied the bed to the wheelchair using the bed-sheets. He then used his good hand to wheel himself, and the bed, slowly on towards the entrance of the ward.

"Shall I hit the button now?" asked the nervous bed occupant once again.

"Hold your horses," said the other one. "I think he's just headed for the toilet."

Hazelhot travelled slowly, dragging the bed behind him, and it clanked against each bed that he passed. He looked neither left nor right, focused intently as he was on his destination. Arriving at the entrance of the ward, he turned, not towards Stott, but in the other direction and toward the bed that was opposite, which currently contained yet another plaster-cast body. Hazelhot undid the sheet holding his bed to the wheelchair, and manoeuvred himself to the side of the occupants' bed. He then turned the wheelchair around and drove himself backwards, along with the occupant's bed, out into the hallway. In pushing backwards, he got a far better purchase than he'd expected to, and got up a decent speed in a brief space of time. He hadn't meant to do it, but got carried away with the sensation, so had pushed on.

"I was wrong," shouted the man nearest to where Hazelhot's bed had originally been. "He's off reservation. Hit the button!"

A moment later, an alarm could be heard going off somewhere distant. Hearing it, Hazelhot remembered his mission and put the brakes on, and though *he* stopped, the bed he had been pushing did not, and it sailed down the corridor with a nervous whimper coming from the occupant as it did so. Hazelhot wheeled himself quickly back to the ward, then manoeuvred his bed into the now vacant position. He hoisted himself back onto it and kicked the wheelchair away. With a flick of his foot, he then launched his bed-card through the air and it landed somewhere distant. Hazelhot then lay motionless, as if nothing had happened at all.

Chaos ensued in the hall-way outside as the bed made the stairs and then took off down them. The occupant bounced like a rodeo cowboy, screaming as he went. Miraculously, he maintained a hold on the bed, and it came to a halt halfway down the stairwell, blocked by the tighter gap between the walls that ran there. When he was eventually retrieved, the nurses returned him to the spot Hazelhot had once been, and where they assumed he had come from. The occupant couldn't tell them otherwise, since by then he'd been injected with opioids to calm his hysterical wailing. No one who had witnessed the incident chimed in to mention anything. They were now more concerned about the disturbing character who had created the problem. Everyone on the ward had been through more than enough drama, and whoever was in the bed that now occupied the front position was clearly dangerous.

As things calmed down again, Hoots arrived back. The floor had been closed off during the event and they had let no one back onto it. This had troubled Hoots, but finding a CCTV monitor on the main desk, he could see that his employer was not involved. Since nothing further was occurring on the ward, he stayed put and observed the situation rather than barge through the police stationed on the floor. But Hoots was not fooled. He noticed immediately that the occupant opposite Stott had been replaced. Something was up, after all. Rather than react, he assessed the situation and chose to let the new occupant reveal his intentions in his own time. As he sat down, he subtly clicked the safety off the gun that was hidden beneath his jacket before taking up his usual position in the chair near to Stott. Conveniently, this allowed him to face the bed with the suspicious new occupant. Hoots returned to his relaxed position, but was ready for whatever might happen next. Nothing happened next.

An hour later, Stott asked Hoots to fetch him some water. Hoots was reluctant to leave his side, but with no nurses around, Stott became animated and insistent. The moment Hoots left, Hazelhot broke his cover.

"What-ho Stott. Did you miss me?" he asked.

Stott jumped out of his skin, and then screamed in a falsetto cry, as the ghost announced itself from across the room.

"You!" Stott managed, somewhat breathlessly, as he descended back down.

He stared aghast at the creature in the bed opposite with a fearful concern that soon gave way to rage.

"What devilish re-incarnation is this! Dragging me around on your mad-cap schemes, then attempting to kill me. Locking me in that room with those menaces-to-society before blowing us all up. You are a goddamn maniac, sir! Where's Hoots... HOOTS!"

Stott began shouting.

"Calm down, grandpa," said Hazelhot. "Do you think I would have ended up in here if I was intent on doing you harm? What kind of idiot blows himself up? I went to get our contact and the place just blew. How was I to know they rigged it?" lied Hazelhot.

Hoots appeared and his gun came out and went up the nostrils of Hazelhot, as his other large hand put a grip on his neck. Hazelhot, unable to speak, gasped for air as he drew in painful, agonised, and slowing breaths.

"Want me to despatch him, sir?" asked Hoots, turning to Stott for the order.

Stott was so impressed that he was momentarily lost for words. He'd got so used to being the one being menaced, that it came as a shock to have someone on his side. A tear escaped to roll down his cheek before he could gather himself. He coughed a few times and tried to clear his throat of the falsetto voice that had returned. He finally got his gruff tone back and answered.

"No, that won't be necessary, Hoots," he replied, but then considered his options. "On second thoughts, maybe apply a little something. This is the man who was with me before the blast, and who, I suspect, knows a hell of a lot more than he is going to admit."

"Very good sir," said Hoots, and put the gun away. He then let go of his grip, and stood back for a moment to observe Hazelhot, who then tried to speak.

"Stott, for God's sa…"

But Hoots had finished assessing Hazelhot's meridians, and put a jujitsu jab into a bit of body showing between cast and plaster. The move would inflict a medium to long-term pain, triggering the nervous system, while putting the opponent clean out. It worked perfectly. Hoots observed his handiwork briefly as Hazelhot lay limp. Then, after checking Hazelhot's still had a pulse, he went and sat down next to Stott.

Stott eyed Hoots with a pride he could barely contain.

"Bravo, Hoots, bravo!" he said, and his eyes watered with happiness, something he hadn't felt for a long time. He hadn't realised just how useful this rather large, and clearly loyal giant was going to be.

"Not sure I'd trust that chap," said Hoots. "Got a nose for the wrong ones, sir. I think you may be better off getting rid of him, to be honest."

He said the last part in a hushed tone, so that no one would overhear.

"Won't be a problem to make it look like an accident in here, sir," he added in a comforting tone.

"Tempting, but best not," said Stott, not eager to despatch anyone.

He knew what danger Hazelhot presented, but he felt it important to stick to his own way of dealing with the world, rather than become more like him. He then explained the situation to Hoots, as he knew it.

"It's Hazelhot, and unfortunately he is legally a third-owner of the company. Getting rid of him at this stage might make me look more implicated in this disaster than I already am," said Stott.

"I fully understand, sir," said Hoots, and he quietly re-engaged the safety on his weapon.

At that moment, powerful computers available only to MI6 were researching information on everybody in The Essex Ward. Information was gleaned from databases around the world, and the AI was busy searching for links to anyone associated with the incident. Sir Stott's name had been connected to Pussy Productions, and Pussy Productions had been connected to the mob who had just recently ceased to exist. Both were then connected to a character by the name of Hazelhot. Because of recent events caught on CCTV - and thanks to new state-of-the-art software that used Facial Recognition to analyse features sometimes even obscured by bandages - the computers had quickly locked in on the potential data relationships and flagged them. The moment that Hazelhot's name came up, one computer went off like a fruit machine and sparks flew out at the back. It finally responded by highlighting him as over 75% likely to be the man behind the *Winston Churchill* alias. As the computer became more convinced of this, it dived and delved further into whatever could be found on Hazelhot. Intersecting connections appeared on the screen that the gentlemen from MI6 soon gathered around. Information about Hazelhot's history of violence, his various perversions, the traceable ones at least. Then came links to various classified military operations that he had once been involved in. The culmination of which was his unceremonious ejection from service, and the reasons for it. Then things took an awkward turn. The dots being connected soon led to long since buried MI6 task force activities. The gentlemen watching the screen at MI6 became nervous. They shifted on their feet uncomfortably as they saw operation names appear that they would really rather forget. Some things were best left buried in the past. Whatever nefarious business Hazelhot had once been involved in, it could now indirectly implicate a variety of high-ranking officials by association. It was an unexpected shock to discover that the computer was now linking *their* names into this madness, indirectly but definitively, albeit all classified, the link still existed. This made the atmosphere somewhat tense.

Sir Michael, never one to miss an opportunity for maximising leverage, pulled suitably pained expressions, and tutted some tutts, while the computers made further connections, going back in time, implicating people that really needed to be kept well out of it.

"Oh, I say, this is getting really rather ugly, gentlemen," he said.

Incidents of cover-ups, sanctioned violence, and extreme sexual deviance now re-surfaced in relation to names, indirectly or otherwise, associated to Hazelhot's various personal campaigns made while under military employ.

"Well, at least we now have confirmation of the likely identity of our *Winston Churchill*. This really looks like our man. Though we clearly have a rather large collateral-damage containment job on our hands," said Sir Michael. "I don't think any of us saw *this* coming. How was this Hazelhot creature ever left roaming the streets is the first bloody question? The man is a top-grade psychopath."

Sir Michael sucked through his teeth at the long report now showing on the screen, as the computers completed their task of gathering all potential connections. The AI software then got on to analysing the potential outcomes of various scenarios. Sir Michael stepped away. He had seen enough to know the situation had crossed a delicate threshold.

"Our next question, gentlemen, without doubt, is going to be what we do to contain this. And if not contain it, then I think we have to be asking ourselves how best to extinguish all threats."

The mood in the room had taken a distinctly dark turn.

One Third Two Much

"Just keep your bloody savage on the leash if you know what's good for you," barked Hazelhot at Stott.

For days, they had been at each other like a married couple. Since neither of them could get off the bed to get at the other, they huffed a lot, sweated a lot, and complained about the behaviour of the other a lot.

Hoots sat disinterested, flicking through a collection of *Secret Service Monthly* that he had brought to read when things became dull on the ward. During a brief lull in the arguing, Rigby and Miss Jones had appeared to discuss plans with Stott. Every decision asked of him was interrupted by a response from Hazelhot from the bed opposite.

"Agreed," he would announce loudly, or, "No, not that, absolutely not."

He was making it clear that he was a one-third owner of Pussy Productions. At first, Rigby had ignored the man's interruptions, as had Stott. When Rigby eventually turned, huffed at him, and then turned back to Stott, this caused Hazelhot to seethe.

"You. Boy. What is your name?" asked Hazelhot.

Rigby froze. The coldness of the voice betrayed an aggression that Rigby had not expected but was familiar with hearing - he'd been made to *kowtow* to bullies most of his life. He looked to Stott for support, but Stott was tired of dealing with the irascible Hazelhot and was feeling pretty irascible himself. Stott sighed, looked away, and in doing so made it clear he was leaving Rigby to fend for himself.

"You, boy. Yes, you. The suit in the cheap tweeds," continued Hazelhot, now feeling inspired. "Turn around and face me like a man when I am speaking to you."

Hazelhot knew instinctively that Rigby was a pushover. He also knew he was going to enjoy bullying him with some regularity just as soon as he was free of his current plaster-cast predicament. And since Stott had signalled that he was happy to abandon Rigby to it, Hazelhot slithered in on his prey.

"What are you, exactly? I mean, other than a nervous and malnourished looking chap in a cheap suit wearing... what the hell is that smell? Lynx? Have you no self-respect? But please enlighten me as to what your exact role is in this company."

Hazelhot was salivating. Rigby was just the sort of person to take verbal abuse indefinitely and do nothing. Hazelhot only cooled off when he noticed that Hoots had started to prickle, his radar tweaked. Hazelhot - not relishing another Hoots grip - reined it in at that point, and waited for a response from Rigby, who was looking like he might cry or wet his pants. Hazelhot hoped for the latter. He was growing increasingly bored trapped on the ward and fighting with Stott was losing its lustre.

It was then he noticed the lady standing behind Rigby. She was shaking in a barely contained rage, and Hazelhot knew in that moment that Miss Jones was in love with Rigby, and that Rigby probably didn't know it. From the look of her, he felt certain she would have launched herself at him in defence of Rigby - like the wild-cat that she was - but for the fact she was hiding her feelings from him. Despite that inner nature being buried beneath the pristine, bookish exterior, Hazelhot knew what he was observing. Given the colour she was currently presenting, Hazelhot felt certain he was right. Hazelhot loved reading people. Especially if he could use the information against them later. It excited him, and he breathed out a satisfied snort and then turned his attention back to Rigby.

"I'm waiting," he said.

Rigby regained some composure but was now steeped in shame - a common condition for him - and finally replied, having realised he had made a huge mistake.

"I am the company lawyer, sir. I deal with the accounts and any legal documents that need signing."

"Got any?" Hazelhot asked.

"Got any what, sir?"

Rigby was tagging the *"sir"* on in a gesture of subservience, and this irked Stott, who broke in.

"Mr Rigby, this is *Mister* Hazelhot. *Mister*...not *sir*. *'Sir'* is reserved for British gentry who have been officially knighted by the Queen, such as myself. Kindly do not refer to this hoodlum in the bed opposite me as a sir, when he is very much a mister, and even that is questionable."

"A recently defrocked and un-knighted *sir*, in your case," said Hazelhot, as the pair arched up at each other again.

But, it was true. News had arrived that - on top of the various club membership ejections and divorce proceedings, Sir Archibold Stott's knighthood had been revoked. He still couldn't believe it, and it hurt to be reminded of it by a plebeian such as Hazelhot.

"Good god, man, will you desist from creating further ruckus!" Stott barked at him.

Stott struggled to calm himself, breathing in deeply, before turning back to Rigby. He *did* have a duty to honour the contractual obligation he was currently stuck in with Hazelhot. However heinous it was, there was a British principle at stake and one honoured one's agreements.

"Rigby, unfortunately, it is true. *Mister* Hazelhot will need to sign off on all documents from this point onward. He has indeed recently become a one-third partner in the company. I have a copy of the paperwork signed by myself on this, which needs to be introduced to the files. He was missing, presumed dead. Sadly, he has now been found to be alive. And yes, like it or not, you will have to deal with us both from this point on regarding all paperwork and signatures."

Rigby looked aghast. Just when he thought a new and brighter day was on the horizon, a nasty piece of work like Hazelhot had shown up to ruin it. Was there no escape? He quickly buried all emotion and then accepted his fate. Composing himself, he nodded to them both. He then apologised in a matter-of-fact way to Hazelhot, after which he excused himself to head to the toilet. Once inside, he locked himself into a cubicle and burst into tears, sobbing uncontrollably into his hands. After that, he wretched twice. A routine he was well used to. After a time, he straightened himself up, wiped his eyes behind his glasses, and then left the cubicle to return to the ward.

The gathered group finished dealing with whatever documents needed attention. Rigby then mentioned an escalating problem that was manifesting in their absence at the Deptford Studios.

"The director, Larry, always had a drug problem, but his brilliance as a director meant everyone turned a blind eye. But since the incident, it has been escalating. Maurice has been bringing him industrial sized bags of cocaine and Larry is up for days, driving everyone into the ground with his insane work schedule and aggressive mood swings. When he isn't in the office shouting down a disconnected phone at non-existent people, he is in the studio shovelling coke up his nose. He's also refusing to speak to anyone directly, but insists on shouting at them through his megaphone. And now he is having paranoia fits. Yesterday we found him hiding in the toilet, said he was afraid of Basher's ghost army coming to get him. Everyone is worried about him. Since Basher's mob is not around to keep him in check, there has been nothing to stop him from going off the rails."

Rigby finished outlining the sorry affair, and Miss Jones nodded vigorously to confirm it was all true.

"Hard to believe they served a useful purpose, but I suppose we best address it. Any suggestions?" Stott asked of everyone present at the porn production management meeting being held on the Essex Ward.

"Send Hoots to savage him. Who can replace him?" asked Hazelhot.

Rigby then expanded on the situation.

"Larry is the connection to the European distributor, or was. At the moment, he is speaking to them on a disconnected phone, but he thinks it's them. It's hard to tell what is going on, as he won't talk without the megaphone, which then makes it difficult to understand him. But the films are still getting made, and though his cocaine use is an issue, his work is definitely still top-notch. Even Lucy thinks so. But I am not sure how much more she, or the other girls, will stand of his behaviour. But without him, the connection for European distribution might become an issue, and there isn't anyone else could do the film work he does."

Stott nodded understandingly.

"Maybe what we need is someone else to take over the distribution side," he said. "Let Larry think he is still doing it, of course. Just keep the phone disconnected and let him have his moment. I presume he is too high to know the difference, anyway."

Rigby nodded to confirm it might work.

"So, do we know anyone else who can deal with the European distribution side of things?" asked Stott.

Rigby waited for others to make suggestions, and when none was forthcoming, he piped up again.

"There is one person. Larry had the task passed on to him when the previous owner, the Earl of Cavendish, got involved with Basher. Basher didn't want the Earl touching anything, so took it off him and gave it to Larry. Everything goes out through Amsterdam, and none of Basher's lot spoke Dutch, but the Earl did, and that gave him an advantage that Basher didn't trust. Larry is part Dutch, but was more easily controlled by Basher with the coke, of course."

"The Earl of Cavendish, hey," said Stott. "That bloody rapscallion is the reason I ended up in this mess. But he may be our best shot for now, unless any of you can speak Dutch?"

When no one put a hand up, Stott turned to Hoots, or tried to, but his condition wouldn't allow him to turn fully. Hoots moved forward so Stott could see him.

"Hoots, maybe you could get the address from Rigby and pay the Earl a visit. Don't be rough with him, but let him know it would be in his best interests to get involved. On second thoughts, if he tries to resist the idea, be persuasive. I doubt he will refuse, since it is going to line his pockets, and with Basher gone, he'll feel safer. See what he says and offer him a temporary contract. Draw that up, will you Rigby?"

"Hang on a minute!" interjected Hazelhot. "I haven't agreed to any of that."

Hazelhot was like a petulant teenager, cutting in as he had done for every decision over the past few days. Clearly not yet tiring of enjoying the annoyance it created in Stott.

"Jesus Mary on a bicycle, what is wrong with you?" shouted Stott. "Do you agree to the aforementioned plan for Hoots to visit the Earl of Cavendish and offer him a job as European distributor to take the weight off Larry?" he added, and waited for Hazelhot to respond.

Hazelhot remained motionless for a moment.

"I do," he finally said.

Stott breathed in and counted to ten.

Hoots made the arrangements to visit the Earl with Rigby, but expressed concern about leaving Stott alone with Hazelhot. Stott assured him it was okay. He didn't think Hazelhot would try anything now that he was out in the open on the ward and gainfully involved with the business again. With the Police not far away down the corridor, he felt safe enough. Hoots was less convinced and spoke to the nurse on the way out to arrange for Hazelhot to get sedated after he left. The nurse had already experienced Hazelhot commenting on the width of her ass, and was more than happy to oblige.

Stott asked Hoots to look in on Larry and see if there was anything that could be done to curb his addiction, or at least make it easier on the other staff. All of this had to go by Hazelhot again, who had insisted on ratifying everything. Hoots finally left, and a nurse showed up shortly after to inject Hazelhot. Hazelhot slept the rest of the afternoon, snoring loudly. When he eventually awoke, he was feeling somewhat docile. Things had quietened down on the ward with Hazelhot asleep. Everyone had welcomed the peace and commented on how much more pleasant it was when the man was unconscious. But the calm on the ward was short-lived, though its arrival was more welcome.

Lucy Lovelips arrived, but she was not alone. Her entourage had been gathered together, and a decision made amongst them to visit the new owners of Pussy Productions. Suddenly, it was like the circus arriving in town. A trumpet could be heard down the hallway announcing their presence as they exited the lift. Red petals appeared on the floor before Lucy as she stepped into the hallway. The dwarfs, dressed as little Roman centurions, started doing flips and cartwheels. Randy Andy, who was dressed as a circus strong-man, flexed his muscles and bent over lewdly, spanking his buttocks or rippling his body muscles, as he postured toward anyone who passed him. Nurses hugged the wall as the troupe made their way along the corridor towards the ward. Janice and Janine danced, skipped, and sashayed ahead of Lucy, as they threw the petals down before her from a basket. Lucy was in her favourite white fur coat and, as usual, had nothing much on underneath. The trumpet faded out as Lucy arrived at the entrance to the ward. She assumed her best Marilyn Monroe pose and then turned to face the beds, letting her fur coat open just enough to show some leg and a hint of cleavage.

"Well now, aren't you soldiers a sorry-looking sight?" she said as a hush fell across the ward.

"And which one of you gorgeous fellows is Sir Archibold Stott?" she asked.

"That would be I," managed Stott, uncertain if he wanted

to admit to it at that moment. He wished Hoots was back, in case this was one of the feminists he had been warned about.

Hazelhot remained strangely silent. This was partly because of the drugs still in his system, but mostly because he was being transported back to his recent visit to Pussy Productions. He recognised Lucy immediately. It was the angel that he had met that day, and he was struck mute by her presence. Though what gave him the huge erection that was now presenting from beneath his sheets was not the memory of Lucy, but of the psychopathic levels of violence that he had later indulged himself in.

Lucy's radar was alerted to the growing situation, and there was little reason for her to assume it was for anything but her, which pleased her immensely.

"Now there's one soldier who is pleased to see little ol' Lucy," she said. "And what is your name, young man?" she asked.

Hazelhot mumbled, barely able to speak, but the sounds he made were familiar to Lucy. She recognised him immediately. It was the man she had been thinking about since the incident in the studio, and he was there in the ward, developing a firm presence just for her.

"Oh my! I know *you*, don't I," she squealed and laughed delightfully, clapping her hands together.

Hazelhot made some more noises, none of which made much sense to anyone except Lucy.

"That's Hazelhot," announced Stott, glad that the potential feminist was temporarily distracted. Though given the sounds Hazelhot was currently making, he wasn't sure why she wasn't terrified.

Lucy turned back to Stott, at which point he wished he hadn't spoken. She made her way towards his bed, and Stott lifted his arm to get at the emergency button, but failed. He needn't have worried. Lucy sat down on his bed and explained the situation.

"We are very pleased to meet you, Archy. You have been our saviour," she said. "Can I call you Archy, Archy?"

Stott nodded nervously but didn't move. Lucy continued.

"I think we met your lovely wife a few weeks ago, but we haven't seen her since. The poor dear was quite beside herself with emotion at seeing all the girls up close. I do hope she's feeling better. But we all wanted to come down here and meet you for ourselves, and say a big thank you for being such a swell fellow. Maybe show you just how glad we are that you are going to be running things now that nasty Basher Bob is gone."

Lucy tapped Stott's bed sheets in exactly the place she knew to tap.

"Righty-ho," said Stott, now nervous for other reasons, but he was pleased to discover she wasn't a dangerous feminist. "You must be *that* Lucy, then. I believe Rigby mentioned you. Very pleased to meet you, Lu..." he froze mid-sentence.

Lucy had moved, and her coat had fallen open. Stott was seeing parts of a woman's body that Stott had never seen before. At least not with a light on, and certainly not that well formed. His mind disengaged from his mouth and he couldn't think properly, but neither could he move his eyes away. Something was happening to him. He then responded like Hazelhot had done, as strange noises emanated from him. Stott was unfamiliar with the effect Lucy was having on him, and he struggled to cover up his discomfort by gibbering. He was fighting with the need to stare, mouth agape, at what Lucy was revealing to him shamelessly. She observed the effect without moving. It was intoxicating for her, too. The sense of power never lessened. Stott then babbled inanities, but could not pull his eyes away however hard he tried. Lucy, in response, opening her coat just a little wider. He deserved it. Stott was now certain that he was under the influence of some sort of female voodoo, caught by an intense, magnetic, sexual tractor-beam that he was powerless to fight.

"And H... H... Hazel.. Hot... hot... hottie... he... he... he's a third partner in the erection business, you know, yes. So he'll be working inside you... alongside you. Yes. That's him. There. In that bed. Over there. The bed. Hazelhot. In a bed. Naked. No. What? Not naked. Just getting abreast of the situation. With huge nipples. My God..."

Stott stammered, stuttered, and said anything that he could think of, desperately trying to deflect her powers elsewhere. The forces emanating from beneath her fur coat were burning images deep into his psyche in ways that he had never known before, but had always feared...

"Sorry mummy..." he finally mumbled.

Stott was hearing echoes of his mother scolding him as a young boy for playing with it. Lucy watched quietly on, knowing exactly what effect she was having.

Hazelhot, still mostly incoherent, was finally coming round thanks to the burst of testosterone that was being triggered by Lucy's presence. His erection was lobbing lazily back and forth beneath the sheet, and was making itself apparent to everyone on the ward. He didn't much care. But for others, the odd lupine noises he was making added a certain creepiness to the situation.

Lucy had worked enough of her magic on Stott that he now fell silent, to stare transfixed by the feminine display so close he could almost touch it. He was gone inside himself, lost in a world of his innocent prepubescent youth, that had now returned to overwhelm him. He completely forgot where he was, as he stared at the goods on display only for him. Lucy then pulled her fur coat shut, but stayed seated on the bed. She knew how to time the exposure perfectly to leave a man confused and lost, but still wanting. Stott floundered in a haze of feelings he had never permitted himself to experience before. His hand weakly clutched at the air in front of her.

"Our friend over there is Mr Hazelhot, is he?" said Lucy, finally getting a name to put on her mystery man.

To be discovering he was a partner in the business, and not just a temporary janitor, was a curious twist, and one that she was pleased to be hearing.

"And there was silly ol' me thinking he was just the hired help," she added, patting Stott gently on the part of his sheet now protruding upward.

"Help?" he mumbled. "He's just gifted in the art of making a bloody mess."

Stott spoke the words mechanically, his mind was split in two. One part of it still staring towards the fur coat, consumed by all he had witnessed there. But hearing Hazelhot being described as *help,* forced him to come around from his stupor somewhat. There was nothing helpful about the creature.

Lucy sat chatting to Stott for a little longer as he came back to his senses, but this didn't make Stott any more at ease. He was now confused and struggling to hide his risen appendage, that refused to go down so long as she was near. Hazelhot, meanwhile, grimaced at them from behind his own appendage, lost, as he was, in a world of sedated deviant recollection.

Lucy stood up and walked around the ward, introducing herself to everyone, asking them who they were, and how they were doing. Most of the ward knew exactly who she was, and some were positively star-struck by her presence, many asking for autographs on their plaster casts. Finally she arrived back at the bed of Hazelhot, who continued to stare at her. His erection firmly in place and pointing her way.

"Well now," she said. "*Someone* is pleased to see me, hey?"

Lucy leaned over the bed to give Hazelhot a peck on the cheek, and she squeezed the place beneath the sheet as she did so. Hazelhot made a groaning sound. Not that he was particularly excited by her. He was not sexually attracted by women at all. But with Lucy, something else was getting triggered. She was inexorably part of the memory of the pathological violence he had unleashed. Though Lucy took the groan as confirmation of his desire for her, she was unaware that he was now being immersed in the graphic recollection of the last few weeks. She continued all the same. Taking the sheet-covered shape in her hand, she following the contour. Playing around the shaft that was protruding so royally, she teased at it.

Her entourage had been quietly loitering in the background, but they knew the drill, and Lucy's act was the signal for them to get busy. A dwarf pressed play on a ghetto blaster, and the *wah-wah* guitar of a 1970s porno soundtrack blasted out across the ward. The dwarfs then started doing flips and cartwheels. Janice and Janine sashayed sexily through the ward, twirling between the beds, and briefly caressing occupants as they floated by them. Randy Andy posed and postured in the entrance like the shiny oiled Adonis that he was. Lucy, subtly at first and then not so subtly, went to work on Hazelhot, who lay there in the remains of his drug-induced stupor. Eyeing the dwarfs hungrily, he panted as Lucy worked her magic. The bizarre nature of the current circumstances was doing wonders, and he gurgled in delight.

Stott, now completely overwhelmed, started praying.

"Oh, Jesus Mary, mother of god, heavenly father, save me."

The blood left his face as it headed towards his lower regions. He recited the Lord's Prayer like an exorcist priest, but it did no good, since it wasn't just him feeling the effects. The sexual vibrations were now taking over the ward. Everyone could feel it, and none could escape it. The *wah-wah* guitar played on.

Lucy climbed on top of Hazelhot and started working her way down onto him. Like catnip thrown on a drunk feline, she began rubbing herself over his plaster-cast body. Stott thought she must be possessed by erotic demons, and his praying got louder in response. But rather than calm the situation, it became a ceremonial accompaniment to the porn guitar, and sounded more like a devilish incantation.

An unprecedented level of debauchery unleashed itself onto The Essex Ward. It wasn't just Hazelhot with a raging erection. The entire ward had escalated in sexual tension, and now every male, and even a few of the females, had raging boners beneath their sheets. The dancing twins stroked them as they passed by, sometimes bowing before them in gestures of honour to the phallic gods that now presented. Going by each bed like whirling fairies, the ward exploded into an uncontrollable sex-magick ritual of Dionysian frenzy.

Stott fought with his Lord against the sexual demons that were rising from within him, as he struggled to stay focused on the task he had set himself. He was shouting the Lord's Prayer at the top of his lungs, unaware it was encouraging the room to reach heightened states. The ward now caught in the maelstrom of a back-firing exorcism that was not working out as intended.

This must be what porn does to a man.

It was Stott's last rational thought, as his mind gave up its defences, to fall into the sexual demonism that had defeated them all from within and without. Desperately confused, an ironic thought occurred to him that his uncontrollable penis was the only thing left pointing heaven-wards. Lucy was obviously the Queen of Porn, and possibly the Queen of the Damned. He'd fought against the forces with all his might, but her power was too much for him, and finally, he gave in to it.

Stott flapped and wriggled on to his front. Anything to hide the shame. His lilly-white ass now revealing itself to the world as he slipped from the bed, where he then feared he might fall to become stranded with penis aloft. His attempts to cling on just meant it was now shaking loose beneath the bed frame. Fighting to pull himself back up, it hooked against the bed frame and thwarted his progress. He wailed in frustration. He could neither get back onto the bed, nor risk letting go to fall onto the floor to be stranded there. Caught in the conflict between shame and hunger, it was a biblical effort he was making, but was doomed to fail. With it rubbing against the cold frame in his attempt to climb back aboard, Stott was soon feeling hornier than he had ever felt in his life. Giving up on the Lord's Prayer, he bit into the pillow as he growled to reduce the tension that was throbbing through his body and his soul. As he thrust against the cold metal, he flailed like an animal trapped in a sexual rage.

Lucy knew what she was doing. Lucy was a professional. She was letting out just enough sexual vibration with all the right noises to trigger the entire ward in orgasmic, mutual unison. The moment then announced by her escalating sexual cries, as they burst out from her body in ecstatic, but well faked, screams.

"Yes, Yes, YYYYYYEEEEEESSSSSSS!"

And what a show it was. As she unleashed her faked orgasm at the top of her lungs, the music turned to a powerful sax solo. Lucy orgasmed from the professionalism of it all, while the rest of the ward went over the top because they had lost all control of their senses. By this time, Janice and Janine were writhing naked between and over plaster-casts. At the sight of the dwarfs fucking one another, even Hazelhot unleashed. Everyone in the ward peaking right along with Lucy, just as she knew they would. Stott, now buried face down into the pillow, was clawing at it violently, his bare ass hanging off the bed, as he screamed in shame and erotic mania his final humps going into the bed-frame as he writhed in the uncontrollable throes of an orgasm. Until finally, it was all over.

Lucy climbed off Hazelhot, unfazed by the event. It was just the average working day for her. The dwarfs unplugged and then stopped the music. Janice and Janine found their clothes and quickly returned to static poses at the ward entrance. The troupe was preparing to make the return procession back towards the lift. Randy Andy adjusted himself, and then took on a suitably vogue statuesque form, catching the light nicely, with one hand on hip, an arm held out, index finger pointing upwards, a wrist slightly limp, as he looked away in the opposite direction. He stood like a Greek sculpture as they waited for the order from Lucy.

"Au revoir, my sexy little rays of love and light," said Lucy to the ward, now in *post-ejaculatus* disarray.

Bodies lay strewn and dishevelled, some on the beds, some beside beds, and some under beds. Everyone coming round from their personal state of incapacitation, discombobulation, and ejaculation. Lucy held a coy pose at the entrance to the ward and adjusted herself before commenting.

"Oops, I did it again," she said, and held a finger up to her mouth.

She then giggled and blew a kiss at Stott and then Hazelhot, after which she turned and signalled the procession to get underway. The trumpet sounded, and they danced and postured their way back towards the lift.

At that same moment, a firmly built and somewhat masculine looking woman was charging up the hospital stairs. She rounded the top of the staircase just after the troupe had entered the lift and the doors had closed behind them. Marching aggressively towards the Essex ward, she arrived at the entrance and stood, hands on hips, looking around. She was baffled by what she saw there.

The woman was an imposing sight to be appearing in the wake of Lucy. Her demeanour suggesting she was not someone to be trifled with. But everyone was too busy trying to recover from recent events to pay her much attention. Everyone except for Hazelhot, who remained on his back, and was still sporting a large, throbbing erection, that despite events had not reduced one bit. It was now showing an unmistakable grotesque pink hue through the wetness of the sheets. He was watching it pulsate, a look of pride on his face.

"Oh... My... God!" said the woman, as her eyes landed on it, her face turning a demonically darker shade of grey.

Hazelhot was getting his senses back. The fucking dwarfs had really worked wonders for him. As far as he was concerned, absolutely nothing was wrong, and everything was as it should be. While he was relaxed and enjoying the afterglow, many on the ward would require years of therapeutic support to unravel what had just happened to them. As far as Hazelhot was concerned, this new arrival was just the next in line to be defiled. He looked up at her. She was staring at his penis, hardly able to believe what she was witnessing. He looked back at his magnificence, then back up at the woman. The strong masculine features, and the dark hairs sprouting from her chin added a certain something that titillated him.

"Just grab some, babe," he offered, smiling, and nodded towards his piece.

The woman's eyes moved away from his member and up to meet his as they closed menacingly.

"You must be the one who runs that disgusting porn company?" she said.

"Sure do, babe. Go on, touch the magic."

"Oh, I can do better than that," she replied, as she pulled an object from her bag and tazered Hazelhot with a pinkie head-shot.

PART THREE

Business As Usual

The months passed, bodies healed, and everyone except Stott and Hazelhot took advantage of the therapy on offer from the hospital to address any psychological re-adjustments required. Hazelhot's penile burns had added a couple of weeks to his recovery time, during which he'd been moved to a private room to recover. Though he was unaware of it, this occurred because of a petition organised by Stott and signed by everyone on the ward. He refused to remain there until Stott agreed to have Rigby visit him on the way out to sign-off on anything regarding the company. Rigby then spent a lot of time running back and forth between them.

At Pussy Productions, the Earl of Cavendish took to his new role with a fervour, becoming the man in charge of distribution to Europe. He was soon taking bi-weekly flights to Amsterdam to liaise with business connections on the continent, which helped to expand the company's reach and income.

Larry's cocaine habit was reduced from a sack a day to a few small bags, and this was overseen by Maurice. Whenever Larry's inner beast tried to strong-arm Maurice for more, Hoots would be called to remind Larry of his position. Larry was easy to manage. For all his dramatic flair, he was a softy. He just needed someone to keep his lines in line. Hoots had a gift for reminding him of his boundaries while doing it with a gentle finesse Larry could respect.

Larry's brilliance as a director was never in question, and the quality of films involving Lucy and her entourage remained their biggest sellers. Their more quirky antics had picked up some additional interest from the US market, not to mention those who had witnessed events on the Essex Ward. Since the conditions at Pussy Productions had changed so much under the new ownership, it became a hive of fun and frivolous activity for those involved, and business was thriving.

Stott and Hazelhot still fought like cat and dog, and Hazelhot was constantly trying to find new ways to gain the lion's share of the company. But Stott was no fool where money was concerned, and he was more than a match for Hazelhot's competitive business streak, even if he was no match for his murderous one.

Hoots stayed on as security guard and personal chauffeur to Stott, though not just for the times when Hazelhot became more psychotic than he already was. He was needed for protection against the feminist group that now occasionally appeared to cause commotion outside Pussy Productions studios, and sometimes picketed the industrial estate. Mostly they were just noise, but sometimes they became aggressive and tried to throw paint or animal innards at the staff.

Hazelhot now had a personal vendetta against feminists after the incident at the hospital, but whenever they showed up, Stott insisted he do nothing more to incur the wrath of the police or garner further attention from the press. Hazelhot longed to reap vengeance on the feminists, but Stott reminded him that the good of the company must come first. They were still under suspicion for the deaths at Bulldog Security, so it made sense to keep a low profile. Hazelhot might have ignored Stotts' request, but for an unmarked van that could often be seen parked a little way down the road on the industrial estate. Hoots was aware of it too. Both men knew Pussy Productions was under observation, but neither mentioned anything to the others.

While Rigby kept the business legal and aboveboard, Miss Jones spent the days quietly pining for Rigby, and Lucy spent her free time wondering why Hazelhot was not following her up. But as business got back on track and thrived with all the new business skills at the helm, everyone was soon doing well out of Pussy Productions and the money was flowing in.

Stott preferred to stay away from the office and studio as much as possible. His ex-wife still refused to take his calls and not a single club would take him back on the books, so long as he ran a porn company. But he had little choice, he was caught between a rock and a hard place and needed income to survive. Pussy Productions was, at least, providing that. He remained housed at the London hotel, hoping that eventually the wife would see sense and let him back into the family nest. While he waited, he became even more overweight and miserable. As time went on, he took this out on the ever faithful Hoots, who took it in his stride like the consummate professional that he was. His loyalty remained unshakable, but the money made it worth his while.

Hazelhot was now camped out at Pussy Productions full-time. He would sit at nights in the main office, tapping into a computer, puffing on a cigar, and creating shadow companies in his attempt to take over Pussy Productions. He was obsessed with the goal of taking over the business for himself. When he wasn't doing that, he was looking for new weaponry on the dark web. He had never been a team player, and since he could not risk focusing his energy on exterminating feminists - and he'd already done away with Basher's mob - he fantasised about war instead. Unfortunately, with nowhere else to direct this energy, Stott and Pussy Productions received the brunt of his focus, along with the occasional knock-out grips he liked to apply on Rigby to keep his hand in.

Sometimes Hazelhot bumped into Lucy at the studio in the evenings, when she would be drifting around with her entourage in tow after a day's shoot. He did his best to avoid her. She now reminded him of being tazered more than anything else. Further confirming that neither women nor consensual sex much interested him. Lucy lingered whenever she got the opportunity, hoping he would eventually pay her some attention. She would march in unexpectedly to the main office, to stand annoyingly close to him, asking him questions. Lucy made him feel odd, and when she was present, he found it difficult to speak. Disarticulated feelings and unfamiliar emotions arose in him, which he disliked and sought to avoid experiencing. So he dodged her as much as possible, but this just made her long for him. She consulted everyone on how *they* thought he felt about her. Everyone but him. She was not used to men *not* throwing themselves at her, and wasn't sure what else she could do. The way he avoided her constantly, yet salivated and gurgled whenever she was near. It made no sense. He confused her.

Hazelhot was sitting alone in the offices the evening after arguing with Stott. His recent attempt to take the company over with *Quaker and Quaker* had failed, and his other business

Stop it, Don't Rock it! had also failed to make much headway. Stott had left after the morning meeting, making it clear he was onto him. Though it was now apparent that Rigby might serve as some kind of bait for the old badger, who clearly enjoyed bullying him as much as Hazelhot loved to bully him. As yet, Hazelhot could not think how best to use this to his benefit. He tapped on the desk, contemplating ideas. When nothing came, he went back to surfing the dark web for weapons, fantasising about blowing Stott up with bazookas and various new war machines he'd found there. So far, it was an un-realised fantasy he was indulging in. Really, what it boiled down to was that Hazelhot was bored.

All this Internet activity was, of course, being monitored by MI6, and it was the main reason they were keeping a van out the front to catch any arrivals or connections that might show up to meet *"the number one suspect for potential terrorist activity in the UK"* at that moment, one Mr R Hazelhot. They had enough to take him in already, based on everything leading up to the explosion at the chemical plant in Essex. They also had him tied into the deaths of Basher's men, and the heinous and brutal murder of Barry Miller. But given the stakes, Sir Michael and the others agreed it was in the country's best interests just to monitor him for now. Maybe he would lead them to a Russian connection, or China, or Iran, or whoever the hell had been behind it all. So far, he had not reached out to anyone at all. But with all the dark web activity, it was clear something was brewing, and they felt certain it was just a matter of time.

Of course, in the absence of him leading them to his contacts upstream, they had needed to charge *someone* for *something*. The press had been baying for a result after the Essex incident. Many reporters had been hurt in the blast, and their primary connection to the incident, Fred, was still missing, presumed vaporised. This led to sustained press coverage and outrage articles, which had eventually forced MI6 to act. Instead of risking alerting Hazelhot's connections by detaining *him*, they chose instead to let Basher Bob take the fall. They could always exonerate him later with a public apology and a small incentive if they needed to. So, he was the moved to an isolated cell in the prison system and refused all contact with the outside world, *"for his own protection"*.

Inspector Stump had been given the task of announcing the arrest and planned trial of Basher Bob to the press a few weeks after the blast. It was a showcase trial and Basher was found guilty before it even began. This meant that the press got their pound of flesh, the public got to feel safe again, and MI6 got to step back into the shadows and monitor the one-man army they suspected of many things, but as yet could not be certain just what. Time, they knew, would tell.

But the months had passed, and even though he dallied and dabbled with barely legal and seemingly pointless business interests, while constantly surfing the web for major artillery, he just never made the move expected of him. MI6 was becoming concerned about what this all meant. Eventually, Sir Michael reached out again to the Inspector, and they arranged another meeting at their usual spot on the banks of the river Thames.

"How are things going with your little project, Roger?" asked Sir Michael, not long after they had sat down on opposite ends of the bench and several joggers had passed by. He was referring to filling the hole that Bulldog Security had left.

"Thought we would see more reaction than we have, to be honest," replied Stump. "So far, no mobs have stepped in to engage any of the business interests left behind. We've had some minor street incidents, but nothing that has seen a genuine attempt at leveraging the racketeering business."

"Minor street incidents?" asked Sir Michael.

"Thugs in hoodies, nothing professional. Religious nuts calling themselves *Sharia Patrol* and uploading their work to the Internet. The idiots were stopping passers-by in the High Street and demanding they behave in an *'Islamic way'*, then filming it. They were pouncing on anyone holding hands, showing too much skin, or who looked the least bit homosexual. That sort of thing. Didn't take long to catch them. Brought five lads in for questioning, and to be honest, they couldn't grass each other up quick enough. Pretty disappointing, really. Not like the old days of the firms," replied Stump.

Sir Michael chortled.

"Well, we've had some similar issues. Some damn fool at HMP Wandsworth set up a violence intervention program. He managed to achieve a hundred per cent success rate. Can you believe it? How the hell are we supposed to recruit fundamentalists for terror if bloody therapists are teaching them how to manage their anger?"

"I heard about that," replied Stump, shaking his head in disbelief.

"Of course we shut that down straight away," said Sir Michael.

They sat together quietly, recalling older, better times. Times when you could trust criminals to behave like criminals.

Sir Michael eventually broke the reverie.

"As to our lone-wolf and Britain's current *Public Enemy Number One*, baffling as it is, he still hasn't made a move. So, not much progress on our side either. Damnably annoying.

Now the PM is getting rather tetchy that we are not bringing in results."

Sir Michael paused briefly before continuing.

"Which brings me to the point of this meeting. I think it is high-time we applied a bit of pressure," he said, and turned briefly to look at Stump.

"How much pressure, exactly?" asked Stump, more than happy to apply a whole lot of it.

Life had gotten boring around Peckham and surrounding boroughs. Worse than that, his income was suffering. The primary source of pocket money in the form of back-handers from Basher's mob was no longer forthcoming. That annoyed him. So far, no gangs had stepped in to fill the Peckham power vacuum, despite his prediction and virtually advertising for the position on the news.

"Maybe reach further out," suggested Sir Michael. "See if you can pique the interest of bigger fish. You have enough connections in other boroughs to stir a bit of interest and get them looking at yours, surely?"

"Maybe," replied Stump, considering who he knew of that he could call on and that might take the bait.

"Again, I think we can help one another here, Roger," said Sir Michael. "The chap we are currently monitoring is, we suspect, a terrorist sleeper cell. A dark past connected to the military and some of *our* chaps' names are tied in to his ops too, unfortunately. We are certain he's the one that did away with your Bulldog mob, and did for Barry Miller, too. He's currently spending his time holed up at the porn studios in Deptford, but has yet to make a move or contact his sources. Other than a brief time on a Russian oil tanker following the aftermath of the blast in Essex, he's done nothing of note. Not a bally peep. Very odd. Very odd indeed."

"I know the guy you mean. Definitely something off with him. I interviewed him at the hospital. So he's still holed up at the studios, is he?" said Stump.

"Indeed. Either way, we really rather wish he would make his move. But we don't want to risk taking him in until we can find out more about who put him there. National Security, and all that. But if we could get a rival gang to push his buttons, maybe it would force him to reveal his connections upstream."

"That might work," agreed Stump.

Sir Michael continued.

"Of course, these things take a bit of time. We understand that. But if you could get some decent sized interest to look at this industrial estate in Deptford, at the same time as addressing your power vacuum situation in Peckham, I think the rest will probably come together by itself. Get a snake to poke a snake, so to speak. I suspect this would support your interests too, would it not? So it might provide a *win-win* all round. What do you think, old chap?" asked Sir Michael, knowing the answer already.

"Not a problem," replied Stump.

He was being given free rein by MI6 to invite larger gangs into his borough. This meant he could milk them for back-handers to turn a blind eye. It was a Christmas bonanza, had it been Christmas.

"I won't let you down," said Stump. "Give me a few weeks. Shouldn't take more than that to drum up a bit of interest if your lot can keep the superiors off my back."

"Of course. And I know you won't let us down, old boy," said Sir Michael. "Just remember to avoid the head of *our* snake when it moves. We will, of course, wash our hands of everything, including connection to you, should things go too far south. So, a bit of a responsibility there, old chap. But I know you want your day in the sun, and frankly, we both know it's long overdue. Good luck, Roger."

With that, Sir Michael clapped his hands on his knees and then stood up. He then turned and walked back towards Vauxhall Bridge while whistling a war-time ditty, as he liked to do.

Stump was finally seeing a way out from the grey poverty trap that the situation had recently returned him to. For the first time in months, he smiled. Things had finally turned around. Staring at the Thames for a while longer, he was so happy that he forgot to keep a check on himself. Moments later, he slipped blissfully into a daydream, but his curious malaise was never far behind. Stump slipped quietly down the bench as he fell into a full-blown episode.

Rearing up in slow motion on a white charger, sweat gleaming on its sides, spurs glinting in the hot Spanish sun. He could hear her voice.

"Señor Stooomp… Señor Stooomp!"

"I am coming, my love, I am coming!" he called to her.

At that moment, along the river path, came a young woman dressed in body-hugging jogging pants. She bounced toward the spot where a man, dressed in tired clothing, was sagging down from a bench towards the ground, all the while voicing drunken sexual profanities.

"… I am coming… my love…" he said.

As she reached him, she paused and turned to face him, still jogging on the spot. His hand was a few inches from her leg as he mouthed the words, but his eyes were distant and out of focus. He was obviously a dirty street bum. The woman checked the path in both directions, and seeing no one coming, she pulled out a bottle of *Lady Mace* and sprayed a large shot of it in his face, making sure it covered him well.

"Bloody pervert," she said, as she continued jogging on the spot while observing the potential rapist with a bitter satisfaction as he writhed on the ground in agony, clutching at his eyes and choking. She spent a moment enjoying the thrill that the defensive attack afforded her as a potential victim before turning and continuing on her way. A sense of pride washed over her for getting one in for *"the girls"*, and it added an extra bounce to her gait.

"It served him right. Bloody men, constantly oppressing us with their unwanted sexual attention," said Sarah to her friend, Angela, after she arrived back at the office and described the nightmare experience she had just been subjected to.

"God, babe, it sounds awful. Are you okay? You must feel totally violated," replied Angela.

Angela was a plump woman, a little shorter than Sarah, with dark brown hair in a brutally shaped bob. Sarah, in contrast, had beautiful, long, golden hair, and a perfectly shaped body with a booty to die for. While Angela's booty was more like a large, square sponge. Angela could only dream of being molested by perverts on the Thames riverbank in broad daylight, and often hung around there in the hope it might happen.

"I do. I really do. It was just so objectifying," said Sarah.

"Bloody men," said Angela dreamily, and they both sipped at their lattes.

A new member of staff came into the kitchen. Sarah turned

to Angela and mouthed the letters,

"O.M.G. H.O.T."

They continued to sip at their lattes and watch the man. He looking at his phone and seemed not to notice them as he faced the counter and made himself a mug of tea. Both women checked out his buttocks and made silent comments and signs to one another about the shape. He turned around, catching them.

"Hi," said the man awkwardly, realising they were there.

He pulled his headphones off and put the phone away in his pocket, then moved and stood in front of Angela, smiling. She stared back at him, hardly able to believe what was happening. The only males that paid her attention were horny Labradors, though she suspected that was a side-effect of the weight loss drugs she was taking to counteract the secret fast-food fetish she had. Sarah seethed noticeably, also unable to comprehend what was happening. How had the hot guy noticed Angela before her? There must be something wrong with him.

"I need something from the fridge?" said the man.

"Oh, my god. Yes. Sorry. Silly me," replied Angela, and she quickly moved aside.

After getting what he needed, he smiled at her again before turning back to finish making his tea.

On his way out the door, he pulled his phone out from his pocket and went back to watching Pussy Productions' latest European release of Randy Andy in a Gay Roman spectacular. It was a Gladiatorial epic titled *Titus & The Dungeon Bears*. Andy played both Titus *and* two of the dungeon bears - one of Larry's ideas to maximise his exposure. They needed a stand-in for the anal scenes, and so used a lot of close-ups, splicing the edit afterwards to make it seem like Andy was doing himself in a three-way. It was a new niche in the gay market. Larry loved it, Maurice too, and sales to the gay community suggested they were correct.

Both women stared into space after the man left, and both were miles away in thought.

Maybe I need to do more Pilates. Is twice a day, seven days a week, too little? Am I eating too much? Are these jogging pants are out of fashion already? Goddamn it! thought Sarah.

What's the best kind of wire to keep a man tied to a bed with to stop him from escaping? thought Angela.

"Are you going to Clammy Frawd's rally next week?" asked Sarah.

"Oh God, yes, wouldn't miss that," said Angela, wishing she could miss it, but knowing Sarah might not talk to her again if she did.

Angela needed a friend, and Sarah was nice to her. She was lucky to have her. Sarah was also her only friend.

"I can't wait to picket that hideous studio up at Deptford," said Sarah. "Really exciting, and after today's experience, I am so glad I got involved with Clammy. She really understands the root of the problem. She changed my life for the better and made me see how evil men are. This Patriarchal bullshit has been going on far too long, Angela. It's time the sisters took over."

"God, yea," said Angela, and she sipped at her latte but was visualising the patriarchy tied to her bed, naked and unable to escape. In her mind, she was in a pinny, cooking dinner for them. Also breakfast, and lunch, and tea, and then cuddling up to them at night to watch *Friends* on repeat, or maybe a food channel.

"Is he gay? Do you think he is gay?" asked Sarah absent-mindedly.

"Who?" asked Angela, but she knew.

"That new guy who was just in here, Chris, I think his name is."

"Oh God, no, definitely straight," replied Angela.

Angela was certain Chris was one hundred-and-ten percent gay, but she saw no reason to inform Sarah of this. Let her feel worthless for a while and see how she liked it. Angela felt better about herself to see Sarah failing to have an effect on a man. She was always pointing her male attracting assets at everything with a penis, while denying it in equal measure.

"Maybe he could come to the rally next week," said Sarah. "Ask him along, would you, Angela? Just don't let it seem like I suggested it. Anyway, see you at lunch."

Sarah then bolted out of the kitchen before Angela could come up with a reason not to. Angela huffed. She felt like Sarah's dog's-body most of the time, but that was the price of having a friend. Though speaking to Chris and asking him to picket a porn studio in Deptford, and to make it look like *she* was asking? Oh god. It was the ultimate shame. But shame was something she was used to. In fact, shame was *all* she knew. She then left to get it over with.

Angela walked out of the kitchen and went to find Chris's cubicle, where she lent over the top of it. Chris was scrolling back and forth on a juicy part. He threw his phone across the room when she coughed to let him know she was there. But she'd seen enough to know that he *would* come to the rally after all, though not for the same reasons that Sarah and Clammy would be going.

"Little secret, Chris. Don't tell anyone, but Sarah and I are going to the Clammy Frawd feminist rally up at Pussy Productions studios in Deptford next week. Wanna come?"

Chris nearly wet himself with excitement as he clapped his hands together. He finally had someone to go with. He'd been dying to stalk the Pussy Production premises where, if he was really lucky, he might catch a glimpse of his hero. Maybe *stalk* was too strong a word when he considered it, or maybe not, he wasn't really sure.

"Oh please, please, please, please, please," he responded, and wriggled in his seat like he'd just got onto the netball squad.

"Great," replied Angela.

And with that, she disappeared back over the cubicle divider to walk down the corridor toward her space, punching the air as she went. For once, she had nailed something. And given what she had just seen on Chris's phone, Sarah would never bag Chris, no matter how well she got that booty of hers working.

Mr Octopus

Inspector Stump took a few days off and blamed it on the flu, rather than admit to having been maced by a female jogger. When he returned to Peckham Police Station, he got to work building up a list of local gangs with plans to entice them into taking on Peckham and some of its surrounding boroughs. He called a sergeant into his office, whom he knew had been involved in collecting that kind of information.

"I need to know heads of all the gangs local to Peckham. We're getting reports of someone trying to muscle in on Basher's old interests and need to monitor it," he said, after the sergeant had entered.

"Certainly, sir," replied the sergeant, who then stood there.

"Well, go on then. Run along and get me that info," said Inspector Stump.

"No need, sir. Got it all in here," replied the Sergeant tapping his head.

"Really, only a few, then?" said the Inspector.

"Quite the opposite, in fact. Got a bit of the Hyperthymisia. Gives me a decent memory for things, sir," replied the sergeant.

"Hyper…? Right you are," Stump replied, not understanding what he was talking about. "Well, fire away then, sergeant. Maybe start with the gangs that are closest to Peckham Rye and work outward."

Stump got his pencil ready, and the sergeant began.

"Well, sir, there's the Black Gang, Ghetto Boys, and Peckham boys here in Peckham to the North. The Shower Gang, DGB, DB, and DM have muscle in the North-East over towards New Cross. Just by them is the IOD, on the Isle of Dogs, obviously. We've got the Maryland Bloods on the Maryland estate, the Monson Bloodset on the Monson estate, and the Tiverton Pirus are on the Tiverton estate. Monson Bloodset also has a small roundabout, a street, and a couple of playgrounds and zebra crossing near to their estate, but not quite on the estate. Makes it annoying when you try to take the underpass for a bite to eat at Hong Kong City actually, sir, in plain clothes at least. Then there is the TMM, and YMM, who are directly south of us, and they own two or three streets and a corner shop, and last I heard they expanded to include a set of swings out at the park, but that's still unconfirmed at the moment, sir. South West in West Norwood is the Gipset. Then at the border of Lambeth going west from there, you have SMS, and Squeeze 4 Pz. Then, of course, directly west of that, you have the Tulse Hill Gang. Now going north to Brixton, well to be honest, too many gangs to mention unless you really want a full breakdown, but the PDC were pretty big there along with the Muslim Boys, the Guns, Shanks, the ABM, and the TN1. East from Peckham is a bit of a no-man's-land. No one seems interested in Hither Green, and it stays that way until you get to the Ferrier Boys in Eltham. Except if you go the wrong way and end up in Tesco's car park or the Argos near Catford bridge then you may bump into the Black Maff or Anti..."

He paused. Inspector Stump had stopped writing and was staring at him with this mouth agape. "Everything alright sir?" asked the sergeant, after a moment.

"Er... thanks, yes, all fine. Interesting skill you have there, sergeant," said the Inspector. "Can I safely assume from the names that most of these gangs are black, have a focused interest in drug-dealing rather than business crime, and are not too large in gang members or reach?" he added.

"Correct, sir. Not like it was in the old days, I am told, and yes, mostly drugs, and most of them an awkward demographic, though we don't officially acknowledge the skin colour now, for obvious reasons, sir."

"Of course, of course. Anyway, thank you, and that will be all for now, sergeant," replied the Inspector.

The sergeant thanked him and then left to go back to his desk. Stump put the pencil down and looked out of the window while leaning back in his chair, considering things. Times had changed more than he had realised. He'd hoped to shop locally to make life simple. Though it was clear there were plenty of gangs around, too many, but with the names he was hearing, it didn't bode well. With a brief check of a few of them on the police database, he soon confirmed it was hooded teenagers and wannabe gangsters, whose primary concerns were looking cool on social media with guns, money, crack pipes, and their 'bitches', as they now referred to them. He needed a proper firm, not a cliché. Sir Michael was right. He needed to look further afield, and it explained why no one had stepped up to take over the racketeering business in Peckham like he had hoped. There wasn't much adult gang activity left, it seemed, at least not near there. Stump was going to have to extend his search, and he considered his old contacts in other parts of London. It had been a while since he had followed any of those leads up. He was clearly going to have to do the legwork and see if he could find any of the old firms.

Stump left the station, headed to Brixton. His first stop was Coldharbour Lane, looking for his old Yardie contacts at pubs like the Mucky Duck. His first mistake was in assuming those places still existed. The Mucky Duck was long gone, and so he walked up Coldharbour Lane until he found another pub he knew, The Prince of Wales, but it was half the size it used to be and looked gentrified. Stump had a pint in there anyway, and waited to see if anyone showed up that he recognised, but it was deathly quiet. He then left and wandered around until he found The Prince Albert, which had a bit more life in it. He was feeling a little more relaxed after another drink, so sidled up to the first person he saw in there who was the correct ethnic shade and looked a bit shifty.

"I'm looking for Yardie Pete," said Inspector Stump.

The man ignored him.

"Excuse me, my man," he tried again. "I was just wondering if you know Yardie Pete?"

"No, I don't, bruv," was the curt reply, and the man turned his back on Stump to continue talking to his friends.

"Alright, just asking," replied Stump, and he went back to the bar stool he had been sitting on and finished his pint.

A while later, having asked several others if they knew Yardie Pete and received similar lukewarm responses, he gave up and left. A few more pints and a few more pubs later, and he wasn't getting anywhere but drunk. It was getting dark, and he figured he might hang around the lane and see if some of the street sellers were about. Maybe they could point him in the right direction. He bought a bottle of water from a newsagent and lent against a wall to steady himself as he sipped from it and watched the street for signs of life. Either the weed dealers knew he was a cop, which was pretty likely given the look of him, or no one sold weed on Coldharbour Lane anymore. He was about to give up when a nearby night club opened its doors, and he walked over to try his luck there. The doorman immediately refusing him entry with a laugh.

"Guest-list only tonight mate, and you certainly aren't coming in dressed like that."

"Discrimination, is it?" asked Stump, feeling a bit wobbly but tiring of the endless kick-backs he'd been getting all day.

"Listen mate," said the doorman, switching to a less amiable tone. "I'm going to tell you this one more time. You aren't fucking coming in here. Clear enough for you?" and with that, he turned and walked back toward the entrance.

"Is it coz I is white?"

Stump said it in a ridiculous imitation patois style, knowing it would create a rise, and the doorman turned back towards him. He then pretended to remember something, and patted at his jacket pockets a few times.

"Oh, hang on," said Stump, finally producing his Inspector ID and shoving it in the doorman's face. "Turns out I am on the guest list, after all."

The doorman rolled his eyes. He'd thought the man might be a cop but had more money on him being a drunk.

"Alright mate, I didn't realise," replied the doorman. "You sure you got the right place, though? This is a night reserved for someone who, at a guess, didn't invite you. Just checking, you know."

"Just fucking let me in, son. If I want questions, I'll book you into an interrogation room."

"Okay, guvnor, you're da boss," replied the doorman, and stood aside to let Stump in.

Stump was beyond niceties. Now he just wanted another drink. The day had started out with a plan which hadn't worked out in the slightest, and he felt like getting properly doused. Coldharbour Lane was not the place that it used to be. He was feeling like a relic from a bygone era, a dinosaur, and he wanted to drink away the sense of grief that it had created, having to spend the day wallowing in the awareness of it.

He headed to the bar. The club was still setting up and empty, but a barman was stocking drinks and eventually came over to him. He ordered a whisky on the rocks. The barman checked his watch and saw they were open, so nodded and got it for him. Stump took a sip. The barman was waiting for payment, but Stump ignored him and sipped again. Realising he had a live one, and wondering how he'd got in, he didn't bother asking again, and pressed a button under the bar, then went back to stacking shelves. Back out where the doorman was, a light began flashing. The doorman, seeing it, rolled his eyes, then wandered through to the main room, pretty certain he knew what to expect. Stump had his back to the barman, who, on seeing the doorman, pointed at Stump and signalled with his fingers that money had not been forthcoming. When the doorman reached Stump, he stood looking at him. Stump smiled back. The doorman pointed to Stump's drink.

"You're going to need to pay for that," he said.

"Tell you what, you tell me where Yardie Pete is, and then I will pay for this drink," replied Stump.

The doorman's face gave nothing away. He knew the name, though he hadn't heard it mentioned for many years. But this changed everything. Now he wondered what the cop was really doing there. It was time to notify certain parties that a drunk cop was in the club asking questions about old gangsters from the hood. The doorman turned to the barman.

"Get him whatever he wants, when he wants it," he said.

"That changed *your* fucking tune, hey?" said Stump, and he shot back the rest of his drink before sliding it toward the barman for a refill.

"Anything for the Fuzz," replied the doorman, and he walked back out to the front entrance, where he pulled a phone from his pocket and dialled a number.

The night filled up. R&B music blared through the club as it came to life. Stump stayed in his position at the bar, every now and again asking people who drifted by him the same question he had asked of everyone that day. He barely seemed to notice when two hours later, and considerably more intoxicated, he was the only white person in a sea of dark faces. Not only was he the whitest in there, he was the worst dressed by far. It could have been a fashion party for the MOBO Awards. Dress sense and style were a priority. Outside, the guest list tailed far down the street and most of them would not be getting in. This was, for the black community of Brixton, the event of the week, and there was not a white person in sight. Everyone in there was sober except for one man, dressed like a flasher, who was knocking back whiskies like he was in the wild west. The fact he was there was odd enough, but the fact a doorman hadn't ejected him was the signal for everyone to leave him well alone. Given who was hosting the *soiree*, this man not being turfed into the street suggested he was not to be trifled with. Stump was seemingly far too drunk to have any concept of his situation.

A group of men watched the man through a one-way mirrored window in an office above the dance floor.

"Raaas blud. This motherfuckin pussy clot ain't no normal five-oh, I am tellin' ya. Look at dat bitch. Him acting like a drunk pale king. I say merk him, blud. He just a dumb ass jake. Him not even from ends," said a foot-soldier who was given to heated exchanges and preferred to shoot people to solve things rather than talk to them. Cops included.

"He is disturbing the guests, can we not just get rid of him… throw him out, I mean?" asked the better spoken club owner, correcting himself rather than wanting to support the foot-soldiers' suggestions of menace.

He turned towards the gang boss, who was stood in the centre of the group, and had been watching the man quietly ever since he'd received the call. The name *Yardie Pete* concerned him. The gang boss was a smooth and well-dressed gentleman, who looked more *money* than *gangster*, and had a calmer refrain than some of the more aggressive and fidgety men that hovered around him in the penumbra of the dark office. When he spoke, it was with a well-educated English accent.

"You definitely heard him asking for *Yardie Pete?* You're absolutely sure about that?" the boss asked, turning to the doorman, who was also in the room.

"Clear as day, boss."

The boss nodded and folded his arms to continue pondering the drunk white man, who stumbled forward from the bar for a moment before righting himself and stumbling back. Still apparently unaware of the wide berth and wary looks that everyone was giving him. But the boss had seen enough. It was time to find out what the cop wanted.

"Get the fool up here," he said. "But better do this masked up. And no pistols. I don't want this going bad. We'll just find out what he wants. So, get all your mash locked in the back room. I'll do the talking. Y'all feel me! *I* will do the talking."

He stressed the last point. Everyone was disappointed to have to put away the guns, but they knew the consequences of disobeying the boss. They began doing as told, while the doorman went back down to escort the white devil up to meet the biggest gang boss in Brixton. The boss grabbed the more uppity foot-soldier who had spoken out previously. He got him in a gentle headlock and rustled his short, dred-locked hair. He did it in a big-brotherly way and spoke in a less English accent as he wrestled playfully with him.

"You behave, ya feel me! I got this. You just let me deal wid this nigga. If we have to *do* him, it be you. *It be you.* But we don't want that. Not yet. Ya feel me. You behave ye'self, blud. *Behave...*" he finished talking and finally let the younger man go while pointing a finger at him.

The boy huffed and wheeled, acting out of bravado, energised by frustration, but did as he was asked and dropped his weapons into the back room. One man locked the temporary gun store to ensure temptation did not overcome anyone. Another then went around with a box handing out masks. They donned their chosen masks and adjusted them, made a few jokes back and forth about the others in the room, then finally took up positions around the office. Well rehearsed positions, that made them look like a well-presented gang. The boss took his seat behind a big, leather-topped oak desk, and finally pulled his own mask down over his face, and then they waited.

The door opened and Stump came in with the doorman behind him. He was feeling the whisky, but he knew what he'd be walking into. He'd known since he first clocked the doorman's reaction after mentioning *Yardie Pete* hours previously. It had been the most subtle of eyebrow movements and only a hint of a pause before replying, but for Stump, it had been more than enough. This was the moment he had since been waiting for. He continued with the drunk act to give himself time to get a read on the room. Finally, he was where he wanted to be for the first time that day. He walked into the black-walled room. The lighting was halogen spot focused but dimmed. He raised an arm up to cover his eyes and peered into the darkness beyond.

"What are we doing in the broom cupboard, Bobo? Are you planning to fuck me in the ass?" asked Stump, then feigning surprise added, "Jesus, there's a fucking whoop in here... Didn't see you in the shadows there. Christ, look at the size of this bastard."

Stump had bumped into one of the larger members of the gang, who was standing in a solid, wide-legged stance. His arms were folded, head tilted back, and he looked at Stump through the eyes of his plastic pig mask. Stump turned, whisky still in hand, to check the rest of the room. He soon spotted the boss, also in a mask, sat in the command position on the other side of the large desk.

"Well, fuck me," said Stump, "Zoidberg here too."

He turned full circle to check out the various other masks in the room as his eyes adjusted to the light, and then he laughed. "You should have told me it was fancy dress, boys."

The boss was unperturbed by Stump's fooling around and was aware of what he was up to.

"What do you want?" he asked Stump.

"'kin blood-clot," seethed the foot-soldier who was currently behind Stump, and then made the sound of sucking through his teeth.

The boss turned his head to stare at him, and the man backed off, looking at the floor in a gesture of submission. He then turned back to Stump, who had briefly turned to check the foot-soldier, and now knew the weakest link in the room. The voice and tone would also be recognisable later, should he need it. Stump smiled to himself at the ease with which he had gamed the situation. The boss knew the play and was annoyed Stump had succeeded.

"The jungle speaks," said Stump, turning back to the boss, and pointing a thumb behind him at the foot soldier, seeing if he could get another rise out of him.

"What the fuck do you want?" asked the boss, said in a tone to imply he wouldn't be asking again.

"Well, for starters, can I talk to a human instead of an... orange squid?" asked Stump, referring to the choice of mask that the Brixton boss was currently wearing.

Stump looked closely at his whisky glass and sniffed it.

"Clearly better than it tastes," he said, but it was all part of the act to appear unconcerned as he turned to the doorman to ask. "What do they put in the drinks here, Bobo? Are you seeing this zoo?"

But his act had run its course, and Stump paused for only a moment before playing his last card. He switched off the drunk display with an immediacy that surprised the less experienced gang members, and then banged his drink down hard on the table, leaned in, and looked more closely into the eyes of the woollen orange mask of Zoidberg from Futurama.

"I have been all fucking day looking for Yardie Pete," said Stump. "I am now thinking he isn't around. Probably dead, or maybe gone back to Jamaica. But what I am also now thinking, Mr... Octopus, is that I have found *exactly* who I was looking for, after all."

Stump held his position, staring into the dark eyes of the man who stared straight back at him. Neither moved, weighing one another up with an intuitive sense that they both possessed. Elsewhere in the room, no one moved an inch. Finally, the boss broke the tension, and he started laughing. A roaring laugh. He leaned back in his chair and lifted a finger that he waggled at Stump.

"I know you," he said.

The gang shared looks at one another. Everyone was confused.

The boss continued, "You're that Dibble from Peckham, involved in the firm that got themselves blown up in Essex… Yea, that's you," but then he stopped laughing as abruptly as he had started. "What the fuck do you want? I won't ask you again, ya feel me?"

The tone could not be mistaken. Stump felt on the back foot for the first time since he'd left Peckham Station that day. He was known to the man, while Zoidberg remained anonymous behind his mask. It wouldn't be hard to figure out who the man was, but he didn't like it. His problem now was going to be getting out of there alive. The other man now took the edge by revealing him. Not to mention the twitchy one behind him, who he could feel bristling and looking for any excuse. Things had got a lot more serious, and he knew he had to get to the point, and hope it was enough. Cop or not, people went missing, and no one from the station knew he was there. He realised he had misjudged the success of his ruse, and his next moves would count for everything. From that moment, Stump was in a play for his life.

"Okay, Mr Octopus," he replied, relaxing his position and stepping back to shift so that the twitchy one would have more difficulty reaching him with a blade if he had one.

Stump then took the opportunity to look around for anything he could use as a weapon. He didn't expect to survive if it went off, but he would make it as difficult as possible for them to clean up without questions being asked later. He looked back at the boss.

"Since you know who I am, I'll get to the point," he said. "Some business interests recently came available under my jurisdiction. I used to deal with Yardie Pete in this manor on these matters, though admittedly, that was a long time ago. Right now, these businesses are looking for protection. The right kind of protection, though, not a bunch of fucking amateurs. It was proper in the days of the old firms to make offers to the right people, and do it in the right order, and that is what brings us to this moment. Yours is the nearest borough with any real weight. Maybe I got the right firm, or maybe not. Maybe everything has changed. You tell me."

Stump had turned to walk towards one of the gang members as he talked, who now stiffened as he pointed to the mask the man was wearing.

"Can I get one of these?" he asked.

The boss continued to stare at him coldly before replying, trying to gauge whether he believed what he was hearing.

"And why the fuck would I want work from a bent copper I don't know?" he asked.

"I thought you said you knew me. The better question would be why the fuck you wouldn't," replied Stump. "You're either interested, or you aren't. I am not here to fuck about, mate. If you have what it takes to meet *our* interests, then our next meeting best be without that fucking mask. Speak to Yardie Pete, if he is still alive, or any of the boys from his day. They'll vouch for me. But you want to be more concerned about who will vouch for you, son. Go ask the right people. You'll soon figure out I am not your average bent copper. I'm dancing with devils so far out of your league, you don't even know they exist."

The boss watched Stump quietly but did not reply for a time.

"Okay, blud," he said eventually. "You give us a list of these business interests. Maybe we'll go check them out. See if you legit, and then - maybe - we'll get back to you. But don't come round here again, you hear what I am saying? If I see you again, I can't vouch for your safety. I don't give a fuck who you think you are, or work for. This is our corner of the jungle... *son.*"

And with that, he looked towards the doorman, then moved his head to the side to imply it was time to see the cop out.

"You give that list to my man here, and we'll be in touch," he said, then he added, "maybe."

Stump breathed a sigh of relief, but gave nothing of it away. He nodded, and then turned to leave, but as he did so, he paused and looked at the weakest link in the crew.

"You might wanna keep twitchy here on a tighter leash in the future. Remember, this works both ways, Mr Octopus. If you knew who I was working for, you'd be putting out a red fucking carpet right now, not this shit. Not your fault though, you weren't to know. But judge this moment for what it is. You really don't want to piss me off."

He looked from the foot-soldier back to the boss, then added, "... *ya feel me?*"

And with that, Stump left the room.

Once outside, he walked calmly up the road until he was out of sight of the club and, after turning the next corner, he vomited over a wall. Standing back up, he wiped spittle from his mouth.

"Fuck me!" he said.

Despite the close call, it had been a worthwhile mission, and he was pleased. He hoped the list of businesses that Basher had once lorded over would be enough to get Mr Octopus interested. The porn production studios in Deptford were high on that list, but not so high as to arouse suspicion, still high enough to be one of the first they noticed. Stump, satisfied with his work for the day, waved down a black Hackney cab, and putting it on police expenses, he went home.

The List

At Peckham Station the next morning, Stump called on the Sergeant and told him everything he could recall about the gang he had met the night before. When he had finished, the Sergeant enlightened him with what he knew.

"That sounds like the Black Bloods, sir. They're run by some fella who's a bit more business driven than the usual gangs, but their income is still the usual drugs, guns, and prostitution. It's mostly drugs, though," said the Sergeant.

Stump had sensed the boss to be a businessman and not just a run-of-the-mill hoodlum. He hoped that would be enough to get their attention regarding his list, but all he could do now was wait and gather information.

"Sergeant, get me as much as you can on these Black Bloods. I want to know who they are, where their turf is, what they shift, and what they are worth. Everything right down to the places they eat and where they shit. Most of all, I need a name for this *Mr Octopus* character."

"Er...certainly sir, though I am currently assigned to..." began the Sergeant, but the Inspector cut in.

"Don't worry about that, Sergeant," he replied. "You'll be

working with me from this point on. I'll arrange the necessary."

Stump picked up the phone and was about to dial when he noticed the Sergeant was looking hesitant.

"You *want* to be involved, I assume, Sergeant? We're going to be gathering intel on some of the biggest gangs in London. This comes from the top, with a chance of recommendations and up-titling if you perform well. Do you have a problem with that?"

"Not at all, sir. No offence, I just didn't know you had the power to reassign me," replied the Sergeant.

"I have the power. Are you in or out?"

"In sir. Most definitely," replied the Sergeant.

"Well, get on with it then," said Stump, and he dialled the private number for MI6.

Stump requested funding and authorisation from MI6. He told them he wanted to set up a small task force and needed their support to stay focused on the gang issue. Only they had the leverage to stop anyone from being re-assigned to other duties, and that request would trickle down to those above him. Confirmation took a few hours to get back to Peckham. Sir Michael had needed to speak to the Commissioner of Police for the Metropolitan area. It had taken an hour to convince him that Inspector Stump - whose file looked far from healthy - was someone they should throw money at for anything. The Commissioner was feeling aggrieved, but that was nothing new.

"Once again, we are supposed to just accept the requests of MI6 at face value, then carry the can if it becomes a bloody great balls-up, I presume?" remarked the Commissioner to Sir Michael, who was sitting opposite him in the

Commissioner's office.

"Of course MI6 will keep you in the loop and help reimburse extraneous costs. I have absolute faith in our man on the ground. He's been in place for years, developing exactly the inconsequential resume you are currently reading there on your screen. We have been priming him for just such a moment," lied Sir Michael. "You have our assurances that if it all goes 'balls-up', we will deal with it appropriately and swiftly. We can provide the distractions required to pull the spotlight from your boys in blue and sweep the whole thing up, containing the press if we have to."

"I don't believe a bloody word of it, but do I have a choice?" asked the Commissioner.

"Only if you want to explain to the PM why you think it should *not* go ahead. Need I use those rather tiresome words we so often have to fall back on at these times, but it is a matter of *National Security*, old boy."

"Just don't fucking fuck me on this Michael," said the Commissioner.

"Wouldn't dream of it, old chap," replied Sir Michael, after which he stood up and they shook hands.

He then left, and a short while later, the Commissioner left the room with signed papers authorising the request. Everything he had just read about Inspector Stump looked like a car crash waiting to happen. He suspected MI6 were far from confident in the man, but he also knew he couldn't go against the PM's wishes. He spoke to his PA after handing her the documents.

"Get me everything on this Inspector Stump chap. I mean everything *not* in this report on him. And I need someone to monitor this small task force that MI6 are palming onto us. I don't trust it. I want to know every move they make, and I want to be ready to act if we need to shut it down."

"Certainly, sir," replied the woman.

Outside in the street, Sir Michael rang a number on his mobile.

"Water Fowl here. Message for Southern Goose. The duck is ready to pluck. Take to the wing."

A short while later, Inspector Stump answered a call, and after putting it down, clapped his hands together in barely containable satisfaction. Things were moving along nicely. It was time for him to head north of the river to a second rendezvous he had been considering. There, he planned to connect with another group of thugs whom he hadn't brushed shoulders with in a long time. He left the station and headed to a pub in Kentish Town.

"Nah, he'd not be interested," said a man with a broad Irish accent after Stump outlined the details of his list.

The thing about the Irish was you could just get down to business over a drink. You didn't need to beat about the bush, and you didn't need to deal with all the preening and posing that came with the black gangs. Stump could understand this level of mobster mentality much better, and he felt less defensive, but he also knew that ambience was not something to take lightly. Once you got involved with the Irish, if you made a mistake, it was your kneecaps they took first, and after that, your family. Certainly, they were friendly on the surface, but they didn't muck about.

"I thought he was always interested in new business opportunities," replied Stump, annoyed by the unexpected knock back.

"He runs the London music scene now. So, what the fock

would he be wanting with some moocky porn trash and a bunch of shit shops south of da river? What fookin planet you bin livin' on? He's the *Gig Father* now, or ain't you heard?"

All the men present, except Stump, laughed briefly before sipping at their pints. The man continued.

"He's been straight up legit since dropping the furniture business and taking over the music venues here from yoos English coonts, who could not run a fooking thing without it losing money hand o'er fist."

The group laughed again.

Stump argued for a while longer, but whatever he tried, the man refused to take his list of business interests to their chief. He was getting nowhere in North London, so he left the pub and called the Sergeant.

"Have you heard of the *Gig Father*?" Stump asked him.

"Er… yea. Irish immigrant, started out in the North London furniture and demolition business, with knee-capping as a side hobby. He moved into the music business a few years ago and went legit, if you can call pushing everyone out with threats of violence, legit."

"Well, see what you can dig up on him, too. Anything we can get on that bastard I want to know about. Legit my ass, those carny crooks were crooks the day they arrived here, and nothing has changed."

Stump flagged down a taxi and asked the driver to take him to Soho. Dealing with mobsters was already giving him a headache.

When he arrived in Rupert Street, he got out, and then wandered into the first clip joint he saw. He hadn't paid much attention on the way in, as he was still mulling over failing to get the Irish on board, and only realised his mistake when he got down the stairs and saw a bar full of cross-dressers. Stump turned on his heel and went back up the steps. Soho had become more metro-sexual since he had last been there. He found another place not much further on, with a scantily dressed woman outside. Briefly checking the signs outside to be sure it was more to his taste, he then ignored her attempts to talk to him and went past her and down the stairs. He was the only customer.

A woman was looking bored behind the bar, and a large man dressed in standard security black clothing was talking to her. It was dark and seedy. The place felt old, and smelt like years of booze had been spilled on the carpets. Any smart person would leave, knowing it for the obvious rat-trap that it was.

Stump found it odd that the clip joints had survived, but London was a mish-mash of hypocrisy and could still lay the odd honey-trap for unsuspecting tourists. No doubt officials were paid handsome sums to leave it all alone. Russian and Turkish mobs ran them, and Stump knew that, which was why he was there.

A barely dressed Russian woman came out from behind a door and walked over to him soon after he sat down. She explained the deal with the drinks and how he would need to buy a drink for her, and how drinks would go on credit, and he could pay later. Stump already knew the racket and agreed to everything, ordering a pint for himself, and whatever the woman was drinking. He then drank the watered down lager and talked to her about meaningless things. Thirty minutes later, a second woman came out and sat with them. Soon they were both laughing at his unfunny jokes until his bill gently clocked up to where both women judged him unable to pay. One then gave a subtle nod to the security, who walked over and asked Stump to pay before continuing. Stump sighed. It had taken an age to get to that moment.

"If you want a girl for pussy, we have pussy next door," said the security guard. "Not these girls, these nice girls. But now you pay, then you drink and talk some more with nice girls, or you go next door for pussy."

"Sure, sure," replied Stump and got up to follow the hulk of a man over to the bar to pay.

The woman there painstakingly tapped the six drinks he had ordered into the till, and then printed the receipt and passed it to Stump.

"Two hundred and fifty pounds and thirty pence," read Stump out loud. "Less than I was expecting."

He then looked for his wallet, patting various pockets. Seemingly unable to find it, he soon got bored with his routine and turned to the security man.

"Just out of interest, what was the thirty pence for?" he asked.

The security man didn't look at him, just shrugged, and then nodded toward the woman behind the bar. "You pay," he said.

"I tell you what," replied Stump, "rather than me paying, how about you both go fuck yourselves?"

He smiled at the man, knowing what was coming next.

They spent the next five minutes scuffling around in the small bar. Stump eventually got the security guard in a jiu-jitsu neck lock that had him crying like a baby beneath him, with his trapped face down on the floor. During the melee, Stump had punched the bar woman in the face, knocking her clean out, and she was currently lying face down a short distance away. He didn't like punching women, but his line of work had long since taught him it was an occasional necessity, especially when they jumped on you while you were wrestling a three-hundred pound gorilla. The other two women, who had come in screaming like banshees ready to jump on him too, had run off when they saw he had no problem with such behaviour. Stump knew he didn't have long before more security arrived, so he got the cuffs on the now unconscious man. He then stood up and stepped over to the prostrate woman and confirmed she had a pulse. She did. After that, he went behind the bar and poured himself another pint, which he held up in a gesture of thanks to a CCTV camera. Stepping back around to the patron side to enjoy it, he waited for whatever was coming next.

By the time a contingent of Russian security came stomping down the stairs and into the bar, Stump had poured himself a double-shot of whisky and found a pen and bit of paper with which to rough up a short list like the one he had given to the Black Bloods. When they saw the cuffs on their man and Stump now casually sat at the bar with his back to them, the men paused. A moment later, a gentleman in a black suit arrived at the bottom of the steps. He had prison tattoos showing on the back of his hands, and looked at the scene calmly, then towards Stump.

"We have the agreement with police. You know this, surely?" asked the man, in a Russian accent, who then turned his head to look at the girl lying unconscious on the floor. "Is she alive?" he asked.

"She's fine," replied Stump, not turning around. "I'm well aware of your affiliations, but this is about... some separate business."

"*This*," said the Russian, waving his hand at the scene on the floor, "is not *good* business. This is *bad* business. Though mostly for you, my friend."

Stump didn't doubt it and laughed.

"*This*," Stump replied, imitating the man in the way he said it, "is the only way to get the right people's attention."

Turning around to look at the man before adding, "This is still London, not Moscow… my friend."

Stump disliked foreigners taking over British businesses, especially when it was the Eastern European mafia. In his mind, they should not be allowed to run crime, or clip joints, in the heart of London. But he knew MI6 could protect him at that moment, enough to put on the display, and it went some way to take a sour taste out of his mouth. He had enjoyed it. It was like the old days of the Flying Squad, when cops got physical because it was expected of them. The girl was collateral damage, but he doubted it was anything that hadn't been done to her by a Russian before. It felt good to be fighting with people again, and he was looking forward to doing a bit more of it. Violence was an underrated therapy.

Stump got up from his stool, walked over to the Russian, and handed him the list.

"Give this to your boss. There are some business interests come available in our area that we want to offer to the right people. He can find me at Peckham Police Station if he has an issue with anything that happened here. Alternatively, my private number is on there if he wants to discuss terms."

Stump didn't wait for a response, but stepped over to remove the cuffs from the man now coming round on the floor, and then he walked towards the exit. The men there blocked his way until the man he had just given the list looked at it, then signalled for them to let him leave.

Back out in the street, Stump breathed the air and flexed his arms and stretched his shoulders. That had felt good. He then turned and walked towards China Town. Pulling his phone from his pocket, he called the Sergeant.

"Add the Russian mafia in Soho to your list. I need to know who the current bosses are, and the same deal; get me names, connections, and any weaknesses we can target. Now, where would I find the head of the Triads these days? I am just nearing China Town."

Stump was walking past Wong Kei and looked around at the other restaurants, trying to recall what he remembered of the area. The Sergeant was wondering what on earth the Inspector was getting himself into, but gave him the information without asking questions. Stump put the phone back in his pocket and then rolled up his sleeves.

He spent the next few days punching, kicking, throttling, upending, and knocking out various villains in various parts of London. Not long after putting the phone down to the Sergeant, he punched a Triad member clean out upon opening the door to him at the gang's headquarters in China Town. They found the man a short while later with a list on his unconscious body. He then throttled a member of the Italian Mafia half to death on a table in a restaurant in Islington, slipping the list into *his* pocket and making a rapid departure when the kitchen staff appeared armed with knives. From there, he went to Manor House and caused a ruckus by throwing a member of the Greek mafia down some stairs, breaking his collarbone and a couple of ribs. It took him a while to get any traction with the Islamic fundamentalists. His first attempt, in Southall, ended with him running for his life down side-streets being chased by men with machetes after barging into a bookshop meeting of the Syrian Islamic Fundamentalist Group For Jihad. Uncertain where to try next to get the attention of Islam, he opted to spend Sunday afternoon at Speakers Corner in Hyde Park. There, he heckled every Muslim he saw. They mostly ignored him, but he eventually managed to get physical with a group that had gathered to try to rein him in. The irony was, the Christians then pitched in to the help the Muslims as they struggled to get the man under control. For a time there was a unity between religions as they converged on Stump, who was by then wildly swinging a ladder he had commissioned by pushing a *Speaker For Christ* off it. His police skills coming to the fore as he cajoled, clobbered, clipped, and deftly rendered unconscious a handful of men from varying faiths. Specifically targeting, where possible, anyone who looked the slightest bit dark skinned or had a beard. He reminded himself that it was for Queen and Country, and their own fault for trying to thwart him. A later press report said the man was heard shouting, *"Say hello to my little friend!"* just before the Christians finally got the upper hand and pinned him down. As they did so, a cheer went up from the Muslim brotherhood. Soon after that, a couple of police officers got him out from under the Christians and into a set of cuffs. This led to the first incident of religious unity seen on a Sunday in Hyde Park in over a decade, as Christians and Muslims could be seen hugging one another and shaking hands effusively as they celebrated the win.

Inspector Stump sat cuffed, dishevelled, bruised, and maniacal looking, in the back of a police van bound for the Hammersmith nick. There, it finally dawned on him he had probably taken the whole thing a bit too far. His insistence that he was working undercover had carried little weight with the arresting officers. Speaker's Corner had been a peaceful gathering, albeit politically argumentative, until Stump arrived. Though once his identity was confirmed - and mysterious orders came from above - reluctantly, they were forced to let him go.

Stump's first outing had irked Sir Michael. It was unprofessional that he had been fool enough to pop his head up like that. Sir Michael called a meeting with him soon afterwards, at the usual place beside the Thames.

"Slightly left-field behaviour, old chap. What exactly was your M.O. there?" asked Sir Michael, looking a little concerned, and checking Stump for signs of psychopathy before sitting down at the bench. He seemed to be fine apart from a few bruises, but one never could tell.

"It's in hand," replied Stump. "Don't worry. I had to put on a show for the Islamic mob. They are hard to get a handle on, and to be honest, I think I am going to give up on them, anyway. All the other gangsters I got the list to, probably checking out the places as we speak. It's going great. Exactly how I expected. Just a minor hiccup, was all."

But the truth was somewhat different. The more he had exercised his dormant lust for violence, the more it had hooked him in, and the more entitled he felt to exert it. The free-pass that MI6 had afforded him then went to his head. And though he didn't know it, the only thing that was keeping him alive throughout his provocation of some of the biggest mobsters in gangland Britain was the fact that his behaviour was so insane, none of the mob bosses could believe it was happening. Until they knew more, they held off from issuing orders to use him for the next concrete mix on the nearest building site in their borough.

"Yes, well regarding this recent dubious escapade," said Sir Michael, "I have heard from a variety of sources that you have single-handedly incurred the wrath of pretty much every mob boss in London. I hope you know what you are doing. Should we be worried, Roger?"

"Of course not. I just needed to get their attention," replied Stump. "All the mobs worth bothering with now have that list. Now we just wait, and enough of them will express an interest in Deptford to put pressure on them. It took something like this to get the ball rolling, that's all."

"Okay, well, I do hope you are right. In the meantime, try not to get arrested again, or killed. You are one of the boys in blue yourself, after all, and it's been damn hard keeping your name out of the press this time. Had to pull a few strings I would rather not be pulling. Can we try to keep it all a bit more incognito from now on? This is really playing havoc with my gall stones. This needs to be managed a little more quietly from here on in. Could you do that? Well, that's it for now, Roger. Pip pip," said Sir Michael, and with that he did his usual trouser patting routine, got up and then left, though he was not in a whistling mood that day.

Suspicious Characters

It was early evening. Pussy Production studios had closed up after a day's shoot, and Hazelhot was the only one left on the premises. He was looking at pieces of torture equipment on the dark web, and part way through a Chinese take-away, when a van screeched to a halt in the road outside and six large gentlemen wearing hoodies and face masks jumped out brandishing baseball bats, then made their way down the path towards the main entrance. Hazelhot sighed, slightly annoyed at being disturbed in the middle of dinner. He put the food down, wiped some remnants from his lips, then got up and calmly left the room.

Further down the road, inside an unmarked van that had not moved for days, an MI6 agent was on the phone to Vauxhall HQ, describing the scene and asking what action to take. He soon received his orders.

"Record audio and video the event, but do not engage under any circumstances," said the voice on the other end.

He put the phone down and then checked the monitoring system was working and then set the camera recording.

The first of the men reached the main entrance and tried

the door. It was glass double doors with a metal frame, and looked like it should open if pulled hard enough, even when locked, but his attempt failed. The next man arrived. He was larger than the first, but tugging on it had the same effect. Eventually, the biggest of them got there and gave it a go. Finally - with most of them having had a couple of goes at tugging on the door - one of the men took a running kick at the glass. It wallowed and sent him flying backward where he landed on the ground while the others tried to stifle laughter.

As they gathered in a huddle to whisper and discuss what to do next, there was a buzzing sound. They looked at one another and then at the door. Once it had finished opening, they all rushed in. It was the Black Bloods of Brixton's first, and only attempt, to strong arm Pussy Productions of Deptford, and it didn't go at all well.

Members of MI6 gathered round a television monitor that had been wheeled in to replay the video evidence taken by the van at the scene. Moments after the hooded men entered the premises, there were a series of flashes, and a mysterious green-white light began emanating from inside the offices. Then there were more flashes, then a pause. Soon after, one by one, men stumbled and crawled from the premises.

"Is that smoke coming from them?" asked Sir Michael, of the agent who had been stationed in the van and was first-hand witness to the event.

"Yes, sir," he replied.

"What in Christ's name did he do to them?"

"We believe it was one of his recent purchases from the dark web, sir, a *Tazer Shockwave Barrier*. We think he has it installed at the end of the main corridor."

"My god, those things work rather well, don't they?" said Sir Michael.

The men present continued to observe the screen as the Black Bloods in various states of smoky discombobulation made their way back to the van they had arrived in. As it took off jumpily and fled the scene, Hazelhot could be seen standing in the office window.

"He looks pretty pleased with himself. What is that in his hand?" asked Sir Michael.

"Remains of a take-away, sir. He'd recently ordered Chinese," replied the agent.

Sir Michael had the agent pause the video, and he peered at the screen, trying to make out the man in the office window, but it wasn't the best quality. He turned to the agent.

"Has there been any further activity after this incident? Has this chap contacted anyone?" he asked.

"Only the staff," replied another man, who had been monitoring the phone lines.

"Could it be that he has some way of messaging that we don't yet know about?" asked Sir Michael, feeling frustrated by the lack of success that the increasingly disturbing events set in motion by Stump were now having.

"Unlikely. Given he is using the Internet with no concern for privacy, and that he hasn't tried to hide his activity at all that we've seen," replied a tech in charge of research. "If he *is* using something, then it's a method unknown to any surveillance team in the US, UK, or friendly countries. We checked with them on the latest spy media. Scanned the premises for signals across the full spectrum. Nothing so far."

"Hmm. So what the bloody hell is he up to?" mused Sir

Michael.

"I think the police are involved, and I think they are testing us," said Hazelhot, as an emergency meeting got underway between the heads of Pussy Production in the office the next day.

"I thought you said it was a hooded black gang," replied Stott, less inclined to believe Hazelhot's flights of fancy after all he had been through.

"There's been an unmarked police van parked near the entrance to the industrial estate ever since we got out of the hospital," replied Hazelhot. "So, why didn't they call it in when that mob showed up, huh? It's still there now, if you don't believe me."

Stott didn't doubt the police were suspicious of them, but needed a second opinion before he was willing to listen to Hazelhot's imaginings.

"What do you think, Hoots?" asked Stott, turning to him.

"Something's not right, and he's correct about the van," replied Hoots, a man professionally trained to assess exactly that kind of situation. "It's hard to judge from this one incident. Maybe they were just looking to rob the place, but it seems a little preempted. Could be they were thinking of muscling in on the porn industry now Basher is gone, but again, it's a pretty dumb move given the exposure we had, unless someone had put them up to it."

There was a brief silence in the room.

"So what's the worst-case scenario?" asked Stott.

Hazelhot shrugged his shoulders, but Hoots had more to say.

"It could be gangs, and it could be police giving them a free rein, but it could also be government. They would use the police for monitoring the premises, but would then rein them in from taking any action to cover up the fact. If the government is behind this, that's big trouble for us. They have the powers to play outside the rule-book. There's nowhere to hide if you are being setup by them. The question is, whoever they are, what is their interest in your business?"

Hoots turned to Hazelhot.

"Did any of the group say what they wanted?" he asked.

"I was in the middle of my dinner and didn't wait to find out," replied Hazelhot. "I heard South London accents and the usual black gangster gibber, so I smoked them. Bloody marvellous bit of kit that Tazer, though, huh?"

No one in the room seemed to be as impressed.

"So why would the police or government be involved with a gang of hoodlums breaking into our premises? I don't understand," said Stott, feeling a little confused.

Hazelhot replied this time.

"Pushing us to see how we respond. I wonder what they will throw at us next?"

"Surely that's the end of it?" replied Stott.

"You really don't know how this works, do you?" said Hazelhot.

"It doesn't surprise me that you do," muttered Stott before turning to Hoots. "You're a man with experience in dealing with this kind of thing. What do you suggest we do next?"

Hoots held up a finger, then walked over to a desk and turned on a radio that was there before putting the air conditioning on full. After that, he came back and waved Stott and Hazelhot in close so he could whisper to them.

"I'll make some enquiries to see what I can find out. We have to assume it will escalate further and should discuss a plan of action, but I suggest we talk no further on these premises. The van is definitely monitoring us, and we have to now assume it is not friendly. We also have to assume this building is compromised. From this point on, we work to a worst-case scenario, and prepare accordingly until we know more."

"And worse case is government?" repeated Stott, just wanting to be clear.

Hoots looked at Hazelhot, who nodded.

"Worst case is government," confirmed Hoots.

When news filtered down to Inspector Stump from MI6 that Hazelhot had tazered the entire Black Blood crew out of the runnings, he laughed out loud. But the amusement soon wore off, when he realised that all his work might still not be enough to deal with whatever currently lurked inside Pussy Productions. That concerned him. He'd promised Sir Michael not to escalate things, but that ship had now sailed. Escalation was inevitable, and now necessary. Given his connection with MI6 was his only access to any kind of genuine power, he would be a fool to jeopardise it. But he also needed this to work.

Stump considered how to proceed next. The Russian mob should prove a better match for the psychopath Hazelhot, but Stump wasn't sure he could risk waiting around to see if they were going to make a move. He began to devise a back-up plan. He needed something that would pit all the gangs against Hazelhot at the same time. Hopefully that would get a better result. He decided to get this new plan ready and in place, and *then* approach Sir Michael for approval to launch it. The Inspector thought it through a little longer, and then slapped his hand on his desk as a good name for it came to him. He then called the Sergeant into his office.

"*Operation Force It In.* Highly confidential, and I am not at liberty to divulge any more than I am about to. We are going to prepare to hit all the gangs at once and take something from each of them. This is still at the planning stage, so it may not get actioned, but we need to be ready. Top brass have requested we prepare it for implementation. But keep it between us for now. We can't afford any leaks."

"Understood, sir," replied the Sergeant.

"Right. I am going to need all the info you have collated on the gangs we have approached so far. We need to work out where and when to hit them. Also, what will they miss the most? If we don't know their routines and movements already, let's find those out, top priority. I also need some recommendations on any lads you trust in the firearms unit. Again, don't go blurting this to anyone, not even them just yet. Just get availability. Understood?"

"Aye sir," replied the Sergeant, excited to be getting into something bigger.

W.A.S.P.

It had been Clammy's first foray into violence on the day she tazered the porn pervert in the penis after breaking into St Thomas's hospital. A cathartic moment and one that had released so much pent up anger that she was champing at the bit to do it again. But this presented a problem. Her ethic had been built on non-violent expression, and that ethic had been a large part of her announced manifesto since she first became an activist. Now she needed to explain how female violence differed from male violence, why it was justified, and why it should be encouraged. Statistics had been the driving force of her campaign since the beginning. Stats were everything. So, she hoped stats would help her explain why it was time for women to fight back. Violently.

She had spent the days after the incident researching the stats for violence, and they proved beyond any doubt that men were responsible for all of it. Of course, there had been some articles on lesbian violence, female driven violence, the effects of emotional terrorism, as well as violence towards children, but they didn't seem relevant, so she ignored them. Women were the clear victims. They had always been the victims and would always be the victims. This was the message. The fact they were also independent, strong, self-motivated and empowered, and were free to do as they wished in modern society, was not in conflict with the idea they were still victims. Their oppression was obviously the fault of the patriarchy, and she gathered all the stats that helped to prove the point. Violence was men's domain, and in no way caused by women. Men were perpetrators, had always been perpetrators, and would always be perpetrators. This was the message. Men may have built, developed, and maintained modern civilisation and millions died protecting it, but that was also irrelevant to the point. Men were mostly violent, toxic beasts. They were the reason Clammy had been forced to become violent. The Patriarchy had caused it. Therefore, female violence must also be men's fault. This was the message. Her problem was solved.

Clammy had always been a tomboy. She was no beauty, and what she lacked in femininity and finesse she made up for in emotionally controlling behaviour. Clammy was, had always been, and would always be, competitive. Especially where men were concerned. She thought she was a gentle, soft, and loving creature. She didn't think of herself as manipulative, but as someone who could emotionally destroy those who opposed her when necessary. Clammy was no victim, Clammy was a *survivor*. This was her strength. Or so she told herself. And it was this strength that had led her to start W.A.S.P.

W.A.S.P. was Clammy's army of hardcore feminists who also believed in the cause. The strength of *Woman Against Servitude to Patriarchy* was in the power of their sisterhood. They would help each other out no matter what the patriarchy threw at them. Their ethic was rooted in community, love, nurture, and support for one another, and they celebrated this togetherness, loudly. Though when a few ex-members had pointed out that the support and nurturing dried up the moment any of them stepped out of line, Clammy had argued that as long as they supported the other women, then they had no reason to be excluded from the group; thus, they had done it to themselves. W.A.S.P. and the sisterhood were considered the real victims in that situation, because departing members were returning to the gas-lighting ways of the toxic patriarchy, so they were bound to attack the women they then abandoned.

Clammy had ruled the sisterhood of W.A.S.P. with a dictatorial flair. She was the queen bee. And pointing this out had led to the first ejection from the group. After that, no one mentioned it again. From then on, everyone agreed it was a group of *equality* and *inclusivity*, and that decisions were made by the sisterhood as a unified group. So long as Clammy approved. Clammy, deep down, knew she was a controlling person, but everything she did, she did for the greater good of women. Besides which, nothing she did could ever compare to the evils of men. She had the stats to prove it.

W.A.S.P. was the sisterhood, and that was the message. The sisterhood needed to be held together by someone, and for Clammy, it had become her life's mission. Women needed to stick together to defeat the testosterone-fuelled over-lording of the patriarchal ape. If it required emotional coercion to achieve it, that was for the best. Women were strongest when in numbers and that was how they would do it - with sheer, loud numbers. And, if she could get away with it, maybe now some violence too.

For Clammy it had been a long war already, but until she had crossed the line and pulled the trigger on the tazer incident, she had never understood the rush of almost orgasmic ecstasy that came from the act of perpetrating violence. Now she knew. Now she wanted more. She'd always had vague fantasies about destroying men. She especially fantasised about obliterating the pervert she had met at the hospital. Deep in her psyche, she felt certain that tearing that particular man to pieces would solve all the problems she'd ever had. Annihilating him might finally free her from the anger and frustration she'd lived under all her life. He symbolised all that made women powerless. He *was* the patriarchy.

Clammy considered herself a modern day Joan of Arc. She was sent by divine feminine powers to put the situation right for women, and W.A.S.P. was the army she would do it with. No male had ever symbolised all that was wrong with the patriarchy so much as the man she had shot that day in the hospital bed. The way his junk had flailed around, wet with semen and lobbing menacingly at her as he leered so grotesquely, had remained with her. This was just the beginning, and she hoped to go deeper. She dreamed some nights of eating him alive, ripping his head off and consuming his life-force, devouring his flesh and drinking his blood, becoming stronger and more powerful, as he became weaker. Rather than concern her, she woke up each morning all the more invigorated by it. She could find no redeeming features in the man. There was nothing. Clammy didn't stop to consider that this might be a symptom of something else that was consuming her, and it soon became her obsession.

When Sarah, Angela, and Chris arrived at the W.A.S.P. meeting point before the planned rally, they were unaware of this. In fact, to Sarah, it seemed like she had found a home in W.A.S.P. They had welcomed her in, and her heart had been filled with the warm sense of being cared for, supported, and nurtured by women that understood her troubles. When they told her that all those troubles were caused by men, and not her responsibility at all, it came as a relief and seemed obvious. For the first time in her life, she felt a part of a sisterhood she had hither-to only heard about. This event was only her third meeting with W.A.S.P., but Clammy had already made a big impression on her. It was Clammy that had appealed to the side of Sarah that felt let down by men. It was Clammy that made her see how men always ruined things, treated her badly, and never did what she wanted without her having to explain it to them. And it was Clammy that suggested she carry mace and never be afraid to use it on a man, just in case he was a pervert. Clammy seemed to understand the problem, and she was not afraid to voice it. That made her wonderful in Sarah's eyes. Clammy was an empowered woman, and Sarah wanted to be more like Clammy. Except for the slightly mannish parts, and the fact Sarah also wanted a boyfriend.

Angela had been to one meeting and saw through the bullshit immediately. She didn't mention this to Sarah, who clearly thought the sun shone out of Clammy's ass. Angela thought Clammy was definitely a sociopath and quite possibly a psychopath. Angela had taken one look around the room at her first W.A.S.P. meeting and realised she was attending what looked like an audition for a local roller-derby team. Then, when she heard them speak, she realised they were out for blood and had some serious daddy issues. But Angela had gone because Sarah was there, and she didn't want to lose Sarah as a friend, so she stuck it out. Now, having Chris in tow might help take the pressure off a bit. Though he seemed blissfully unaware of what he was walking into, she hoped his obvious gayness would save him if W.A.S.P. saw him as a threat.

It was an overcast Saturday as they arrived, though there

was no expectation of rain. Everyone was gathered in a public car park near the industrial estate in Deptford. Clammy was standing on a small podium preparing to address the group. She had a megaphone in one hand and looked out over the faces, clearly basking in the experience. Many had billboards or banners, and the small crowd already amounted to a hundred or more protesters. Still more people were arriving thanks to the messages sent out on social media encouraging others to join the fifteenth wave of feminism and its stance against porn. Angela noticed several men had now shown up, and she breathed a sigh of relief not have to defend Chris against the feminists. She knew they would have turned their wrath on her more than they would on him had she tried to defend him. Clammy soon announced the intentions for the day. They would make the short walk to the Pussy Production studios, where they would stage a picket outside the front, and heckle anyone coming in, or going out.

"She said nothing about keeping it peaceful. Aren't they supposed to do that?" mused Angela, as Clammy finished raising the rabble.

"Of course it's going to be peaceful. It's women, silly," replied Sarah, tutting at Angela's obvious ignorance. Angela looked at Chris, who shrugged and rolled his eyes knowingly. She was starting to like him.

Angela wasn't sure how she felt about porn. She only knew that she hadn't seen enough of it to judge it fairly. She would have liked to, but didn't know where to get any. Angela's fantasies had more hugging and eating going on than sex, though they always involved being naked and tied up. But that was mostly to stop the men from getting away rather than for any lewd business. She felt the naked part or the tying up might qualify as porn, but wasn't sure.

The march began, and as they walked, Angela wondered about her fantasies, while those around her shouted.

"PORN KILLS LOVE, FIGHT FOR LOVE!"

"STOP THE PORN, STOP THE RAPE!"

Chris couldn't care less what the feminists thought about porn. He loved it and was just super excited to be getting the chance to see Randy Andy in the flesh. He kept grabbing Angela and thanking her for inviting him along. Sarah soon noticed this and wondered why he was being so touchy-feely with her safe friend. It made little sense, and it was threatening to ruin her day. Chris had not once cast an eye on her butt, or glanced at her new yoga pants that especially accented the vagina. She already knew her tits were too small to get male attention, because the only men to comment on them had been derogatory exes. Working out thirty times a week on her legs and ass, rarely eating, and spending a lot of money on jogging pants that were wedged up her butt crack, had finally turned those tables. Now men stared at her all the time. But not Chris. What was wrong with him? What more did a girl have to do to get noticed?

Bloody men, she thought, *he must be gay*.

But the doubt still crept in, and she wondered if getting breast implants might be the next step.

As the group of over three hundred protesters rounded the corner to the industrial estate, a van parked nearby contacted Vauxhaull HQ to let them know there was trouble brewing. As usual, they were told to monitor the situation, film it, but not under any circumstances to act. If things got nasty, they were to drive away, or as a last resort, abandon the van and run. After receiving the news, Sir Michael contacted the Commissioner to ask why there was an unauthorised protest occurring in Deptford that was, at that moment, headed towards their person of interest.

"Nothing came through to us. No request has been put in for it," replied the Commissioner, as surprised as Sir Michael to be hearing about it. "I'll get a car up there now and find out what is going on," he added.

"Just don't send the riot squad," replied Sir Michael. "We don't want our chap going off and the press thinking the police caused it. He's a loose cannon and armed to the teeth with god knows what. Tell your boys to stay well back and let's pray we don't have an escalating problem. You really have no idea who is behind it?"

"None yet," replied the Commissioner, already on the other phone trying to get hold of someone to find out.

"Well, whoever the hell is behind the march needs to be contained, so let's find out who they are so we can get some damage control in place. Keep me posted."

Sir Michael put the phone down, concerned that the press would be over it before he was. How the hell was he going to contain the fall-out if Hazelhot unleashed an industrial-sized tazering event on the public? He wondered what other god forsaken contraptions he had stashed away in his lair, delivered to him via the dark-web.

Hazelhot was watching the arrival of the protesters from his office window. He was the only one in the office. When he saw who was at the head of the pack, he smiled, clapped his hands together, and then left to make sure the *Tazer Shockwave Barrier* was fully charged and armed. Once the device was ready, he checked that the front door was unlocked in case anyone wanted to try for an entry. He then went back to the office and pulled his chair up to the window so he could watch the crowd as it gathered. Grabbing the phone, he called Stott to let him know they had a feminist protest outside their offices.

"Oh dear god, that's all we need," said Stott after he had been informed of the situation. "How will that effect this afternoon's shoot?" he asked.

"No idea, depends if they get violent or when they plan to disperse, I suppose. But I recognise the bitch from the ward who had no qualms about tazering me, so I imagine it won't remain peaceful."

Hazelhot already had plans to make sure it wouldn't.

"One moment," said Stott, and he put his hand over the receiver while he consulted Hoots.

Hazelhot was annoyed that Stott now constantly referred to his guard dog and not to him in matters of company decision making. It was why he was so adamant in his plans to eject Stott, if he could only figure out a way to do it without incurring the wrath of Hoots. He swung the phone receiver around in the air as he watched out the window at the woman who had zapped his nether regions. An erection developed in his trousers. Her propensity for violence was attractive. He wondered if there was a way he could separate her from the herd and show her some of his own. As he considered ways to achieve it, Stott's voice crackled over the phone. Hazelhot let the over-fed stoat hang for a little while longer, then lifted it to his ear.

"Mm, hmm," he said.

"Bloody hell Hazelhot, are we having a conversation or not?"

"Mm, hmm."

"I think we should call off today's shoot. Reschedule for tomorrow. It's a cost, but better than risking our team getting hurt. Do you agree?" Stott asked.

Stott had learnt to confirm every decision verbally with Hazelhot on any matter, even though he bypassed him completely when making it.

"Mm, hmm."

"I'll take that as a yes. I'll call Rigby and get him to cancel everyone. Are you okay to stay there and man the fort, or should we get you some re-enforcements?" asked Stott.

Though he felt certain that the only people who should be concerned for their safety were the ones outside Pussy Productions at that moment.

"All good this end," Hazelhot confirmed, which made Stott feel even more nervous about what might occur, but Hazelhot was best left to his own devices and with any luck he might get himself arrested.

"Okay," replied Stott. "Can you please try not to kill anyone on the premises?" he added.

But he was talking to the air as the receiver made its way back to the handset.

Hazelhot stood up and pulled a set of high-power binoculars from a desk drawer. The crowd was only a hundred feet away, but he wanted a really close look at his target.

Clammy was chanting with the others and waving a fist at the offices. She was feeling disappointed. It looked like they had chosen the wrong day to show up. Her inquiries had led her to believe that Saturday was a shoot day, but so far, not a soul had arrived. She could make out someone in an office window, but that was it, and the car park was mostly empty. There was no security on the main doors either, and she wondered why. Surely a porn warehouse needed guarding. She kept chanting as she considered the situation. It would be a boring day if no one showed up for them to shout at. Secretly she'd been hoping for it to turn into a riot, and that was the main reason she had lied to the rest of W.A.S.P. about putting in the request for a protest to the council. She would deal with the consequences of not informing them later. Play the victim, cry in court. It usually worked. Meanwhile, in the rucksack that currently lay at her feet was a tazer, a kosh, and a set of knuckledusters she had picked up on a trip to France. But all this required porn people to use them on, and so far, there were none.

After an hour, the crowd were losing their angry edge, and some protesters broke out thermos flasks and sandwiches and sat on the path and on the grass outside the studios. A food van soon arrived that served coffee, then a Taco truck, and finally an ice cream truck, which completely stopped the protest for forty minutes while everyone queued for sweet refreshments.

Hazelhot stood back from the window, waiting for the right moment to reveal himself to the woman he had been studying like a hawk. He was hoping for explosive results the moment she figured out who he was. Though he had been covered in bandages at the hospital, he felt certain she would recognise him. From the way she guarded the rucksack at her feet, he suspected there was weaponry within, which excited him all the more. For now, he stayed in the shadows, like a lurking python, biding its time and waiting for opportunity to strike.

Sir Michael had received word from the Commissioner that the protest had been organised by a feminist group going by the name of W.A.S.P. Their head was one Clammy Frawd, who was the same woman who had broken into the hospital and tazered their person of interest. This connection concerned the Commissioner, but Sir Michael then relaxed. Feminists were of far less concern than agents of higher powers, and would allow for a nicely tailored story for the press if the time came that he needed one. The only risk now was that the woman might cause Hazelhot to react violently in response to seeing her. From the illegally monitored phone lines of the various Pussy Production staff, Sir Michael already knew that Stott and Hazelhot had agreed to cancel the day's shoot. But Sir Michael knew better than to let the Commissioner know that he already knew a lot of what he was hearing, instead he allowed the Commissioner to feel like he was being useful. Since most of the information gathered by MI6 was achieved outside of the law, it was simply good politics to appear to be uninformed, until informed, by the less informed.

"Are the press at the site yet?" asked Sir Michael, also knowing full well that they were not.

"We're keeping them out at the moment. We have a small, but present force monitoring roads in and out, but are keeping a distance. Some food vans we permitted through, which seems to have helped pacify the crowd. The crowd is a manageable size so far, but if you want us to go in and disperse them, we can," replied the Commissioner.

"Hold off for now. It sounds contained and peaceful enough, so let's try to keep it that way. Hopefully, they'll get bored and disperse by themselves before long. We have heard through other sources that the studio cancelled the planned shoot, so with any luck we won't have any antagonised femmes finding an excuse to react further."

Sir Michael paused and tapped his chin twice as he thought about something.

"On second thoughts, maybe let the press through. They will only make it about the boys in blue otherwise, and then accuse you of militant handling of minorities. I don't think our man is going to react openly if he sees the press outside. After all, he is trying to lie low. So unless you can think of a good reason not to, I suggest we let them in."

"I agree," replied the Commissioner, feeling a little better about himself to have been asked his opinion by MI6.

The day continued with relatively little action and there was a distinct loss of gusto in the crowd without any porn people to harass. By early afternoon, many had left, including the press who had been and gone after seeing there was nothing worth writing about. This left the die-hard W.A.S.P. crew who knew better than to leave before the leader of their loving, nurturing, and supportive sisterhood said they could.

Sarah had also wanted to stay. She was eager to suck up to Clammy who had so far been ignoring her, unaware that this was one of her tactics. Clammy liked to test a potential member's response for the subservience required to become a member. Chris was happy to hang around forever if there was the slightest chance of seeing Randy Andy, so he didn't complain. And Since Sarah and Chris were showing no sign of wanting to leave, this meant that Angela was once again trapped in other people's dramas, since it was that or spending the day alone.

Hazelhot continued to lurk in the shadows. It was 3 pm when the moment he had been waiting for finally presented itself. The W.A.S.P. crew had given up chanting, and even Clammy no longer urged them to keep at it. Before she called an end to the day's events, and frustrated by its failure, she decided to check out the premises and see if there was a way in. Picking a moment when no one was looking, she picked up her bag, and then wandered around to the back of the warehouse alone.

Hazelhot, who had not taken his eyes off her the entire time, and as soon as she headed toward the building he walked over to his computer, moving the mouse to wake it up. He switched views between the CCTV monitors as he observed Clammy prowl around the side and to the back of the premises. He had ensured the front was the only point of access, though now he wished he had left a door open back there. Pussy Productions was currently one of the most secure and well defended strongholds in England. There was no way for Clammy to get in without help.

Clammy tried the fire exits and any entrance points she could find, but to no avail. Completing a full circuit of the studios, she finally appeared at the front again. Just as she was about to head back to where the remaining protesters were gathered she paused, then turning, she walked towards the front door. Hazelhot froze like a crouching cat, a bead of sweat growing on his brow in excitement and tension as he waited, his finger hovering over a trigger. If only she would check it, she would realise it was wide open and she could stroll right in. Clammy peered in through the glass of the main entrance. She leaned against the outer door just enough that it moved, but not enough to realise it was open.

Then, turning to look up at the building, she walked towards the window where she had briefly glimpsed the only person seen on the premises that day. When she got to the window, the overcast light obscured whatever lay within. Clammy cupped her hands up to the glass and lent against it to peer inside. She saw a man standing in a strangely erect posture, his arms straight down by his sides, and staring straight at her. Her body froze, not just at the sight of his disturbing smile, but because there was something familiar about him. His face grimaced as he stood there motionless, beaming at her, waiting as he was for the moment to land. A slight motion of the hands that had been vertical at his sides now drew her to look as they pointed toward his mid-section. And then she saw it. *That* penis. Something about it was unmistakable. It bobbed, semi-erect and goading her, taunting at her, daring her to try for it.

The change that occurred in Clammy was immediate and startling. She backed away from the window like a bull, her rucksack coming off her back, as she fumbled inside it without once taking her eyes away from the glass. A moment later, she leapt forward and began violently punching the knuckleduster into the window. The rage that drove her was a hunger desperate to get at the creature and its appendage on the other side, that now stood behind the window and laughed at her as it wallowed. He'd long since had all the glass replaced with impenetrable bullet-proof material. Hazelhot roared like a demon and began to masturbate, revelling in her impotence. The rage that consumed Clammy on seeing him spanking it made her stop punching the re-enforced glass, and instead she began to smash herself into the window.

By the time W.A.S.P. and the others got to Clammy, she had a broken hand, and blood was streaming from her head and nose and covered her face and clothes. Three of the women held her to stop her from rushing at the glass again. Others now staring inside to figure out what had caused her to lose her mind, but could see nothing other than a man sat at a desk. He shrugged his shoulders and raised his arms to imply he didn't know what was going on, either. Clammy stopped, and gave up fighting the urge to keep going, but she was gone inside, now babbling about *"wanking cocks"* and *"the electrocuted penis of that dirty goddamn motherfucker"*. Her eyes glazed over as her spent rage mixed with her developing concussion. All the women agreed they had never seen her lose her cool like that before. Something was definitely wrong with Clammy.

And so ended the largest W.A.S.P. protest to date as the organisers went to the hospital to take care of their leader. Meanwhile, back on the premises of Pussy Productions, Hazelhot wiped tissues across the top of his trousers, and laughed.

Angela, Sarah and Chris went home, and though Clammy Frawd recovered from her physical injuries, mentally and emotionally, the doctors were concerned. Her brief sashay into physical violence having to be put on hold as she took an extended holiday in a mental asylum.

Going Rambo In Deptford

For the next few weeks, MI6 and several agents at the Pentagon monitoring global Internet activity observed an up-tick in purchases of weapons, ammunition, and torture devices from the dark web. This correlated with a spike in delivery vans seen arriving at Pussy Productions. Large wooden crates were offloaded from the back of trucks, deliveries coming from far-flung lands labelled as "machine parts" which were then deposited into the warehouse. Customs had noted they were all for a *Mr Zingbang*, but it was Hazelhot who signed off for them on site, then taking them to the storage area, where he'd recently had new locks and a security door fitted.

Stott was being updated one afternoon at the hotel where he was still holed up. Hoots was present, as he always was. They were hearing the long list of the Earl of Cavendish's most recent expenses, which were becoming far too extravagant and needed reining in. Rigby was expressing his frustration.

"It's one thing charging European hotels and sundries to the business, but to be blatantly putting '*Hookers and Cocaine*' down, I really don't think there is a tax kick-back for that in the British system, not legitimately at least. It's making it very difficult to keep it all above board," he said.

"Tell him to disguise his disgusting habits with something more official, and if he says he can't, assure him that Hoots will be happy to see that he does," replied Sir Stott.

Stott was in a bib and tucking into a large turkey sandwich with all the trimmings. He was watching the stock market news on a television as he listened to Rigby.

"And the last item," began Rigby.

Stott braced, knowing who it would likely involve. Rigby continued.

"Hazelhot has been receiving numerous deliveries which are now locked in a storeroom. He won't let anyone in it, and just growls if you go near. Really, he actually growls. He has changed the door and the locks to the area, and it looks more like the entrance to a safe house or bunker than a store cupboard. He's also now taken to dressing like a Vietnam soldier and behaving as if readying for combat. I am really rather concerned it is creating a tension in the other staff members, and everyone is worried about what is in those boxes. They arrive for a *Mr Zingbang*, coming from third-world countries, and are mostly unmarked. It is all very suspicious, and I am surprised we haven't had a visit from Customs and Excise yet."

Hoots paused half way through peeling an orange with a military knife. His large shoulders bounced as a chuckle came from him, and he shook his head.

"What do you think that bloody homicidal maniac is up to now?" Stott asked, turning him.

"Prepping," replied Hoots.

"Say what?" said Stott. "Prepping for what? On second

thoughts, don't tell me. The man is a world class lunatic, I can guess. Any suggestion on how best to deal with it?"

"For now, I say just let him," replied Hoots. "It's keeping him occupied, which means he is leaving you alone. He hasn't tried a stunt like the attempted takeover since the gang incident. But with suspicious boxes of 'machine parts' getting through without a problem, that confirms government involvement. That van parked outside is there to monitor *him*, I expect. Incidentally, I drew a blank with my contacts, which means whoever it is, they are working in the shadows, and that suggests government, probably MI6. It would make sense after the Essex incident. Hazelhot is probably their top person of interest. Customs knows damn well what comes into the country. He probably has Interpol, MI6, *and* the Pentagon watching those offices right now."

Hoots finished his orange and looked up before adding,

"But this is going to attract all the attention towards *him*, not you, sir. Ultimately, if something goes down, that is exactly what you want. So, my suggestion would be to leave Hazelhot to incriminate himself, and we all do our best to stay out of the way until he achieves it."

Stott nodded. "I agree," he said.

When Rigby returned to Pussy Productions later that evening, Hazelhot was sitting at this desk completing more online purchases with a credit card. Rigby stood beside his desk, waiting for him to finish.

"Did you tell them what I told you to?" asked Hazelhot.

"I did," replied Rigby, looking at the name on the credit card Hazelhot was using. "Who *is* Mr Zingbang, or should I not ask?" he asked.

"I don't suppose you have ever had a need for a false

identity, have you, Rigby?" asked Hazelhot as he finished the order.

"No, I haven't," replied Rigby.

"It's an old trick. You get a copy of a birth certificate from public records for a child that died not long after being born, and around the same year you were born. And then you simply assume their identity."

"It can't be that easy?"

"Actually, it is. You get a library card first, then build up an existence until you are convincing enough to open a bank account. After that, you can borrow money. Small amounts at first, building up a good credit rating until you can get bigger loans and pay them all back. Grow it as large as you want after that until one day... POOF!" Hazelhot made a sudden movement startling Rigby. "You cash it all in and disappear."

Hazelhot turned back to his computer screen and hit the send button.

"Or, in my case, buy everything you need on the dark web to deal with what is coming at you."

"What's coming at you?" asked Rigby.

But Hazelhot didn't reply. He stood up and stared at Rigby.

Hazelhot was dressed in combat gear with the arms of his military green t-shirt turned up at the shoulder. Adjusting his red headband, he puffed on his cigar and then blew it in Rigby's face, who coughed.

"So, what did the over-fed stoat have to say? And what did that jar-head Hoots suggest?"

"They said to let you carry on. They figure it will mean you are more likely to attract all the flack if it's the government monitoring us. Hoots is now convinced it's MI6, but said his contacts have drawn a blank."

"I think he's right," replied Hazelhot. "Though I can't figure out why they are waiting. Letting me buy up an arsenal of weaponry without moving on me? Very odd. Customs should have been here a long time ago. So that is the question, Rigby. Why are they waiting?"

Hazelhot considered this as he looked out of the window at the white van that was still parked at the entrance to the industrial estate. He puffed on his cigar again and raised himself up and down on his toes several times as he contemplated it. His hands clasped behind his back, he watched on calmly.

"Can I ask why you are being so casual about this? I thought you said we were being monitored, so why are we having these conversations here?" asked Rigby.

Hazelhot continued to look out of the window, but his left arm pointed up to the corner of the room. Rigby looked up and saw a device that looked like a small satellite dish he hadn't noticed before.

"That blocks scanners, and I have a few other things stopping any devices from penetrating the building," said Hazelhot. "It's perfectly safe to talk in here. In fact, you are standing in one of the most secure locations in Britain right now, Rigby. Frankly, the powers out there *should* be impressed."

Sir Michael was tapping a pen nervously on a table as he waited for the room to settle. He was present with the same high-ranking officials that had sat in on the meeting after the Essex blast.

"He is stockpiling, gentlemen," he announced as the last of them took a seat. "We also have the Pentagon and Interpol asking us what the hell an unknown terrorist sleeper-cell is doing in Deptford and what our plans are to contain it. As of this moment, I have no answer to give them. He has contacted no one outside of the country, but is clearly preparing for something big. We have no idea what. We *could* take him in, but he is highly unlikely to give us very much at all. His past form rules out torture, since he is likely to enjoy it. The latest psychological profile on him, you have in printouts before you. I'll give you a moment to get acquainted with it, if you aren't already. In short, we have every reason to be extremely concerned."

There was a rustling of paper and murmurs around the room as they studied the content of the handouts. Sir Michael gave them a moment before continuing.

"This a *Jason bloody Bourne* and we need to contain him. So, I've gathered us here to discuss the next step. With the US and Europe pressuring us to act, it is time for us to make a decision. Do we take him out and risk losing the chance to get a sniff of those who put him in our midst, or leave him there and risk him going Rambo in Deptford at any moment? As you can see from the list of his recent acquisitions, things could get extremely ugly, pretty damn quick. Either way, gentlemen, it's decision time."

For the next hour, they mused over tactics, war manoeuvres, siege methods, and past strategies that had worked, as well as those that had not. Finally, they came to a mutually agreed decision on how best to proceed.

It was essential they contain any damage and loss of life to the Deptford industrial estate, but any loss of life within that boundary was acceptable. Everyone working or directly associated with Pussy Productions was to be considered collateral-damage and expendable in order to keep the situation contained. Counter Terrorism Command would be prepped and put on standby and sent to the site to help achieve exactly that - ready to go in *"fangs-out"* with maximum force at a moment's notice. The PM would be notified by Sir Michael immediately after the meeting, but he said he already had full authority to, *"Do whatever must be done to get this nipped in the bud."* He then shared with the room the other comment from the PM to the effect of, *"The Pentagon has a set of pliers and a blowtorch on my balls as we speak"*. Finally, there was the matter of who they could use as a scapegoat to pin everything on in the event of things not going to plan. Sir Michael then saying that he had that well covered.

"Now *that* is all decided," he said. "Let's not take up any more of your valuable time, gentlemen. I thank you all for coming. To Queen and Country!"

Everyone stood up and echoed the words before departing. As the last of them left the office, Sir Michael pressed the intercom and spoke to his P.A.

"Set up a meet with Southern Goose for tomorrow morning, the usual place. Thank you."

Sir Michael had been left with no choice. It was time for Inspector Stump to be embroiled, garnished, and fattened up, ready to be presented as the lamb fit for slaughter if things went badly, which Sir Michael now felt certain they would.

They met at the usual place. Sir Michael arrived, feeling pensive. He did so hate setting people up, especially a friend. He'd always had a soft spot for Roger Stump. They had been childhood chums, though their paths had separated because they came from different sides of the street. Sir Michael was the posh end of it; born as he was into large detached houses, multiple cars, security gates, nannies, chauffeurs, fox hunting, and polo tournaments. He'd gone to Dragon School, followed by Eton, then on to Cambridge with a scholarship, until climbing the ranks to reach Government Intelligence after a brief spell in the Armed Forces.

Roger Stump had lived in the nearby council estate and gone to a local comprehensive school. He left education at sixteen to join the Metropolitan Police from a recruitment drive he'd seen in Peckham High Street. The two men had met as young boys, no older than ten, at a creek in a local park in the summer and instantly bonded, unaware of the class differences between them. They'd spent the rest of that summer chasing frogs and collecting newts together. They'd stayed in touch and grown up as firm friends, and it was only as life took over that they separated to become the remarkably different people they now were. But beneath it all, they were as close as friends could be. Unfortunately, when national security became threatened, that was not enough.

"Oh, for the simple days of our youth," mused Sir Michael as they sat together on the bench and looked out over the Thames.

Stump nodded. He'd always felt awkward discussing emotions, especially ones that meant something to him, but he felt the same way. They sat for a while in a nostalgic reverie. There were no words required between men whose friendship existed without the need for emotional indulgences. They both knew where they stood and how they felt. Finally, Sir Michael breathed a reluctant sigh and set the ball rolling.

"Our man has been stock-piling, but still hasn't contacted his sources. How are you positioned if we needed to push for a result?" he asked.

"I thought this might happen, so I took the liberty of preparing *Operation Force It In*. It's ready to go. Just say the word," replied Stump.

He then picked up a Tesco carry bag that was between his legs and placed it on the bench. Sir Michael checked no one was coming before picking it up and pulling out the contents to flick through an A4 dossier. He scanned the pages briefly, then put it into his briefcase.

"You have my full authorisation to set it in motion. I'll green light any activity from this point on. Consider your path clear for all of it. But we're in the final stages now, and all records of activities and authorisations are going to be scrubbed as soon as they are made. There will be nothing that traces back to us, Roger. Do you understand your position here?" asked Sir Michael.

Knowing he was cutting his friend adrift, he felt a gulp of emotion rise in his throat. Disguising it with a cough and a movement of his gloved hand, he soon returned to his more composed stature.

"I understand," replied Stump, who continued to stare out over the water.

Sir Michael then outlined the situation.

"CTC are being prepped to take up a position on the industrial estate. We're going to lock it down with a *shoot to kill* policy until the snake is in the bag. I'll let them know to allow you through, but for god's sake, keep your phone on you at all times. That way, our GPS boys can know it is you on the site. A mistake will get you killed just for being in that zone, and not a soul will hear about it. Hmm?"

Sir Michael paused to make sure Stump understood before continuing.

"It gets tricky from here on in, Roger. We can't be seen to have contact again, and I have to disassociate myself from this operation completely after our chat. We won't talk again, and possibly for a very long time, old boy. The Pentagon has eyes on us now, and Interpol, too. Some things are beyond even our reach to control. So from now on, *Southern Goose* is going to be alone on the wing. For God's sake, make sure you clear things up on your end so that no one can join the dots. Complete your operation, destroy all evidence of misbehaviour, and do what you can to get the hell out from under this entire bloody mess when it's done. You are a good friend, Roger, but this is going to fall hard, and when it does, there is nothing I can do to help you."

Sir Michael paused again, and a sigh came from him.

"We've had had a good journey together, my friend. You have been loyal to Britain and the right people know that, but until all this all dies down and is forgotten, you are on your own out there. Sacrifices must be made. Our burden, never to be known, is the price we must pay for Queen and Country to remain safe. I think we both knew it would come to this one day. Our connection was written in our fates, so to speak."

He pulled a small sealed document from his briefcase and pushed it along the bench towards Stump.

"This has an authorisation code. Any action you need to take while your operation is underway, give it to the police or officials to bypass their authority. While it is live, MI6 will confirm and sanction any act through me, but remember what that means - all bridges burn after this event as if they never existed. We intend to bury anything and everything, and everyone along with it. I mean that literally. No one will know who allowed this, Roger, and no one will admit to anything when the awkward questions get asked later. Do what needs to be done. And for Christ's sake, stay safe. When it all comes crumbling down, don't be standing under it. This may be for Queen and Country, old boy, but we will show no mercy, you understand?"

He looked again at his friend, knowing there was every chance that he would be forced to deny all connections to him before long. From the look of *Operation Force It In*, along with the recent behavioural traits being exhibited by Stump, there was a juggernaut full of things likely to go wrong. *Operation Force It In* looked like a recipe for absolute chaos. Unfortunately, that was exactly what MI6 now needed to take the heat off them in these final stages. They needed fall-guys. Stump had the capability, and now the authority, to flush out Hazelhot, and when it was done, they would bury him for his service. They had no choice. Stump and Hazelhot were two forces in directly opposed motion. He was perfectly positioned for the task. And though that was the saddest thing - *ours not to question why, ours just to do or die.* In the end, all that mattered was that Queen and Country survived. There were no rules in *that* game, and they both knew it. Sacrifices must be made. It was their job, if not their destiny, but it was no longer their choice.

"For Queen and Country," replied Stump.

Stump knew exactly what was being asked of him, but as a result, for a brief time, he was going to be *above* the law because of it. *Operation Force It In* gave him true power, and he intended to employ it with one singular goal and purpose in mind - fuck Queen and Country, he planned to use it to save *himself*. He breathed in to control his unconscious reaction to the excitement he was feeling - and hiding - from Sir Michael. As he did so, he heard the echo of her calling to him, *"Señor Stoooooomp."*

Sir Michael stood up and turned to his friend. Their eyes met, and a sense of deeper understanding was there between them. A brotherly love. Two men who were bound together by the fates, yet would only ever be thought of as evil men by the people who did not know the full extent of their sacrifice for the greater good. Only *they* would ever know, and maybe that was enough. The moment had arrived.

As Sir Michael left their final meeting, Stump felt fear mix with his excitement. He stood up to leave, but only managed a few steps before dropping to his knees on a nearby patch of grass, then falling headfirst into a flowerbed, he disappeared into a catatonic vision.

From his white horse he saw her, his sweet *señorita*, so close as she was now, they were almost touching. He could smell the jasmine of her perfume. As back down on earth, he shook violently in ecstatic abandon as he let go to the vision. For the first time in a very long time, he had entered it with a feeling of hope. Victory was now so close he could almost taste it.

Operation Force It In

Hazelhot stood watching the latest events unfold out of the window of Pussy Productions when Lucy came in to the office. Her eyes caught what he'd absent-mindedly left open on his computer screen. Hazelhot knew she was looking at it, but didn't turn around. He was getting used to her presence, and it didn't have the same impact it once had. An awkward silence hung in the air as Lucy took it in.

"I was never interested in women," said Hazelhot. "What I enjoy is considered, by most, to be beyond normal human acceptance. I was probably born like it, though I'm sure the wars played a part."

He'd been avoiding her for weeks, but in this moment of opening up to her, he was also explaining to her why. Lucy held no judgement. Though it had caught her off guard to see such debased acts of heinous sexual deviance, it also didn't surprise her. Until that moment she hadn't known the precise nature of Hazelhot's kinks, but now she did. She had seen enough in her line of work not to be easily shocked, still it was confronting. Before she could reply, Hazelhot changed the subject.

"Does it seem odd to you that the men moving a new business into the property over the road are all built like soldiers?" he asked, noticing more vans arriving to offload more men than equipment.

Lucy moved over to the window. It was an excuse for an opportunity to get nearer to him. She didn't think he was born like it. Nothing she had just witnessed on that screen was enjoyed by someone "born like it". He could be fixed. She felt certain of it. It just needed the right woman to love him. A strong woman, an understanding woman, a woman like Lucy. She smelt the pheromones coming off him. Possibly a little stronger than was necessary, but in his current Vietnam phase, he hadn't washed for days. She swooned, not just from the body odour, but from finally being permitted in close to the man she had obsessed over for months. She meant to have him. Nothing was going to stop her. Not even those acts she had just witnessed on the screen. She lent in a little closer. Hazelhot lifted his arm, and for a moment she thought he was going to put it around her, but he put a mobile phone to his ear and pressed a speed-dial number. When a South African accent answered, Hazelhot spoke.

"You better come here and bring that fat badger with you. We have a major problem developing," he said, then put the phone down before waiting for a reply.

At the hotel, Hoots turned towards Stott.

"This is it, sir," he said.

Hoots had finally received word from one of his contacts that MI6 *were* behind events, and the lives of everyone at Pussy Productions were now in danger. This had changed the game plan, and after some discussion with well-trained peers still active in the services, Hoots decided they were going to be safer *behind* Hazelhot than they would be out in the open. It was risky, but they had no choice. They were all of them about to become targets for government agents. Stott hated the idea, but Hoots said they were sitting ducks where they were and would not last the week.

"If Interpol and the Pentagon are also involved, there is nowhere to run," replied Hoots.

"I don't like it," replied Stott. "We are for Queen and Country, Hoots. They should know what side we are on. Hazelhot is the maniac here, not us."

"You own a porn company, sir. They won't care to hear it, and we already know what the public thinks. We'll be collateral damage and part of the cleanup. It's standard practice. Happens all the time. We'll be lucky to get out of this in one piece at all, but running right now? We won't stand a chance. Our options have become extremely limited."

"Surely we can make it abroad? I find it hard to believe this is our only option. I mean, it's Hazelhot, for Christ's sake! He's guaranteed to get us all killed. The madman *wants* to die. It's his thing. Dressing like a Vietnam vet? What more signs do we need to know he has gone completely off the rails?"

"Normally I would agree with you, sir, but circumstance dictates a lack of choice at this stage. He has the firepower to fend them off long enough that we might establish a rapport with the people involved and bargain our release. If we stay here any longer, they'll take us out. I have it on good authority that whatever it is they are planning is about to be unleashed."

Hoots had good contacts, and a plan was already formed in his mind, not all of which he thought necessary to share with Stott.

"Trust me, sir. My job is to keep you safe, and I will give my life to achieve it. But sometimes we have to head into the jaws of the dragon in order to escape it."

"I just don't like it, Hoots, but my god man, without you by my side, I wouldn't have survived this far. I trust you absolutely. If you say it's our only option, then we must do what we must. Deptford it is, then."

Hoots gathered their things, and they left the hotel.

"Sergeant, on me!" barked Inspector Stump as he marched boldly into Peckham Police Station. Then he walked into his office and shut the door behind them.

"Operation *Force It In*. It's in full effect as of this moment. How quickly can we gather the team to strike?"

The Sergeant was trying to take it all in. He'd barely finished a recently fetched croissant from a local bakery.

"Um…I can get on to it now. Probably have some of them ready by tonight or tomorrow morning, depends what they are all involved with at this moment," he replied.

"Okay, action it and keep me posted. As soon as the team is ready, I want to hear about it. We are against the clock on this one now, Sergeant. I expect good co-ordination and rapid response. We have a green light for a limited window of time only. Drop everything else and make it clear to everyone that this comes from the top. The very top. Right? Any authorisation required, I'll have it arranged. Just let me know. Now, I want to look again at the information we have on all the targets, to be sure we have this tightly wrapped. Let's get started. Well, what are you waiting for? Go, go, go!"

The Sergeant hurried out. Stump sat down to consider his next moves, but most of all, his exit strategy. While doing so, he unconsciously played with the slip of paper in his pocket that held the power for him to do anything he wanted at that moment and get away with it. Shutting his eyes, he breathed in. He needed to get it all dead right. He could afford no mistakes from here on in. So long as Hazelhot was holed up in Pussy Productions and alive, he had the power to use the code, but how long that would last, he didn't know. Timing was paramount.

The Sergeant arrived back with a pile of papers and dropped them onto Stump's desk.

"This is everything I've got on the firms, as requested, sir," he said.

Stump went through the papers and had the Sergeant send someone out to get coffee and more croissant for them both.

The Sergeant soon received word that most of the requested team members could drop what they were doing to engage in the operation. By the time he got this information, the Inspector had sectioned the gang dossiers individually out across his desk and he explained the plan.

"So, we have a task force of ten men not including ourselves. We'll hit each of these over the next few days. By the look of it, all of them will have movement of illegal goods going on during this period, assuming that they follow their usual routines. Are you confident of all the information provided here, Sergeant?" asked Stump, wondering if it really could be as easy as it looked at that moment.

"As accurate as was possible to get, sir. We have been tracking them for a while, and they really don't deviate from their schedules much. The only question is *what* they will have. It's been virtually impossible to be certain what they are dealing in. But given these are mafia level, it probably won't be legal goods, and we should be able to get an airtight case with most of them."

Stump didn't enlighten the Sergeant to the fact that their operation had nothing to do with the legal system, and that none of the gangs would see the inside of a courtroom. No air-tight case would be necessary.

"Very good, then Sergeant," he said. "Then here are the times and chosen targets. I have circled the ones I would like you to action in red. Confirm the men can be ready for those dates and times and if they can, then our first will be tonight at twenty-one hundred hours in North London. We'll meet for final prepping here at the station, get everyone in room six at nineteen-hundred hours. Is that clear?"

"Crystal clear, sir!" replied the Sergeant, excited to be seeing some action finally.

Later that evening, two police cars and a large black van left Peckham Police Station and headed for a location just north of Kentish Town. They arrived at exactly 8:55 pm and parked near to the first premises on Stump's list. Two police officers set to work blocking off the road, and the rest of the men, clothed in black, wearing bullet-proof vests and helmets, got out of the van and ran low, following the line of the wall towards their intended target. When they reached the doors, one man counted down silently with a hand signal to the others. A fourth man then rushed up with an Enforcer, smashing it into the door and it caved in on the first hit. The rest, armed with semi-automatic carbine machine guns, stormed into the premises, shouting their presence as they went.

Inspector Stump and the Sergeant waited a little way down the road, both armed and wearing bullet-proof vests, for the signal that it was clear for them to go in. Five minutes and fourteen seconds later, Inspector Stump and the Sergeant entered the premises.

"Are ya off ya fookin head, son?" said an Irishman, as he

tried to look up at Stump from beneath the jackboot of an officer who was currently confirming his cuffs were in place. It was the same man Stump had met with in the pub a few weeks previously. Stump didn't reply as he looked around the office and head-quarters of the *Gig Father.*

"So, is he here?" he asked, idly looking through paperwork on a desk and spotting a pile of money that was partially stuffed into a counting machine.

"I don't know wot yoos tink yoos ah doin..." replied the man, but Stump motioned to the officer, who pressed down with his boot.

"JESUS MARY MOTHER OF GOD!" the Irishman shouted.

The officer eased up.

"No, he is nat fockin heer." he then exclaimed, getting the message.

But Stump didn't care, he was happy with what was there. Pulling open a desk drawer, he smiled to see a set of hard-back cashier books. He took them out and flicked through them quickly. After that, he had every room searched for drugs and guns, but all they found was more cash. Stump took his sergeant to the side.

"Take these boys down to the local nick and book them in there. I'll go with the evidence back to Peckham. Call me if you run into any problems, but you have the authorisation code I gave you and the number for them to contact if they have an issue with taking these crooks in. Don't be afraid to use it."

"Er...yes sir. One question, sir. Why are we putting them in the local nick, but taking the evidence to Peckham?"

"That's two questions, Sergeant, but I will answer both. We don't have the cell space for the entire operation in Peckham, and the local stations can hold them much better.

That authorisation code will see to that. And the evidence, well, we need to accumulate it all in one place for it to be accountable, and that place will be Peckham nick until higher powers are ready to move it elsewhere. That is my arrangement with the higher-ups."

Stump was going to leave it there, then thought it best to push the point home.

"You can't just trust the entire police force with a load of uncounted cash, drugs, and guns," he said. "See the problem, Sergeant? It's a temptation. We've been trusted to see this operation through by the highest level of authority, and I don't intend to have some low rank scally-wags stealing cream off the top. Now, if all that meets your approval and is okay with you, I think we should get on, don't you?"

"Of course, sir. Sorry sir, stupid of me not to see the obvious. I just wanted to be clear that I had understood," replied the Sergeant.

"Of course. Clarity is important in an operation of this nature, Sergeant, so commendable that you are asking. This may seem unorthodox, but this is not your usual street bobby stuff. Things work slightly differently in the upper stratospheres, Sergeant. So, are we good?"

"We're good, sir," replied the Sergeant.

"Right then. I'll take our car back. You can ride with the others, but make sure you oversee them getting signed-in properly and then head home. Good work, Sergeant, and thank the lads for me, won't you? I'll see you all tomorrow morning. It's the same room for the brief. 11 am. Good night."

The Inspector had the money bagged and tagged, then took it with the account ledgers to the car and put them in the boot. After that, he drove home. Back at his flat - a small council estate affair - he opened the evidence bags and removed a large amount of the cash, sealing the remainder in fresh bags and re-labelling the contents. When done, he put the stolen cash and the account ledgers into a large, recently purchased safe that stood in his front room. He then took the remaining evidence on to Peckham nick and signed it into a storage area setup specifically for the operation. Returning home after that, he went via an off licence and bought himself a cheap bottle of red wine. Pouring himself a glass, he put some classical music on the stereo, took off his work clothes, and then whistled as he sashayed about the room in his socks and well-worn boxers.

The money he'd lifted amounted to nearly ten thousand pounds in twenty-pound notes and appeared to be genuine. After a while dancing with himself, he sat down on the sofa and put the wine down so he could have a good look at the account ledgers. As he did so, he laughed.

"Oh, you bloody villain," he said as he read through them. "Strong arming your way to the top of the music business. I've got you by the balls, you rotten bastard."

Stump had seen enough to know he now had power to wield with the information in front of him, and he snapped the book shut, then got back up to dance again to a rousing section of the music. He was happy with his haul, and it made up for the losses incurred by the demise of Basher's mob. He was also safe from any comebacks from the man known as *the Gig Father*. But Stump was just getting started.

The next morning, the team met at Peckham Police Station, and Stump congratulated them on a successful first sting. They were noticeably excited to be in on some real police action, and feelings were running high. Much of their time was spent preparing for events that never transpired, so to be seeing the list of strikes planned for that week, it was a dream come true for the officers involved. Stump knew they would be eager, and he made the most of it by outlining the details of the rest of the operation and what he had planned for them. He made it clear that a little extra violence would not concern him if they felt the need to administer it. It was top level villains they were dealing with, after all.

At 2 pm that afternoon, the team entered through the back of a restaurant in Islington owned by the Italian mafia. Once inside, the exits were sealed off, and they stormed the flat above. The haul this time was even bigger. They found counterfeit money, as well as real money, and some paintings wrapped in brown paper Stump noticed leaning against a wall. The reaction from one of the Italians when Stump went to move them was enough for him to take them in as evidence, too. He had initially thought it was rubbish, but clearly, they had some value. Once the place had been searched to his satisfaction, Stump told the Sergeant to take those arrested to the local nick, while he would take the haul to Peckham and the lock-up there.

Back at his flat, Stump took around twenty thousand in the counterfeit money and another fifty thousand in real money, and put them in his safe. He then removed the brown paper from one of the paintings, and placed it on his kitchen draining board, then sat at the table to look at it. He couldn't see why the Italian had reacted, but then he was no art expert. Standing up, he grabbed the picture, then walked into his living room and swapped it out for one that hung on a wall. Once done, he stood back again to look at it.

"A bit moody," he said.

Stump then wrapped his own picture back up in the brown paper. It was of a horse and barge, and he recalled buying it at Peckham market for five quid when he'd first moved in. After that, he gathered up the remaining money, along with the second painting that was still in its wrappings, and the newly replaced picture, and then headed to Peckham with it all.

The next day, the team hit the Triads in Chinatown. This time, they met some resistance and shots were fired when someone threw a kitchen chopper and a glazed duck. But the standoff lasted for only a few rounds, and once the mobsters realised it was the police, they surrendered. The haul was eight blocks of heroin and some computer code on printed sheets that Stump glanced at, but could not make head nor tail of. He grabbed one of the Triads who was being led out in cuffs.

"What's your name?" asked Stump.

"Nakamoto Satoshi," replied the man.

"And what the fuck is this?" he asked, holding up the sheet of code to the man's face.

"Grocery receipt," replied the man.

But Stump knew it was more important. He could tell when a man was lying, and the way the man's pupils dilated belied his true feelings. It had value. He stared at the man briefly, then waved the officer to take him away.

"Grocery receipt, my ass," he said, looking at it again.

Back at his flat, Stump struggled with a decision, but in the end kept two blocks of the heroin which he put into his safe, and everything else, including the mystery receipt, he signed into the store.

That evening, the team stopped a van in Manor House containing members of the Greek mafia, and though there was a fair amount of money, it was mostly bags of cocaine.

Lots of cocaine, in fact. Stump had expected to see more cocaine in the other raids, and had been surprised to find there was none. The Greek raid made up for the lack of it elsewhere, and when he got home, he put all fifteen kilos of uncut cocaine into his broom cupboard, and then took out fifteen similarly packed kilo bags filled with baby laxative and talcum powder that he'd been keeping ready for a swap. He took those, and the small amount of cash from the raid, on to the station.

When they hit the Black Bloods of Brixton, Stump was excited to be going back into the same room where they had tried to intimidate him previously. None were hiding behind masks this time, and he got to meet Mr Octopus in the flesh. They had timed the raid to perfection. The room was full of street ready meth, ice, crack, and a host of assorted weaponry, mostly guns and machetes. He had them open up their storeroom, and in there he found a bizarre-looking device.

"What the fuck is that?" asked Stump.

"That is one brutal fucking weapon, blud," said the boss, and all the boys murmured in agreement as they recalled their personal experiences with a machine just like it.

Stump was disappointed not to be taking anything for himself from the haul, but there was nothing worth taking. He didn't want to hold more drugs, and the weapon would not fit into his car. So they had to call in a van to collect the guns and drug haul to fit everything in.

The last group on the list, they hit the next day. It was the Russian mafia who were running the clip joints in Soho, but it was a bitter disappointment. Stump had hoped for more money, but all they got was a van full of noisy and unmanageable Eastern European prostitutes. He wasn't about to put them up in his flat or take them to Peckham nick, so he had the Sergeant arrest everyone and take them to the local Police Station.

But Stump had now run into a problem. He was nowhere near the amount of money he had hoped to gather from the raids. He could shift the fifteen keys of cocaine, which might then push it over a couple of million in total value, but he'd figured he needed at least five million, and preferably more, to get away clean and start over with a new identity abroad. As he drove back home from the Soho raid, he knew he still had time before MI6 revoked his powers. So, he needed to conjure up one more big hit, a huge one, but who and where?

He was miles away in thought when he slammed on the brakes, nearly hitting a man at a zebra crossing. An old fella dressed in a large black hat and ring curls in his hair smacked his arms down angrily on the bonnet of Stump's car that had stopped just millimetres from his leg. He shook a fist at Stump and shouted obtuse foreign swear words. Soon, several similarly dressed men had appeared out of nowhere and gathered around his car to bang on it. But Stump wasn't listening or paying attention. He pulled his phone from his pocket, calling the Sergeant, then putting a finger in his ear to block out the din.

"We have one more job. It wasn't on the list," he shouted into the phone. "Gather the team together, tomorrow 11 am, same room. Be ready to go. I'll explain it all then."

They hit a jewellery store in Hatton Gardens at exactly 1 pm and several orthodox Jews were cuffed and on the floor ten minutes later. Stump knew it was going to cause trouble, but he had no choice. He had to push the limits now, and it was a matter of survival for him to do so. There were small velvet bags containing diamonds of various sizes, and he bagged them all up, ignoring the objections coming from the men lying on the floor. Once done, he took the haul to Peckham Station, but not before he'd swapped out most of the diamonds for diamante glass broken out of trinkets bought the night before in a night market at Elephant and Castle.

The haul in lock-up at Peckham was creating a lot of interest, given the contraband building up there. But Stump had finally hit his value target, and it was time to action the next part of the operation. He had to act fast, as things were certain to get heated after the Jewish arrests. But given no news had yet come from events building up at Pussy Productions, he still had a window of time to work in. But he was against the clock and MI6 would not like what he had just done. He needed to act before they could revoke his authorisation code.

Stump left Peckham Station after depositing the last of the official haul and went home. There, he transferred everything from the safe and cupboards to his car and drove it to a garage that he rented under a false name outside of Peckham and was paid up for the next five decades. Being careful to make sure no one saw him, he emptied everything into the garage and an even larger safe that was in there. The only thing he didn't take from his flat was the picture that still hung on his wall, only because he had forgotten about it.

Once he locked the garage door, he breathed a sigh of relief. Everything had come together. All that was left of *Operation Force It In* was to send the confiscated goods from Peckham nick to Deptford under MI6 authorisation, then let the gangs know where it could be found. After that, he could inform Sir Michael, or rather notify MI6 through the coded message, that his work was complete. There was, of course, a high chance MI6 would lose their minds over the Jewish incident and want answers, so come looking for him before any of that could take place. But with the stash safely locked away, he could now relax a little. He'd deal with whatever they threw at him, safe in the assurance that when the time came, he had enough money to make his escape. He had enough dodgy contacts to convert the contraband to cash, and after that, he could disappear forever and go in search of his *señorita*. All he had to do now was to survive whatever happened next.

Release The Hounds

Sir Michael received a call in his office and put it onto loud speaker.

"Another code request from *Operation Force It In* needing authorisation, sir," said his P.A. on the other end.

"What this time?" asked Sir Michael, wondering when Stump's foray into chaos was going to finish.

So far, the complaints to MI6 had been coming from police stations where mobsters now languished in cells, as overpaid lawyers fought to get them released. In many ways, Stump was cleaning up where the local constabulary had failed to. His antics had been mild compared to his Hyde Park soiree, where he'd pitted the entire Muslim and Christian community into a field battle against him. Sir Michael had even wondered if Stump had lost his touch. Until that moment.

"Some Jewish gentlemen from a Hatton Garden jewellers are being signed into Holborn station charged with handling stolen diamonds. Their lawyers are already at the station and a crowd of orthodox Jews are gathering outside. They claim their diamonds have been stolen by the police during a raid. The Commissioner is a friend of some of the lawyers, sir, and I rather think he might be on his way over here."

"Ah," replied Sir Michael, now wondering why he had been foolish enough to think Stump would not achieve dizzy new heights. "Then, somewhat predictably, our man has finally gone off reservation. Okay. Give it the green light all the same and please show the Commissioner into my office when he arrives. Assuming he stops long enough in his rage to acknowledge the fine job that you are doing. Thank you."

"Sorry sir, did you say to *green light* the arrests?" asked the voice on the other end, surprised and wanting to be certain she had not misheard.

"If it is *Operation Force It In,* green light it. Thank you."

Sir Michael ended the call and lent back in his chair, wondering what Stump was up to and how he might best explain the situation to the Commissioner. He was still sat like it when the Commissioner stormed into his office twenty minutes later. The first thing Sir Michael noticed was the shade of red that the Commissioner was exhibiting. The next thing he noticed was how loud he could be when enraged.

"ARE YOU OUT OF YOUR FUCKING MIND!?" shouted the Commissioner, completely forgetting himself.

Sir Michael did not move an inch nor bat an eyelid, and continued to peer at him calmly. It was enough to make the Commissioner remember himself, and he mumbled an apology then began pacing back and forth across the room. Sir Michael was used to dealing with moments of extreme distress in members of the upper echelons. He also knew how challenging it was to deal with Hebrew lawyers. Sir Michael quietly listened as the Commissioner paced and explained the situation.

"A task force, supposedly commissioned, or at the very

least under the authority of MI6, has just raided a perfectly legal jewellery store in Hatton Gardens. Their lawyers are regular dinner guests of mine, for Christ's sake, and are baying for blood. What the hell is going on, Michael?"

The Commissioner looked like he might have a cardiac arrest if he kept pacing.

"Sit, please, Commissioner," offered Sir Michael, pointing to a chair.

"I'll stand right here. Thanks all the same. Please explain to me what the fuck is going on before I hand in my resignation. The press are going to crucify us over this. It is bloody unfair. You didn't give me any warning about this."

Sir Michael considered the veiled threat and whether the Commissioner was the type to blab to the press if he lost his job over the incident. It took him less than a second to decide that he was not a threat of any consequence. If necessary MI6 could easily muster a male prostitute willing to tell a court that he was regularly paid by the Commissioner to fulfil bizarre homo-erotic fantasies that the press would then lap up. The Commissioner was not a threat, but he was more useful placated, if possible. Sir Michael began an attempt to placate.

"*Operation Force It In,*" he said, and paused for effect. "It's been a matter of National Security, but given the circumstances, what you didn't need to know has now become something you *do* need to know. Please, sit, Commissioner, and allow me to enlighten you on what has been happening. We will need your help on this one. Though your timing is excellent because I have to take a conference call in..." Sir Michael checked his watch, "Right about now, in fact. Maybe things will become a little clearer after that. Can I get you some tea while we wait?"

"What conference call, and why should that matter one jot?" asked the Commissioner, reluctant to give up his position for fear he might appear an easy push-over. Though his anger was already waning and turning to excitement at the prospect of being privy to an MI6 conference call.

"Tea first, then all will become clear, I am certain," said Sir Michael, and he held up a finger to pause the Commissioner as he tapped on the phone and spoke to his PA on the other end.

"Can we get a pot of Earl Grey in here, please?" he said. "Lemon, no sugar, if I recall correctly," he said, looking at the Commissioner with a raised brow.

"Er… yes, that's correct," replied the Commissioner, surprised to find that Sir Michael cared enough about him to know how he took his tea. It was, of course, just one of Sir Michaels' tricks used to disarm a man when required.

"Did you get that?" asked Sir Michael of his PA.

"Yes sir, and just to let you know, the conference call is ready and they are waiting for you."

"Marvellous," replied Sir Michael. "Please do patch us in."

There were a few clicks and a beep and then a longer tone which signalled Sir Michael's phone was now on the call.

"Gentlemen, are you there?" he asked, and waved again for the Commissioner to sit down, which he finally did.

A guttural American voice broke through.

"Hi there, Michael. With you here, from the US of A."

A French accent then followed.

"Bonjour Michael, ca va?"

"Good day, gentlemen. Just letting you know we have the Police Commissioner for the Metropolitan area here with us this morning. There has been an unfortunate escalation of events on the operational side of things. Not the target, but it's now involved the Metropolitan Police in other ways, so we are currently in damage-control, and understandably he has questions. He is, as yet, not up to speed on the whole saga, so this will be an enlightening moment for him. Commissioner, allow me to introduce you to General Bingham of Special Intelligence at the Pentagon, and the mighty Pierre Farrah from Interpol."

Sir Michael smiled at the Commissioner, who was looking visibly impressed and at a loss for words. For a moment, he almost forgot he had the entire London Jewish community chomping at his heels. Sir Michael continued,

"Let me start by asking, has anyone gathered any new information about the terrorist sleeper-cell currently holed up in Deptford?"

No one had any new information.

"Okay, well to bring everyone up to speed here, as you know the British PM authorised us to action an undercover operation titled *Operation Force It In*. The main purpose of which is to trigger the terrorist sleeper-cell that is currently dug in on an industrial estate in Deptford and has over the last few weeks been stock-piling some rather serious artillery there. Crucially, he has not yet contacted whoever put him there. On this, we are still in the dark. We discussed previously our operational man on the ground, one Inspector Stump, who has been in place for a number of years working in the Police force undercover. He has now been actioned specifically for this operation."

Sir Michael looked at the Commissioner as a spoke to be certain he understood this to be the man behind the current Jewish problem. The Commissioner nodded, then Sir Michael continued.

"The main purpose of which - and bear with me now,

Commissioner - was to steal items of value from several large gangs in the Metropolitan area. The intended effect being to then quietly point the blame towards this terror cell, and let the gangs do what we, legally speaking, cannot. This was going splendidly right up until our chap targeted some Jewish friends in Hatton Gardens, which is what brings the Commissioner to be here today."

The Commissioner, now reminded of the Jewish contingent, was turning the same shade of red he had been on arrival. Sir Michael held up a hand to suggest he let him finish his explanation before unleashing. The Commissioner restrained himself, but his grip tightened on the arms of his chair.

"Our dear Commissioner is, understandably, deeply disturbed by this turn of events. He is now in the firing line of some of the most artful and aggressive Hebrew lawyers in the Northern Hemisphere. And though MI6 were not informed of this part of the operation by our man in the field, given the sensitivity and difficulty of the task facing Inspector Stump, we have absolute trust in him to know what he is doing. Of course, we will make immediate enquiries and do whatever we must to contain and placate our Hebrew friends, but with other circumstances now facing us, this is actually the least of our troubles. I think you'll agree, gentleman."

There was the sound of confirmation from both men on the other end of the line.

"Which brings me to the updated list of weaponry, which I am about to show to the Commissioner."

Sir Michael passed a dossier to the Commissioner with a breakdown of the capabilities of the weaponry purchased by Hazelhot. There was a long silence as the Commissioner read the list and finally uttered the words.

"Dear God in Heaven! How the hell did he get hold of this stuff?"

"You see our predicament," replied Sir Michael.

Everything changed in that moment. Sir Michael was now the person who the Commissioner would look to for rescue. Some items on the list were the stuff of nightmares, but knowing it was in the hands of a terrorist currently holed up in Deptford was unthinkable. Though Sir Michael was also rather good at navigating people to where he needed them to be. The Commissioner was nearly there.

"Don't worry Commissioner," he said. "You now know why we have been speaking with our friends at Interpol and the Pentagon, and why we have had to employ such unorthodox methods that have now so upset our more Orthodox friends. Take heart in the fact we have great minds on all sides of various ponds working on bringing it all to a safe and, hopefully, uneventful close. Unfortunately, we have had to engage an old but workable tactic: *Escalate, Contain,* and then *Terminate*. You join us today mid-process. I need not remind you that not a word of what is on that list, or what you hear today, can be spoken of outside of this room."

"I completely understand," replied the Commissioner, and his hand shook as he placed the dossier back on Sir Michael's desk. "I had no idea," he added.

"Quite," replied Sir Michael. "But now you do."

"Whatever you need from me, gentlemen, just say the word," said the Commissioner, realising he was going to be required to support whatever they needed to do next, however heinous it seemed, and regardless of who it might upset in Hatton Gardens, or elsewhere.

"Welcome to *our* world," said Sir Michael, and he raised his eyebrows once again in a gesture to the Commissioner regarding the sense of burden they all now carried. Something which the ever complaining public would, and could, never know of.

Sir Michael then quietly opened a desk drawer. Pulling out two glasses and a bottle of the finest Scotch, he poured it high, handing one glass to the Commissioner who shot it back while he stared straight ahead, still trying to comprehend how much worse things had got.

"I am now showing the Commissioner the list of contraband and the gangs it was gathered from," said Sir Michael, passing a second dossier across his desk toward the Commissioner.

After the commissioner read through it, he held his hand up to ask a question. Sir Michael bid him to ask away.

"Just so I am clear. You authorised this Inspector Stump chap to gather all this by performing raids across London, and you plan to now use it as bait to encourage these gangs to target this terrorist chap in Deptford?" The Commissioner was still coming to terms with the kind of manipulation tactics that would have him crucified for thinking about, let alone ordering done.

"Correct," said Sir Michael. "Completely illegal, but authorised from above, Commissioner. The very top," he added as he waved a hand in the air to suggest it was a deity that was ordering it. "I understand it to be quite the haul, including now, of course, our Jewish friend's diamonds."

"And members of these gangs are also being held across the Metropolitan area?" continued the Commissioner, joining it together piece by piece.

"Ah, the awkward part. Yes, they are, as we speak, dotted around stations under your command across the Metropolitan area, and without your knowledge. The rather impressive coercive force of the Jewish lawyers got your attention quicker than we expected. Our plan was to release all of them without charge before bothering you with the nuts and bolts of it. We are waiting now on Inspector Stump to give us the signal that he has completed his part of the operation, at which point we will send the gathered booty to Deptford and after that release the hounds, as it were."

"Is setting these gangs on the terrorist not likely to set him off and make him use all that stuff on the list?" asked the Commissioner feeling a little stupid for asking, but now concerned for his family and half of London if events took a turn.

"Of course, manoeuvres such as these can prove tricky," replied Sir Michael. "But years of experience, and the latest in computer whizz bang, can predict outcomes to a very high accuracy these days. Meticulous planning has been spent bringing us to this point. Normally, of course, you would not be privy to any of it, for the very reason that these decisions do seem somewhat risky to burden others with. But such is our task and why we exist, you understand? This is not new for us, in the same way it might be for you. This *is* us."

The Commissioner didn't understand. The entire plan sounded insane, but he didn't say that part out loud. Sir Michael read it in his facial movements all the same, and he needed the Commissioner properly placated, so he continued.

"*Escalation, Containment, Termination*," repeated Sir Michael, slowly, to let it sink in to the Commissioner. "Think of it as a controlled explosion, Commissioner. We have escalated the situation deliberately in order to manage it. We can't have some maniac choosing the time or place that those weapons get used. *Escalation* has been achieved, now it becomes about *Containment*. Whatever happens next will happen in Deptford, and not outside the Houses of Parliament or, god forbid, Buckingham Palace. Then finally, we will arrive at the *Termination* phase of this operation. Whatever is not achieved by the gangs on arrival at the industrial estate in search of their booty will be addressed by our CTC boys, who are currently in position on site awaiting our signal. After what we fully expect to be the equivalent of a modern day *shootout at the O.K. Corral,* snipers stationed in buildings nearby will be given permission to unleash. That specific order is simple - *let anyone in, but no-one gets out.*"

"Good god, it's going to be a massacre!" said the Commissioner, handing his glass back for a refill that went a little higher this time.

"Sadly true, but it's a numbers game, you see," continued Sir Michael. "Our job is to decide *not* how many to save, but *who* to sacrifice. Our singular aim is to reduce the final tally regarding members of the public. Such are the stakes at *our* table. This way it will be hoodlums and gangsters, and *not* innocent civilians, which of course is our prime concern and directive, as it must be yours, Commissioner."

He'd led the Commissioner to the point of no return. He now understood that there really was no alternative. But this led the Commissioner to his next worrying thought.

"When you put it like that, yes, of course, I completely understand. But presuming you will not be coming forward to the press after all this is over, what part will the police play in carrying the can?" asked the Commissioner, realising that he was likely to get all the blame when it was over.

"And right that you should ask," said Sir Michael. "Of course, we have considered the operational aftermath. To put it plainly, Inspector Stump is our lamb for to sacrifice. He knows this and has been prepared for it. As has often been the case at such times, *cometh the hour, cometh the man.* He put his hand up the moment we proposed it to our various agents in the field. He knows his survival chances are next to zero. We will, of course, work with you to prepare anything required to appease the public and the press when this is all over. We had thrown around some headline ideas - '*Old Skool British Bobby Sacrifices Himself For The Nation*', that kind of thing. Along with detailed explanations and maps showing the extent of the potential damage, had he not. We feel certain it will pale into insignificance in the light of what *could* happen to our fine capital if the terror cell and associated gangs are not engaged head-on. Is it a little clearer now, Commissioner?"

"Hmm," replied the Commissioner, at which point Sir Michael knew it was his career survival he was thinking of next. Sir Michael was prepared.

"We had also briefly discussed accolades for those involved in the operation. Though we obviously don't wish to jinx it at this stage, it is always important to acknowledge those superior commanders who show excellence, bravery, and due diligence in times of national, and international, importance. Those commendable souls willing to carry the burden of duty and stay the course."

The Commissioner straightened up in his chair, becoming more officious looking, and Sir Michael knew he had played his cards well. It was time to push the advantage home a little more overtly.

"This is likely to be a win-win for you, Commissioner, whichever way it falls. Of course, MI6 will quietly work behind the scenes to honour our side in this ghastly affair, but if it all goes south, we have Inspector Stump to pin it on, a man who volunteered for that very role. But of course, the PM will need someone to thank if we achieve a satisfactory result. We hoped you might step up when the time came for the boring task of receiving medals and knighthoods, and whatnot?"

Sir Michael stopped to give the Commissioner a moment take it in. He was watching for signs in his facial movement as he assessed how he might get nothing but royally fucked.

"…for Queen and Country," Sir Michael added, gently, to give it a final bit of top spin as it headed toward the wicket.

A few moments passed, and the silence in the room was deafening.

"You can count on me," said the Commissioner, finally.

Sir Michael smiled briefly, then took the opportunity to suggest he leave them to the boring task of "dotting the I's and crossing the T's".

The Commissioner agreed, then thanked everyone and apologised for interrupting their meeting. After a few moments of dithering, he finally left just as the Earl Grey tea was arriving. There was a moment of further dithering at the door while the Commissioner apologised to Sir Michaels P.A., and then he left.

The men on the call sat in silence for a moment until Sir Michael let them know he was alone.

"He bought that then?" asked the General.

"He bought it," replied Sir Michael.

"So, how are we really placed, Michael?" asked Pierre.

"Stump has gone off plan. Hitting the Jews has given him access to a lot of diamonds. I thought he might do something like this, but I have faith that he will complete the job. He'll likely be hoping that we lose track of him in the ensuing melee, and this will be part of his trying to fund an escape. He's correctly assessed he's expendable. But as long as he delivers the rest of the contraband to Deptford as planned, and then makes the call to the gangs, I don't think we need to worry further about whatever he is up to. He'll get the job done. The Commissioner will now field the fall-out from Hatton Gardens. In short, we can continue on with our plans without being too concerned about our rogue inspector. I'll revoke any authorisation on other stunts of this nature, but I think that will be the last from him. Look at it this way, gentlemen, we now have the wrath of the Israelites coming to the party. They will hit hard, and I think our inspector deliberately upped the ante, knowing it would improve our odds."

There was a brief pause on the other end of the line. The General spoke first.

"Well, goddamn Michael, you need to put it into perspective. You guys currently have zero public losses and zero public loss expectancy if this plays out, too. If it keeps to trajectory, regardless of this Stump fella going off reservation, that's one hell of a goddamn score sheet. Christ, we lost over three thousand and trillions of dollars just starting the whole terrorist angle back in nine eleven, and we have done little better since. You guys pull this off, and it's going to be used in strategy planning for future operations the world over. Let me tell you, this is a damn fine operation so far. Damn fine. We here at the Pentagon are pretty impressed. How about you guys over there in France, Pierre? Same story, I imagine."

"Absolutement, Generale," replied Pierre. "Public collateral damage is very difficult to contain. Really, all eyes are on you at this moment, Michael, and from our side too, as you English say, I think, *a damn fine job, what?*"

"You really are too kind, gentlemen, too kind," replied Sir Michael.

Deals Between Devils

Inspector Stump sat at his desk in Peckham Police Station knowing that everything, including his survival, rested on the final stages of *Operation Force It In*. He was thinking about how best to play it when the sergeant came in.

"Sir, the seized contraband is in crates and labelled as per your request. I still don't fully understand why we are making it for the attention of *Mr Zingbang*, or why it needs to appear as if it came from North Korea. This is all very odd, sir," said the Sergeant.

"Need I remind you we are working under conditions of national security, Sergeant? We have our orders, and that is all we need to know. I am as in the dark as you, if it is any consolation," he lied.

"Do you wish me to come with you, sir?" asked the Sergeant, trying to be helpful.

"That won't be necessary, Sergeant. I'm really just there to get a signature officiated and confirm that the target receives the contraband. Call me when it's on the truck and they are ready to leave."

"Yes, sir," replied the Sergeant, and he left to complete the task.

Stump breathed deeply and then went through his mental check-list one more time. He confirmed that his mobile phone was fully charged. The last thing he needed was to be shot by CTC snipers before he even delivered the goods. The industrial estate was now on lock down with a shoot to kill policy in place. Given no officials had yet showed at the station looking for him, he took it that Sir Michael had covered for him over what was likely one of the biggest diamond heists Britain had ever seen. Sir Michael would know full well what he was up to. The question on Stump's mind now was how far he would let him get, and there was every chance he'd order a bullet put in the back of his head after delivery. He only hoped that Sir Michael's friendship went as deep as he believed it did. He could not blame Sir Michael if he took him out as part of the cleanup. Duty trumped friendship in their game. It was par for the course, and one accepted it. At least CTC would make it quick, clean, and painless. But other than in terms of strategic planning of his next moves, these issues no longer concerned Stump. His trajectory was set. It was death or glory for him now, and too late to turn back.

The Sergeant appeared in the doorway again.

"They're ready for you, sir," he said.

Stump stood up. As he reached the door, he paused, looked around the office once, and then turned to the Sergeant and put a hand out to him.

"An excellent job, Sergeant, well done. Been a pleasure working with you. Thank the lads for me, won't you," he said, and not waiting for a reply, he left to find the truck.

The Sergeant watched him go.

"Well, that was weird," he said, before heading back to his

desk.

As the security truck carried Inspector Stump and two large crates towards Deptford, he thought about Sir Michael and their many years of friendship. Though they came from different sides of the street, Sir Michael had always felt like an older brother to him, and he hoped it would not play out like Cain and Abel. Rather than think about the consequences of his actions, he tried to focus on how he was going to handle what lay ahead. He shut his eyes and tried to find a meditative place to run through the scenario again.

As they reached the industrial estate, it was just getting dark and there were workers in the street leading up to the entrance. One of them spotted the truck and waved it to a stop. The man then went round to the driver's side and tapped on the window. The driver wound it down.

"Can't go through at the moment, sorry gents. We have a sewage main burst under the street, shit everywhere and a total health hazard. Where were you trying to get to?" asked the man.

The Inspector lent forward so the man could get a better look at him in the darkening light.

"I'm Detective Inspector Roger Stump. Authorisation code Five, Nine, Hector, Buffalo, Swamp-Rat," he said from the passenger seat. On hearing this, the man relaxed and gave a subtle salute.

"Very good, sir. We tracked your phone on the way in, but just needed to be sure. I'm Colonel Savage, CTC, in command on site here. Just give me a moment, would you, sir?"

The man then spoke into a hidden radio microphone in the lapel of his work clothes and waited for confirmation from the other end.

"Okay, we have a green light for you," he said upon receiving it. "To update you on the situation as we know it. We have eyes on the premises from the building opposite. We also have some sound, but it's been difficult to catch anything as he has scrambling devices in place. He's built a safe house in the back warehouse, which neither satellites nor high-tech scanners can penetrate. The scary stuff is in there. This guy knows what he is doing, but I am sure I don't need to remind you to exercise extreme caution."

"Of course, and thanks for the update," replied the Inspector.

"We are going to need the truck to leave as soon as delivery is made," said the Colonel. "And please park down the side of the warehouse, and not directly in front of the building, so our snipers can keep the sight-line clear."

The driver nodded.

"So, is there anything you need from us?" the Colonel asked Stump.

"Yes, actually there is," replied Stump. "There's been a last-minute change of plan, Colonel. He's likely to react once he sees what is in the crates, and I've been asked to attempt a negotiation. We know the risks, but it's our last chance at talking him down peacefully. I plan to get the driver and the truck out before he opens the crates, but if you can give me an hour to process a negotiation strategy, that would be ideal. I assume you won't be able to monitor conversation in the back of the warehouse, given what you said?" asked Stump, wanting to double-check the safest place to start his discussion with the target where he would not be over-heard.

"Er… we haven't had that authorised, sir. If you are on the premises, we cannot guarantee your safety at all. We are on a shoot-to-kill policy here as of a few hours ago," replied the Colonel, looking concerned.

"I'm aware of the risks, Colonel. Run it through to MI6 first, if you like. It's been authorised, I can give you the code for it," replied the Inspector, though in reality he had no idea how Sir Michael would respond. He was gambling on them still needing him to deliver the goods and notify the gangs.

"That won't be necessary sir, we have already been advised to give you anything you need. Will there be anything else, sir?"

"No, that will be all, thank you," replied Stump.

"One hour then. Good luck, sir," replied the Colonel.

"Thank you, Colonel, and to you and your lads. See you in an hour."

They drove into the industrial estate. Stump pulled a baseball hat from the glove compartment and then put on a jacket that had the delivery company logo emblazoned on it. He checked himself in the mirror and pulled the hat down a bit. He knew Hazelhot might recognise him from the hospital ward visit and wasn't sure what kind of response that might create. The truck pulled into the main driveway that lead to the rear of the warehouse. High power sensor lights came on along the side of the building as they did so. Coming to a halt, Inspector Stump jumped out and walked back towards the front doors of the premises, carrying a docket on a clipboard. He made sure his hands were visible enough that it wouldn't alarm anyone inside; he didn't want them thinking he was armed. His jacket was loosely open, as wasn't wearing a vest either, and he wanted to appear relaxed.

This was it. The key moment it had all been leading up to for him. He felt afraid but excited, his heart thumping, and he breathed in deeply as he reached the main doors, trying to calm himself. He pressed the buzzer and waited until the speaker crackled to life. Hazelhot's voice came from it.

"Who is it?"

"Delivery for Mr… *Zingbang*. Two crates. We've brought a forklift, so we can drop them straight down the back if you could open it up for us, sir. Need a sign-off first though, please. I have the docket here."

There was silence for a while, then Hazelhot spoke again.

"I wasn't expecting a delivery. Where is it from?" he asked.

Stump looked at the docket, moving it into the light coming from the entrance, and making a show for the camera that was there watching him.

"Er… *Doctor Wing Hong Woo Poo Sang Wong How…Chong, North Korea*. We can leave it outside, but it's going to be hard to shift without the lifts, and it looks like it might rain," he added, trying to sound as casual as possible but hoping Hazelhot would not refuse the delivery.

Once again, he was met with a long silence. The camera above him moved. Like a prying eye, it looked around the front area as if checking for more people. When it seemed finished with that, it homed in on Stump and he could see the lens focusing in and out, getting a good look at him. It was a high-tech contraption and nothing he'd seen before. A short while after it stopped moving, Hazelhot's voice came on the line again.

"Are you armed?" asked Hazelhot, but he had already x-rayed Stump and knew he wasn't.

"Excuse me?" replied Stump, staying in character.

"It's a simple enough question. Are you armed?"

"Um… no sir, we just deliver goods. We don't carry weapons, sir. This is England, not Lebanon," replied Stump, trying to think what the average driver might say.

He was then met with an even longer pause before the voice came on again.

"Who else is with you?"

"Just my driver. He's in the truck. Look, can we get on with it? We still have one more delivery tonight and the traffic's awful out there, which is why we're late. M25 at the A3 turn off was back to back when we came through."

"Okay, the door is going to buzz to let you in. Only *you* come in. You understand. No one else, or you'll regret it."

"Certainly, sir. I only need a signature and we can drop everything round the back and get out of your hair," replied Stump.

The door then buzzed and Stump entered through two sets of doors and into Pussy Productions reception area. Hazelhot was standing in the doorway a little further down the corridor, out of sight of any potential sniper action. The front doors would have stopped most calibre weapons, but he didn't want to take the risk. It was dimly lit, and Stump could only make out his silhouette, but could see that he had what looked like a British Army issue machine gun, and was casually pointing it at him from his hip.

"Hold it there, please. Open your jacket," said Hazelhot.

Stump did so without speaking, but as he let his jacket close again, he held his hand up to his lips. Hazelhot caught the move and stood observing him. Stump then further motioned as if making talking movements with his hand and pointed casually to his ear. Hazelhot understood, but continued staring at him for a time, weighing him up.

"Okay, come through," he finally said. "I'll show you where you can drop the crates."

Hazelhot then motioned Stump to walk to where he was.

Stump did so. Hazelhot then followed on behind him, prodding him once in the back with it to make sure he understood he wasn't trusted. They walked through the warehouse towards a secure door at the far end. When they got to it, Hazelhot used a key from around his neck to open it while keeping the gun levelled on Stump. He then motioned him into the storeroom before pulling the door shut behind them.

Hazelhot stepped to stand in front of Stump, the gun held at his belly. He stared at him for a moment, testing to see how he would react. Stump now saw the Vietnam clothing and caught his musky odour, and wondered if Hazelhot was sane, but he avoided reacting to the challenge. When he didn't respond to the test, Hazelhot pulled Stump's jacket down over his upper arms to make it difficult if he changed his mind. He then checked him thoroughly for weapons, ramming his hand into every crevice, more for his own amusement than a need to check. Stump braced against the urge to turn around and punch him. He had to allow the indignation, reminding himself it was a matter of survival. When Hazelhot had finished, he stepped back around to the front of Stump and re-lit his cigar while keeping a watchful eye on him from far enough away that he could react if Stump made a lunge. The gun remained at his hip, pointed casually toward Stump's genitals.

"We can talk in here," he said. "You're the cop from the hospital. What the fuck do you want?"

"Roger Stump, Detective Inspector at Peckham nick. I've been part of the operation since you took out Basher's lot. They are from my... *were*... from my manor. This site used to be under my jurisdiction while they strong-armed it..."

"I suggest you get to the point, unless you want a lead scrotum," said Hazelhot, not interested in hearing backstories.

"Right. Well, there *are* two crates addressed to Mr Zingbang on board the truck out there. But they're not from North Korea. They contain contraband taken from several London gangs by a squad I've been in charge of over the last week. All of that was authorised by MI6. At least they are supposed to contain contraband. I swapped most of the valuable goods out and have it all safely stashed away elsewhere. That is the bit they don't know about. Right now, CTC is outside with snipers, and they think I am in here to make a last attempt to negotiate with you on behalf of MI6. While MI6 thinks I am delivering the goods to you. Those goods are the bait to bring the biggest gangs in London down on your head. Which is happening whether you take delivery or not. And… well, it's a longer story, but they are planning to take me out when all this is over. You probably guessed they don't intend to let you leave, nor anyone associated with this business. To put it plainly, you are already dead. All of you. When the gangs arrive, they are expecting them to set you off. The gangs being here gives them a cover story for whatever shit you unleash in their attempt to take you *all* out. That gives them a nice story to tell the press. But… I have a plan that could get us all out of this situation. I don't particularly wish to be the fall-guy for MI6."

Hazelhot looked at him and blew a puff of smoke into the air.

"And I'm supposed to believe that crock of shit?" he said.

"I don't know. I really don't have a choice. Between you and MI6, I've become embroiled in this shit show. Whatever the fuck you think you were up to, all I know is you caused me a lot of problems."

"And what do *you* think I have been up to?" asked

Hazelhot.

"MI6 thinks you are a terrorist sleeper cell with plans to take out half of London. Judging from the look and smell of you - no offence, mate - but you strike me as just another nutter who watches too many Stephen Seagal movies and is off his medication."

Hazelhot laughed, but Stump didn't. He wasn't joking.

"Whatever you *are* up to, right now, without me," continued Stump. "You aren't getting out of here alive. None of you are."

"That's a pretty bold statement to be making," said Hazelhot.

"There's nowhere for you to run, man. Interpol and the Pentagon are working with MI6 on this, and the gangs are about to be let out and given directions where to find their stolen goods. I presume you saw the Hatton Gardens incident on the News, that was me, and there's been plenty of others. The stash is worth millions. You have some serious problems about to head this way."

Hazelhot continued to look at him but didn't reply. Stump was getting desperate and needed to convince him. Time was running out. He continued.

"I've asked CTC to give me an hour, but that really depends on you. If they don't see my driver leave, then the moment the first of those gangs arrive on this estate, it's over for everyone in here. I need the truck to drop the goods and leave. That was part of my agreement with CTC when we came in. We need to do that. It buys you time. The gangs are coming regardless of whether the goods are out there in the street or in here with you, and if one of you tries to drive it out, you are going to catch a sniper bullet in the skull," said Stump.

"This stinks like a setup. Probably a bomb on that truck. And what's stopping me from torturing you for the location of the diamonds and whatever else you have stashed away?" asked Hazelhot.

"You know I won't tell you that," replied Stump. "The only thing stopping you from killing me already is that bit of information."

Hazelhot lifted the gun and pointed it at Stump's forehead, then looked at him down the barrel. Stump braced, but held eye contact. He felt sweat dripping down his body, and it tickled his skin.

"Why the fuck would MI6 use a nobody dibble like you? It's a great story, but I really don't buy it," said Hazelhot, moving the gun down to point it at Stump's groin again.

"The fact I am expendable and caught with my hands in the till. They didn't give me much choice. But I also have an old acquaintance who is at the top of MI6. He's been parting the red sea for me like Moses, all the way through this operation, and keeping me updated. Though the diamond hit was my idea, not theirs. I've been navigating toward this meeting the entire time. It's my only way out. They know I'm a bent copper and Basher Bob is going to end my career when he talks. They have him under wraps, ready to deliver him to the press at the end of all this. So they have me over a barrel. My contact in MI6 has been using me as their man on the ground, and I'll be their other fall guy when it all ends in carnage. The bent copper angle. They'll blame me for the contraband haul. I've been doing their dirty work the entire time. They offered me a deal to risk my neck with the promise they'd not investigate me at the end. But it's MI6, isn't it? About as trustworthy as a two-headed snake. All they care about is not having chaos reign over London and some nutter loose with whatever psycho equipment you have in here. Hence my predicament, but also my opportunity. The stash I have tucked away is more than enough for us all to get away and disappear. It's got to be upwards of ten million, probably a lot more."

Hazelhot laughed, then pushed a button on an intercom and a South African accent answered.

"What do you make of that load of bollocks?" asked Hazelhot, and Stump realised their conversation had been monitored elsewhere.

"I'll make some enquiries, but it wouldn't surprise me," replied Hoots on the other end. "May as well take the delivery and check the crates. If they *are* booby-trapped, it's going to take the building out where it is, anyway. Get him to open them and see if he sweats. Then let's talk after that."

"Agreed," said Hazelhot.

He stepped over to Stump and pulled his jacket arms back up over his shoulders.

"I've got artillery in here you wouldn't believe, and you won't make it off this industrial estate if you try to run," said Hazelhot. "Bring the truck round the back and offload the crates, then it can leave, but *you* stay. And if anything seems out of line, I'll kill you and anyone in that truck. You understand me?"

"I understand," replied Stump. "But you don't need to worry. There's no tracking devices or explosives in the crates. I had them packed myself at Peckham."

"Well, let's go find that out," said Hazelhot.

They made their way back to reception, and Stump left to take the truck around the back of the warehouse and offload the crates. Once it was done, the crates stood in the middle of the warehouse as the truck left and the shutters closed. Hazelhot moved to the edge of the warehouse, keeping his gun trained on Stump, then gave him a nod to open the crates. Stump prised the lids off with a crowbar and then threw the crowbar away to the side. Hazelhot walked over to peer in, and soon after Hoots appeared in the warehouse. Hazelhot then went over to a box that had lights on and turned a dial up. Pink noise crackled from strange looking speakers raised up in the corners of the warehouse. After that, he nodded at Hoots to let him know he could now speak.

"His story holds up," said Hoots.

"That doesn't mean much," replied Hazelhot. "Watch him while I check the contents."

Hazelhot pulled a large knife from his back and cut into one of the cocaine satchels. He tasted it and then spat it out. After that, crushing some fake diamonds underfoot. The buzzer went off on an intercom by a wall, and Stott could be heard rasping into the other end unintelligibly. Hazelhot tutted and walked over to it.

"Step back from the speaker, you idiot," he said. "We can't make out a bloody word of what you are saying."

There was a pause in the crackling, then a couple of coughs, and Stott tried again.

"I just wanted to know what is taking so bloody long?" he asked.

"Just sit tight and keep your wig on, old man," said Hazelhot, who then ignored Stotts' further questioning and pushed a button, cutting him off mid-sentence as he liked to do. Hazelhot turned back to Stump and levelled his gun at him again.

"You've got five minutes to convince us you are not setting us up, and if you fail, I'm going to shoot you in the ball sack and leave you here to bleed to death."

Stump then detailed the situation in full. He told them how the whole thing had started, what he knew, how he had played it, and why. He explained that the only reason they were all currently still alive was because Interpol, the Pentagon, and MI6 needed to know who had put Hazelhot in place. When he finished, Hazelhot's expression hadn't changed, but Stump could see he was thinking.

"That all sounds like a typically colossal balls-up by MI6," said Hazelhot. "They got some of it right. But I've never been under orders of a terror cell, or had help in dispatching anyone. I deserve more credit than that. It's insulting, really."

Hoots shook his head, unsurprised to hear that Hazelhot's biggest concern was his own ego. Until that moment, neither Hoots nor Hazelhot had known the full extent of it, but their guesses had been close enough. What Stump had told them tallied with the info Hoots had, and it confirmed to them he was probably telling the truth. The three men stood silently, contemplating the ramifications of what lay before them. They were dead men walking, and they knew exactly what that meant. They'd be used to cover up the mess conjured into being by the powers that be once they discovered how wrong they had got it. Admittedly, Hazelhot was the cause of most of it, but at that moment, it didn't much matter. Anyone closely tied to Hazelhot was going to be killed by the government in the clean-up job. That was a given.

"We have no choice but to trust him," said Hoots.

"I don't like it," replied Hazelhot, "but I agree. There's no other way out of this."

Stump knew it was best not to say anything else, but to wait for them to make their decision.

"If you are fucking with us, I'll make you regret it," said Hazelhot.

"I got that bit," replied Stump.

A moment later, Hazelhot lowered his gun.

"Alright, I'll go with it. Welcome to Hell," he said.

A six-foot-six South African security expert, a Detective Inspector from Peckham, and an ex-Armed Forces psychopath looking like extra from *Apocalypse Now*, stood in a porn production warehouse in Deptford, discussing plans to make their escape. Meanwhile, outside, professionally trained killers and a handful of snipers, under the authority of MI6 and Her Majesty's government, waited for the command to open fire. One order stood between them and chaos. At that same moment, some way outside the stratosphere and circling the planet, multiple satellites monitored the industrial estate for movement and signs of life. There were not just American satellites. Some were Russian, some were Chinese, one was French, and one was North Korean. There was even one bleeping loudly, held together with superglue and duct tape, which belonged to a teenage hacker in Southern California. Further afield, in secure underground bunkers in countries across the globe, teams of military officials with breasts full of medals watched large screens and discussed potential scenarios, risks, and outcomes, as computers whirred and spat out statistical possibilities as information accumulated. Submarines with nuclear capability, aware of the co-ordinates of the industrial estate in Deptford, waited in readiness, just in case. Powers around the planet were at that moment poised, waiting for three men to make their next move. A computer deep in a bunker in China then spat out a calculation. A man looked at it and his face changed colour.

"Sir, you better look at this," he said in Mandarin to his

superior officer.

"What is it?"

"We fed the new AI every possible scenario, and this is the result."

The senior ranking officer put on his reading spectacles and looked at the piece of paper.

"60% chance of total world annihilation? This cannot be correct. Run it again," said the senior officer.

The man bowed and did as he was asked, but the result came out higher and he passed it to the senior officer with an even lower bow. The senior officer's face went a new shade of grey and he picked up a phone preparing to advise more senior people of the situation.

"Fuck it. Let's just go for it," said Hazelhot, as the three men finished considering all the possible ways they could get themselves out of their situation. "I don't see that we have a choice," he added.

Hoots confirmed with a nod, and Stump shrugged his shoulders. He'd not been part of the final decision making and was surprised he had got as far as he had. Hazelhot stepped over and pressed the intercom.

"Stott," he said into it. "How much do you know about art?"

Stott could be heard *umming* and *ahhing* on the other end, but before he launched into a long-winded explanation, Hazelhot shook his head and said, "Just meet us in the warehouse storeroom, you bumbling buffoon," he said, cutting Stott off again right after.

They gathered in the warehouse to stare at the piece of artwork, now removed from a crate and unwrapped. Hoots had placed it under a spotlight on some boxes near a wall.

Though Stump was clueless, Hazelhot had known it was of value the moment he saw it. Stott was nodding and spoke first.

"Ah yes, well. Were this the original, it would be the most wanted piece of stolen artwork on the planet. This is unmistakably *Vermeer's 'The Concert'*. Stolen around 1990. A priceless artefact. Priceless. Looks like an excellent copy, mind you. Meticulous to detail..."

He moved in to inspect it, then froze before turning to look at the others.

"Dear god, this is the original!" he said, looking at Inspector Stump. "What the hell is it doing here?"

Stump was now wondering about the picture that he had left on the wall in his flat.

"It was lifted in a raid on the Italian Mafia," he replied. "There was another one with it that had some guys in a boat bouncing around in a storm..."

Stott broke in, "Bloody hell man, that sounds like Rembrandt's painting of *Christ in the Storm on the Lake of Galilee*! That was stolen in the same robbery. You realise that between these two paintings, you are looking at an unfathomable fortune in stolen artwork. They would fetch absolute millions on the black market."

Stott was visibly excited and turned back to inspect the painting.

Stump looked at his watch.

"I better get going," he said. "So, are we good?" he added.

Hazelhot looked at Hoots, who nodded.

"Run me through it one more time, just so I know we are clear," replied Hazelhot.

"I'll leave here, and let them know you are open to negotiation," said Stump. "That should buy you some time while I get the keys to my lockup and finalise my part of the operation to launch the gangs this way, so MI6 don't get suspicious. In the meantime, Hoots is going to arrange the exit vehicles with his people. And if I am not back within two hours, you'll know something went wrong and action the escape plan, regardless. But it would help me if I could know what part of the coast you plan to leave from, in case I get delayed."

"Nah," said Hazelhot. "If we told you that, you could sell us out to save your own ass, so no can do. You just make sure you get back here in time."

Stump understood. Hazelhot was right. They all needed to keep hold of some leverage if they were to trust one another. Despite them having the painting - which was an oversight on Stump's part - Stump had enough value in contraband to fund everyone's escape for a long time, and Hoots had the connections and the resources to get abroad undetected. They were of value to each other for now, but it was a tentative connection. Deals between devils often were. Once Stump had left, Hazelhot spoke to Hoots.

"With that painting, we don't need him," he said.

"He's a connection back to MI6 if we need it later to sort things out," replied Hoots.

"That makes him a liability, not an asset," replied Hazelhot.

"And if we can't shift the painting?"

"Hmm," replied Hazelhot.

"Look, let's just get this underway now, and if he makes it back, we can decide after we see what's in his lock-up."

"I don't think you can trust him, he's a bent copper, but if you think that's the best approach, I don't have a problem with it for now," replied Hazelhot.

Hoots then went to make the arrangements for their extraction.

Allah Be Praised

Inspector Stump left Pussy Productions and gave a subtle thumbs-up to CTC across the road. News immediately travelled back to MI6 that the Inspector had left the building and appeared to be unharmed. The truck he arrived on had long since left, but Stump ordered a taxi, calling it from the Pussy Production office, knowing that CTC would set up an intercept. The car arrived and he could see a well-built man squeezed into the driver's seat. He approached the vehicle and got in the back, watching the driver nervously, uncertain whether MI6 were done with him now that the contraband was at its destination. The driver didn't speak as the car left the industrial estate and soon pulled up where Stump had previously spoken to the Colonel. He got out and was told to enter a worker's prefab hut that was beside the road. He felt his heart pounding as he opened the door, then breathed a sigh of relief. Inside was a mobile command post with various soldiers sat monitoring screens. After entering, a soldier handed a two-way radio to him. The Colonel was on the other end, talking from inside the industrial estate from where they were monitoring the warehouse. He asked

Stump how he was doing, then asked him how it went. Stump had half expected to be shot the moment he entered the hut, so he had to gather himself before replying.

"They took the crates and opened them, but they weren't surprised to hear the story," said Stump. "They knew you were out here and setup across the road. I've convinced them I'm their best bet to settle the situation down. They are expecting me to head to MI6 to set up negotiations. So they seem to be willing."

"Okay Inspector, thanks for the update. You don't think they are likely to make a run for it, or attempt to shoot their way out?"

"Definitely not at this stage. They're under the command of the primary target, but he's playing the long game. As long as no one moves on him, he won't react. That's my assessment. He wants to negotiate a deal, hence his allowing me to leave," replied Stump.

"Okay Inspector. My understanding is that you will unleash the main event this way after you get back to the station. Is that correct?" asked the Colonel.

"That is correct. We need to keep the pressure on the target, so we won't be cancelling that. I plan to inform the gangs at twenty-two hundred hours," said Stump as he checked his watch. "I expect you'll see them arrive an hour or two after that."

"Very good. Thank you again for updating us, Inspector. Good luck at MI6," replied the Colonel.

Stump handed the mike back to the soldier and then left in a genuine taxi, ordered while he had been talking to the Colonel. He returned to Peckham Police Station, where he saw the Sergeant.

"It's time to release the hounds, Sergeant. Can you please

call all the stations holding the various gangs, and have them put back into the wild without charge. Please do this at precisely twenty-two hundred hours, and not a moment before," he said.

"Yes sir. Is that it then, with the operation?" asked the Sergeant.

"It is, Sergeant. It's with MI6 from here on in. Again, good work Sergeant, I am sure praise will come from on high when all this is over."

A satisfied, and somewhat relieved, Inspector Stump left the station by a rear door and got in another taxi, asking it to stop near a telephone box on the outskirts of Peckham. Stump paid the driver for the fare, but asked him to wait while he made a couple of calls. The driver agreed and then settled into his seat and turned the radio up. Stump crossed the road and entered the phone box. He took a small notepad from his pocket and looked through the list of gangland bosses he had recently had the pleasure of targeting. He pulled out a pencil, readying to tick them off, then lifted the receiver and dialled the first number.

"*Si?*" said a gruff Italian voice on the other end.

Stump covered the receiver with his hand and spoke into it using a barely intelligible accent.

"The police raid was a setup. If you want to find your stolen goods, they are at..." Stump began.

A white transit van swerved across the road and screeched to a halt beside the telephone box. The side door flew open and several masked men jumped out. One opened the door of the telephone box as another stepped in and hit Stump over the head with a kosh, and he dropped to the ground like a rag doll. The other men lifted the unconscious Stump up, threw him into the van, then jumped in after him.

The side door of the van pulling shut as they tore off up the road. A moment later, a mobile phone flew out of the passenger side window and exploded on the road. The taxi driver was relaxed, slunk down in his car seat with his eyes shut, singing to Magic FM Seventies nostalgia as it blasted from his radio, and had missed the entire event.

Stump came round to a throbbing headache. He had a hessian bag over his head through which he could make out some light and some figures. He was lying on a hard stone floor and his body hurt. His hands were tied behind his back, making it even more uncomfortable, and cable-ties were cutting off the circulation in his wrists. There were five people dressed in black clothing sat around a circular table. They spoke in a mixed Arabic with London accents cutting through occasionally. He tried to ask for water, but his throat was dry and a husky sound came out. One man noticed he was awake and barked a command to another man, who left and returned a short time later with a bottle of water. He put it down beside Stump, then helped him up to a sitting position, and pulled the bag from his head.

Stump could see he was in a cellar. One light hung down over the round table where the men were sitting. All of them were wearing balaclavas, put on before the bag was removed from his head. The man who had helped him up now helped him drink from the bottle. The water tasted chlorinated, like London tap water. Stump assessed he was still in London, or at least near to it. He listened for traffic or other sounds outside, but the cellar was soundproofed by design or because it was below ground. There were some steps in a corner that led up, but he couldn't see where to. The men looked at him quietly, waiting for him to speak. He coughed to clear his throat after drinking enough.

"You fellas have made a big fucking mistake," he managed, but the men looked at one another and then laughed.

"There are no mistakes under Allah's will, brother," replied one man in such a way that Stump now knew he was the man in charge.

"What the fuck do you want?" asked Stump. "You realise you have kidnapped an officer of the Law?" he added.

The man pushed around some items on the table and then picked one up and read from it.

"Detective Inspector Roger Stump," he said. "Would that be the same Inspector Stump that arrested our Brothers of the Sharia Patrol for doing the holy work of Allah in Peckham High Street? And the same Inspector Stump that broke into our place of worship in Luton during a peaceful meeting of our Muslim brothers there? Yes, we know who you are. We have the right man."

"Then you're a bunch of fucking idiots, with no idea what you have just done," replied Stump, now more concerned about the situation that would be developing elsewhere in his absence. "I need to use a phone. I have to make some essential calls," he added.

The men looked at each other and then burst into laughter again.

"You are a funny guy," said the man.

"What time is it?" asked Stump, ignoring him.

"For you, it is time to become a servant of Islam. That is all that matters," he said, and the other men laughed again and nodded their approval.

"You stupid pricks," muttered Stump. "Oh, this is so fucked."

"Please, hit him," said the man, annoyed that he wasn't getting the fearful response he was used to when kidnapping infidels.

The man who had given Stump the water pulled up a sleeve and then punched him sideways across the face. Stump fell hard onto the floor and blood filled his mouth and throat. He spat out part of a tooth as he was pulled back into a sitting position.

"Maybe I haven't made the situation clear," said the man at the table. "Today you will become a Muslim. Nothing else should matter, it is a very honourable position to be in. You are a very lucky man."

Stump wasn't paying attention. He had noticed a watch on the arm of the man who had just hit him. Struggling to focus, he made out the time and date from the digital display. It was nearly midnight. So, the deadline had passed, and the gangs would have been released by the Sergeant, but without the information on where their stash was to be found. That was not good. He tried to think through the scenarios, but this wasn't something that he had accounted for.

"Who put you up to this?" asked Stump.

He was wondering if it was a setup by MI6 to keep him on ice until they decided what to do with him, or maybe just have him whacked by the fools he was currently in the basement with. Though given what they had said, it seemed unlikely.

The men looked at each other, a little confused, and the man at the table spoke again.

"This is Allah's will, none other. You should be grateful to him. You are to be saved. Allah be praised!"

All the other men shouted in unison, *"Al-hamdulillah!"*

"What a fucking shit show," replied Stump, spitting out another mouthful of blood.

"Do not blaspheme while we are giving honour to Allah!" said the man in a dramatised rage as he stood up menacingly.

But Stump wasn't paying attention to his theatrics. He was too busy trying to figure out what would be happening back at Pussy Productions. His head throbbed and his mouth felt broken. It was hard to think. The man moved in closer to tower over Stump, who was still more concerned by events outside the cellar than in them. Frustrated by his failure to be intimidating, the man turned again to the one holding the water.

"Please, hit him again," he said, waving a dismissive hand toward Stump.

The punch landed the same way, and Stump went sideways down onto the hard floor again.

"It is time to prepare him," said the man, after Stump had been brought back up to a sitting position.

They dressed Stump in a thawb and a keffiyah, and after that, the men stood back to admire their work. One of them whispered something to another, who laughed, and he left the cellar and returned a short time later with glue, scissors, and a toilet brush. Amidst bouts of laughing so hard that none of them could breathe, they eventually glued a square of black brush onto the chin of the Inspector. After that, they positioned him along one wall with a prayer mat placed in front of him, and they tried to teach him how to pray. Stump's constant refusal leading to the inevitable.

"Please, hit him again," said the main man, once again motioning toward Stump with a frustrated wave of his hand. The one tasked with the job of punching Stump obeyed.

They set up a video camera, some lights, and then filmed Stump, hoping to get enough they could cobble together something to make it appear he was doing as they had asked. Stump's lack of compliance meant they spent a lot of time recording each scene, but also a fair amount of time punching him in various places for not doing his part. All of which took their toll on the Inspector. After a take, the men would jump up and jostle for position behind the camera to see the resulting playback. Most were admiring themselves in the shot.

When they were done filming, Stump was left barely conscious and slumped forward with blood and drool falling from his mouth as it pooled in the lap of his once white thawb. He remained there, motionless, with his head hanging down. After the group confirmed they had the footage needed, the men were told to take the camera upstairs and edit it on the computer there. They did so, leaving only the main man in the cellar with Stump. He pushed a foot against Stump, who didn't respond, after which he turned on a small television on a shelf in the corner, and sat back down at the table to watch. The News came on. As he watched, he occasionally spoke to the semi-conscious Stump, who remained hunched forward.

"You are now a Muslim, my friend, and soon the world will see this. Another infidel serving the true faith," said the man. "Allah be praised!"

Upstairs, the men responded in unison, *"Al-hamdulillah!"*

Stump tried to mumble something, but the man couldn't make it out.

"What is that, my friend? Are you trying to say *'Allah be praised'*?"

Again, the men responded in unison in the distance, *"Al-*

hamdulillah!"

Stump made a noise, and the man, still unable to hear him, leaned in, putting his hand to his ear.

"Speak up, brother," he said.

"Turn... the fucking... volume... up," managed Stump, and he spat more blood onto his thawb, while his remaining good eye looked up at the television.

The man turned to look at the television and, seeing what was on it, did as Stump asked. A male reporter's voice came on.

"Riots have broken out across London as rival gangs take to the streets. As yet, we are unsure what has triggered this unexpected chain of events, but we are hearing similar reports from other boroughs throughout the capital. I can confirm London is in riot."

Gunfire broke out behind the reporter, and then a petrol bomb whistled through the air, hitting a police car and bursting into flames. From his crouching position with the camera still on him, the reporter listened to an ear-piece with one finger in his ear, clearly disturbed by events, but wildly excited, too. He continued.

"We are just getting reports of similar events in Soho, Islington, Brixton, and ...yes... we are going now to Hatton Gardens, where Jessica Langdon is with us to report on events there. This is Edward Mutton reporting live from Kentish Town in North London. Over to you, Jessica."

Before the camera switched away from Edward Mutton, a group of men wearing balaclavas, dressed in dirty jeans and t-shirts shouting in Irish accents, could be seen to grab him. After that, the camera shook violently and blacked out. The scene switched to Hatton Gardens.

Behind Jessica Langdon - who was standing facing the

camera with a microphone ready - could be seen a wall of Orthodox Jews marching up the street towards riot police that were attempting to stop them. A scuffle broke out between police and the front line as they reached the shielded barricade. Then chaos reigned. Jessica stopped an Orthodox Jew who was running past her, getting him to stay long enough to ask what he thought the reason was for the rioting.

"Our people are sick and tired of being oppressed by the British police," he said. "We come to this country in good faith, bringing our wisdom and God's good word. And for this, the police target us and steal what little we possess; raiding from our shops, throwing our brethren in jail like common criminals, then refusing them access to their lawyers. The Jewish people will not stand for this harassment any longer."

The men upstairs had heard the commotion on the television and returned to the cellar. All of them stood watching the small television.

"Why have we not been told about this?" asked the main man, holding his arm out towards the television and looking at the others in the room who all shook their heads. "Once again, we are the last to know about a riot. Do we not also constantly fight the Infidels, but here the Jews and the Irish know about it before us, and they get all the glory?"

He shook his fist at the television., then turned to the other men.

"Have you published the video on YouTube, brothers?" he asked.

The men nodded.

"Allah be praised," said a voice, and in unison all the men responded with a fist in the air,"*Al-hamdulillah!*" before realising none of them had said it.

They turned to see a maniacal looking Stump, his hands by his sides, fists tightly clenched as an intense rage shook his body. There was blood and spittle hanging down from his chin and a dark pool of blood around his crotch area that contrasted with the white of the robe to make a disturbing sight. Though the stuck-on beard helped lend credence to the Arabic theme, he now looked more like a castrated escapee from an asylum for the criminally insane.

There was a brief pause as the men took the situation in. After that, events escalated so fast it was hard to know what was going on. The hanging light broke first as Stump launched himself across the table. He'd aimed for the main man and caught him square in the chest, as they then fell back into the television which itself then fell and exploded, sending the room into darkness with a singular loud flash. A scuffling, ripping, breaking, and crashing followed. After that came blood-curdling screams, shortly followed by the sound of feet stamping up the stairs and the door flying open. A soft yellow light shone down into the cellar as a figure exited above. There was the sound of kicking at a locked front door, which seemed to end without success. That was followed by another brief pause, and then the sound of smashing glass as Stump exited through a window. After that, there was silence, except for the groans coming from bodies that could now be seen in the soft light of the cellar as the men got up from the floor.

"Okay, who forgot to put a cable-tie back on the infidel?" asked the main man.

A voice could be heard to apologise from the darkness.

"Never mind. Is everyone alright?" he asked as he struggled to get to his feet.

Each man responded that he was.

"Well, at least we are alive. Allah be praised," he said painfully.

Though the response that came was a far less enthusiastic, *"Al-hamdulillah."*

London's Burning

By the time Stump found a phone box and had reverse-charged a call the Sergeant, London was burning and in a full scale riot.

"Where the hell have you been, sir? It's bloody chaos out there," said the Sergeant.

"Never mind that now. I need you to get a list of all the gang's numbers and contact them anonymously from a phone box somewhere away from Peckham. It's essential they know where the contraband is," said Stump between breaths.

"Certainly, sir, though everyone has been called in to deal with the riots. After we let the gangs out of the cells, it all escalated pretty quickly. I think they assumed rival gangs were behind it all. There are literally shoot-outs going on in the streets."

"I know. I saw the news."

"I'll get on and call those numbers now. Are you coming back here, sir?" asked the Sergeant.

"No, I have to deal with something else, but make sure they don't suspect you are police when you contact them," replied Stump.

At that moment, a shout went up behind Stump. He had been spotted by a gang of football hooligans who were marauding the area, enjoying the opportunity the riot afforded them.

"Get it done soon as you can, Sergeant, for all our sakes. Gotta go!" shouted Stump down the phone.

He then took off up the road, still dressed in his Arab regalia, sporting a toilet brush beard and bloody crotch, as fifty Nationalists in white t-shirts, braces, jeans, and doc martin boots, chased after him.

The Sergeant borrowed one of the remaining unmarked squad cars and drove through a rioting city to find a phone box in a quiet cul-de-sac that had avoided the action. He made the relevant calls, putting on a deep voice and covering the phone with a cloth. By the time he was done and heading back to the station, gang members were answering mobile phones and pulling their crews out of the rioting, preparing them to head towards Deptford.

Meanwhile, somewhere near Southall, Stump had kept ahead of the mob and was running through traffic until he reached the front of the queue at a set of lights. He wrenched the door open on the front car that had no passengers in it. He grimaced blood and missing teeth at the driver as he lent in, un-clipped his seat belt, and then pulled the man out and threw him into the road.

"Police emergency," he said, as he jumped in.

In a squeal of rubber and smoke, he took off, barely missing some oncoming traffic as he went through the lights. The mob appearing in his rear-view mirror slowed their gait. It had been a close call. Flicking a bloody finger on the

GPS on the dashboard, he punched in the Deptford address. It was clear from the traffic alerts that most of London was in chaos and many of the roads were going to be impassable.

"Fuck!" he shouted, and punched the steering wheel, but the GPS eventually found him a route.

Navigating through back roads and side streets, sometimes having to reverse all the way back up ones he'd gone down, he eventually neared his destination in Deptford.

Sir Michael was fending off calls from high command who were demanding to know how the situation had got so out of hand, and how he was planning to put things right. It was getting so chaotic that he had to screen calls and ignore anyone not ranking above him. That included the Police Commissioner, who had reverted to his distressed and vocally abusive state. Rioting was now consuming the city he was supposed to be in charge of, which definitely had not been part of his remit. So he needed to blame someone, and Sir Michael, apparently, was that someone.

"Put any calls from the Commissioner's office onto permanent hold, please, thank you," said Sir Michael to his secretary as he lifted and put the phone down on a shouting Commissioner for the third time without speaking to him.

A call then came through that Sir Michael could not ignore, and it took all his powers of discipline not to shout down the phone at the PM to shut his damn stupid mouth. Instead, he calmly replied to the same questions he had heard over a hundred times that night, that were always delivered in a loud and demanding tone. As placated as the PM would ever be, given the circumstances, Sir Michael finally ended the phone call. No sooner had he replaced the handset than his PA came in carrying a laptop.

"You need to see this," she said and didn't wait for an answer.

Putting the laptop down on his desk and hitting the space bar, she stood back. Sir Michael looked at the screen and couldn't quite believe what he was seeing.

"This is…" he turned to his PA and then looked back to the screen again. "This is Roger!"

It was rare to see Sir Michael exhibit unconditional shock, but Stump had finally achieved it.

"Yes sir, that is Inspector Stump. Face recognition software picked it up fifteen minutes ago on a YouTube channel hosted by the *Islamic Jihad for the Support of Conversion of the Infidels*. Its already had half a million views. Is he a Muslim, sir?"

"He is not a bloody Muslim. This must be some sort of… CGI trickery, or done under duress," replied Sir Michael, still struggling to understand why he was looking at Stump in a beard and full Arab dressage praying to Allah. Then the video showed him dancing with a group of Islamic gentlemen, all wearing masks except for him, but he was clearly dancing with them. The ridiculous beard he was sporting made little sense either, though the fact the video was being broadcast went some way to explain why he had gone missing before completing *Operation Force It In*.

Sir Michael sat back and considered events. He was already thinking of ways he could use the footage to reduce MI6's involvement when the dust settled on the riots. Unfortunately, it would not favour Stump one bit, assuming he was still alive. As he considered what to do next, his PA took the laptop and returned to her desk outside his office. She soon contacted him again on the speaker-phone.

"CTC Unit from Deptford on the line," she said.

"Patch them through, please." replied Sir Michael, feeling exasperated by the heady speed with which events were unfolding.

"CTC Command Deptford here," said the Colonel.

"Hello Colonel, bloody chaos here. What's the current situation with you chaps?" asked Sir Michael.

"Well, sir, it's been absolutely quiet here since the Inspector left, but we just had three vans pull up on the estate and they are currently watching the premises. It looks like the Irish mob, and we expect the rest to be following on. Just letting you know it looks like we are finally underway."

"Oh, thank Christ! That is good news. Most of bloody London is burning in the meantime, but at least it's finally happening at your end. Has there been any further sign of the Inspector?" asked Sir Michael.

"No sign of the inspector, sir. We lost his GPS signal about an hour after he left. Last signal was from just outside the Peckham area, after that it went dark. Nothing since."

"Very good Colonel. I suspect you will be busy from this point on. Stick to plan and good luck. Let's speak again when the storm has gathered."

"Very good, sir," replied the Colonel.

Sir Michael put on a television that was in a wall cupboard in his office, and let the News play quietly in the background. Before long, his desk phone was lighting up, and he was back to fending calls from top officials demanding he explain the rioting across the Capital, why it was happening, and just what the hell he planned to do about it. This time, he was advising them to come immediately to MI6, and he would provide the answer when they got there.

Hazelhot's Alamo

Lucy blinked awake and looked around the room. One benefit of being a queen of the Porn industry was that you could have small corners of production warehouses made into sound proofed living areas for yourself. She often slept in her dressing room after a long shoot and it had become a home from home. It was decked out like a small apartment and had everything she could need. She also had her trusty entourage with her, as she often did. Though on this occasion they had been called in to an emergency meeting by Hoots, but it was all very cloak and dagger mysterious. He'd asked her to trust him, and to get everyone to stay put in her dressing room until he could tell her more. He assured her it would not be too long. They'd all fallen asleep after discussing what they thought it might be that was so important.

Stretching awake like a cat, she checked the time. It was all taking a bit longer than was appropriate. She then put on her extremely gorgeous silk dressing gown and stepped over the still sleeping dwarfs, and Janice and Janine, and left to have a walk and stretch her legs. She decided to see what Hazelhot was up to. He was always awake at ridiculous hours, satisfying his base curiosities on the Internet.

She walked through the warehouse and past the open crates. Looking into one, she saw bags of what looked like cocaine and a variety of other items. She assumed it to be props for one of Larry's new ideas. Continuing on towards the front of the warehouse and out into the main corridor, she heard voices and could smell cigar smoke. Checking herself to make sure everything was revealing enough, but not too much, she entered.

Lucy quietly stepped into the doorway and lent seductively, but casually, against the door frame. She momentarily checked her pose was just right before letting out a delicate cough to announce her presence. The room hushed as the men within turned to see her glamorously adorning the entrance. She lit it up beautifully. Men, previously deep in discussion on serious matters, became suddenly lighter, and the mood became warmer, as they first acknowledged her, and then welcomed her in. Hoots fetched Lucy a chair, and Stott forced himself to stand until she had sat down. The only one who did nothing and ignored her completely was Hazelhot. This dismissive attitude had, of course, been what attracted her to him.

"We were just about to wake you," said Hoots once she had settled. "We have something we need to discuss with everyone. It's an unfortunate business, but something that we have all, by circumstance, become caught up in."

Hoots then outlined the situation to Lucy, along with his plan on how to get them all out, as well as what would happen if he did not. He explained the current situation with events that were unfolding outside of the warehouse, as well as the danger they all faced at the hands of the gangs, or worse, the government. When he had finished, everyone turned to look at Lucy and await her response. She was no stranger to drama, on set or off it. Drama was something she took it in her stride, but this didn't just involve her.

"Can you give me a moment to discuss this with the others?" she asked.

"Of course," replied Hoots.

Lucy returned to her dressing room to wake her entourage, and she appeared back in the office a short while later.

"Whatever you need from us, you have it. We have more than enough costumes available, so everyone will find something. It's going to be fun," she said, knowing that the men would feel better thinking they would be occupied with costumes instead of bothering them with questions.

In reality, the entourage had been terrified by what Lucy had told them. It was hard to digest and harder still to believe, but they knew Hoots was not someone given to lying. They had little choice, but the fact he had a plan gave them hope.

Hoots thanked her, and Lucy nodded and then left. Soon after, Hoots received a call on his phone.

"Mm-hmm... Yup... Great... Great... Okay... Yup... Thanks."

He ended the call, looked at his watch, and then turned to Stott and Hazelhot.

"It's time gentlemen. We can't wait any longer for the Inspector."

"I told you. Never trust a copper," said Hazelhot.

"But where the hell are Rigby and Miss Jones?" asked Stott.

"They aren't coming," replied Hoots.

"Why the hell not? Do they not understand the situation?" asked Stott.

Hoots shrugged.

"I told Rigby it was life or death, but he was adamant he'd rather stay and risk it, and when I told Miss Jones that Rigby wasn't coming, she said neither was she. There wasn't much else I could do. Larry and Maurice were the same. Larry said he'd rather die than live somewhere without cocaine."

"Doesn't that rather put the rest of us at risk?" asked Stott. "Rigby is bound to blab everything at the first sign of trouble, and Larry, too."

"They don't know the plan. I told them to come here to discuss it, but other than being aware they are a target out there, they know nothing," replied Hoots.

"Very well," said Stott. "Though God help them all," he added.

"We better get ready," said Hoots.

They headed to the back of the warehouse and to Lucy's dressing room. All except Hazelhot, who diverted off to walk towards his locked storage area. Hoots, noticing he wasn't with them, walked back out of the dressing room to see what he was up to.

"I'm not coming," said Hazelhot, after Hoots asked him what was going on.

"You won't stand a chance here," replied Hoots.

"I don't expect to. If I get out, do you think MI6 will leave it at that? I'm the one they want. They will hunt me to the ends of the earth for what I've done. Besides, they need to hang this on someone, and I'd rather go out fighting. You guys go on, I can at least provide a suitable distraction," said Hazelhot as he admired some of the high-end weaponry he had there, stroking it like a stash of treasure he adored. Hoots knew better than to try to persuade him, and after a moment of deliberating, he put his hand out to him.

"Then good luck, bru, and see you on the other side," he said.

Hazelhot looked at the outstretched hand and considered ignoring it, but then relented and shook it.

"Go on," he said. "Get them out of here."

After which, he lifted a large black machine gun into the air and clicked a magazine into the underside of it and grinned at Hoots.

Hoots returned to Lucy's dressing room, and as he walked in, Lucy stopped him.

"What's he doing? We need to get ready?" she said.

"He's not coming," replied Hoots.

Stott over-heard this and stopped what he was doing then looked up. He was sitting in front of a stage mirror dressed in a costume that appeared to be a large mole. Randy Andy was part way through adding whiskers to him, while trying not to laugh. He looked ridiculous. Stott brushed Randy Andy's hand away and waddled out into the warehouse to where Hazelhot was busy setting up his chrome killing machines.

"I hear you are not joining the party, old boy," said Stott, gearing up for a speech.

Hazelhot had his back to him and was leaning over a large device, adjusting part of it with a spanner. He paused for a moment, then carried on preparing the weapon without turning around. Stott continued.

"I know we have had our disputes in the past and, well frankly, you are a bloody maniac, lets face it, but I have to say I am in awe and respect on this one, Hazelhot. Didn't know you had it in you. Really quite impressed. If there is anything you would like us to do for you, you know, last requests and wot not?" asked Stott, and he finished by mumbling something incoherent.

Hazelhot tightened the last nut and stood back. Turning to look at Stott, he laughed.

"Well, don't you look bloody ridiculous? An appropriate last memory of you, at least," said Hazelhot.

Stott looked down at himself. He was feeling emotional knowing that Hazelhot, who had for so long been his nemesis, was now sacrificing himself for the greater good. He cleared his throat and tried to cover his vulnerability.

"Hmm, yes well, still very touched, old boy, that you are doing this for us," replied Stott.

"Oh, for Christ's sake, save the emotion for my eulogy, you over-fed badger. It really isn't for your benefit," replied Hazelhot.

"Mole," corrected Stott.

"What?"

"It's a mole. The costume. A mole, not a badger."

"Right. Either way, I've enough to do here without listening to your blubbering," replied Hazelhot.

"Well. Thank you anyway, old chap. Damn sporting of you, all the same. And god bless you sir, god bless you indeed."

Stott was feeling tears form, and a gulp rise in his throat. He wanted to say something meaningful that might get through to Hazelhot. Hazelhot continued to ignore his outstretched hand, and so he gave up, then shrugged and turned to walk back to the dressing room. He stopped once and turned, as if he had finally found what he wanted to say, but never got it out, whatever it was. Hazelhot watched him go and then got back to his work.

"Bloody idiot," he said.

Lucy appeared in the doorway of the dressing room and

stood watching Hazelhot from a distance. A tear ran down her face and she wiped it. Hoots appeared beside her.

"Funny, the people we end up caring about, isn't it?" said Hoots.

Lucy wiped her eyes again and then laughed a little awkwardly.

"Yes, Hoots, it certainly is. The man is a psychopath, and yet I'm in deliriously love with him."

Hoots put a hand gently on her shoulder, then turned and went back into the dressing room.

Outside, three vans were parked up and watching the premises. A man sat in the front of the leading van made a call and spoke in a strong Irish accent to the voice that answered.

"On da site now, boss. There's definitely people in there... Nah, doesn't seem suspicious. What d'ya want us a do? Hol' up... what the fook is this now..."

Just as he was talking, two more vans arrived on the industrial estate. The Irish ducked down to peer over the top of their dashboards. The new arrivals sped onto the estate and took up positions some distance from them, the men inside then watching towards the Pussy Productions premises.

"Boss, we just had another crew turn up. Looks like them Jewish fellas. Yea. Them. Alright, boss. Will do."

The man put the phone down. Everyone in the van looked at him as he went back to looking out of the window.

"Well?" asked one from the back.

"Well, what?" asked the man.

"Well...what the fook did he say?"

"Well Seamus, he said he wants yoos to go on over to them

Jews and sort them out," replied the first guy.

"Just me, or all of us?" asked Seamus, falling for it.

"He said we's wait, yoos stupid fook," replied the first guy, turning around and clapping Seamus across the head.

The Jews had noticed the Irish crew ducking down when they drove onto the estate. After they parked up and watched the premises for a while, the driver in the front Jewish van pulled out a phone and made a call.

"We are at the premises. But we have another three vans here. Looks like the Irish. Maybe they know about the diamonds? What do you want us to do?" he asked, and listened to the reply.

"Okay. Will do," he said, and put the phone down, then went back to watching the premises.

"So, what did he say?" asked a man from the back of the van.

"He said he wants you to take some pretzels over to the Irishmen in that van."

"We don't have any pretzels," replied the man, looking about for some, and everyone else hit him with their hats.

"He wants us to wait for the others, and then we go in," replied the first man after it had calmed down in the back.

At that moment, another two vans came careering onto the industrial estate, but the moment they spotted the vans already there, they put on the brakes and slowed down to a crawl.

All the men in the Jewish and the Irish vans ducked down as the Italians drove slowly past them to park up closer to the Pussy Productions' main entrance. They would have hung back further, but there was increasingly less parking space on the road leading up to the premises.

The driver in the leading van dialled a number and soon

after spoke in expressive terms as he informed the person on the other end of all that was going on in the industrial estate. He was throwing his arms in all directions inside the cab and shouting. Suddenly reducing his tone to a soft level, he said, "okay, ciao," and put the phone down.

Someone in the back asked a question, and the driver pretended he had not understood. So, the man in the back repeated his question with a little more elaboration, which created an outburst of mozzarella and pepperoni comments from the front, while pointing to the other vans. Some snickering came from the other men in the back.

Hazelhot had finished priming most of the weapons, and was placing them in strategic positions around the warehouse. Hoots went to the main office to check how things were developing outside. He saw the vans and checked his watch, then returned to the warehouse. Everyone else was in the dressing room waiting for Hoots to tell them what to do next. The mood was glum, except for Hazelhot, who was polishing his death machines and dancing as he went between them, singing to himself. Hoots watched him for a moment, then shook his head. He pulled a mobile from his pocket and made a call. After that he stepped over to where Lucy was quietly watching Hazelhot, lost in thought, and said something to her. Lucy's face lit up, and she nodded and then hugged Hoots.

The Chinese and the Greeks arrived next on the industrial estate. The roads were now full of vans. There was a growing tension as they all eyed one another across the darkness, but mostly they kept a watchful eye on Pussy Productions. None of the vans had so far noticed the men lurking on the roof of the premises opposite.

The CTC Colonel was on the roof and was patched in by radio to Sir Michaels' office at MI6. He was waiting for the signal for his men to unleash. Looking through night-vision binoculars at the vehicles, he was informing Sir Michael of what he saw there, which was then being relayed live via a loudspeaker in the MI6 office.

In the office with Sir Michael were several high-ranking officials. Those present included the Police Commissioner, the PM's personal attaché, a selection of military men of high standing, and various representatives from various offices that had clout in the upper echelons of British Intelligence, as well as the US and French connections. They were all listening as the Colonel described the scene. A hired server came in and wandered through the group offering nibbles from a tray and taking orders for drinks, as the voice of the Colonel came through the speaker and finished describing events, then advised they were ready to act as soon as MI6 desired.

"Very good," said Sir Michael, "just hold tight for a moment Colonel, while I have a chat with our chaps here."

Sir Michael pressed the mute button on the speaker and then looked around the room.

"Well, ladies and gentlemen, it has been a long and painful journey to get to this point, but we are finally here. Our target inside the warehouse has still not contacted *Daddy*, which is, of course, extremely frustrating, but we are in the Last Act and all the gangs have gathered. They will approach the warehouse at any moment, and no doubt, carnage will ensue when they do. As we planned and expected. We will then... er... 'tidy up'...shall we say... using our CTC boys to ensure no one leaves. Our plan is to go with the original headline suggestion to the press tomorrow morning of, '*CTC Foil Terrorist Plot And Gangland Sympathisers*'. Does anyone wish to add anything before we give the Colonel the green light to proceed when he sees fit?"

No one had anything to add.

Sir Michael looked next toward a group of American military men and European diplomats who were setup along one wall and talking into phones.

"Any requests from our American or European friends?" he asked.

He received confirmation that they were all fine for him to proceed. Sir Michael finally looked to the PM's attaché, who was also at that moment on a mobile phone re-iterating to the PM word-for-word as Sir Michael spoke.

"So, if the PM would like to give us the go ahead, then we can get this rather detestable business under way," he said, but just as he did so, the speaker-phone crackled and a voice came over it.

"Um, sir, are you there? It looks like we have a rogue arrival," said the Colonel.

Sir Michael held his hand up to bid everyone in the room to silence so that he could un-mute the button. Once everyone was quiet, he did so and spoke into the speaker.

"Go ahead Colonel. What are you seeing?" he asked.

"Were any Muslims advised of this event, sir? It seems we have one coming in via car at high speed. Hell's bells! This looks a suicide bomber. He is in full Arab gear and bearded... what the fu... oh sweet Jesus..."

Before the Colonel could finish his sentence, the speaker rattled with a background noise that grew so loud it drowned out the shouts of the Colonel. First some crashing could be heard, then gunfire, then explosions, and after a while sounds that could only be described as full spectrum cacophony that escalated to the point the speaker-phone on

Sir Michaels desk began vibrating violently and moving around the desk as it tried to convey the sounds it was picking up, but was wholly struggling to transmit. It ranged across the spectrum of frequencies, including some that were colour more than sound, all of which were interspersed with human shouts and screams, followed by further explosions and then more gun-fire. Utter chaos was raining down in Deptford.

Everyone in the room at MI6 HQ stood motionless, transfixed, watching the speaker-phone as it danced around the desk. A cigar dropped from a half-open mouth, a half-bitten sandwich folded and fell to the floor. War had preemptively unleashed, and everyone was waiting to see when it might end. The speaker bounced around the desk, conveying the intensity of what it was experiencing for what seemed like an eternity, until a moment hinted at a pause, and there was a gradual diminishing in noise, then the speaker stopped moving and a painful silence descended. But from within this hush, there grew a curious sound. An escalating whistle began, until it reached a level that hurt the ears, at which point the speaker gave up, popped a small puff of smoke, and died. A second later, as everyone stared at the cloud of smoke rising from the speaker, someone pointed out the window and said.

"What the fuck is that?"

The entire building then rattled, as if being shaken by an earthquake. All present grabbed for solid objects to steady themselves as the London skyline lit up with a greenish white hue, before gently returning to night-time black. A loud bang was heard as a shock wave hit the building. Then, gradually, it stopped rattling, as an eerie silence descended across London.

"Oh dear God," said Sir Michael. "What the hell has that

mad bastard done?"

Armaggedon Lewisham

In the days that followed, war tacticians, forensic experts, and demolition teams from around the world were flown in to make sense of what had happened. Many breathed a sigh of relief to discover it was not a nuclear event. But the mystery remained to figure out what had exploded in the final blast, and what went on in the time leading up to it.

What became known as *"Armageddon Lewisham"* in the press was titled *"The Battle of Deptford"* in the history books. And what transpired in those last few minutes before the entire industrial estate and everything in it was reduced to a melted glass-like material, would become the subject of urban myths and old soldier's dinner conversations. Decades later, men would scare the grandchildren with stories about the *mad terrorist* of Deptford. Whatever the truth of it was, those few moments became a pivotal turning point in military strategy and was given a place in war journals to be studied in Military School for years to come. It wasn't for the tactics, but for the sheer amount of carnage that was created by so few, and yet had affected so many. The start of it all was believed to be a mixture of two coincidentally synchronised events.

It began with the unplanned arrival of Inspector Stump back onto the industrial estate. He was so determined not to be left behind by the Pussy Production team that he completely forgot the danger that his arrival might represent. As he rounded the corner of the industrial estate entrance in his stolen car, he saw the vans waiting. Realising that nothing had begun, this stirred an irrational sense of hope that he was not too late, if he could just get himself into the warehouse. It was foolhardy. But given events that had transpired for him leading up to that point, it was understandable for him to assume that he might get away with it. Stump was concussed and had lost a lot of blood, so whatever was going through his mind was anything but rational. Given he was now within metres of his destination and potential escape to freedom, he forgot what had led him to be in his predicament in the first place. Not to mention how fate was rarely forgiving, and more often than not, preferred to be ironic and really rather cruel.

And so it was, that with an increased sense of purpose and determination, Stump stepped on the accelerator after he rounded the corner, and made directly for the front door of Pussy Productions with his car. His plan was to pull up, jump out, and gain entry before CTC or the various gangs could react. However bad an idea that was, he knew he had little choice. So he went for it.

The Colonel, upon seeing the vehicle speed up, could only make out what looked like an Arab covered in blood, speeding towards the warehouse. The man had such a look of such maniacal determination on this face that the Colonel, of course, assumed it to be a suicide bomber. Not that it mattered much, since events were about to be unleashed by

Sir Michael, anyway. All that Stump achieved was beating them to it. But it was the secondary event that really brought things to boiling point.

At the rear of the warehouse, just as Stump was putting his foot down, there was an explosion that sent bricks and mortar flying into the air. Dust and rubble appeared over the top of the warehouse and out from the sides of it. Through the breach in the rear, moved army vehicles that later - after satellite images were studied and compared - were thought to be the latest edition of a military vehicle known as the *Marauder*.

As Stump sped up across the grass, he got a good view of one of them just before it disappeared behind the building and into Pussy Productions. Realising their appearance confirmed that he was not too late, he chose that moment to leap from the car. After performing a roll for a few yards, he was then up and running towards the back of the warehouse.

The sight of an Islamic militant tearing hell for leather toward the premises triggered all the waiting gangs into action. Fearing that it was the competition intent on gaining access to their contraband ahead of them, they gave up waiting for the okay from their bosses and responded accordingly. It's believed that the Jews reacted first, pulling out an arsenal of machine guns, then throwing a side door open, as they unleashed fury toward the Arab. This barrage of bullets caused Stump to give up his sprint for freedom and dive to the floor to take cover. Soon, every gang member had grabbed a weapon and jumped from their vehicles to do what they could to stop the Jews or the Arab from taking the lead. Cacophony followed, and in the carnage and chaos, everyone began shooting at everyone else.

Inevitably, some of the stray bullets ricocheted and hit the building where the CTC were currently housed. Thinking they were now under attack, CTC was forced to open fire. The Colonel shouting orders to, "gun down anything and everything that moves!" It was then that the gangs realised they had a whole additional issue behind them.

As CTC unleashed, some of the gang members turned to take them on. Soon there was so much heavy gunfire in all directions that the air hung thick with smoke. With the added problem of drifting brick dust, it became impossible to know what was going on, or what direction to shoot in. Amidst coughing and dust blindness, men stopped taking aim and instead held onto a trigger while spinning in circles, hoping for the best.

The Marauders, that had been parked briefly inside the warehouse, now reversed out the same way they had arrived. Though it was difficult to see much, since the power had now gone out on the industrial estate and several smoke grenades had been thrown, that added to the obfuscation. In the skies above, the US, Chinese, North Korean, and Russian *eyes-in-the-sky*, all of which had the latest vision enhancing hardware, could no longer make out what was going on either. Effectively, Deptford industrial estate now became a blackout, or rather white-out, for information. As such, they missed the Marauders exiting.

One may have been of the mind that, with the Marauders exiting, it would have been the start of things calming down. But alas, no. The main event had not yet started. In fact, none of the many weapons that Hazelhot had spent so long studying, selecting, purchasing, and stockpiling, had yet seen any action at all. But this was about to change.

Remarkably, very few people outside the warehouse had been hit by bullets, and even more incredibly, there were just minor casualties. But as the gunfire slowed, and some of the smoke and dust settled, a sound began emanating from the centre of the warehouse that was picked up by monitoring radar and would later be described as "like a gigantic kettle coming to the boil". As this sound increased - with some grainy footage later gathered and collated from the combined satellite imagery - what looked like a giant Catherine Wheel began spinning to life in the middle of the warehouse. What could also be made out were small missiles that were subsequently launched in all directions from the contraption, some even going vertically.

What was left of the warehouse above, to the front and to the sides, was then decimated under the rain of exploding missiles that came from the device. Though the remaining walls soon gave way, the whistling missiles did not. Projectile after projectile came shooting forth from the infernal machine and hit nearby targets on the industrial estate, including the premises opposite.

By the time the monstrous device began to show signs of slowing, there were very few vans left, and large smouldering holes in all the buildings within a line of sight of Pussy Productions, though all the gunfire from the road had now ceased. Everyone, including those inside the remains of the CTC building, were either lying on the floor covering their heads and praying for it to end, or were dead. Finally, it seemed like there was going to be a pause in the battle.

Though it would have been difficult to see much beyond arm's length, and the field of conflict would have looked more like Dresden circa 1945 than an industrial estate at this stage, some of the remaining gangs took the opportunity to attempt entry to the remnants of the warehouse. This proved to be a mistake.

As they crossed the threshold of what was once the

entrance, they were immediately met with another of Hazelhot's purchases. This one was well known to a small group of men in Brixton, who knew better than to trust a lull in events where Hazelhot was concerned. It was why they had chosen not to join the attempt to recover their stolen contraband, considering it to be a foolhardy mission and doomed to failure. It seemed they were right. Through the thick smoke, it was later estimated that around thirty of the remaining gang members of varying denominations stalked their way like combat soldiers in towards their goal. As they crossed the point of no return, the black night devoured them until the weapon located them. Then came the eerie sight of men being lit up green and white in electric silhouettes as they were struck by the now infamous *Tazer Shockwave Barrier*. But this was not the end, either. It was just the end of the beginning.

There came next the sound of rapid machine gun fire, this time bursting forth from somewhere deeper inside what was left of the building. It was the speed of fire that concerned the Colonel as he heard it. Somehow he had survived the earlier barrage and collapse of the CTC building, and was now looking toward one of his men - a weapons expert - who shrugged his shoulders, clearly not recognising the sound either. It was indeed strange, but it was nothing compared to the weapon's capability. The thing was just warming up, and as it got to full readiness, it unleashed its ammunition load. Bullets came at such a speed that it was beyond anything anyone had ever witnessed before. It was a fanned-out stream of gunfire that cut down anyone standing, or more precisely, disintegrated them. In assessing it later, military studies would conclude it to have been a bespoke version of a piece of futuristic artillery capable of shooting over one million rounds per minute. This device had been adapted by Hazelhot to move in a semi-circular trajectory as it distributed its load. The result was disturbingly successful. By the time it chugged to a stop, not a man, van, nor wall was left standing.

Miraculously, there were still some survivors. These comprised those men wise enough to remain lying down through the previous events. As the machine gun spluttered its final round, another silence descended upon the industrial estate in Deptford. The smoke lifted on the devastation and men could be heard coughing amongst the rubble. Some dared to get to their feet to look around. The Colonel picked himself and shook some of the dust from his hair and clothes. He looked around for a communication device to contact MI6. It was then that a new sound was heard coming from the direction of what now felt more like the gates of hell.

"Oh, Christ!" said the Colonel as he caught sight of Hazelhot's *pièce de résistance*.

A dazzling array of colourful lights began to glow and sparkle through the smoke. This increased in intensity along with a whistling sound until the bomb reached the point that it finally exploded. In a split second, it melted all solids within a five hundred metre radius while sending bright light, followed by a shock-wave, out in all directions. This event was felt over forty miles away. Though, thankfully, the worst of the devastation was localised to the half-kilometre range around the industrial estate. Other than that, there was some structural damage to buildings and windows in the forty-mile zone as the shock wave passed through them. In the flick of an eye, the industrial estate, along with everything and everyone in it, was turned to glass, melted and atomised. Few biological fragments remained.

One item that somehow survived the blast was a safe buried

deep in Pussy Productions storage that was found during the clean-up operation. Miraculously, it was in one piece, though certainly looked the worse for wear. It was taken to MI6, and a few days later, the lab there finally broke into it. The press had also mysteriously got wind of the safe being found, and in the interests of transparency, had forced the hand of MI6 to demand to be present when it was opened. Public interest in the event had become so huge that MI6 were now under scrutiny to prove they had not been involved. So they were hardly in any position to refuse without making matters worse.

The resulting find came as a shock to everyone, most especially MI6, when official documents found inside the safe - later confirmed to be either incredibly accurate forgeries of more likely the real thing - exonerated Sir Archibold Stott, proving him to have been a key figure working with MI6 the entire time, helping them bring down the terrorist sleeper cell that had been working at Pussy Productions in Deptford. A revelation that was neither confirmed nor denied by MI6, though they breathed a sigh of relief that nothing more incriminating had been discovered in the safe.

the press needed a hero, and in the late Sir Archibold Stott they found their man. Especially poignant, since they had spent so long trying to destroy him. The fact he was now presumed amongst the dead made it the perfect hero story. They waxed endlessly lyrical on that *True British Spirit,* noting how not once had he sought to make amends by revealing his true identity. For England, and for Queen and Country, he had allowed his honour to be destroyed. What bravery to carry the shame they had so woefully burdened upon him to his grave. How wrong they had been, they said.

The story of Sir Archibold Stott the Hero ran the front page for weeks. Several best seller books were written about the life of the character and the man who sacrificed everything for his belief in Empire. He was toasted in mess halls, in private schools, at political dinners, and at events country-wide. His name now held in the highest regard, where once it had been the lowest. Sir Archibold Stott became the ultimate example of a true British Gentleman and the epitome of an absolutely top-notch chap. GQ did an article on him, and claimed him to be the kind of man others could only ever aspire to be, but never hope to emulate. He was posthumously returned his knighthood, then granted a second knighthood, and then a third for good measure. The Queen making a twenty-minute speech in which his name was mentioned three times. A statue in his honour was made by an eminent British sculptor and placed at Ground Zero in Deptford, depicting him astride a large horse, rearing up, prior to making its battle charge. In one hand, he held a book of justice, and in the other, a bolt of lightning. It was a powerful piece, everyone agreed.

School children and tourists flocked in bus loads to visit the site, and a downloadable audio app told of the details and the more child-friendly elements of Sir Archibold Stott's life. He was a man amongst men, a hero who helped MI6 to save Britain from a terrorist. He was a man willing to sacrifice himself and his honour for the call of duty.

Sir Archibold Stump was also posthumously re-awarded eternal membership to all the clubs he had once been a member of before the initial sorry story of his fall from grace had him expelled from all of them. Most placed plaques near to seats in which he might have sat, or tables where he might have eaten. One was even put up inside a toilet cubicle at the Hell-Fire Club. The only person who seemed wholly uninterested in forgiving Sir Archibold Stott, or even talking about him, was his ex-wife.

As for what remained of the Deptford site, it was impossible to get much from forensics, given the atomised state of everything. The final body count was assumed to be above two hundred but less than four, and amazingly, none were believed to be civilians. All were gangs, criminals, soldiers, CTC, and several sex industry perverts who had been part of the now disintegrated company once known as Pussy Productions. The only survivors were an accountant called Rigby and a secretary by the name of Miss Jones, both were believed duped and coerced into the job. Larry and Maurice, who were both so hysterical about the event, no one could believe they had been complicit in it. There was also an Earl of Cavendish association, but he had since disappeared somewhere in Eastern Europe and was presumed hiding out in shame over some curious purchases associated with his name when business accounts came to light.

But there had been one survivor from the scene, which was unfortunate for him. Found hours after the blast, running barefoot and half naked down a road, was what appeared on first sight to be a castrated Muslim. Men from MI6 were on the scene before the press and it was they that found him, but rather than be taken to a hospital, the soon to be ex-Inspector Stump was bagged up and hustled into a van then taken to cells deep inside an undisclosed location. There, flashing lights and loud nursery rhymes were pumped round the clock for several days, before a thorough interrogation began. His discovery was covered up. The press failed to confirm reports on the alleged sighting of an Islamic militant running away from the scene before the blast, at least none that made sense, so they ignored it. It eventually became the stuff of conspiracy theorists, but was ignored by the mainstream media and the public. The other conspiracy theory that remained equally mysterious and unanswered was to do with some army vehicles seen entering the site but never seen leaving. But with no evidence to the contrary, it was assumed they went up in the blast.

The now deceased terrorist was discussed at length in the press and on TV. MI6 had released details of his name and some of his acts, but not enough to create a full profile of the man. None could seem to decide whether Hazelhot was a specially trained super-soldier, or simply a natural born psychopath. What everyone could agree on was that he was a terrorist, and had been the ring-leader behind it all. Several Islamic groups tried to claim responsibility for the event, but none came up with a good enough description of Hazelhot to be believed. MI6 confirmed or denied nothing and everything. All they would say was that *"National Security"* was the reason for not divulging any further information. Their new AI Software recommended this course of action, suggesting there was an 80% chance of it all blowing over within four months if they refused to confirm or deny anything.

The saddest loss was the entire CTC unit, including the Colonel, all of whom were praised for their sacrifice and posthumously honoured with medals, plaques, and a war memorial in Central London. Every man lost in the line of duty had his name printed on a piece of stone and a personalised letter was signed on behalf of the Queen by her secretary. This was then sent to the families to thank them for their service and duty to Great Britain.

The Pentagon and Interpol sent flowers and cards of congratulations to Sir Michael for a job well done, and even the Police Commissioner thanked him profusely for bringing him in at such an early stage. He had since been commended for his part in saving London from a terrorist sleeper-cell. The PM was happy because it showed how well the government and the Metropolitan Police could work alongside MI6 and foreign counterparts to bring about a result that saw zero civilian casualties and had saved the nation.

To those in the know, despite it triggering one of the worst riots in British history and laying waste to an industrial estate in Deptford, as well as leading to the loss of two to four hundred servicemen, it was still considered a total success by higher powers who knew what real failure looked like. Weighing up the cost against the result, there was no question of its success. It was also considered as one of the most successful gang clean-up operations in modern history. That alone was credit enough for the Commissioner and enough to have his name committed to a place in history, and that sat very well with him.

Sir Michaels' only regret was that his old friend had inevitably, and irrevocably, set himself up as lamb for slaughter. Sir Michael knew that once the dust settled, he might be able to help him, but not before. He could not risk drawing attention to his connection by showing concern. He knew that Roger Stump likely had a larger part of the original stash tucked away somewhere, and that would be his focus for surviving whatever was going to be done to him during his interrogation. Since everything had been melted into glass when the industrial estate went up, it was beyond forensics to confirm the existence of anything much at all, which had made the entire contraband haul a write-off. Something Sir Michael himself had signed-off on. Once the press attention died down, and the public forgot all about *Armageddon Lewisham,* Sir Michael would visit his old friend and see what could be done to get him out, maybe broker a deal. Hopefully, Stump would survive the torturing. Until then, he'd suffer mercilessly as they sought information from him he likely didn't posses. Though this saddened Sir Michael, he felt certain Roger was tough enough to get through it with aplomb.

And that was the end of *Operation Force It In*, *Armageddon Lewisham*, and *The Battle of Deptford*, as well as Roger Stump's career as a Detective Inspector. It was also the end of Pussy Productions, and most of the people involved in the company, as well as the psychopathic creature known as Hazelhot. Everything that had been associated with the event soon passed into history, and though everyone involved closed the book on the event, that wasn't quite the entire story.

PART FOUR

Arrivals From The Underworld

A few days after the explosion that turned a Deptford industrial estate to molten glass and lit up, then shook half of London, a small circus troupe arrived by Hercules aircraft and bounced onto a runway in Sierra Leone, West Africa. Signed off on the arrival docket as *"Entertainment for the troops"*, the authorising signature provided by a South African security expert who was in charge of the detail. They passed through customs, which amounted to one bored-looking soldier who waved them through without asking to see any papers.

Unless someone knew what to look for, there was no record kept of their arrival at all, and a week later what information there was went up in smoke when the airport was attacked by rebels for the third time that year. Their arrival and subsequent failure to depart the country went unnoticed. All records of the Hercules transport leaving the UK went much the same way. There was a departure list of mostly consumable goods bound for an African charity's support team, and *"Entertainment for the troops"* written above a list of random names involved in providing some entertainment. This file also met an unfortunate end thanks to a visiting General's blood hounds being left temporarily in a filing room for longer than they appreciated.

"Damn hounds, they rarely misbehave like that," said the General on being notified of the incident. "Send any clean-up bill for the damage to my department and please apologise to the staff for me. Was much lost?"

"They seemed especially interested in the West African transport section, sir. We presume it was tainted with honey we often receive from there in unsuitable containers. Gifts from various tribal leaders to the Queen, and so on. It can get awfully sticky in the customs department."

"Yes, that certainly might have been what set them off. Well, as I said, send the clean-up bill to my people and we'll get that addressed. Now, I think we have a dinner dance to attend this evening in... er... where the blazes was it again?"

"Aldershot, sir."

"Aldershot, that's right. Well, best get on."

And that was that. All evidence of their leaving the country was erased.

After leaving the airport in Sierra Leone, rather than heading to the local camp and the faked show that they were claiming to provide, the truck containing the circus troupe took a detour. A week later it arrived in a small African village in the country of Togo, having travelled across rugged terrain and through obscure border crossings using falsified papers or US dollars. It stopped only for supplies and fuel, or for everyone to sleep. Each day, at sunset, it would pull off the road and tents would be pitched deep in the bush. Catering would be setup and all occupants would be fed. Local soldiers, hired cheaply, would then stand guard through the night, and by the time the first slither of sunlight was breaking across the sky the next morning, the truck would be packed and bouncing down dusty roads on its way to its final destination. Eventually, it arrived in the centre of a small tribal village deep in the heart of Togo, and there it pulled to a stop. The dust settled, and the morning became still once again, but for the sound of crickets and several hens that were clucking at the intrusion.

Hoots got out from the cab, stretched, and then walked down the side of the truck, banging lightly against it as he went. He opened the rear, and a group of tired and bedraggled looking individuals gradually alighted. This was watched idly on by a growing numbers of sleepy black faces that appeared in the doorways of huts around the village.

First to appear from the back of the truck were the armed soldiers. They were followed by a large and muscular white man. He jumped to the ground with a thud and a small cloud of dust rose around his feet. The sight of him stirred voices and drew excited finger-pointing from the huts. He was dressed in a leopard-skin leotard, and on seeing him some children came running out from behind their mother's legs to circle him and grab his hand as they jumped up and down. Recognising the signature of a warrior who had killed a leopard with his bare hands for its skins, they wanted to hold his warring hand in the hope they might gain some of his strength and power. Randy Andy loved kids, so it was a pleasant enough welcome for him as he was dragged around the centre of the village by small insistent hands. With more children chasing after him, shouting their joy, the village was now awake.

Lucy appeared next, and she checked herself in a small compact mirror before looking around for someone to help her down from the truck. Hoots was on hand, and he carefully took her by the waist and turned to deposit her gently on *terra firma*. Seeing Lucy, the young women who had stayed modestly in doorways now talked animatedly, and called to others who had remained hidden inside the huts. Soon every female in the village was at the door and seeing a white woman, of Lucy's calibre, for the first time in the flesh. There was plenty of flesh. Most of the village women were used to modestly dressed charity workers and had only seen more racily clad white women in colour magazines imported from the USA dating back to the 1970s. There was great excitement in discovering one of these revered white queens was now in their midst, and discussion was already turning to how best to celebrate and honour her arrival.

Two dwarfs climbed down from the back of the truck next, though not without a fair amount of satirical difficulty. Hoots knew better than to offer to help and smiled knowingly. They were used to navigating such situations and turned it into an acrobatic display to compensate, which amused the kids that had remained. The laughter now drew older men to appear in the doorways, roused to wake by the noise, and they became quite animated themselves in recognising two pygmy tribesmen. Even more auspicious was to see they were from the rare albino tribe. This omen generated excitement in the older generation, and runners were called and sent to wake the more senior tribal elders and inform them of the immense blessing bestowed that morning on them all by the gods of the Underworld. That they had ordained to send not one, but two albino pygmy tribesmen to visit their humble village was going to be big news. It required appropriate interpretation, and that required the elders.

The elders had not risen yet because there was nothing in the human realm that could be so important that they needed to check on it directly. This news, of course, now transcended the human realm, but the elders still took their time. Though they soon appeared wandering at a suitably dis-interested pace towards the centre of the village, most of them aided by canes and ornate walking sticks.

Janice and Janine were helped down next. They were dressed in see-through fairy costumes adorned with translucent multi-coloured wings that shimmered in the light, yet somehow had remained intact throughout the journey. They looked like naked pixies from another realm, and they rubbed their eyes and stretched their bodies like cats, then walked over to stand with Lucy as they looked about sleepily. This signalled to the tribe that it was a powerful white queen from the other world who was in their midst, since she had arrived with two winged emissaries. They would now need to celebrate for many days, if not an entire week, just to honour this situation correctly. With this news, more runners were called and then sent out to chase the runners that had already been sent, to update them with the new information. They were also told to increase the number of chickens and goats that would be required for the celebratory feast.

A curious creature appeared at the rear of the truck. It *harrumphed* and *guffawed* and turned this way and that, then tried to reverse down but struggled to get a footing, eventually falling backwards and landing unceremoniously onto its arse in the dust. Some children ran over to dance around what they knew was a giant *skonku* sent from the Underworld to amuse them. They shouted and danced and held their noses and laughed, and it struggled to get up as they teased it.

Hoots spotted Stott flailing around, hopelessly stuck on his back, and ran over to help him get upright. Of course, this meant he complained about being helped and, in his embarrassment, became quite vocal. Dark make-up was smeared across his face, and his body-hugging black outfit made him look like a rotund mole that had been crying for days. The children had never seen a mole, but they *had* seen and smelt a skunk, which was what they sang and danced as they circled Stott playfully from a safe distance.

With all bodies now down from the truck, Hoots signalled to a couple of tribesmen, and they came over to help him remove a large box from the back. They placed it carefully on the ground, and Hoots popped open the lid. He checked inside, and satisfied all was well, left it there and went to greet the chief of the village. The chief had just appeared regaled in ceremonial dressage, ready to officially welcome the beings that had arrived from the Underworld. When he saw Hoots, his face lit up in recognition and they hugged one another. Hoots spoke in a *Fon* dialect to the gathering group and the chief nodded as he heard the story of how, and why, they came to be in their midst. When Hoots had finished summarising the situation, the chief clapped him on the shoulder, then barked some orders, which sent men running to prepare huts for their guests.

Stott was already feeling the heat of the morning sun and looked around for shade and somewhere to escape the children. Spotting a suitable place, he wandered over to an area that had a small black and white television housed under a tree branch. It was covered by a tarpaulin to create a large shaded area beneath it. A man was adjusting the television set and trying to get a reception on it, as the chug of a petrol generator behind the large tree provided the means of power. Slowly, the old television produced a picture. The BBC World News appeared, catching Stott's eye. The man, satisfied with the grainy picture, then pulled open a metal folding chair for Stott to sit on. Stott sat without breaking his gaze from the television and thanked the man. Some clean drinking water was fetched and placed on a table next to him.

Not long after this, with his eyes still transfixed on the television, Stott started to cry. Now and then he stood up and pointed to the TV, or looked around as if wishing to convey what he was feeling, but didn't know how. Whatever words he was trying to form made a strange sound, and that was all he could manage, and all that came out of him, as the tears streamed down his face, blurring his make-up even further.

"Why does the skunk cry?" asked a man in his native dialect. Hoots looked around to see Stott standing up, then sitting down, then pointing at the tv, while blubbering incoherently.

"His people no longer think him guilty of the crime of which he was accused," replied Hoots in the same dialect.

He had been aware for a few days from a radio broadcast in the cab that the documents he'd had forged and planted in the safe at Pussy Productions had been found. He knew it was a matter of time before their desired impact exonerated Stott from his complicity in the affair, and had hoped it would re-instate him to the respectable position he had lost. It seemed to have worked.

As the gathered elders went back to discussing the logistics of housing the guests, a scream went up from the children near the box, that looked suspiciously like a coffin. Those who had been peering into it went running in all directions. A moment later, a hand came out and grabbed one side, then another. A body then appeared, sitting upright. The coffin's inhabitant was dressed in a black cape with thickly oiled, jet-black hair, and ghoulish white make-up. It sat up in the coffin and took a deep gasping breath, as if coming back to life. The creature looked around slowly. The village froze motionless in silence, as only the clucking of hens, the noise of the television, and a continually blubbering Stott could be heard. It put a hand up to its mouth, and a moment later, removed a set of fangs it then threw on the ground. Followed by a spitting and flicking of its tongue, as it grimaced like a cat with a trapped fur ball. It glanced once more at its surroundings, then finally it spoke.

"So, this is Hell," it said.

Turning in the box to get a better look at its surroundings, the creature spotted Hoots. There was a moment's pause as it took it in.

"You fucking bastard!" shouted Hazelhot. "I didn't agree to this at all!"

Hoots excused himself from the elders and walked over to the coffin, to stand towering over Hazelhot.

"Morning, bru. Welcome to Togo."

"This is a bloody liberty!" shouted Hazelhot.

"It was Lucy insisted we take you, but we all voted on it and agreed it was the right thing to do," said Hoots.

"I can't move my fucking legs. What have you done to me?"

"We had to keep you drugged until we got here in case you kicked up a stink. It'll pass in a few hours. Sorry, but we couldn't risk being caught, or you going crazy on us. We've been travelling for a week as a circus troupe, hence your current situation there."

Hoots was referring to Hazelhot's Dracula outfit. He continued.

"This is Africa, bru. No one is going to touch a dead body, especially when it looks like you do. It was for your own good. We can stay here until everything calms down back home, assuming it ever will."

"Right… yes… well, how did that go?" asked Hazelhot, calming down slightly, and recalling his last conscious moments.

"You can catch some of your handiwork on the television, over there. It's been on the World News since we left. They are still trying to figure out what happened, but so far it's being blamed on you and that Inspector Stump fella. God knows what happened to him, but it seems like he was trying to get back when we left the scene. Everyone on that site is dead, us included. But that blast, man, your fucking weapons were something else. Insanity, bru, absolute carnage."

Hazelhot didn't seem overly impressed and looked down at himself in the coffin.

"There's a week of bowel movement in this box. I stink," he said.

"We kept you as clean as we could," replied Hoots. "We let the drugs wear off enough to feed and walk you a bit. It shouldn't be too long before you can use your legs again. I'll get some guys to take you down to the river and get you washed up properly. Just watch out for the crocs, hey."

"Do you know these people?" asked Hazelhot.

"I was brought up in this village before the Missionaries took me to South Africa," replied Hoots. "My parents were hunters, got killed by lions. This tribe found me and took me in. These are my people."

"Well, I hope you aren't expecting thanks from me for this," said Hazelhot, gradually returning to his old self. "Don't suppose I'll be going back to England, though," he added, looking around at his surroundings.

"Maybe everything you could need came out with you," replied Hoots, as he looked toward Lucy, who was surrounded by young women daringly touching her skin and giggling, trying to make sense of what she was.

"I was happy to let you have your death-wish fulfilled, but not her. She saved your life, man," he added.

"Hmm." replied Hazelhot, seeing Lucy, but other thoughts arose. "So, what was the final head count on site?" he asked, clearly coming back to himself.

Hoots looked at him and shook his head, then pointed to the television area again.

"Check the News for yourself, hey. You took them all out. The blast even rocked houses and broke windows over forty miles away. Turned everything in the industrial estate to glass, they are saying. Forensics can't make head nor tail of anything."

Hazelhot smiled beneath the make-up.

"Wonderful! So, you got everyone out then?" he asked. "I honestly didn't think any of you would make it once my toys got going."

"We got most of the way out before your crazy damn weapons got started. My squaddie buddies got us some serious vehicles, else we'd have been toast too. I'd put you out by the time they arrived, and we threw you in the back of one. The girls dressed you on the way. Took a Hercules out of an air-base and headed for Sierre Leone, then we drove the truck here. I've taken care to cover our tracks. No one is going to know we are out here. I doubt they even know we are alive. New names and passports should be ready in a couple of weeks, but we'll need to give it a while to let the whole affair settle down back home. Meantime, no one leaves this village, right, else it could put us all at risk."

"And how are we paying for this little venture?" asked Hazelhot, as he slapped at his legs trying to get some feeling back in them, then waved to a couple of tribesmen to come and help him up, but they didn't budge.

"I've sent word to some private art dealers discreetly. Turns out that picture is worth a few million on the black market. We can discuss the split when everyone is more settled, but I don't think any of us need to worry about money for a while."

"So what do you think happened to the inspector?"

"Judging from what they have been saying, he was trying to get back to us. Too late for him now, though, that's for sure. He's either dead, or getting grilled by the finest terrorist interrogation the US can offer. He's being blamed for helping you set the whole thing up, but you have the starring role my friend, MI6 saw to that. We'll have to be careful that no one sees us here, but you most of all. You may be dead, but your face is all over the World News right now and charity workers come by here often enough. You can trust all the people in this tribe, though. They think you are all from the Underworld and won't be talking to any white folk about that. Anyway, I'll get someone over to help you get washed up and situated. There'll be some grub soon. I hope you like meat. It's all they eat round these parts."

Hoots left Hazelhot, and walked back to talk again with the elders, who were in a heated discussion with a concerned tribal witch doctor about the ramifications and requirements of hosting a demon related to *Papa Legba*.

The village celebrated the beings from the Underworld with traditional Vodou rituals that went on day and night for over a week. Over one-hundred chickens and ten goats were slaughtered, and their blood spilled in libation. They did this in honour of the various deities that had sent the beings into their midst. As was traditional, the dancing and celebration included liquor, smoke, and the imbibing of various intoxicating substances. They offered these to the gods first, then everyone else. The witch doctor was tasked with keeping a close eye on the one Randy Andy had jokingly called "Baron Samedi", and was the only one to insist on staying in costume after they had helped him to clean up in the river. He'd been wobbly on his feet for a long time after the drugs wore off, since atrophy had affected his muscles. Everyone gave him a wide berth except the witch doctor, who followed him wherever he went, shaking rattles and charms, and inhaling various smoking substances, but always from a safe distance.

As was common in ceremonies of this nature, things got pretty strange deep into the night, when reality became blurred. The effect of being in deepest Africa, and being dead, had its impact on the new arrivals. It was a curious time. By the end of the week-long session, everyone had been possessed by spirits of the *Lwa*, at least once. Stott seemed to be a particular favourite of the spirits, and had clocked up over fifteen possessions, often forcing him to dance around the fire, wildly throwing shapes. When the spirits brought him back and sat him where they had found him, he seemed blissfully unaware that anything had happened. This was not uncommon in the antics of the spirit realm. He'd smile and clap, and toast his drink to someone, completely unaware he had just been part of the performance. By the end of the week, they had become a part of the village. Having been initiated into it, they now fit in.

They stayed in the village for many months. Supplies arrived to give them more familiar comforts than the village lifestyle could offer, and new huts were built to house them. These looked like huts on the outside but were better equipped. All of this done to help hide them from the prying eyes of charity workers, religious zealots, and annoying back-packers that insisted on wandering uninvited into the villages looking for their African fix.

While they lived amongst the tribe, they were treated like kings and queens from a far-away mystical land, which to some extent they were. Lucy and her troupe enjoyed the down-time away from the cameras, but entertained themselves with ease, and they began putting on small shows for the village. Often what they performed was then interpreted as communication from the gods in the Underworld. This then became incorporated into the many Vodou rituals that were a part of daily life there. And that went both ways, with a new wildness emerging in the performers that often ended in some risqué animistic renditions.

Eventually the News coming from England moved on, and though the incident was not forgotten, and never would be, the site at Deptford was now a popular tourist attraction. This meant that soon they could consider their options.

Hoots had the stolen Vermeer sold at a private auction in Germany, and split the proceeds equally. Each receiving a private off-shore account under their new identities with over a million USD dollars in each, though they had little need of money where they were. Once they had adjusted to the menu options, life just seemed to happen one day at a time. It became a simpler existence, never having to be concerned about the future much beyond the day's events. Though everyone quietly wondered what the future would hold, and there was always a hint of nostalgia and grief at the loss of their old lives. But they avoided discussing it too much and got on with living in the place they found themselves.

Curiously, Hazelhot had adjusted better than anyone to life in a remote African village. He'd even begun a Vodou apprenticeship with the witch doctor. Who, after his initial scepticism, now saw in his protégé a remarkable gift for helping the unwell and old get to the other side.

Stott was the other person who changed considerably. At first, grumbling endlessly about the horrific diet, he ended up losing a lot of excess weight. Then, attuning to village life, he became much more amenable to everyone, especially the children, who would sit on his lap as he made up wild stories of his days in Borneo as a soldier. The stories were completely fabricated, but that didn't matter because the children didn't understand a word of it, anyway. To them, he remained the giant *skonku* that had come from the Underworld for their amusement, and in that they had been correct. But in reflective moments alone - which were pretty few in a village of that size - Stott wondered about the day that he might return to England's green and pleasant land. He had no foolish ideas that his ex-wife would take him back. Despite being fully exonerated and posthumously re-knighted, he realised she could never forgive him.

But Hoots had assured Stott, as he had the others, that the day would eventually come, that they could return, but not to hold out for it. He suggested avoiding the pain *that* longing would create, and to counteract it, they should immerse themselves in the village life of Africa. And so they did.

A Year Away

After nearly a year spent as guests in a small tribal village deep in the heart of Togo, Hoots returned from one of his trips to the outside world and called a meeting. Everyone was soon in the shaded area except for Hazelhot, who was performing a Vodou ceremony in a nearby village and wouldn't be back for a day or two.

"I have news," said Hoots, with a look of grave concern after the group had gathered, but then his face brightened and he announced. "We can finally go home!"

There was a brief pause while everyone took in what they had just heard, and then a cheer went up as the group jumped around and hugged one another. Hoots waited for everyone to calm before continuing.

"There are a few caveats," he said, bringing the mood back down to earth. "The Inspector who never made it back to us is alive, but locked up and will be for a long time. My sources have told me they never got him to talk, so it seems we are safe on that count for now, though it is an area of concern that I will look into. Hazelhot, as you all know, is considered the terrorist behind the event. The press and the public all believe he is dead. Which brings me to the issue we face in returning. I caught up with him before I arrived back here, and it turns out he had no plans to return to England with us. He says he has found an excellent teacher in Mbtungo the witch doctor, and plans to stay on with the tribe and learn the ways as one of their *houngan*. I think most of you know he's been taking a lead in a lot of the Vodou ceremonies here of late, and seems to have really found a place where his 'unique skill set' is appreciated."

There was a murmur of amusement from the group. Everyone had done their best to avoid Hazelhot's extremist nature back at Pussy Productions, but his gifts had really come into their own on his arrival in Togo. He had risen through the tribal ranks and was one of the best goat and chicken sacrificers in that part of Togo. It had also been noted by the elders, the speed with which he could manifest the deity *Papa Legba* during important ceremonies. The deity had clearly taken a shine to him, and he was now getting offers of work from nearby tribes whenever a tricky situation arose that suited his particular flair. This local popularity reflected well on the village. Hazelhot never cowered in the presence of the *Lords of Death*, and the locals very much admired this about him. His abilities meant suffering family members rarely lingered long between this world and the next, leading to a reduced cost for the remaining family in terms of provision of sacrificial animals while trying to find out which direction their loved one was headed. Hazelhot loved his job, and he relished the opportunity to help. The others had even nicknamed him *Médecins Sans Scruples,* which he quietly enjoyed. He'd barely had a day to himself since Mbtungo had discovered - through divination - the true purpose of his arrival in their midst. So, it seemed Hazelhot had found a place where he was appreciated.

"As for Sir Stott," said Hoots. "As we all know, he has been posthumously exonerated and re-knighted, and there is a statue in Deptford acknowledging his part in helping MI6, which is quite the tourist attraction."

Everyone cheered and clapped, as Sir Stott stood up to give a lordly bow, followed by a royal hand wave. Hoots waited patiently for the excitement to abate before carrying on.

"And so, the time has come to reveal to the world that we are very much alive. But..." he said, holding a hand up to stop them all cheering again. "It is going to cause intense emotional reactions that won't all be in our favour. People will be suspicious and we will be interrogated by the press, the police, MI6, and probably Interpol and US Government agencies too. It will not be a walk in the park.

"So, we have to make an agreement here today that we will never discuss Hazelhot again. Ever. As far as anyone is concerned, we left him to his fate in Deptford, as was his wish. We absolutely must stick to this story, and we must do it for the rest of our days. There can be no exceptions. The consequences do not bear thinking about if it gets out that he was with us out here. If just one of us breaks and shares this information, none of us will survive the day it comes out."

Hoots paused to let the group consider it.

"I don't need to remind you," he said after a moment. "For all his psychopathic mania and insane behaviour, we have Hazelhot to thank for our being alive at all. The government, as we know, was planning to clean up their mess using the most extreme methods, and had no intention of letting us leave that industrial estate. Other than the Inspector - or I should say ex-Inspector - we are the only ones left alive who witnessed what happened that day in Deptford. We absolutely must stick to our stories even on our deathbeds. Is this clear?"

There was a murmur of concern, as everyone now wondered how they would avoid MI6, should they or the gangs decide to finish the job. Hoots was quick to put their minds at ease.

"There is going to be minimal risk to us, so long as we all stick to the game plan. I have confirmed with sources involved with the operation, who have access to the redacted details of the op, that there is a way through this. We will negotiate our way through it together. They are also aware of the parameters in place for dealing with unexpected new information if it arises. We are going to be that unexpected new information. I assure you, beyond the initial interrogation, which we have to expect, we have nothing to fear from the government or the gangs. Not that there is much left of the latter.

"I plan to get us full press coverage from the moment that we land back in England. This public exposure will protect us from the outset. Once it enters the public realm, it will be international news within the hour. The government will then be forced to take a hands-off approach. MI6 have no reason to want anything other than to see the end to all this, believe me. If the truth got out, they would be in far worse public shape than they are going to be with us appearing back from the dead. All they will care about is their public image. So long as we do not present a threat to them, they will not become a threat to us. Again, I cannot state how important never discussing our friend is to our survival and future good health. Not even with them.

"There will be much for us to deal with, good and bad. We are going to be made famous and our lives will never be what they were, but we *can* go home and we will rebuild. There will be book offers, and I expect everyone to take them up, but again on a few provisos - we never discuss a certain person, and we never discuss the location of this village, or this country. Never. If anyone asks, it was Sierra Leone. We also never dispute the story that MI6 gives us to share about what happened. After they grill us, they will brief us. Whatever they ask us to do, we do. We do *not* want to have that beast waking up to come looking for us again. Make no mistake, all our lives will depend on us adhering to this plan. Are we clear?"

Hoots paused again to let it sink in.

"Before we leave, I will go into greater detail of the plan with each one of you, such as how we explain the off-shore bank accounts, and so on. Just remember that together we *can* face what happens next. Our unity will be our strength. We have been through a hell of a lot together already and shown what we can do."

Someone held a hand up and asked if they could use their real identities on return.

"Yes, we can. I'll field all the press questions regards the fake passports and the escape plan. The military will understand my position as Security Adviser and that Stott's survival was my primary objective above all else. It's going to make me look good that I kept all of you alive, so it should be fine on my side of things. As far as anyone is concerned, you have all been living this time in Sierra Leone, in a small village there, the details of which we will go over in the coming days. Not that any of you would know where the hell this is, anyway, and we'll keep it that way when leaving, too.

"A truck will arrive in a few weeks to take us back to the airport in Sierra Leone. From there we will return directly to Heathrow, and from the moment we land, our lives will become a paparazzi frenzy. I don't expect that will let up for at least a few years. But this is *it*, folks. We are finally going home."

It was an apprehensive yet exciting time for everyone. In the village, celebrations were once again called for. The beings from the Underworld were now leaving. The tribe felt honoured to learn that their other-world visitors were leaving behind them the gift of *Papa Bwa*, the name now given to Hazelhot by the elders.

Then one morning, a truck, much like the one that had brought them, arrived in the centre of the village and came to a halt, creating a swirl of dust. Everyone soon appeared dressed in European clothing that had been sourced for them by Hoots. All except for *Papa Bwa*, who stood with the villagers a little distance from the truck, ready to see it off with an appropriate dance, ceremony, and to despatch some chickens and a goat. He was dressed in his tribal regalia - a loin cloth covering his waist and a large spear in one hand that he lent against. A bone and cowrie-shell necklace hung around his neck that was a gift from a local elder whose injured son he had helped over to the land of the ancestors, and similar bracelets adorned his wrists and ankles. He had markings on his face, and his body was covered in dried mud. Fresh tribal tattoos covered him like Scout badges, given to him after achieving certain levels of skill during ceremonies. He was a fully initiated *hougan* now, and a member of the tribe, as if he had always been one. Next to him were his two young wives, a recent gift from a local tribal chief, and they stood an appropriate distance away, happy to serve him and look after his various needs. Some of those needs Hoots had beseeched him to curtail, at least until everyone had left, so they would have only fond memories of him. Hazelhot, or rather *Papa Bwa*, had agreed.

Lucy walked over to him as the others boarded the truck,

and they stood looking at one another for a moment.

"I'll miss you," she said.

"You can always come visit," he replied, in his matter-of-fact way.

"It's quite the trip, but who knows, maybe one day," she said. "Won't you miss England? It's your home, after all."

"What's to miss? There's nothing for me back there. I aimed at hell and ended up in paradise. Why would I leave this place?" he replied.

Lucy laughed, then looked at his new wives behind him, who had their eyes on the ground as was customary when their master was in conversation with another woman.

"How many do you plan on collecting?" she asked, a tone of sarcasm in her voice.

"You should know, there are no limits," replied Hazelhot.

"Riiight," said Lucy, realising it wasn't going where she had hoped. "Well, you take care... *Papa Bwa*," she added, and then turned to walk away.

"Lucy..." said Hazelhot.

Her name had escaped his lips with an urgency. He'd never called her by name before. She stopped and turned, not sure what to expect. Hazelhot was uncertain what he had meant to say, and fumbled for the words, then gave up, and said.

"Thank you," and a moment later added, "I'd like it if you came back sometime."

It was as close to emotion as anyone was going to get from Hazelhot.

"I'll do that," replied Lucy.

She stepped back over and kissed him, and they stood together with their lips touching awkwardly. After a while she pulled away, but lifted a hand to touch his face, before dropping her gaze and turning to join the others. Reaching the back of the truck, she turned once to smile at him, knowing that would be the lasting memory he held of her. Then Randy Andy and Hoots lifted her up, and she disappeared inside the truck with the others.

A moment later, the vehicle manoeuvred around in the dirt. Children moved behind it, ready to chase it up the road. As it turned near to where Hazelhot was, it came to a stop. The window wound down and Hoots lent out, offering a hand to him. Hazelhot stepped over and took it.

"Goodbye then, bru, and good luck," said Hoots.

"You look after them," replied Hazelhot. "And you know where I'll be, if you need anything," he added.

"I do," replied Hoots. "Take care now, and stay gone, you hear?"

They looked at one another. Two soldiers who performed the dark deeds that needed to be done. The dirty work required, so that other, more civilised folk, might never have to. It had been quite the journey they had taken together. They held a look for a moment longer. Then the man, formerly Hazelhot and now known as *Papa Bwa*, nodded before stepping back. Hoots gave two loud taps on the roof of the cab and the truck roared to life. Leaping forward, it moved through the village, followed by singing children, tribal elders, and a myriad of dancers. And so began the journey to return the beings from the Underworld home.

Epilogue

"I don't see why *we* have to get her," said Angela to Sarah, as the car turned into the driveway of Bethlem Royal Hospital.

"Because we are the sisterhood, and sisters need to help each other out," replied Sarah. "I am finding your negativity very distressing," she added.

"So why is Chris here?" asked Angela.

"I really don't mi…" began Chris from the back of the car, but Angela gave him a look and he stopped speaking.

"Because Chris is a feminist and an ally," replied Sarah, and she turned to reverse into a parking space, bouncing over the curb and getting the car momentarily stuck, before revving violently enough to shoot forward and try again.

"… an ally," Sarah repeated, while giving Angela a look to imply she was not.

Turning huffily, Sarah repeated the manoeuvre, this time parking the car successfully.

Angela did not like the idea at all, but she liked the idea of Sarah spending time with Chris even less. Sarah still hadn't figured out Chris was gay, but it irked Angela all the same. She did not want to risk leaving him alone with Sarah in case he changed his mind. Knowing from experience that she would lose them both if they got together. She felt it was unlikely, but she couldn't risk it. They were her only friends. Meanwhile, Sarah's continued obsession with W.A.S.P. had got worse. She completely idolised Clammy Frawd in her absence, and had taken advantage of the momentary loss of their leader to make herself as useful as possible to the other W.A.S.P. women in order to get closer to Clammy when the time came she was released. That time was upon them. They got out of the car and entered the building.

They appeared again two hours later, after signing all the release forms and confirming with the doctors that they knew exactly what order Clammy needed to take her medicines in. Chris and Sarah helping Clammy into the back of the car while Angela stood watching with her arms folded, still sulking.

"I think this is a terrible idea," she whispered loudly at Sarah across the top of the car as Sarah opened the driver's side to get in. They'd been fighting the entire time.

Chris was in the back trying to get a seat-belt on Clammy, who was still dazed from her last injection and trying to focus her eyes on him.

"She needs our help," said Sarah.

"She's a fucking maniac," said Angela, finding Sarah's naivety concerning.

Sarah huffed, and before she ducked down, said, "I can't talk with you when you are like this."

Then she disappeared inside the car.

Angela shut her eyes and shook her head, then got in. She knew it was a bad idea, but there was going to be no getting through to Sarah.

"Is this him?" asked Clammy, as saliva dribbled from her

chin to settle on the hospital gown she was still wearing.

"Who?" asked Sarah, turning to look.

"Big penis bastard," slurred Clammy.

Sarah looked at Angela, who shrugged her shoulders.

"Show me your penis," said Clammy to Chris.

Chris looked at Angela and Sarah and pulled a face. They both shook their heads.

"It's probably the drugs," mouthed Sarah.

Clammy turned to lean against the window and dribble down it.

"Penis," she said.

As they drove back to the city and Sarah's flat, where Clammy was going to be staying while she got better, Clammy started coming round. But it was clear she was still deeply upset about something, and they soon heard all about it.

"So where is he, then?" asked Clammy.

"Who?" asked Sarah, watching the road, but able to see Clammy in the rear-view mirror.

"That disgusting pig I tazered," replied Clammy.

"Tazered?" repeated Sarah, looking at the others, but neither Angela nor Chris knew either.

"He's a pig," mumbled Clammy.

"If you mean someone from that porn company we picketed, it blew up some time ago, they are all dead," said Sarah.

"He's not dead," replied Clammy.

"Do you think she means that terrorist? Maybe that is who she saw before... you know. This happened," said Chris.

Clammy was trying to focus on Chris, but was still effected by the narcotics. She put her hand out to grab at his penis for the umpteenth time, and Chris picked her hand up and placed it back in her own lap.

"Pig," said Clammy, leaning into his face. "He's not dead," she repeated, turning to look out of the window again. "I can feel him out there."

Chris made a gesture to Angela to imply Clammy was clearly mental, even without the drugs. Angela was glad she was not alone in being concerned about Sarah's plan. But Sarah had seen the gesture.

"It's going to be fine," she said. "It's only for a few days until she gets back on her feet."

"*If* she gets back on her feet," replied Angela.

"Show me your penis," said Clammy.

"She's obsessed," said Angela.

"I'd know that penis anywhere," confirmed Clammy. "It's still out there. I can feel it," she said.

"Everyone from that industrial estate is dead," said Sarah to her again in the rear-view mirror.

"He's alive," said Clammy. "I can feel it in MY VAGINA!"

She shouted the last part right at Chris. It was so loud and so sudden that Sarah nearly drove them off the road, and narrowly missed hitting another car. Jumping on the brakes, they came to a halt in the middle of the road.

"Oh, this is so fucked," said Angela, as they all caught their breath and car horns started going off around them.

"It's fine, we are helping a friend," repeated Sarah, trying to convince herself more than Angela at this point.

"My vagina will find him, and I'm going to kill him," said Clammy.

"Yea, I am sure it's going to be fine," said Angela to Sarah, just as Clammy shoved her head down into Chris's lap and bit with full force.

* * *

A man lay alone on his cell bunk inside HMP Wandsworth Prison, scratching at his skin as he mumbled incoherently. He'd been found wandering naked in a London park many months before and been taken to the local police station, whereupon he became quite animated. Unable to calm him, they called a doctor who had then tried to get a name, or anything sensible from him, but failed. The final decision was to have him sectioned in a mental facility, but there was an issue with the handover, so they sent him to Wandsworth prison for holding while the system processed the paperwork. He was entered under *John Doe,* to be held there for monitoring in the hope that whatever was wrong with him might just wear off. Then the system forgot about him. As he lay on the bunk where they had left him, he became increasingly vocal.

"Rats, the rats, they are coming for us. Big as houses and glowing eyes. Genetic experiments. Those plaster-cast bastards! They are coming from Mars, to Mars we go. Up Uranus. Tra-la-la... k'BOOM! Freddy. Freddy, what are you doing Freddy, you naughty boy? Come here now. Mummy must hit it with a ruler to make it behave."

He'd been babbling like this for hours that morning when the notification sounded for everyone to return to their cells. The man stood up shakily from the bed and the blanket fell from him. He was naked, with his skin an awful white and in an emaciated state. Covered in fresh scars, he had large burns from a recent fire. It was clear he could not look after himself. On shaky legs, he made his way to the cell door and looked out through the small view hole. As he did so, he continued to mutter to himself, his eyes following a new prisoner that was being walked past his cell. After watching the prisoner pass by, he turned and shuffled back to lie down on his bed again and continued to gibber.

A man who had spent the last few months in orange overalls, being heavily interrogated, while continually denying any involvement in the crimes being put to him, was now dressed in prison clothing and being walked toward his new cell by two large prison guards. Heavy-duty cuffs were on his arms and legs that were chained together, and he was shuffling his way down the prison corridor. All eyes watched from the cells as he passed. Inmates could be heard making pig noises, and one hummed the song of the *Duelling Banjos*.

"See you in the shower block, piggy," a voice shouted.

But the man did not turn or break his gaze. He just looked straight ahead, unaffected by anything they tried to intimidate him with. When he arrived at his new quarters, one guard made him stop as the other opened the cell door and checked inside.

"On your bed," said the guard in the doorway to the prisoner who was currently standing in the cell, just staring at them. This prisoner was holding a tough-guy stance, with his head titled slightly back, and his chest puffed up and out. His arms lifted a little at his sides as if his muscles were full of helium and hard to keep down. He remained in that pose for a moment, then suddenly relaxed and did as he was told, quickly diving onto the bottom bunk as ordered. The guard shook his head at the histrionics and then stepped back to let their detail enter his new cell.

Roger Stump, ex-Detective Inspector at Peckham Police Station, and now a man looking at three consecutive life sentences for his part in an alleged terrorist plot, shuffled into the cell and turned to have his cuffs removed. Once done, the door was shut and locked behind him and he stood there facing it, not moving. He listened to the sound of the guards as they walked away, their footsteps echoing down the prison corridor. When they were gone, he turned and stared at the man lying on the bottom bunk, who stared back at him.

"He isn't dead," said Stump after a moment.

"Who isn't dead?" asked the man on the bottom bunk.

"The man who killed your crew," replied Stump.

Basher Bob sat bolt upright as if he had just been electrocuted.

"You tell me where he is. I will fucking destroy the cunt!" he shouted.

*

Other books by Mark DK Berry

The Road To El Palmar (Travel journal)
Seven Nights In Morocco (Travel journal)

Rock Star (Fiction/Humour)

Infinite Time (Fiction/Sci-fi)

Broke (Poetry)
Leaving Town (Poetry)
A to Z (Poetry)
The Black Book (Poetry)

For the latest publications visit www.MarkDKBerry.com